"**M**aybe he's a saint" Chet shot h[...] supposed to mean?"

"I mean, like, the bodies of saints are supposed to be incorrigible."

"That's 'incorruptible,'" Chet said, looking like he wished he could gag Tony. "Now just—"

"Right. That's what I meant. When they dig them up years and years after they've been buried their bodies are in perfect shape."

Yeah, right, Pam thought.

"Tell that to Joan of Arc. Believe me: Phil was no Mother Teresa."

Chet pointed to a chair in the corner and said, "What's that magazine over there, Tony?"

Tony got an embarrassed look. "Um, Sports Illustrated. I read it while I'm waiting for—"

"Bring it here." When Tony complied, Chet laid it on Phil's chest.

"What—?" Pam began.

"Just in case there's a skeptic among us, this will prove that it is really and truly hot in there." He looked like he wanted to say *fucking* hot but held back.

After the retort was sealed, Chet positioned her before the tempered glass plate of the monitoring window. The nozzles spewed jets of natural-gas flame from above and all sides, and she watched the magazine blacken and dissolve into ash while Philip Sirman's body remained totally unaffected.

THE
UPWELLING

BOOK I OF THE HIDDEN

BY F. Paul Wilson

GORDIAN KNOT BOOKS

MONDAY

1

Pamela Sirman walked into the Landry Funeral Home at the appointed hour and spotted the head man—Chester "Call-Me-Chet" Landry—as soon as she stepped inside the door.

"Oh, Mrs. Sirman," he said. He looked troubled. "I was just about to call you."

"Really? Wasn't this the time you told me I could pick up Phil's ashes?"

"Yes...about that."

Now he really looked troubled.

"Is something wrong?"

"Yes. That's why I was calling you. It appears we've had a problem with your loved one's cremation."

Loved one...that was a good one. She and Phil hadn't been each other's *loved one* for years, but...

"What sort of problem?"

"It's your husband's body."

"What about it, damn it?"

He cleared his throat. "It won't burn."

It took a few seconds for Pam to make sense of those words, and then they made even less sense.

"What?"

"The attendant loaded him into the retort and turned on the flames, but when he looked through the observation port later to check on the progress, your husband's body was completely unaffected."

Pam stared at him, mouth agape. Finally she found her voice.

"There's got to be some mistake."

"Exactly what I thought when the attendant called me down

to the crematorium and showed me an unblemished body amid the flames of the retort. The first thing I did was check the temperature gauge, but it read just shy of seventeen hundred degrees, exactly as it should have. The next thing was the timer which read sixty-seven minutes. The cremation process usually takes somewhere around two hours, but after more than an hour at that temperature, he should have been, well, halfway there."

What was it with the fucking world? Everything was going to hell. No, check that: Everything had fucking *gone* to hell a long time ago. Couldn't anybody do their job right? *Ever?* For the first twenty-five or so years of her life she'd sort of assumed competence in others—or at least in those most folks assumed were competent—but then reality had stepped in and totally kicked her ass. And in the seven years since that butt blow, the message had been brought home time and time again: Nobody knew what the fuck they were doing.

But this...this was fucking unbelievable.

"Can I pick 'em, or what?"

"I beg your pardon?"

"Of all the funeral homes in Monmouth County, I pick a Mickey Mouse joint that doesn't know what the fuck it's doing!"

As a rule she kept Potty-mouth Pam in check when she was with strangers, but now the old girl was breaking loose. And with good fucking reason.

"Now, you listen here, Mrs. Sirman! We know exactly what we're doing. Our attendants are highly trained, skilled professionals. And that crematorium is top of the line."

"'Skilled professionals'? What kind of skill does it take to stick a body in a toaster and turn up the heat?"

A thought struck her. Wait a minute...wait just one big fucking minute. Was good old Chet running a game on her?

Yesterday he'd tried to talk her out of the cremation bit and insisted on showing her his array of caskets. To make it worse, Chet felt he had to do all sorts of mansplaining about the difference between a coffin and a casket—as if she cared—but she'd feigned interest about how a coffin has six or eight sides compared to a four-sided rectangular casket.

She'd somehow managed to keep her eyes from glazing over during this riveting discourse as he rambled on and on about his deluxe bronze-and-copper model because it offered the most "protection." Seriously? Thirty grand to protect Phil from what? The worms? The guy's fucking dead and eventually the worms are going to get him no matter what kind of box he's in. Why put them off? Worms gotta eat too.

Pam had called an abrupt halt to the pitch. Phil was going to be cremated and that was that. And all they needed for that was a cardboard coffin.

Chet had wanted to know about arranging for a viewing. Well, forget that. The truck that T-boned Phil's car had pretty much flattened his head on one side, so who'd want to look at that? Pam had barely recognized him when she went to identify the body. The medical examiner had taken one look at him and saved Monmouth County a few bucks by declaring the cause of death obvious, no post-mortem necessary. Yeah, that bad. About all they did was some bloodwork to determine if he'd been impaired in any way. The guy who'd plowed into him had been totally fucking wasted on booze and oxy, but Phil proved clean.

And as for catering to mourners, there wouldn't be any. Both her family and Phil's were all dead, and the people they'd once called friends had given up on them long ago, so what was the point of a viewing, even with a closed casket? She'd told Chet she wanted to have Phil cremated the next day. Which was today. But now he was trying to convince her that wasn't gonna happen.

This guy was running a game: Tell the dumb wife her husband's body won't burn so she'll have to buy a coffin and bury him.

No way. No fucking way.

"Where's the body?"

"Downstairs, in the cremation center."

"I want to see it."

"I don't think—"

"I want to see it, Chet. I mean, how do I know you're telling the truth? For all I know you really did cremate him and now you're going to dump his ashes in one of your overpriced coffins and tell me you're burying his uncremated body."

"Are you calling me a liar?"

She spoke through her teeth. "I. Want. To. See. Him."

After a long pause, he said, "Very well. Come this way."

He led her to an oversized elevator—freight model, she guessed, big enough to move coffins to and from the basement. When they arrived below, the crematorium lay only a few steps to the right. A squat, burly guy stood discreetly off to the side.

Chet said, "I had the attendant wait until the body had cooled enough, then slide it out of the retort."

Pam stutter-stepped and froze at the sight Phil's body, naked and supine.

"Where are his clothes?" she said, her voice hushed. "Did you just dump him in the casket naked?"

"They burned away. That ash you see around him is all that remains of his cremation casket. Everything burned away except... him."

She continued to stare at the body. "How is this possible?"

"I would love to have the answer to that, Mrs. Sirman. My father started this funeral home, and as a boy I'd help him prepare the bodies. I learned at his feet, which means I've been involved in the undertaking profession for most of my life. What you see here today is... I want to say 'impossible' but obviously it's very possible, so I'll go with unprecedented."

She edged forward and took hold of Phil's wrist. He felt cold. She lifted his arm and then dropped it.

"He's not stiff."

"No, he wouldn't be. He's long past the rigor mortis stage."

She leaned closer and looked him up and down. This was Phil... really Phil. She straightened and turned to Chet.

This couldn't be real. She and Phil had met in college—what... fourteen years ago—and fucked each other's brains out. And then they got married and kept on fucking each other's brains out until... until they stopped. They did everything together... until they didn't. They hadn't been getting along for years now, but...

"I *know* this man," she said. "He's normal flesh and blood through and through. Why won't he burn?"

"Normal flesh and blood burns, Mrs. Sirman."

She noted the slight added emphasis on *normal* and felt her shoulder muscles bunch with anger.

"We've been together over fourteen years. Don't try to tell me I've been married to some kind of fucking android!"

"All I'm saying is that human bodies *burn*. The temperature in the retort was almost seventeen hundred degrees this morning and your husband spent over an hour in there with no damage."

"Is that hot enough?"

"Fifteen hundred is enough to cremate a human body, Mrs. Sirman."

All fine and good, she thought, but this could all be staged.

"All right. Show me."

"Pardon me?"

She waved the body toward the toaster. "Slide him back in there and light up your burners and let's see what happens."

"Oh, I don't think—"

"I need to know the truth."

"I am *telling* you the truth."

She leaned toward him. "But I need to see for myself. You get that, don't you, Chet. What you're telling me doesn't make any fucking sense, so I need to see for myself."

His expression said he got that. He turned to the attendant and said, "Put him back in, Tony."

Tony must have been listening because he was already stepping forward. She watched as he began to slide the body back into the chamber—what Chet called the "retort."

"Maybe he's a saint," Tony muttered.

Chet shot him a glare but Pam said, "What's that supposed to mean?"

"I mean, like, the bodies of saints are supposed to be incorrigible."

"That's 'incorruptible,'" Chet said, looking like he wished he could gag Tony. "Now just—"

"Right. That's what I meant. When they dig them up years and years after they've been buried their bodies are in perfect shape."

Yeah, right, Pam thought.

"Tell that to Joan of Arc. Believe me: Phil was no Mother Teresa."

Chet pointed to a chair in the corner and said, "What's that magazine over there, Tony?"

Tony got an embarrassed look. "Um, *Sports Illustrated*. I read it while I'm waiting for—"

"Bring it here." When Tony complied, Chet laid it on Phil's chest.

"What—?" Pam began.

"Just in case there's a skeptic among us, this will prove that it is really and truly hot in there." He looked like he wanted to say *fucking* hot but held back.

After the retort was sealed, Chet positioned her before the tempered glass plate of the monitoring window. The nozzles spewed jets of natural-gas flame from above and all sides, and she watched the magazine blacken and dissolve into ash while Philip Sirman's body remained totally unaffected.

2

Chan Liao stood on the high-rise balcony of his Margate apartment and stared northward at the spot where the hotels and casinos of Atlantic City had once lined the Boardwalk. Where he'd consulted on the online gaming at the Xìngyùn Casino. Where nothing stood now. The high rises in Ventnor and Marvin Gardens between him and the city had been knocked down and lay in piles of rubble, but Atlantic City itself had been scoured flat.

Two months since the disaster—the Atlantic City Upwelling seemed to be the preferred euphemism for the complete destruction of a city and the disappearance of 25,000 people along with it—and he still couldn't believe it. He found himself out here every day, staring at the devastation. The whole city... gone.

Along with his job. The Chinese owners of the Xìngyùn had loved Chan, their wonder boy. US-born of Heilongjiang immigrant parents, he was Ivy League educated with a major in computer engineering, who spoke both English and Mandarin without an accent. Really, what was not to like?

They'd started him off developing bettor profiles for their high rollers and he was just getting a handle on the whole operation when the pandemic struck. Like all the AC casinos, the Xìngyùn had to close its physical doors in early 2020, but its virtual doors remained open. That was when Chan took the reins of the online betting and sports book that kept the casino afloat. Upon reopening later in the year, the grateful owners gave him free rein to streamline all their computer operations.

Oh, yes. Only twenty-six years old, but Chan Liao had been on his way up in the gaming world—way up, like with a jetpack strapped to his back. Not that he was happy. He'd never, ever been truly happy in life. It simply wasn't in the cards for him. But these past few years in AC had brought him within sight of that elusive state.

And then, on June 22, disaster. Total destruction. Even the online betting was gone.

As natural disasters go, the Atlantic City Upwelling didn't hold a candle to the historic floods in China which purportedly killed millions. But upward of 25,000 Atlantic City guests and locals were listed as missing. Not officially confirmed dead, but vanished without a trace.

He remembered how the morning-after reports blamed the devastation on a tsunami. But all sorts of experts in varying fields started calling that into question. A tsunami is the result of a sudden displacement of water from a seismic event or a massive collapse like a landslide, but nothing like that had been recorded in the Atlantic or anywhere else that day. Also, the ocean will recede from the shore as a tsunami nears, and that never happened at Atlantic City. Nor could the flooding be blamed on a storm surge because the violent storm didn't make landfall until after the flooding had begun.

By all accounts, the ocean simply rose and flowed into the city with no great velocity. In addition to the city proper, it inundated the lower part of Brigantine to the north and southward almost to Marvin Gardens as it flowed twenty miles inland through Pleasantville and Absecon, washing out the Garden State Parkway, inundating the AC Airport, and flowing into Hamilton Township where it flooded Mays Landing but spared Egg Harbor City. It penetrated past Route 50 into the Pine Barrens, then, after a brief pause, it receded, leaving unparalleled destruction in its wake.

The current theory was an unexplained upwelling from the Sohm abyssal plain—the ocean's relatively flat bottom between the edge of the continental shelf and the mid-Atlantic ridge. Where exactly on the plain it originated no one could say since the Sohm Plain has an area of approximately 350,000 square miles and is one of and least explored regions on Earth. Its averages about four miles in depth, and even deeper in the trenches.

An "upwelling." That was all Homeland Security would say about it. The city proper took the most damage.

People who had evacuated or been out of town wanted to return to see their property or find a loved one. But DHS had quarantined the ruins—easy to enforce since AC was basically an island and all its bridges had been destroyed. The reason given was an unspecified microbe causing an equally unspecified infection. But aerial photos from drones and news helicopters made it abundantly clear to the whole world that no intact property remained to visit, and no lost relative had survived to be found.

The Atlantic Ocean had done what the pandemic could not: put Chan out of work. But he was one of the lucky ones. He'd taken the day off to meet with old friends. Virtually everyone he knew had been taken from him, because they'd all been involved in the casino industry, and they'd all been working that Friday night.

He wasn't broke yet, but he would be. The thrifty mindset imbued in him by his industrious parents, however, had served him well. They'd run a butcher shop in Cincinnati's Chinatown—growing up he'd learned how to butcher everything from a duck to a side of beef—where nothing went to waste. Saving was a habit that had left him with a financial cushion that would hold him for a while. In retrospect, this high-rise apartment had been an extravagance—that and the BMW M2—but he was single and unattached with few other expenses. He'd lost the BMW in the disaster and was still waiting for the insurance money. As a replacement he'd picked up a much saner used Nissan Sentra. And jobwise he'd been reduced to keeping busy with temporary ad hoc IT gigs here and there around the state.

All of which gave him more time to spend working on his killer music app, which he should be doing now instead of staring at the ruins.

Ruins...normally the thought of ruins conjured up images of crumbling jungle temples or archival black-and-white footage of Berlin after the war, where skeletons of burned- and bombed-out buildings stood stark against the sky. At least those places still had standing remnants. AC had *nothing*. Whatever happened there had leveled it.

The *whatever* was perhaps the worst aspect of the disaster: No one knew what had caused it. Or at least no one was saying what caused it. And if the government agencies on the scene there—DHS and FBI and NSA and even the CIA—had a clue as to the cause, it would have leaked by now. But nothing... not a word. Which meant no one knew how to prevent it from happening again, because how do you take measures against a threat you've yet to identify?

Chan was well aware that he had become obsessed with that night. He didn't fight it. He'd filled the wall above his desk with clippings about it. He embraced it. Because he'd lost two longtime friends in that disaster.

And he didn't know how.

He'd joined Danni, Mac, and Aldo—all fellow alums from U of P—at the Hard Rock Casino on the Boardwalk for a night of eating too much, drinking too much, and gambling too much. Less than twelve hours later, Atlantic City was gone, and Mac and Aldo with it.

And he couldn't remember a goddamn thing about it. Neither could Danni. Somehow they'd survived but they didn't know how. Ten hours had been erased from his life and he wanted them back. He'd given up hope of seeing Mac and Aldo again, but those ten hours... he knew they were floating out there somewhere. All he had to do was find them.

Danni had lost those hours too, but she'd gone incommunicado. Where was she?

3

FBI Special Agent Danielle Boudreau sat alone in the meeting room of the Brigantine Public Library, reading the NDA she was expected to sign before her briefing. After the disaster, the library had been commandeered by the Department of Homeland Security as a base of operations. Brigantine sat just north of the ruins of Atlantic City and had been only partially damaged by the Upwelling. The meeting room sported a few empty bookshelves along one wall, a desk with an open laptop, a monitor on the wall behind it, and an array of stackable chairs before it. Danni sat in one of those chairs. Morning light came through the windows behind her.

Her life had been co-opted by the government. After almost eight weeks of being shuttled between the Hoover Building in downtown DC, the Walter Reed complex in Bethesda, NSA's Black House HQ in Fort Meade, and Quantico and Langley in Virginia, she was glad to be back in New Jersey. But instead of returning her to her apartment in the Ironbound District of Newark, they'd placed her in a furnished Smithville garden apartment over the weekend. Looked like they wanted her on a short leash.

Her own damn fault for opening her yap. Why did she have to blab to her bosses that she'd been in Atlantic City the night of the Upwelling? That was all they had to hear. They'd been delighted to have a witness who was one of their own; that is, until she told them she remembered nothing of the night, nor most of the afternoon of that day. That triggered a raft of suspicions that placed her on the Acela to DC for debriefing.

They hadn't believed her at first, and subjected her to intense interrogation, polygraphs, and multiple psychiatric evaluations.

After weeks of grilling and having her mind probed by a battery of shrinks, they came to the brilliant deduction that she was suffering from post-traumatic stress disorder complicated by event-specific dissociative amnesia. Nice mouthful, that.

She opened up about losing her friends, Mac and Aldo, but through it all she never once mentioned Chan. Because Chan suffered from the same memory loss and she didn't want him subjected to what she'd endured.

She sensed that she'd become some sort of pariah. One of their own had been on the scene of this massive disaster and could tell them nothing about it. She was sure some of the old boys had said that this was what you had to expect with a female agent—simply can't handle the stresses of the job. But she loved this job. She saw it as restoring order to chaos and wanted to spend the rest of her life doing this. But right now, she couldn't see how she had much of a future with the Bureau.

A man in his mid-thirties entered—maybe ten years older than she. He had light-brown skin, dark wavy hair combed straight back, and wore jeans and an FBI windbreaker over a T-shirt. Danni wore pretty much the same. They'd told her to dress casually for her briefing.

He rested his tall Starbucks cup on the desk and extended his hand. "Agent Boudreau? Special Agent Abel Benigno." As they shook hands, he added, "Did you sign the NDA?"

She handed him the sheets and he looked them over— checking for her signature, no doubt—then dropped them next to the laptop on the desk.

He smiled. "Helluva NDA, huh?"

She nodded. "I'll say. I'm thinking of having my vocal cords cut just so I can't slip up."

He made an attempt at a polite laugh, then said, "When we finish here, you'll understand why it's so strict." He stared at her a moment. "I was attached to the resident agency in AC which, like everything else that used to be part of the city, no longer exists. I was safe at home here in Brigantine watching the storm that night with no idea what was happening. I hear you were actually there."

"That's true."

And now came the questions she never could answer.

Instead, he said, "I'm told you have memory loss associated with PTSD."

"That's what I'm told too. A lot of people don't believe that."

She'd encountered nothing but skepticism since she'd opened her yap. She prepared herself for more right here.

But again, he surprised her by saying, "I believe it. The people who don't believe you haven't been on site and don't know what I know. You'll find it's different with the folks here. Something hellacious happened that night. We still don't know what, but it had to be traumatic."

Danni could only nod as she bit back a sob. She'd wanted so badly to be believed. She'd grown so tired of the suspicious looks and the skeptical attitudes. Was the doubting over?

Benigno seemed to understand.

"Okay, Boudreau, this is your briefing and it's going to be brief. In the course of a few minutes I'm going to give you the results of the team's nine weeks of digging. I can do that because, basically, we still don't know shit."

Well, that's hardly encouraging, she thought.

"The first thing to know is it wasn't the water that did the damage, although publicly we're blaming the Upwelling. It's true that water welled up from the Sohm abyssal plain—there's plenty of evidence to confirm that that's where it came from—but we've had NOAA all over this and not one of their oceanologists have a clue as to why."

"But affecting just Atlantic City?" she said. "You'd think half the eastern seaboard would be affected by something like that. Why such a localized effect?"

"As you've no doubt heard, that oddity hasn't been lost on the fundamentalists of both Islam and Christianity. They're calling it divine payback for the city's sins of gambling, alcohol, and prostitution. But the fact is, yours is another question that begs an answer that none of the oceanologists seem to be able to come up with."

"But you said the water didn't do the damage," Danni said.

"Right. It didn't. By all accounts of the evacuees who made it out as the ocean was coming in, the water *flowed* in rather than arriving like a wall. This was *not* a tsunami. And once on land it flowed at a velocity of no more than ten miles an hour."

Danni did a quick calculation. "That's not exactly slow. That's almost nine hundred feet a minute, which is..." Another calculation. "...about a six-minute mile. You can outrun that, but not for long."

"Right. But the really strange thing is the way the water behaved. Give me a second here."

He ran his index finger over his laptop's touch pad and the monitor on the screen came to life with a map.

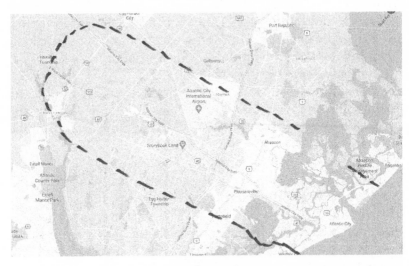

"What am I looking at?" she said.

"It's something the team has been working on. That's the flood zone."

"Okaaaay."

"Notice anything?"

"Not particularly."

"See how limited the flooding is? Water doesn't behave like that. That dotted line represents the edges of the flooding and the path of the storm that accompanied it, but there's no reason it should have been limited to that area."

"How so?"

"The elevations. Egg Harbor Township is at sea level. It should have been entirely flooded, but it wasn't. Only its northern half. The water flowed in over a two-hour period, engulfing everything within the dotted line there, reaching all the way into Hamilton Township—the westernmost point is about twenty miles from the ocean. The storm came with it, but then the storm broke up and dissipated and the flood receded. But while it was here the flood didn't behave like normal water, by which I mean, flowing toward the lowest point. It flowed west, confining itself to a path it shouldn't have followed—*couldn't* have followed without breaking a bunch of physical laws. Totally unnatural." He sipped his coffee. "So you see what we're dealing with, don't you?"

Danni saw, and didn't envy the team. "You're tasked with explaining the impossible. Are you sure your data is accurate? You know what the computer folks say: Garbage in—"

"—garbage out. I know. We've checked and rechecked our measurements."

Danni leaned back and studied the map. "Does chaos theory come into play here?"

Benigno shook his head. "A flood certainly qualifies as a complex system, but chaos affects predictions only in those systems with a sensitive dependence on initial conditions. I don't know if a flood qualifies. But even if it did, it's a moot point since we're not predicting here. We've arrived after the fact, so I don't see chaos in play."

"So what happened after the storm died and the water stopped moving west?"

"It started receding almost immediately, but a lot slower than when it advanced. Took about six hours to drain back into the sea. So the whole disaster lasted maybe eight hours, although we're pretty sure the city was flattened during those first two hours."

"Speaking of the storm," Danni said, "where'd that come from? Clear skies were predicted, as I recall."

"It just appeared. Storms around here tend to come either up the coast like a nor'easter, or in from the west. This one formed directly off shore without warning and moved in. Nothing on radar until it started gathering and then its dBZ went from zero to sixty-five in just a few minutes."

"What's that mean?"

"It's how they measure precip with Doppler radar. Like *that*—he snapped his fingers—"it went from no rain to giant hail. One of the meteorologists called it 'unnatural' and none of them can explain it."

"That's the second time 'unnatural' has been used."

"Yeah, and not the last. Get used to it. Some of these so-called experts say the flood did most of the damage as well as triggering the storm."

Danni was dubious. "You buy that?"

"I wish I could buy *some* of the theories coming out of the team, but not that one. We clocked the flood at fifteen feet per second on what little workable CCTV footage we could find, which is plenty fast enough to knock you off your feet, and certainly enough to mess up a ground-floor lobby, but it can't knock down a ferro-concrete high-rise."

"Knock down?" Danni said. "If they were just knocked down we could still see them lying on their sides over there. They had drone footage on the news early on and none of the buildings were lying on their sides."

Benigno nodded. "Exactly. They didn't just fall over, they were *crushed*. All the hotels and apartment buildings and all the houses and tenements are flattened. Not even the marina district casinos were spared—the Borgata, the Golden Nugget, Harrah's—anything in the path of the storm got flattened, as in pancaked and pulverized. They're now gravel."

Crushed…flattened. Danni couldn't get her head around that. From the look of the city from here in Brigantine—more like the *non*-look, because nothing was there—she'd suspected something like that, but to hear it from someone who'd been on the scene…

"The drones never got close enough to the ground to show that."

"That's because they were shot down as soon as we spotted them. DHS has a team dedicated to detecting drones early and blasting them out of the sky."

"But what flattened the city?"

"We don't *know!*" he said through suddenly clenched teeth

as frustration escaped for an instant. "It happened during the storm that landed during the tide, when visibility was effectively zero."

"Somebody must have a theory."

A rueful smile twisted his lips. "Well, there's the daikaiju theory."

"The what?"

"That a massive, Godzilla-style monster waded ashore and stomped the city flat."

"But that's silly!"

He laughed but she could hear no humor in the sound. "Of course it is. But some of us have had a running debate—facetious, of course—about which particular Japanese monster did it. I think it shows how desperate we are for an answer. The truth is that the city is flattened, but nothing *stomped* it flat. The USGS oversees a whole network of seismometers—I mean, all over the place—and something coming down with enough force to pound a high-rise into the ground would set them all off. Something that big couldn't even *walk* ashore without raising a ruckus. But not a peep. The seismos stayed flatlined all the way."

"So, no monster. How about a divine hand descending from the heavens and crushing the sinners?"

"Yeah, God might have been able to do it without a seismic footprint, but no one can think of anything else. And we keep the monster talk strictly between ourselves. I mean, can you imagine what would happen if it got out that some of us were theorizing about something like that?"

"What *are* you theorizing about?"

"We're still looking for hard evidence to go on. Trouble is, we've got nothing. *Nada*. Over twenty-five thousand people are missing and assumed dead, so you'd think there'd be plenty. But they're gone without a trace. Every single one, and still not a clue as to what happened to them."

...over twenty-five thousand people missing and assumed dead... her dear friends Mac and Aldo among them.

"Well, unless the Rapture came to AC, they didn't just disappear. They've gotta be somewhere."

Benigno shrugged. "So you'd think. The current theory is they were either devoured or carried off to the Sohm Abyss in the receding tide, or a combination of both, which is as good as nowhere. Survivors along the fringe of the Upwelling are pretty consistent in their descriptions of the *things* that came in with the tide: things with claws, things with tentacles, things with claws *and* tentacles. Little things the size of baby crabs and things the size of manta rays and every size between. What CCTV we could find shows the tide flooding in and reveals shapes moving in the water. Then the storm hit with its blinding hail and rain, and the cameras were flattened along with everything else."

"But there has to be *some* trace."

"No, Boudreau," he said with a slow shake of his head. "That's what you'd think. But we've found nothing organic so far. Not a blood smear, not a *cell*. Even the rats and insects are gone. Not even bacteria. The ruins are *sterile*."

That rocked her. Not even bacteria?

"But wait," she said. "DHS has quarantined the area because of infection risk. If it's sterile—"

"The infection risk is bogus."

She nodded. "I had a feeling about that. Why?"

"It helps keep people out. Ever since COVID-19, infections are an easy sell, especially since everyone in the investigative team wears hazmat coveralls whenever they're on site."

"Hazmats? But if the ruins are sterile…"

"We've been unable to isolate a virus or bacteria, but there *is* risk. At least there might be."

"I'm not following."

He fiddled with his laptop again and a middle-aged man's face replaced the map on the wall monitor. Watery blue eyes peered through wire-rimmed glasses; he wore his hair in a comb-over. His toothy smile looked friendly, though.

"This is Pastor Anton Seward, founder and leader of the Church of the Received Word. Don't rack you brain for anything you might have heard about them, because you won't find it unless you're a student of tiny, weirdo Christian sects based in Salem County. Two nights after the Upwelling, when we were all still getting our bearings, he sneaked in, pitched a pup tent on the beach right in front of where Bally's used to be, and spent the night praying. His intention was to perform an exorcism on the ruins at dawn. His explanation for the Upwelling, as he explains on the video, was at odds with that of his fellow religious leaders who were calling it retribution for the city's sinful ways. He said the city hadn't been evil *enough* for Satan who sent a horde of his haunts—"

"Haunts?"

"Yes. It appears the Church of the Received Word has its own mythology. According to him the destruction left the 'blasted heath' more evil than ever, thus the exorcism."

"What's a 'blasted heath'?" Danni said.

"'Heath' is an old term for an infertile wasteland, which I guess fits AC these days. And it certainly appears blasted. But anyway, he made a vid recording of his night-long prayer vigil. Maybe he thought he'd put it on YouTube or something."

You're not going to make me watch a night-long vigil, are you? Danni thought. Please, no. Please-please-please, no.

As if responding to her silent plea, Benigno said, "I won't subject you to that. We've had psychologists and psychiatrists and anthropologists and linguists watch it time and time again. I've fast-forwarded through it myself and it's a huge bore for most of its length. Until dawn approaches, that is, and then it gets stomach-churningly violent."

"He was attacked?"

"No, he attacked himself. But first he started speaking gibberish. His endless chants in English appealing to God for guidance in cleansing this 'blasted heath' go on all night. But as dawn approaches he starts talking about seeing the 'haunts' and how awful they are. And as he talks about them he starts inserting nonsense words into his speech. Just occasionally at first, and then more and more until he'd spouting pure word salad—or at least what *seems* like word salad."

"What do you mean, 'seems'?"

"Our linguists swear he's speaking a real language, but not one any of them have ever heard. They couldn't even find roots to other human languages. But then things get nasty. He becomes more and more agitated, starts screaming in that unknown tongue, and then, still in front of the camera, he gouges out both his eyes."

Danni couldn't help recoiling. "Oh, shit. Really?"

"Really. He's screaming with the pain, his hands are covered with blood, but he keeps working at it until he rips both of them out. And then…"

Danni waited, then said, "And then?"

"And then he eats them."

"Aw, no." Her stomach writhed. "Now you're kidding me."

He reached for the laptop. "I can show you—"

Danni waved her hands frantically. "No! No, I believe you! It's just…"

"I know. It's totally gross. But it doesn't stop there."

"It gets worse?"

"Not really. Hard to get worse than that. But after he finishes with his eyes, he starts biting off pieces of flesh from his forearms and eating that too. We found him wandering around the ruins, covered in blood and screaming in that unhuman language."

"Did he survive?"

Another nod. "We've got him over at Wharton State Psychiatric Center in Hammonton."

"Wharton? I thought they closed that."

"They're in the process. You know, winding down. The type of patients who end up in Wharton can't be just let out on the street or put in group homes. The place still houses a few patients and a skeleton staff, and we wanted to keep him close by. The pastor's bite wounds have healed but he's got to stay wrapped up in a straitjacket to keep him from eating himself. He doesn't seem interested in eating anyone else—he's got no zombie thing going on—just himself. And here's the really weird part."

"Oh, really? Like this hasn't been weird enough already?"

"Try this: If he can't eat himself, he won't eat anything else. For almost nine weeks now he hasn't eaten a thing, hasn't drunk so much as a drop of water, and yet he hasn't lost an ounce."

Danni laughed. "I've been on that diet!"

Benigno frowned. "This isn't a joke, Boudreau."

"How can it not be? That's impossible."

"But it's true. He's under constant video surveillance because he's such a danger to himself, so we know no one's sneaking him food. The doctors there are totally baffled. I've simply added him to my list of Shit That Just Can't Happen associated with the Upwelling. But wait—there's more. In all that time, not only has he not eaten, he hasn't shut up. He keeps babbling on and on, twenty-four-seven in that unhuman language."

"He doesn't sleep?"

"Oh, didn't I mention that? Sorry. No, he hasn't slept a wink in almost nine weeks."

Danni sat and stared at the smiling, happy face on the screen and tried to imagine it without eyes. She failed.

"What happened to him out there?"

"That's what we'd like to know. But it's not unique to him. We've put animals out there in cages all night, and they do fine until it nears dawn, then they start chewing at themselves. They usually bleed to death before we get to them."

"My God. Is it some sort of radiation?"

"If it is, it's a new sort, because we've detected nothing. Time of exposure seems to be the key, so we limit our excursions onto the ruins to one hour or less, and only in full hazmat gear. So now you know the reason behind the phony infection warning and why DHS can't have people picking through the rubble. And that's why the extremely restrictive NDA. You understand we can have no leaks about this."

Danni nodded. "Totally."

"And now you understand why your memory loss is no surprise and so easy for us here to accept. It's rather prosaic compared to the rest of what we're dealing with."

"I guess so. Doesn't make it any easier for me to deal with, though. I still want those hours back."

He stared at her. "Do you, Boudreau? Be careful what you wish for." He closed his laptop. "Anyway, take a break and then we'll fit you out with a hazmat suit for your first trip onto the blasted heath."

Danni had been looking forward to investigating the ruins in person since she got word that they were attaching her to the Atlantic City team. Now she wasn't so sure.

4

Pam sat in Chet's office opposite his desk and stared at nothing. Well, her gaze was fixed on the edge of his desk, actually, but that was pretty much the same as nothing. The wind had gone out of her. She felt weak. Mentally and physically deflated.

What the fuck? Seriously, what the fuck had she just seen? Phil's body engulfed in flames and he wasn't even the slightest bit scorched.

She remembered the good times, when they'd been close, the feel of his skin, the muscles moving beneath it, the rhythmic beat of his heart as she lay with her ear against his chest. A normal guy with normal hang ups, with a normal day-to-day existence until life fucked him over—fucked them both over. That was when everything changed for them.

But none of that could have changed him into some sort of *thing* that wouldn't burn.

That attendant's words came back to her: *Maybe he's a saint...*

Could it be? No. She discarded the thought immediately. She didn't need any of that religious bullshit clouding the waters. This was the real world and Phil's body *really* wouldn't burn.

God, she needed a cigarette, but she didn't have the energy to get up and walk outside to have one. And she would definitely have to go outside, what with the *No Smoking* signs all over the place.

She also needed a drink. A little too early—make that way too early—to hit the bottle, but today she might make an exception. Oh, yeah. A *big* exception.

Chet sat on the other side of the desk, saying nothing. Probably afraid to speak. Probably thought she was some crazy rage monkey and didn't want to set her off. Well, she had damn good reasons for her rage, and they started long before Phil's senseless death. But he didn't need to know them. She didn't need to explain herself to him or anyone else.

An insane question had been growing in her head since she'd watched Phil's body lying untouched in the flame. She had to ask it.

"This may sound a little crazy—or even a lot crazy—but could this have anything to do with Atlantic City?"

She could tell from his expression that he hadn't seen that coming.

"Why do you ask?" he said after a pregnant pause. "Did your husband work there?"

"No, and he never went there. He hated the place, thought gambling was stupid. 'Might as well just throw your money out the window,' he'd say. And I agreed with him. But you know how people lately try to connect anything weird that happens to whatever went down in AC. And you've got to admit that this is weird as all fuck."

He nodded. "Oh, it definitely is. Connecting one inexplicable occurrence to another is natural, I suppose. It's how conspiracy theories get started. But since we don't understand what happened to AC, how can we connect it to this?"

"Gotcha." They sat in silence until she managed to say, "What do we do now?"

"I've been thinking about that," Chet said. "I'll have to call the medical examiner and see what he says."

She lifted her head. "The medical examiner?"

He shrugged. "Under the circumstances, I don't see any way around it. This is now a coroner's case."

"But we know his cause of death,"

"But all sorts of abnormal circumstances have suddenly cropped up. I mean, I've got a body that won't burn. That alone is enough to warrant a post-mortem."

Well, damn. That meant dragging out all the drama. Not that she had a problem with someone cutting Phil open. He was dead, after all, and neither of them belonged to any church or gave much thought to religion. She was pretty sure that if the cause of death hadn't been so obvious—if his head hadn't looked like a dropped melon—the medical examiner probably would have insisted on slicing and dicing him before releasing the body.

Yeah, not only did she not have a problem with post mortems, after what she'd just seen, she wanted one. Very much so.

"How do we arrange that?"

Chet said, "Not your worry. I'll take care of it. I'll call over and explain what I can—"

"Yeah, well, good luck with that."

He flashed a brief smile—the first time she'd seen him smile since she'd walked in here yesterday. It changed his face.

"I'll ease into it—start off saying I noticed some 'irregularities' and expand from there. I'll let you know what they find."

She rose. "Please do."

"You'll know as soon as I do."

Maybe Chet wasn't such a bad guy. But what the fuck was up with Phil?

5

Danni's excursion into the ruins turned out to be very brief and very disturbing.

It took her a half hour to get into her Level B hazmat suit—and that was with Benigno's help. Damn, it was complicated. It seemed that during the weeks since the disaster the team had learned that a Level B suit with a self-contained breathing apparatus appeared to offer sufficient protection. No one who had ventured out into the ruins had come down with an illness or a taste for their own flesh like Pastor Seward. At least so far. Maybe a Level C suit without the SCBA would be just as effective, but nobody had volunteered to try it, and no one was pushing.

The suit came with a two-way, voice-activated radio—encrypted, of course—and an earpiece. Each hood also had a body cam mounted on it to record whatever they saw. It should have come with an air-conditioning unit too, because this contraption was not designed with an August jaunt to the beach in mind.

Once they were all suited up, they boarded a skiff that took them across the Absecon Inlet to the area that had once been the Atlantic City Aquarium. Before the Upwelling, a bridge had arched over the water from Brigantine to the Marina District, but that had been crushed along with everything else.

As they stepped ashore, Danni could only stop and stare. She, Chan, Mac, and Aldo had gathered in AC twice a year to spend a weekend together. They made a point of staying at a different casino-hotel each time, from the relatively small Golden Nugget to the absolutely cavernous Ocean, and she'd become fairly familiar with the city's skyline.

Now...no skyline. Absolutely flat.

The famous boardwalk and the Steel Pier—gone. The soaring oceanfront hotels—gone. The restaurants, fast-food joints, banks, drugstores, department stores, high-rise condos and the tenements behind them—gone. The massive hotels that dominated the Marina District—gone.

Through the salt haze from the pounding surf Danni could see all the way south to the Margate high rises where Chan lived. Looking west, the view was clear to Absecon and Pleasantville and beyond. The vast, undeveloped wetlands before her must have been what early humans saw when they first arrived here. The ocean still crashed on shore, the seabirds still wheeled in the sky, the grasses along the edges of the inlet still grew lush and green, but no trace of humankind remained.

"I can't believe this," she said.

"And you've only been a tourist," Benigno squawked in her ear. "I used to work here. Commuted every day via the Brigantine Boulevard bridge to the resident agency office. Now the bridge is no more, the office is no more, the whole damn city is no more. I still can't believe what I see here. Or rather what I don't see."

She walked about thirty feet or so into what Pastor Stewart had called "the blasted heath" and kicked at the multicolored rubble that resembled crushed stone.

Benigno came up beside her. "It's a mix of pieces of asphalt, concrete, steel, wood, and plastic, no pebble bigger than one inch across."

"The whole city is reduced to this?"

"Yep. And it goes deep, pushed way, way down, like a great weight descended on it all."

Danni thought she caught movement among the pebbles. She bent for a closer look and saw an oblong shape, brown and shiny with long, bobbing antennae, struggling up to the air from beneath the gravel. A cockroach.

"Look," she said, pointing. "You said the place was sterile, but something survived."

"Well, I'll be," Benigno said. "You're right. Figures it would be a cockroach. The damn things are indestructible."

Normally cockroaches disgusted her, but she took a strange delight in this one. Any sign of life on this blasted heath was a cause for celebration. A few inches away, a second roach struggled up to the surface.

"Here's another! And another!"

More and more were appearing. A dozen, then two dozen, then fifty. Danni gradually slipped from delight to concern, and from there to consternation. The ground was now acrawl with literally hundreds of cockroaches, scuttling this way and that, over and under one another. And then, as if on cue, they all froze in place, all facing the same way: toward her.

"What's going on?"

"I don't know," Benigno said. "They all seem to be looking at you."

His words chilled her, more so because they really *did* seem to be looking at her. "But why would they do that?"

"I have absolutely no idea. I've never seen anything like this."

And then they came for her. In a shiny, brown, undulating wave, a carpet of insects flowed toward her. Danni stumbled back and almost fell, but managed to stay upright. She couldn't help a cry of revulsion as they swept over her, flowing up her legs and spreading over her torso. She frantically batted at them, but they were too many. Benigno tried to help but was just as ineffective. Why weren't they crawling over him? Why just her?

Now they were *all* over her, blocking her faceplate. She bit back a scream.

"Head for the water!" Benigno said. "We'll drown them!"

Great idea, but...

"Which way?" she cried. She kept sweeping them from her faceplate but they covered it again in an instant. "I can't see!"

Strong hands grabbed her arm and wheeled her around.

"Straight ahead. I'll guide you."

Trusting him—what choice did she have?—she put one foot in front of the other and blindly stumbled forward.

"You're doing great. Keep it up. We're almost to the beach."

After a few more steps she felt sand squish beneath her boots, and suddenly her faceplate cleared. She looked down and her hazmat suit was bug free. Turning, she saw the wave of roaches flowing back to the ruins, to the blasted heath, to disappear again into the rubbled remains of the crushed city.

"What just happened?"

"As soon as you set foot on the beach it was as if you stepped through a curtain that swept them off you."

They both stared back at the rubble. It looked exactly as it had when they'd arrived.

"Did that really happen?" she said.

"It did. I'm finding it hard to believe I didn't imagine it, but that was real. Our body cams will back us up."

"But why only me? Why not you? It doesn't make any sense."

"Nothing about this place makes sense."

She raised her arm to point back at the blasted heath and noticed countless tiny pinhole rents in the fabric of her suit.

"My God, they were biting me!"

Had they wanted to eat her?

"Get me out of here," she said. "Please?"

6

Pam finished her car cigarette before she got home. Once inside she lit up another before she realized she didn't have a single ashtray in the whole fucking house. As an outside-only smoker she hadn't needed one. She grabbed the cup from her morning coffee, still sitting on the kitchen table, and used that.

Smoking in their front room...weird. Not anywhere near as weird as Phil's body not burning, but still weird. The whole house had taken on a weird vibe. The place had been big for two people, and now enormous for one. Four bedrooms, to hold the big family they'd planned. One of many plans that never panned out.

Just her now...Phil would not be coming home from work. He would not sit in his fucking La-Z-Boy and watch TV at night. He'd started out as an accountant, but then after their lives exploded, he found he couldn't handle it. He'd always been handy and so he decided he wanted to work with his hands and hired out as a carpenter. He made decent blue-collar money—which they didn't really need after the settlement their ambulance chaser wrangled from the hospital for them. The shark took a third for himself but that still left plenty.

Now she had the house and the settlement all to herself. No more arguing over what to watch at night. She stared at the empty La-Z-Boy. Would she miss him? They hadn't got along for years. No big fights or shouting matches. No throwing things. Just a sort of cold war. Peaceful coexistence—isn't that what they called it?

Yeah. No more Phil.

Which meant another hole in her life.

For no good reason, Pam began to sob.

7

Danni started at the blare of her intercom buzzer. This was the first time it had sounded since they'd moved her into the apartment. She fumbled with the buttons on the console in the kitchen until she found the right one.

"Who's there?"

"Boudreau?" said a scratchy voice from the tiny speaker. "It's Agent Benigno. Can I come up? I need to speak with you."

He'd driven out to her place? At night? Oh, hell. Was this going to be a pass?

Men had stopped being a problem at the Newark office. Word had finally got around that she wasn't into men. One guy had still persisted, obviously thinking she'd simply never met the right guy—namely, him. She'd been forced to dress him down loud and clear in public, shouting, "Didn't you get the message? I don't do dicks—literally and figuratively—which makes you a two-time loser!"

That had been the end of that.

Her love life, though, had been trapped in the pits. She'd meet someone and there'd be sweetness and passion and sparks, and then she'd start finding things wrong and it would end, usually on a sour note. *It's not you, it's me...* such a cliché, but in her case it almost always was Danni. And being dragged off to the DC-Maryland-Northern Virginia area for two months hadn't helped in the least.

And now what? Was she going to have to circulate a memo around the Brigantine office—*Agent Boudreau doesn't do dicks?*

On the plus side tonight, he'd announced himself as "Agent Benigno," and hadn't called her "Danielle."

Still, she said, "It's kind of late."

"It's kind of important."

Shit. Didn't sound like he was going away. She pressed the entry buzzer.

She'd been sipping a glass of white wine to settle her nerves. She was still shaken by the cockroach incident earlier. Her body cam recording had been compromised by the roaches obscuring the lens, but Benigno's had picked up every horrific detail. It had been... surreal. The only word for it. She stashed both the glass and the bottle out of sight. She was *not* offering him a drink.

She looked around to see if she should put anything else out of sight. The Bureau had rented the place furnished so nothing here was hers except her beloved Pollock print. Like a big hotel suite, except no room service.

When she opened the door he stepped inside without being asked. He looked rattled.

"A situation has arisen," he said, "and I didn't want to get into it over the phone. It needs face to face."

"Oh?" That had an ominous ring. Where was this going?

"I got word from the Wharton psychiatric facility—from Pastor Seward's doctor out there."

"Oh?" She hadn't wanted to say that again, but didn't know how else to respond. She was glad he was sticking to business, though.

"He told me that today Pastor Seward spoke in English for the first time since his arrival there. He said only eight words, then went back to his babbling. The words meant nothing to the doctor. He thought it was just more nonsense, except in English this time. But he felt he had to report it to someone, so he called my office."

"What did he say—the pastor, I mean?"

"He said, 'I need to talk to the cockroach girl.'"

Danni felt a sudden need to sit.

"Are you okay?" Benigno said, all solicitous. "Can I get you a drink of water?"

She waved him off, annoyed with her reaction. "No-no, that's okay. I'm not the type who gets the vapors. It's just that... he's talking about me, isn't he?"

"Well, yeah. Who else?"

"But how can he know? Do you have a leak?"

"Absolutely not. It was just you and me out there, and the call came in before I'd filed my incident report. And listen: Even if we did have a leak, Seward has no contact with the outside world."

"He's got to have attendants. One of them might have—"

"First off, it happened only a few hours ago. Second, he spends the whole day alone. He's watched on CCTV, of course, but they stopped trying to feed him weeks ago when they realized his total fast wasn't affecting his health. And because nothing's going in, nothing's coming out, so he has no toilet needs. They bathe him once a week and today wasn't the day. His doctor had just stepped in to do his weekly checkup when Seward stopped his babbling long enough to say, 'I need to talk to the cockroach girl.' Then he resumed his usual."

Chilled, Danni rubbed her arms. "God, that's weird. I never even heard of him before today. What do I do?"

"Talk to him, of course. Or rather, let him talk to you."

Danni shook her head. "I don't know...I mean, he's got no eyes..."

"Look, he'll be safely trussed in his straitjacket and they keep his eye sockets covered all the time to protect them. If he sits there and continues his unhuman babble thing, we'll call it quits and write it off as nice try but wasted time. But if he does switch back to English, maybe we can find out what's going on in his head and what he saw—or thinks he saw before he gouged out his eyes."

"And maybe find out how he learned about 'cockroach girl.'"

God, was that how she was going to be known by the team?

"That too." He did his staring thing, then said, "You're connected to that place and what happened there, Boudreau. I don't know how, I don't know why. Maybe the reason for your memory loss is at the root, but you're definitely connected. The cockroaches are proof enough for me. Seward lost his mind there, so he's connected too. And somehow, maybe because of that, you and Seward have formed a connection. It makes a strange sort of triangular sense while, at the same time, making no sense at all."

That seemed to sum up the situation perfectly.

"What do you say?" he said. "Meet with Seward?"

Her first day with the team and this happens. Well, she wanted to prove herself an asset. She could wind up the only person the crazy, eyeless pastor would talk sense to. Wow, what an honor. Not.

"Okay." She hoped she wouldn't regret this. "When?"

"As soon as I can arrange it with the hospital. I'll get back to you tomorrow with the time."

She saw him to the door where he turned and gave her a crooked smile. "Sleep tight, Boudreau."

Yeah, if I sleep at all.

Once he was gone she retrieved her wine and gulped the rest of the glass. Now she *really* needed a drink. When Benigno had appeared she'd been worried about him making a pass at her. Now she wished that had been the reason for his visit. She'd have found it much easier to deal with.

TUESDAY

1

Who the fuck was ringing her doorbell at this hour of the morning?

Pam glanced at the time on the cable box as she stumbled past: *9:38*. Oh. Okay, not so early after all. But she felt like absolute crap—head throbbing, stomach queasy. Self-pity had once been her big thing. She'd wallowed in it. Then she'd come out of it. But she'd relapsed last night and hit the Luksusowa bottle a little too hard. She was paying for that this morning.

She checked through the peephole and recognized the funeral guy. His name had fled her head. Chet—that was it. What the fuck did he want?

She glanced in the oval mirror next to the door and gasped. Not that she cared to make any sort of impression on the fucking undertaker, but she looked like warmed-over shit, and that red mop of hers... she finger-combed some of the flyaway strands and pulled open the door.

"Now what?"

He blinked, obviously taken aback by the warmth of her greeting. "Um, I need to speak to you, Mrs. Sirman."

"I'm guessing some new shit has hit your fan."

"Pardon? May I come in?"

"The place is a mess."

"I'd rather not discuss this out here."

Uh-oh. That didn't sound good. She couldn't help a pang of apprehension as she stepped back to let him pass.

She shut the door. "Is this where you tell me Phil's body turned to ash overnight?"

"I wish that were the case. The truth is, your husband's body is missing."

Did he say...?

"Wait. Did I hear you right? Missing? His body's *missing*? You fucking lost Phil's body?"

"Yes, it's missing, no, we didn't *lose* it. We went to transport him to the medical examiner's office this morning and he was gone."

She stared at him, tried to say something, failed, then tried again.

"Seriously? *Seriously?*"

"I didn't want you to hear it on the news, so—"

"Wait-wait-wait. Why would I hear it on the news?"

"Well, I've just spent an hour with a couple of cops. They'll be filing a police report of the crime, and news of this sort will inevitably find its way to the media which—"

"Great! Just fucking great! You lost his body and now there's going to be a media circus."

His expression turned sour. "I wish you'd stop saying 'lost.'"

"Well, how would you put it?"

She asked out of pure curiosity, because she didn't give a rat's ass what he wished.

"His body was *stolen*, Mrs. Sirman. Someone *stole* your husband's body."

The words landed like a punch. She tried to process that: stolen?

"You're talking about body snatchers?"

"And very skilled. I sent Tony home early last night and closed up—checked the door locks and set the alarm myself. And as is my habit, I was the first to arrive this morning. The backdoor was locked and the alarm still set, just as I'd left it. The thieves entered and left without leaving a trace."

"But why would someone want to steal Phil's body?"

"The only reason I can think of is that it's somehow related to the fact that it won't burn."

She still hadn't fully processed that fact yet, and now this new one. But yeah, they had to be related.

"You mean...someone doesn't want a post-mortem on him."

He nodded. "Exactly."

Movement outside the front window distracted her. She

peered through the sheer and saw a small panel truck pulling into the curb. *NEWS 12 NJ* blared along its side.

"Well, they didn't waste any fucking time!"

Chet stepped up beside her. "They'll be looking for an interview. I advise against it."

"If I tell them I don't know a fucking thing, they'll go away."

"Can you talk to them without using the F-word?"

*The F-word...*seriously?

"Who, me? Fuck yeah."

They both had a little laugh at that.

"You have a nice laugh," he said. "You ought to try it more."

He wasn't coming on to her, was he?

"Not much to laugh about in my life."

"Yeah, I guess not."

You don't know the half of it, brother.

He said, "Why don't you just stay out of sight in here. Don't say a word to them."

"You think they'll have to bleep me a lot, is that it?"

"Yes, and they'll have a ball doing it. Which will bring them back for more."

She'd pretty much always had a sailor's mouth. "Potty-mouth Pam" had been her high school nickname, along with Garbage-gums Gunning when she still used her maiden name. But the habit had grown so much worse over the past few years, in direct proportion to her generalized anger at the whole fucking world.

A woman she recognized as one of the channel's on-location reporters stepped out of the passenger side and approached the house. Maybe Chet was right: Keep mum. If that reporter got her pissed, she'd let loose with a stream that would melt her ears.

He added, "I should talk to them."

"But they're not here for you."

"True, but when you get down to it, it's my problem. You entrusted your husband's remains to my care and he was stolen from under my nose. I've got a personal stake here. My reputation is on the line."

Not to mention your fucking business, she thought, but held that back.

Pam said, "We should both keep our yaps shut."

He sighed. "I guess you're right."

There came a triple knock. They stood still and silent. Then another triplet. Then: "*News 12*, Mrs. Sirman." The reporter's voice was faint through the door. "We'd like to talk to you about the theft of your husband's body, if it's all right with you. We have the funeral home's side of the story, so we'd like yours."

She saw Chet stiffen. "'Funeral home's side'?" he said in a hushed tone. "What the hell?"

Anger exploded in Pam. "You fucking talked to them already?" she shouted.

"Not a word!" He leaned toward the door and shouted. "I happen to be the funeral home director and you did not speak to me!"

"We spoke to an attendant named Anthony Vallone."

Chet closed his eyes and grimaced. "Oh, shit. Big-mouth Tony." He reached for the door handle. "I'm going to straighten this out right now."

As the door slammed behind him, Pam thought that maybe Chet wasn't such a bad guy after all.

And then a sudden symmetry descended with crushing weight: Phil was gone, erased without a trace.

Just like Julie.

2

True to his word, Benigno texted Danni directions to the Wharton State Psychiatric Center first thing in the morning.

They've set up a meeting with the pastor for 11 AM. I'll meet you there. I know it's not far from your place, but leave yourself plenty of time. It's easy to get lost out there.

Despite her dread of meeting the self-destructive loony who called her "the cockroach girl," she left early and made her way to the White Horse Pike. She took that into Hammonton, which liked to bill itself as "The Blueberry Capital of the World."

Since she'd had a little free time earlier this morning, she did some research on the psychiatric center and learned that the town of Hammonton grew up along the old Pennsylvania line that ran from Philly to Atlantic City. The psych center started out as a huge Victorian mansion belonging to one of the area's blueberry barons. A Philadelphia psychiatrist later purchased it and added large extensions to house his mental patients. After his death, the state took it over. Since it bordered the Wharton State Forest, it seemed only natural to adopt that as part of its new name.

Benigno's suggestion about leaving herself extra time turned out to be a good one; she lost her way more than once among the vineyards, blueberry fields, and vast turf farms. But she arrived fashionably early at ten forty-five. She didn't know enough about Victorian architecture to identify its particular design, but the old structure exuded an appropriate Addams Family vibe.

Benigno appeared almost instantly after she gave her name at the front desk and led her down a long hall to a monitoring station. He introduced her to the technician sitting at a console who gave her a wary look. Was he wondering how she'd earned the name "cockroach girl"?

Benigno said, "This is where we'll be monitoring and recoding everything Seward says to you." He led her around to where she could see a color monitor showing a figure sitting at a long table. "That used to be their group therapy room, back when they had enough patients for groups. Seward's already there."

The straitjacketed man wore white pads over his eyes, secured by gauze wrapped around his head. But something about his mouth... his teeth were exposed, almost like a skull's.

"Can you get closer on him?" she said.

The tech worked a lever and the camera slowly zoomed in on his face. She gasped when she realized he had no lips.

"God, what happened to him?"

"He ate his lips," Benigno said. "Chewed them off."

"Oh, joy."

Wow. She didn't know if she could do this. This guy was too—

No, she *would* do this. She wasn't going to allow herself to wimp out. She was not Clarice Starling going in to meet Hannibal Lecter. This wasn't some evil genius, this was a poor, weirdo preacher who'd lost his mind out there on the blasted heath. Not to be feared. Pitied, if anything.

"If he does start speaking to you," Benigno said, "you'll have to listen closely. Without lips he can't say 'B' or 'F' or 'M' or 'W,' or the like. As I said, we'll be recording everything, but you'll need to understand him in order to respond. Comprende?"

"Got it."

"We don't know what he wants with you, but here's what we want to know from him: What happened to him out there? What did he think he saw? What made him rip his eyes out? Do you need a list?"

"No, I think I can remember. Let's get this over with."

"Yeah, let's. He's right around the corner."

He led her back to the hall, a few steps to the left, then opened a door for her. She stepped into a good-sized room with ornate light fixtures hanging from the high ceiling. Sunlight filtered through leaded glass in tall, narrow, pointed-arch windows, giving it a chapel feel.

Pastor Seward had been babbling when the door opened but stopped and rose from his chair. "The cockroach girl! Greetings!"

She swallowed. Okay. You can do this.

"Gree—" The word caught, then shook free. "Greetings, Pastor."

"Sit, sit," he said, nodding to the other side of the table.

As she settled onto her chair, he returned to his. Benigno stayed standing beside her.

"I need to talk to you," he said. "Alone."

"Not gonna happen," Benigno said.

Seward leaned back and began to babble in his strange tongue with bizarre syllables. This had to be the unhuman language Danni had been told about. She looked at him: a skinny, blind, middle-aged guy in a straitjacket. What did she have to fear?

"I'll be all right," she told Benigno.

His dark eyebrows lifted. "You're sure?"

"I'm not sure of anything, anymore, but...yeah, pretty much."

"Okay. I'll be right outside."

As soon as the door closed behind Benigno, Seward switched back to English.

"Alone at last." She thought he might have been smiling but, without lips and his teeth constantly exposed, who could tell?

"You wanted to speak to me?"

"Yes."

When he didn't go on, she tried one of Benigno's questions. "Why did you blind yourself?"

"I saw then and didn't 'ant to see then any-'ore."

Saw then? Oh, right. He couldn't pronounce "*m*."

"Saw whom?"

"Those who 'ait 'or us."

"Wait for us where?"

"In the endless night. I see the haunters uh the endless night."

"But where *is* that?"

"Out there." He leaned back and directed his sightless gaze at the ceiling. "'Ehind the curtain. They're hungry 'or us." He sobbed, then screamed, "I tore out 'y eyes *and I still see then!*"

He's totally off the wall! What the hell am I doing here? What am I accomplishing?

She gave him a few seconds to calm down, then, "Tell me, Pastor, was this part of your beliefs as a member of…" What had been the name of his sect? "…of the Church of the Received Word?"

He shook his head. "No, that's dead. I now ser' the Owner."

"The Owner? Who is the Owner?"

And why did it sound vaguely familiar?

"It owns us. It touched 'e."

It?

"It 'touched' you? How? I don't understand."

"You do. You *do* understand. The Squatter touched *you*."

Okay…how did she respond to that? And again, that twinge of familiarity. Why?

"The 'Squatter'? Who is the Squatter? I'm not familiar with anyone by that name."

"Don't lie! It touched you! The Squatter touched you and now you're unclean!"

A ripping sound, and then his right hand suddenly appeared through a rent in the fabric of his straitjacket. He tore the bandages from his eyes, revealing raw, empty sockets.

"I see you! I see the Squatter in you! Tear it out! Tear it out!"

Danni jumped from her seat as he launched himself across the table and grabbed her arm.

"Die, Squatter! Die!"

Danni heard the door open behind her and Benigno yelling as her hand-to-hand training at Quantico came back to her. Grabbing Seward's pinky, she peeled back his fingers from around her wrist and twisted his arm behind him, depositing him face first on the table, kicking and gnashing his teeth.

God, he was strong—the strength of a madman. Lucky for her he'd managed to free only one arm. Benigno charged up to pin his legs and they held him there until orderlies arrived with extra restraints.

As they led him away, he sobbed, "I tore out 'y eyes and still I see then... still see the haunters!"

Benigno gave her his patented stare. "You handled yourself pretty good there, Boudreau. Pretty damn good. Looks like you were paying attention down at Quantico."

She jammed her hands into her pockets to hide her trembling fingers. Her insides were shaking from the adrenaline rush. The pastor had scared her half to death.

"They said it might come in handy someday. I guess today was the day."

"Let's take a break and then we'll review the video of the encounter."

Seriously? she thought. The last thing she wanted to do was relive this encounter.

3

Chan's phone dinged its email chime.

"I'll be damned," he muttered as he checked it: One of his Google alerts had scored a hit. He'd set up a string of them six weeks ago. "Body stolen"... "body missing"... "body snatch"... "corpse theft" and a few other variations on the theme. They'd been silent until today. Looked like "body stolen" got the hit. He opened the email and saw a link to *NJ.com*. He hit it and it took him to a news headline just hours old.

BODY STOLEN FROM FUNERAL HOME

Holy crap. A real hit. A click on the link took him to the article itself.

> *Lincroft, NJ—Between the hours of 10 PM last night and 6 AM this morning, a body was stolen from the Landry Funeral Home on Newman Springs Road. The remains of Philip A. Sirman were scheduled to be transported to the county medical examiner but when attendants went to transfer the body, they found it missing. Mr. Sirman was the victim of a fatal two-vehicle collision this past Friday. He is survived by his spouse who was not available for comment.*
>
> *According to police, there were no signs of a break-in. A full investigation is pending.*

Philip Sirman...Chan shook his head. The name rang no bells. He glanced at the newspaper clippings that covered a section of the wall above his desk. Most concerned the Atlantic City Upwelling, but a small cluster concerned the death and subsequent disappearance of one Kurt Maez. Maez, too, had died in a highway accident. Coincidence? But Maez's death had involved an impact with an abutment and a ghastly car fire. Chan had witnessed it and felt somewhat responsible.

He shrugged and returned to the online article.

Police note that corpse theft is an unusual crime, rare in the United States. If it occurs it is usually committed after burial, an act known as grave robbing. There is no record of a body ever being stolen from a New Jersey funeral home. (In 2015 the body of Julie Mott was stolen from a private viewing room in a funeral home in San Antonio, TX, and never recovered.)

Chan noticed how they neglected to mention that Kurt Maez's body had disappeared from the Atlantic County morgue just two weeks ago. Although, to be fair, a morgue was not a funeral home, and none of the reports Chan had read referred to the disappearance as a "theft." Apparently the powers that be had listed it as "misplaced" or "misfiled." How do you "misfile" a corpse?

Was it worth investigating further? Probably not, but he'd promised himself to look into any body theft that occurred no matter where.

Another unusual aspect of the case was revealed by crematorium attendant, Anthony Vallone. "We tried to cremate the body yesterday," Vallone says, *"but it wouldn't burn. We tried twice at full throttle but nothing touched it. That's why we were sending it to the medical examiner."*

Wouldn't burn? No! Couldn't be!

He jumped to his wall and yanked down the Maez articles, sending the tacks flying. He scanned through them until he found: Despite the inferno of the crashed vehicle, the victim's body was miraculously unscathed when it was removed from the wreckage.

"Holy shit!"

He'd been so intent on the theft of the body... Maez, a

mysterious man doing mysterious things in a remote section of the pinelands had died on the road right in front of Chan and his body had disappeared overnight. What had happened to it? The question had so consumed him that he'd pushed the undamaged state of the body off his radar. Chan had seen that car fire, and "inferno" was not an exaggeration. He'd seen the unburnt body but had thought his eyes were playing tricks on him, though the newspaper article confirmed it.

Unburnt...just like Philip Sirman in the cremation chamber—twice, according to the attendant.

A mix of excitement and dread blasted through him, every nerve in his body tingling. He'd created those alerts without ever expecting a hit. But this was more than just a hit. This was a *connection*, goddamn it! A definite connection.

He printed out the Sirman item and tacked it up with the rest. Clearly now, he was going to have to make a trip to Lincroft. He knew where it was—a straight shot eighty or so miles up the Parkway. He'd save that for tomorrow. He'd do some research on this Sirman fellow and see if he could get the wife to talk to him. But in the meantime...

He looked at the life-size portrait on the wall next the balcony doors. It showed a middle-aged Chinese man from the waist up wearing a brocade tunic and a beaded cap. He had a high forehead and cold green eyes. A marmoset sat on his shoulder. The infamous Dr. Fu Manchu.

He'd seen it at an artist's table at one of the Atlantic City Comics and Anime Conventions and had to have it—with one change. He told the artist that if he could remove the mustache, he'd have a sale. The artist said no problem, but why? Chan explained that never in any of the books had Fu Manchu worn a mustache. Ironic, right? The namesake of the Fu Manchu mustache had always been clean shaven.

The artist called the following day: The mustache was gone. And so Chan became the proud owner of a portrait of Dr. Fu Manchu.

"What would you do?" he asked the painting.

He knew the answer: He'd send one of his minions out to the Pine Barrens and get to the bottom of this. Chan had no minions, so he grabbed his keys and headed down to the garage. He was sure the answer—or at least part of the answer—hid out there. He simply had to find it.

Two fireproof bodies, both stolen…the link was undeniable. It meant this Phil Sirman of Lincroft was somehow linked to Kurt Maez who was linked to that mysterious spot in the Pinelands… where Chan and his friends had been headed when his memory blanked. Time to go back for another look.

Pre-Upwelling, the fastest way there would have been via Route 40 or the Atlantic City Expressway, but as the saying goes, You can't get there from here. DHS had everything blocked off. So he had to take the slow, roundabout way via Margate Boulevard and county roads all the way to Mays Landing where he could pick up 50 North and from there veer off into the wilderness.

This was the last thing he remembered from that fateful day: Turning off Route 50 onto an unnamed road and heading west into the Pine Barrens. The pavement had started off as cracked and crumbling asphalt; an occasional small, secluded ranch house would be visible off to the side through the trees. Then the asphalt disappeared and the houses as well. Soon the sandy path narrowed to a pair of ruts with fire trails branching off left and right. The forty-foot scrub pines grew closer and closer together, crowding the edges of the path, leaning over it, their crooked branches forming a kind of scraggly roof.

Chan had been back along this route a number of times since then, searching for answers, and each time the growing sense of isolation permeated his psyche. He'd read up on the Pine Barrens since the AC disaster: a million-plus acres of wilderness, large swaths of it unmapped because they were still unexplored—all nestled in the heart of the most densely populated state in the US. New Jersey averaged 1200 people per square mile—the Pine Barrens averaged a single human being every eight square miles.

He turned off onto one of the fire trails. Years ago these paths had been cut through the dense trees to allow firefighters access to the woods when they periodically caught fire from lightning strikes during dry spells. They crisscrossed and branched with no sane pattern. The first time Chan had come here—well, the first time available to his memory, anyway—he'd seemed to know which branch to take when he came to it. Not a hundred percent. He made wrong choices because every trail looked like every other, but when he took the wrong trail he knew it almost immediately. He didn't know how he knew, he just *knew*. Had to be his subconscious at work. He'd had no conscious memory of being here before, but some part of his hindbrain remembered.

During his first trip back he recorded the GPS coordinates to help him find the place again, but got a bizarre reading at the spot—telling him he was in Honshu, Japan. He had to move off a ways before he could get an accurate reading. But on return trips, even with the coords, he never failed to make a couple of wrong turns before he found the spot. But he knew when he found it—didn't know how he knew but, again, like everything else related to this insanity, he just *knew*.

But he'd always been like that. Intuitive. Like a sixth sense. Not that he could see dead people like in the movie, but he could sense things other people were blind to. He couldn't ever put his finger on exactly what it was, but he blamed his perpetual uneasiness on it.

His mother had called him a *xiānzhī*. Like so many Chinese terms it could be interpreted a number of ways. Her family used it to mean a sort of seer, a talent that traditionally skipped generations. His grandmother had had it, then it skipped his mother to land on Chan.

He wished it had skipped to someone else, because it left him with a perpetual malaise. He sensed the background noise of the world and it wasn't a comforting sound. His *xiānzhī* sense could be helpful in sniffing out the wrongness in a place or situation and avoiding it, but it also sensed a wrongness in existence itself.

He'd been raised a Catholic. That was why his folks had left China: Despite supposed detente with the Vatican, the Beijing government was hostile to the Church and harassed Catholics on a habitual basis, especially members of the underground church like his folks. Finally they'd had enough.

They'd sent him to Catholic grammar school in Cincinnati,

and there the priests had presented an orderly, tidy universe with God the Father above and Satan below. Satan was trying to get you but the Good Guy upstairs had your back. A comforting view of the cosmos because everything was so nicely balanced and Someone was watching out for you.

But that wasn't what Chan *felt*. He felt chaos, an unsettling background noise, a malevolent Muzak that never ceased. He heard it from the moment he awoke, and it hummed a dissonant lullaby as he tried to sleep.

His friends tended to make fun of him—"Oh, no, Chan's got another of his *feelings*"—so he often kept them to himself. It wasn't always easy being a *tairongo*.

Wait... *tairongo*? Where had that come from? The word was *xiānzhī*. *Tairongo* seemed to mean something but he couldn't recall ever hearing it. It had simply popped into his head. Was it even a word?

More weirdness. Where would it end?

He spotted the camera affixed to a tree along the fire trail and that double-confirmed he was in the right place. Shortly after the Upwelling he'd found his way to this remote spot in the pines and somehow knew it was linked to those missing hours. How? Because he was a *xiānzhī*?

Whatever.

He'd spent a good deal of money he couldn't afford on a motion-activated camera with a satellite link to send all its images to his laptop. He'd faced a small photovoltaic collector south on a neighboring tree to provide a trickle charge to the battery. The phone took only still images and the area was so damn deserted, the camera was hardly ever triggered.

But it did trigger on occasion. And that was how he'd met the late Kurt Maez...

4

Six weeks ago...

For the first few days Chan's camera caught images of passing deer and not much else. Not a single human or car. And then one day he happened to be at his desk, working on his app—with his workplace obliterated, he had loads of time for that—when his Dropbox announced it had a new image. Expecting another deer, he checked and found a series of photos. The first showed a gray, aging multi-passenger van. What? Was someone taking a tour into the pines? The next showed a thirty-something fellow stepping out of the driver door. The third showed the rear doors open with him bending inside.

This was happening right now. Which meant if Chan hurried his ass and if his luck didn't go south—which it seemed to be doing lately with hellish regularity—he might be able to catch this guy and ask him what he knew about the spot.

Off he went, driving like a madman. One benefit of the disaster, if anything connected to it could be considered even remotely beneficial, was the sudden lack of traffic in the area. Twenty-five thousand people had been obliterated along with the city, and so, with the local population so drastically reduced, and the remains of the city sealed off and no longer a gambler magnet, his Sentra had the roads pretty much to itself.

He made it into the pines in record time and gave a little whoop when he saw the van still there, parked directly across from his camera. As he pulled in behind it, he noticed a new sign off to the right of the fire trail.

Restricted Pinelands Wildlife
Research Project Area
New Jersey Agricultural Experiment
Station at Rutgers University

Well, here was a new wrinkle. Rutgers? What kind of agricultural experiment was the university running out here?

He got out and inspected the van—a GMC Savana. A peek through the side windows showed two rows of seats behind the driver, all empty. Looked like it seated eight. Odd thing to have out here. And somehow oddly familiar. Through the window in the rear door he spotted a hodgepodge of spades and a toolbox in the space where a third seat row might have been installed.

Okay: A van had arrived, and a new sign had appeared, but where was the driver? Maybe he was putting up more signs along the fire trails that bordered this "restricted area."

Chan returned to his car, cruised to the first branch on this fire trail, then bore right. Sure enough, another new sign had been installed, an exact copy of the first. And up ahead, a man crouching in the tall grass along the edge of the corner of the next trail branch. Chan pulled to a stop and got out.

The guy looked up. He was lanky with dark brown hair on the long side and brown eyes. He wore a faded T-shirt, jeans, and an Astros baseball cap.

"Help you?"

"Yeah," Chan said, approaching. "I was out here a few days ago and none of these signs were here. What's up?"

He finished hammering a small metal stake into the ground, then wired a ceramic plaque the size of a playing card to it through a hole in the top. Chan noticed a symbol on one surface. As he finished the job, the guy rose and Chan noticed a sling hanging from around his neck. He slipped his right arm into it.

"The university asked me to put them up," he said, sweating in the July heat. All these trees seemed to absorb any attempt at a breeze.

"No, I mean, what's the experiment?"

He shrugged. "Damned if I know. They sent me out to put up the signs and adjust the corner markers."

Chan craned his neck to see the symbol:

Some sort of glyph. Why did it look vaguely familiar? Even this guy seemed a little familiar, but that could be because he was pretty average looking.

Damn, he seemed to be in a constant state of déjà vu today.

"What's it supposed to mean?"

Another shrug. "Nothing to me, but I guess it means something to the eggheads at the school."

This guy was a veritable font of information.

"I noticed some similar markers down the other end, but they're attached to trees. You're lowering them?"

"You're just full of questions, aren't you," he said, but with a grin.

Chan's turn to shrug. "That's how I learn."

"Okay. Here's what I was told." He swept his good arm toward the area behind the "restricted" sign. "The scientist guys are running some sort of tests on the pines. I don't know what. But, no surprise, they don't want anyone messing with whatever they're doing. So they're adding these signs."

"And the markers?"

"They're on all the corners of the plot. They've decided that the markers are too conspicuous on the higher poles. I mean, they're not mile markers, so they don't have to be visible from the trails here. There ain't many people through here, but when someone does happen by, they can't seem to resist taking one of these weird little markers as a souvenir. Must think they're folk art or something. And that gets the eggheads all upset because the markers have something to do with their experiments. Don't ask me what, they just do. So they hired me to take them off the poles and switch them to little stakes hidden in the grass."

Okay. Simple enough. Just a workman doing his job.

The guy stared at him. "Anyone ever tell you you look like Bruce Lee?"

"All the time," Chan said.

He couldn't see it, but he'd heard it enough that there must be something to it. He heard it even more now that he'd let his hair grow a bit longer. But he suspected a lot of young Chinese men looked alike to white folks.

As for the markers, Chan could see someone being interested in them. He'd spotted them before and had wondered about their purpose. Though oddly familiar to him, their symbols weren't even remotely like Chinese characters, or cuneiform, or Egyptian. They seemed almost otherworldly. And as much as he wouldn't mind having one them, the thought of removing it from the area struck an uneasy note in him.

"Will you permit me one more question?" he said.

"Ask away."

Chan hurried back to his car and pulled a three-by-four-inch slip of paper from the glove compartment. He unfolded it and handed it to the guy.

"Do you have any idea what this is?"

He held it in his free hand and tilted it this way and that. "Which way is up?"

Chan leaned over for a look and adjusted the orientation so that the torn perforations were along the top.

Pinelands

The guy cocked his head left and right, then shrugged and handed it back. "No idea. Who drew it?"

"I did."

Now a squinty look. "You? You drew it and you don't know what it is?"

Chan pulled the little spiral-topped note pad from his back pocket and held it up. "I know I drew it because that's my handwriting and it came from this, which I always carry."

He had a habit of jotting notes to himself. He'd tried using his phone but he frequently forgot to check for them. Forgetting was a lot harder with the pad.

"But you don't remember?"

Okay, he didn't want to tell him about his big blackout, but he knew he'd drawn this at some time during the missing ten hours. He felt sure it was linked to this place, and the word "pinelands" in his handwriting bolstered that.

"I had too much to drink one night and when I woke up I found this in the notebook."

The guy grinned. "Been there, done that. Look, I've got to keep moving on this."

"Oh, yeah, of course," Chan said, backing away. "Sorry to interrupt." He pointed to the sling. "What happened to your arm?"

"Dislocated my shoulder a couple of weeks ago. I can use it some, but it's still not right."

"Well, feel better."

As he turned away he noticed the browning underbrush on the far side of the trail.

"Is that from the flooding?"

The guy nodded. "Yeah. Looks like the seawater stopped there."

"And the salt's killing the trees?"

"Not the trees, no. It's damaged the undergrowth, but it'll come back. These pines, though... they're almost unkillable. Even after one of the regular fires out here you'll see these bright green baby branches popping through the char. You can burn them to ash and even then the roots stay alive and shoot up new growth. You've got to completely uproot them and *then* burn them before they're really dead."

Chan waved again and started up the Nissan, but instead of going back the way he'd come, he decided to make a slow circuit of the fire trails around the "restricted" area. He counted seven turns before he returned to the Savana. Seven corners, three of which still had visible markers on trees.

Nothing more to see here, so he headed back, but he'd traveled only a few hundred yards when something occurred to him. He'd counted seven corners on the Rutgers plot... and the polygon on his sketch had seven corners. Could it be...?

He hit the brake and pulled out his phone. He had the nearby GPS coordinates, so he plugged them into his map program, then called up an aerial shot. The satellite view filled the tiny screen. He moved it around until the image was centered on the area he'd just left. And there it was:

"Holy crap!"

He gaped at the same seven-sided, equilateral polygon—a septagon, he guessed. Idiot! The map and the coordinates had been available all along but he hadn't thought to put them together till now.

Suddenly he had a whole new set of questions for the sign guy. He whipped the Sentra into a K-turn and rushed back. But the van was nowhere in sight. Maybe the sign guy had moved it around to the far side of the septagon. Chan made the circuit of the seven sides but found no sign of him. And the three remaining tree markers remained untouched.

Plenty of daylight left. Why would he leave without finishing the job?

He hadn't used Chan's route, otherwise the van would have passed while he was checking the satellite image. Must have gone another way. But which trail?

Then Chan remembered the heavy rain that had blown through last night. It would have washed out any old tire tracks. He eased his car along. All he had to do was find fresh ones in the sand of a fire trail and—

Here we go: fresh and deep, just like a heavy van would make. He followed. The tracks angled this way and that along the branching trails but he finally caught up as the van was approaching Route 50. He honked and waved his arm out the window to get the guy's attention. He could swear he saw the driver turn and look back, but instead of stopping, he accelerated onto Route 50 and zoomed north along the two-lane blacktop.

"What the—?"

Chan had to wait for a couple of southbound cars to pass before he could follow. Not much traffic so he hit the gas. The speedometer climbed until he was doing eighty-five—on a fifty-limit road—and gaining only slowly on the van, which meant it had to be doing at least eighty. Damn. All he needed now was to trigger a cop's speed gun.

But what was up with the sign guy? Chan wasn't out to hurt him, just wanted to talk to him. Why was he running?

An overpass appeared ahead, which meant they were approaching the onramp to the AC Expressway. Was that where he was headed?

And why am I chasing the guy? he wondered.

Chan could stay behind him indefinitely, or at least until one of them ran out of gas. But then what? If he didn't want to talk...

He took his foot off the gas, but his quarry kept running, speeding up behind some SUV poking along under the speed limit. The van swerved into the oncoming lane to pass it just as a car pulled out of a side road. The van veered to avoid a collision, wobbling as it kept on moving left. The right-side wheels lifted off the pavement and then its front bumper hit the metal barrier on the median before the overpass. Becoming airborne, it smashed headlong into the concrete support abutment and burst into flame.

"Oh, fuck!" Chan shouted as he coasted past, horrified at the sight.

He slammed on his brakes, pulled onto the median, and ran back. The car was totally engulfed in flame. Other people stopped and joined him. They all wanted to help but what could Chan or anyone else on the scene could do? He tried to approach but the heat kept him from getting near the wreck. It looked like the gas tank had exploded. And judging from the intensity of the blaze, it must have been nearly full.

Eventually the Egg Harbor Fire Company showed up and foamed it down. All but a few of the onlookers had left by then. Chan felt remotely responsible. If he hadn't followed the guy, he wouldn't have panicked and would still be alive. He felt duty-bound to stay. He didn't see any signs of life and didn't expect any. Really, how could anyone survive a blaze like that? He didn't want to see what remained of the corpse, yet still he hung around.

Finally, they pried open the driver's door. The two firemen who had done the prying called their fellows over. They seemed excited. Soon all the firemen on the scene were clustered around the driver's door, either muttering or staring with dropped jaws. One of them crossed himself.

Chan's curiosity was running wild, and soon it got the best of him. He sidled up to see what was so fascinating. Peering between the firefighters he spotted the victim's body still in the front seat...in perfect condition. Blackened by soot, clothes burned away, but otherwise undamaged.

"Is he alive?" he cried.

One of the firefighters said, "No, we checked for a pulse. He's dead. But why isn't he burned?"

Chan staggered away, asking the same question.

The next day he searched online and found the story. It made mention of the undamaged condition of the body, and gave the driver's name: Kurt Maez. He was listed as an Uber driver. Originally from Enid, Oklahoma, currently of Wantage, NJ.

Wantaugh? That was way at the top of the state. Mr. Maez had come a long way to fix those signs—and not even finish the job.

But that started Chan thinking about the "restricted area" signs Maez had been putting up. Why? What sort of research was Rutgers conducting there? So he called the university and got in touch with the Agricultural Research Station there. It took him an ungodly amount of time and numerous call transfers to learn that Rutgers was conducting no research of any kind in the Pine Barrens.

Okay, now Chan's antennae were up. Kurt Maez was installing those signs either on his own or on someone else's behalf. But whoever it was, Rutgers University was not involved. He'd flat-out lied. Why? And why the phony signs? Unless he had his own reasons to want people to stay out. Again, why?

So Chan did some searches on Kurt Maez. Not much there. No criminal record. No social media accounts. He found a two-year-old obituary on one Andrea Maez of Enid, Oklahoma, survived by her husband Kurt. No children mentioned. The obit said she'd died of leukemia.

A later search revealed that his body had gone missing from the hospital morgue. He'd been scheduled for post-mortem exam but his remains couldn't be found. A clerical error rather than foul play was suspected.

Ongoing daily searches found no reports of him ever being found. An inquiry to the Atlantic County Medical Examiner's office revealed no record of an autopsy on Kurt Maez.

Now *that* was interesting. Corpses didn't simply evaporate. If they're not cremated, they have to *be* somewhere. And it's not like you can mislay one or walk off with one in your pocket; they can't slip behind a cabinet or roll under a couch. They're big and they're heavy. Chan became convinced that Kurt Maez's body had been stolen.

For the hell of it he created a string of online alerts to see if it happened to someone else. And that eventually led him back…

5

...to where he'd met the mysterious Mr. Maez.

So now Chan stood once more before the septagonal plot with its bogus "restricted" signs and reviewed what he knew. And damn if it wasn't even hotter here now than last time.

This Okie taxi driver named Kurt Maez loses his wife to leukemia and moves east to north Jersey where he works as an Uber driver. But that's not his only gig. Two weeks after the Atlantic City disaster, he's out here in the middle of the wilderness, miles and miles from the ruins of the city, putting up bogus signs on a plot of land outlined in a drawing Chan had no memory of making... a memory lost in the ten-hour black hole during which Atlantic City was obliterated along with two of his closest friends.

Somehow, some way, it was all connected. And Chan sensed that if he could uncover those connections, he could retrieve the memory of the ten lost hours. Tomorrow he'd investigate the connection between Maez and Philip Sirman. But today...

Today he'd explore the septagon.

He left his car and walked to the nearest corner where one of those odd little markers was attached to a tree—one of the plaques that Maez hadn't replaced. Like its fellows at the other six corners, this card-size marker was inscribed with an odd glyph:

One of Maez's lies had been that he didn't know what they meant and that the Rutgers "eggheads" used them to mark their experiments. Bullshit. Rutgers wasn't involved. These things had to mean something, even if only to Maez. He'd put them here for a reason, but just what that reason might be remained to be seen.

Chan stepped past it and immediately felt a change in the air. Cooler... as if the temperature had dropped ten degrees. Quieter too. The insect sounds abruptly seemed muffled. And something else... something that went beyond temperature. He did a slow turn. Was somebody else here? Watching him? He saw no one. And yet the feeling of being under observation persisted, along with a tingling... not on the skin, but under it. Not painful, simply *there.*

And then it came to him...the realization delayed because he was experiencing an *absence* of a sensation. The perpetual malaise from his *xiānzhī* sense had faded away. The ceaseless, malevolent Muzak had gone silent.

He didn't understand this, but it was wonderful. And disturbing, as well. He couldn't remember a minute without that malaise.

Something going on here. Maybe this little exploration wasn't such a good idea. Maybe he should go, leave it for another day. Maybe come back with someone else along who could stay by the car and keep watch while he explored. Danni, maybe. She was the only friend he had left, but she'd been out of touch since the disaster. She always used to answer her phone, now it kept going straight to voicemail. If he had her along—

No. He was overdue for this. This odd-shaped plot of land needed, at the very least, a walk-through. He needed to do exactly what Maez's signage had tried to prevent: He needed to *trespass.* He needed to know why Maez had wanted to keep people out. It might turn out to be something as mundane as a still or a meth lab, but Chan thought not.

So he forced himself forward into the pines. The underbrush was thick near the fire trail where it had access to lots of sun, but thinned quickly once he moved into the shade under the trees. Overhead the branches of the hardy barrens scrub pines formed a thick canopy while their fallen needles lay in a brown carpet below.

The feeling of being under scrutiny intensified as he moved deeper among the trees. But so far no sign of anything out of place. Whatever Maez had been tending in here—if anything— would go untended from now on. Untended, at least, by Kurt Maez. It seemed unlikely that he'd be alone in this. He had to have a partner or partners, and most likely they'd stolen his body from the morgue. Had he known Philip Sirman? Had Sirman helped steal Maez's body? But then—

Did it just get darker?

Chan looked up but couldn't find the sun through the pine-needle canopy Probably just a cloud drifting across it. But no... the ground itself looked dark. It *was* dark, almost as if a black fog were seeping from it. He could no longer make out the pine needles that lined the floor—nor find his feet.

Okay. That did it. He was done. Had to get out of here, back to his car. The black fog continued to rise as he reversed course. Waist-high now. No, not a fog. Simply blackness, impenetrable, light-eating blackness. A deep uneasiness bloomed in his gut as he quickened his pace, wending a path through the trees. The black quickly rose to chest level, then to his throat, and then engulfed him. The woods around him vanished.

He stifled a cry of panic as he thrust his arms out before him. He couldn't see where he was—

He slammed into a tree trunk. As he stumbled back he tripped and landed on his butt. In total blackness now he rolled over onto his hands and knees and realized he was no longer in the woods. Instead of dead pine needles, his hands pressed against cold, damp, uneven stone.

What had happened? Where was he? This wasn't the woods anymore. Had he passed out and been moved?

No, he was sure he hadn't lost consciousness. But where were the pines? How had he ended up on rock?

If only he could *see*, damn it! Something, *anything*. But the air remained dark and still around him.

And then he did see something. Off to his left. It looked like...a speck of light. He fought the urge to leap to his feet and dash for it. He could make out no details of his surroundings. A gaping chasm might wait just a few steps ahead.

The stone floor of wherever he was angled slightly upward. Remaining on his hands and knees, he began a slow crawl toward the glow, one hand after the other, reaching as far ahead as he could to warn of any unpleasant surprises in his path. He made steady progress and soon was able to see that the glow was actually a patch of blue sky. Closer now, the light filtering in revealed some of the features of his surroundings. He seemed to be in some sort of cave, and the rocky floor ahead of him looked unobstructed.

Chan rose to a crouch and hurried forward, reaching the opening and bursting through—

—onto a wooded hillside.

A cool, clean breeze caressed his face under the midafternoon sun as he took in the lush mountainous vista stretching out before him.

What the fuck?

6

Danni was sick of watching that video. She, Benigno, Seward's psychiatrist—a Dr. Hudson—and the technician had post-mortemed the encounter for almost two hours now.

"Okay," Hudson said. She had black skin and short, natural black hair, and peered at the world through wire-rimmed glasses. "I've got rounds to make so let's sum this up."

Thank God, she thought.

"Let me ask the big question," Benigno said. "What have we learned?"

Hudson leaned forward. "We've learned that Pastor Seward can speak English when he wants to. That's not a big help to you regarding AC, but it's enormous for me. Now I know the babbling is a choice. I still don't know how he keeps it up twenty-four hours a day with no sleep, and still no explanation as to why he's not dead from malnutrition and dehydration, but at least now I can be pretty sure he understands me when I speak to him, and that he can answer if he chooses to." He looked at Benigno. "What have you folks learned?"

Benigno flashed Danni an evil grin. "Well, I've learned that Agent Boudreau here has been 'touched by the Squatter.' How did that feel, exactly?"

Danni considered flipping him the bird, then reconsidered. The shrink saved her from a response as he spoke to his tech.

"Did you have a chance to look that up? Were you able to find any mythology associated with 'the Squatter'?"

The tech cleared his throat. "Well, a squatter is obviously one who squats. It's also a person who lives on a property to which they have no title, right, or lease."

"Hardly mythological," Hudson said.

"But I went a step further and found something called 'the squatting man,' which is a petroglyph going back seven thousand years or more and recurring around the world. They've found similar figures in Africa, Arizona, the Middle East, all over." He tapped his keyboard and the monitor lit with a new image. "Here's a typical squatting man petroglyph."

"Squatter" still had that familiar ring for Danni, but the figure meant nothing to her.

She said, "Seward didn't say 'squatting man,' he said 'the Squatter,' as if there was only one, and he referred to it as 'it,' not 'he.' Seward said he'd been touched by 'the Owner.' If we go back to the earlier definition, there's naturally a conflict between a squatter who lives on a property to which they have no right, and the rightful owner of that property. Could that be what's in the pastor's head?"

"I think you might be onto something," Hudson said, nodding vigorously. "Yes, this could be the basis for the mythology he's created. This could be very helpful."

"The Owner sure seems to have it in for the Squatter," Benigno said. "'Die, Squatter, die!' indicates that their beef is something more than just a tiff."

The tech said, "But what about...?" He checked his notes. "What about these 'haunters of the endless night' he says he sees even without his eyes?"

Hudson said, "That tells me that they're hallucinations, originating in the visual cortex. His eyes may be gone, but his visual cortex is intact. These 'haunters' exist only in his brain, and therefore he doesn't need his eyes to see them."

"Well, I think our work here is done," Danni said, sending a pleading look to Benigno.

Benigno got it, and five minutes later they were out in the parking lot.

"We need to talk about this, you and me," Benigno said. "But not now. I never mentioned your memory loss to Hudson and he has no clue as to why Seward calls you 'cockroach girl.' I'm keeping that on a need-to-know basis, and he doesn't need to know."

"Then why were he and that tech giving me these sidelong looks?"

Benigno sighed. "I didn't want to tell you before you went in to see Seward because you already had enough strangeness on your mind, but..."

More strangeness...just what she needed.

"But what?"

"As we were sitting there, waiting for you to arrive, the tech had the monitor on with Seward at the table droning his gobbledygook in the background. Suddenly he goes quiet. We all look at the screen and see he's staring in the direction of the parking lot. He says, 'Oh, good. She's here,' then resumes his babble. I go to the window and see this Volvo pulling into a parking spot. Who gets out but you."

Despite the baking heat rising from the parking lot's asphalt, a chill ran over her entire body.

"Really? You're not making that up?"

He raised a hand, palm out. "Swear to God."

"I guess I'm glad you didn't tell me."

That definitely would have rattled her before meeting Seward.

Another of his stares, then, "You did well in there, Boudreau, both in the encounter and in the post-mortem. You made some good observations. I think this is going to work out. You've definitely got a future in the Bureau and I'm glad to have you on my team."

They shook hands and started walking in different directions. Danni's heart was singing. She'd been afraid she was on the outs with the Bureau, and now she was on the ups.

"See you back in Brigantine?" she said.

"Nah. You've done enough today. See you tomorrow."

Even better.

She reached her car. The insurance money for the one she'd lost in the Upwelling had arrived last week, so she'd picked up a used Volvo S60 over the weekend. She got in but didn't start it. The inside was an oven from sitting in the midday sun, but it felt good so she just sat there. Everything about Pastor Seward chilled her through and through.

Touched by the Squatter...what did that *mean*? The thing of it was, if she had been "touched," then Chan had been too. He'd been calling her. Time to call him back.

But his phone went straight to voicemail. Had he turned it off? Where was he?

7

Where the hell was he?

The trees rising around Chan were birch and maple and cedar. He didn't know his location, but the air was definitely cooler. Obviously he was a long way from the Jersey Pine Barrens. Far down the gentle slope of the mountainside, through a gap in the trees, he spied a thin ribbon of blacktop with a double yellow line down the center. As he watched, a car zipped through the space. A road meant civilization and the chance for a ride.

To where? *From* where? Where on Earth was he?

Wait. His GPS locator would know and show him on a map. Give him the time, as well. He pulled out his phone but the screen lit with a *No Service* message.

He noticed a path leading downhill from the cave mouth. Not terribly well worn, but obviously people came here now again. Or was that a deer path? Either was okay with him, as long as it wasn't a bear path.

It seemed to lead in the general direction of the road, so he started walking down the slope. He had a bad moment as the trees closed in around him, but it passed.

How did he explain this? He'd been walking through the woods on the South Jersey coastal plain, and seconds later he found himself in a mountain cave. If he'd been on the *Enterprise* he could guess that he'd been teleported, but he'd been in the woods, damn it, and anyway, teleportation was impossible. So what had happened?

As he kept making his way downhill along the path, the trees began to thin until he came to a level clearing. A couple of dozen or so small, rustic-looking houses of maybe late twentieth century vintage were arranged in a semicircle facing up the slope toward a large, stone castle-like structure. Children of varying ages—all girls from a variety of races—frolicked in a playground in the central area while a number of adult women—their mothers, he assumed—clustered at the perimeter and watched.

People. Yes!

He angled toward the play area. As he approached, a couple of the women noticed and began pointing at him. They all wore ankle-length skirts and loose, long-sleeve patterned tops that buttoned to the throat. His first thought was some kind of commune or religious community. One of them, a slim, thirty-something woman with long chestnut hair pulled back in a ponytail, hurried forward and intercepted him.

"What are you doing here?" she said with a French accent. Not exactly a snarl but a definite note of hostility.

"I'm lost. Where am I?"

A second woman with short blond hair joined her. "You're not supposed to be in here. And don't say you didn't know that because you had to cut through the fence to get in."

"I haven't even seen a fence. I…" Oh, brother, this was going to open a can of worms if he had to explain. "I came from that cave up there."

A narrowing of both pairs of eyes.

"What do you mean, 'from' the cave?"

Okay, here goes: "I…I found myself inside it. I don't know how I got there, I just… I was someplace else and somehow I wound up there. Where am I?"

The narrowed eyes went wide. They looked at each other and spoke in unison: "Translated!"

The brunette gave the blonde a little shove. "Quick! Go get Samuel!"

She ran up toward the stone fortress.

Translated?

"Hey," Chan said. "What's going on? And will somebody tell me where I am?"

"Alberta," she said. Her whole attitude had changed—from dark suspicion to something he could only describe as elation.

"Canada?"

A lighthearted laugh. "Everybody asks that. No, Alberta, New York. Do you know where Hunter Mountain is?"

"The ski resort?" He'd been there once in high school. "Yeah. Vaguely."

"We're just about ten miles northwest of there. You're in the Catskills."

Wonder seeped through him. He was in New York State... the Catskills... the Jewish Alps... the Borscht Belt... *Dirty Dancing*...

"What day is it?"

She frowned. He was just beginning to notice how pretty she was. Maybe half a dozen years older than he but he felt a growing attraction.

"You really don't know?"

"I know when I woke up this morning it was Tuesday. I don't know if I've done a Rip van Winkle or what."

She laughed—a pleasant sound—and laid a gentle hand on his arm. "Don't worry. It's still Tuesday."

Well, at least he hadn't time travelled as well.

He noticed the blonde hurrying back with a broad-shouldered, broad-faced man with longish brown, gray-streaked hair close behind her. He was shorter than the blonde, maybe five six.

"And the time?"

"Of day? We don't pay too much attention to that here. Don't you have one of those phones?"

Well, yeah, he had "one of those phones"—he didn't know anyone who didn't. "Oh, believe me, I tried it but it doesn't work up here."

"Of course it does," she said in that delightful accent. "It just won't work close to the cave. Try it now."

He wriggled it from his pocket and swiped the screen: 2:32.

My God! Less than half an hour since he stepped into the septagon. And here he was in upstate New York, well over a hundred miles away. Didn't matter if it was only a hundred feet away, it was still fucking impossible.

"How did I get here?"

She beamed. "You were translated!" She said it like that explained everything.

"What does that *mean*? To me, translate means, like, changing English into French. What do *you* mean by it?"

"It still means changing, but in your case it means changing from one location to another. Where did you start out?"

"I was in the Jersey Pine Barrens—South Jersey—walking through the woods when suddenly—"

"Oh, here's Samuel," she said.

"Yes, I'm Samuel." The man stopped before Chan and thrust out his hand. "And you are...?"

"Chan Liao," he said, shaking the man's. He had a firm grip.

"Daphne tells me you woke up in the cave?"

"No, I didn't wake up. I just appeared there."

Samuel was nodding, his expression avid with interest. "I see, I see. Tell me about the circumstances. Be as detailed as you wish."

It hit home then that these people weren't looking at him as if he'd grown another head—a response he'd fully expected when he tried to explain how he'd been in New Jersey one minute and in New York the next. They were perfectly comfortable with the idea.

So he told them about the septagon, the markers, entering the area, the rising blackness, and then finding himself in the cave. He kept saying "finding myself" because he'd had no sense of motion despite traveling all those miles in an eye blink.

The three of them were grinning and nodding as Chan finished his tale.

"Yes!" Samuel said. "You were translated. This is wonderful!"

Wonderful was hardly his reaction and didn't answer any of his questions. "But what exactly—?"

"Tell me," Samuel said. "How did you feel as you passed the marker?"

How did he know about that? "A tingling under my skin, but strangely at peace. I... I've never felt so at peace with the world."

"You're a tairongo. Welcome to the Family."

That word again—the second time today. When he'd been

thinking about his intuition, his *xiānzhī* sense, it had popped into his head.

"What, exactly, is a tairongo?"

"A sensitive."

"In my family we call that person a *xiānzhī*."

"Yes, the Chinese term for it. Lorenzo, our longtime tairongo—or *xiānzhī*, if you wish—passed away last year and we've been searching for a new one."

"Sensitive to what?"

"The Mountain, of course. The Mountain brought you to us."

This all seemed to make perfect sense to them but it sent Chan's head spinning.

"How do you feel?" the brunette said, laying a hand on his arm again. "Are you okay? Did being translated affect you? I'm Nicolette, by the way."

So that was her name.

"Not at all. At least not physically. But I'm totally confused and nonplussed by this. I've just been transported—or 'translated,' as you call it—a hundred-some miles or so in an instant by... a *mountain*? Which mountain? This one?"

All three were nodding vigorously.

"Yes," Samuel said. "Our Mountain—*the* Mountain. Come up to the fort where we can sit down and you can gather your wits."

"I really should be finding a way to get back to Jersey."

"Please," said Nicolette, giving his arm a little squeeze. She really was kind of pretty. "We can help you with that."

As he followed them up the gentle slope it occurred to Chan that he'd been worried they'd be put off by the crazy, outrageous truth of how he got here. But he was realizing they were already crazy in their own way.

The Mountain brought you to us.

Yeeesh.

But then, after what had happened to him—losing his memory, losing his job, losing his *city*—what was "crazy" anymore?

"What is this place?" he said, gesturing around as they walked.

"It's our community," Samuel said. "For want of a better term, we refer to ourselves as the Family, even though none of us are related."

"So…like a commune?"

"Not in the traditional sense. We don't share everything, and we're not the least bit self-sustaining. Those that feel up to it can grow their own produce, but most of our food comes from the general store in town. We try to have regular communal meals to foster friendship and relationships, but on a day-to-day basis, meals are individually prepared at the family level."

The big stone structure that Samuel called "the fort" looked cold and forbidding. Like something transported from medieval times.

"This seems out of place here," Chan said.

"Indeed it does. This area was settled and abandoned and resettled in colonial times, so if records as to its origin ever existed, they're long gone. The accepted theory is that it was built during the Revolutionary War to guard the valley."

"The British were interested in the Catskills?"

Samuel shrugged. "As I said, the records are lost in time."

As they approached he noticed that the fort seemed built flush against the side of the mountain. The big wooden door at the entrance stood open and they entered a large front room with long tables down the center and maybe thirty or forty chairs.

"I gather this is where you hold your family dinners."

"Along with indoor activities for the children in bad weather and during the cold months. It has numerous side rooms where we hold classes."

"Home schooling?"

"Of a sort."

"No windows," Chan said.

"Well, it was a fortress, after all. The second floor has windows, but the First lives there."

"First?" Chan said.

"Our elder, so to speak. His wisdom guides the community."

Chan supposed all these cultish groups had at least one elder. Sounded like they revered him. Better than warehousing the old folks in a nursing home, he guessed.

The dank, stony gloom was relieved by wrought-iron electric chandeliers suspended from the high ceiling.

"Not the original equipment, I assume," Chan said, pointing.

"You assume correctly," Nicolette said with a laugh. "We used to depend on multiple generators but Samuel arranged for an underground cable from Central Hudson Gas and Electric. We keep the generators just for backup now."

Samuel led them to a small round table off to the side. As they sat, Samuel said, "Would you like coffee, tea, something stronger?"

Chan shook his head. He didn't want to get involved in a kaffeeklatsch here, he wanted to get back home. But he was thirsty.

"A glass of water would be much appreciated."

Samuel looked at the blond woman. "Daphne, would you mind?"

"Not at all," she said and hurried off.

Chan said, "I really should be looking into arranging a ride back to Jersey."

"Where do you live?" Nicolette said.

"Margate. Officially it's called Margate City. Just south of Atlantic City—or rather, where Atlantic City used to be."

Immediately he regretted saying that because mentioning proximity to AC unfailingly triggered a deluge of questions about the disaster, and he didn't feel like talking about that now. But oddly enough, they let it pass without comment. Had they so isolated themselves from the workaday world that they hadn't heard? No, they must have. It seemed as if they didn't care to acknowledge it.

Samuel said, "There's a Hertz rental office in Catskill—that's a town about twenty-five miles from here."

"Twenty-five…"

"Not a problem. One of us will drive you. But first I want to invite you to join the Family."

Me? Chan thought, biting back a laugh. Join a commune? Not in a million years.

But if one of these folks was going to make a fifty-mile round trip to the Hertz place so he could rent a car, he didn't want to blow them off. He wouldn't say no, just temporize…

"Why would you want me?"

"As I said, you're a tairongo. That's why the Mountain brought you here—you and only you. Anyone else in that special patch of woods would have wandered in and out without incident. But you… you're a tairongo. One can't learn that. One must be born that way. The Family needs someone like you to keep tabs on the mood of the cosmos."

Daphne returned with a glass of water. Chan thanked her and gulped half of it down, then said, "'The mood of the cosmos'…I have to confess that makes no sense to me."

"Let me see if I can help," Samuel said. "Just for a few seconds, lean back and close your eyes and open yourself to the Mountain."

Open yourself to the Mountain…totally meaningless to Chan. How did he "open" himself to a giant mound of rock? But he played along: He slumped in the chair, let his head fall back, and closed his eyes.

Now what?

As if reading Chan's mind, Samuel said, "Okay, just try to empty your mind, banish all thought, and let the Mountain in."

Easier said than done. But he tried, reaching for the feeling he'd get as he was falling asleep, and felt…

Nothing but the lack of discordance and malaise that had plagued him all his life… he'd lost it on entering the septagon and it hadn't returned. Otherwise…

No, wait…a vague feeling creeping in…directionless… all encompassing… a feeling of…

"Peace…welcoming peace." He blurted the words and opened his eyes to find Samuel, Nicolette, and Daphne staring at him.

Samuel nodded, his expression grim. "Yes, that fits."

Chan couldn't help a frown. "How can a mountain be welcoming?"

"You'll understand when you join us." Samuel's use of "when" instead of "if" was not lost on Chan. "And this proves that you are meant to be with us. You are attuned to the

Mountain, which is, of course, why it brought you here."

Chan leaned forward. "Yes...about that. How—?"

"All in good time, dear fellow. Take the time you need to get your affairs in order, but don't tarry too long. We need you here. And when you join us, all will become clear—and it will change your life. I guarantee it." He clapped his hands as if to say his time with Chan was done. "Now, who will drive our new tairongo to the Hertz office?"

Nicolette's arm shot up. "I will." She turned to Chan and said, "Wait out front here and I'll bring the van around."

And with that the three of them walked off, leaving Chan alone in the fort.

8

He closed his eyes as he waited for Nicolette...so peaceful here, so homey. Man, he could get so used to this. He might even find happiness here.

The van turned out to be a GMC Savana which Chan found more than a little disturbing. Unlike Kurt Maez's, this one had the third passenger row installed. He debated saying something as Nicolette drove him past the playground area with its children and mothers, but then he noticed that all the kids were boys now. They'd been all girls there when he arrived. Then it struck him that Samuel had been the only adult male he'd seen since he'd arrived.

"Where are all the men?"

"Working," she said with a smile. "We're sort of old fashioned that way: The wives raise the children and the husbands bring home the bacon, so to speak."

"What does your husband do?"

The smile faded. "He died."

"Oh, I'm sorry. How long has it been?"

She gave him a strange look. "Long enough."

The dirt road steepened as they left the plateau and soon they came to a gated entrance with a small guardhouse on the right. An eight-foot chain-link fence ran off into the trees on each side. A man stepped out of the guardhouse and waved. He wore matching light gray shirt and pants, and a pistol belted around his waist.

"Armed guards?" Chan said, startled as Nicolette waited while the gate pole swung up. "You folks don't encourage drop-in company, I take it."

"We've had guards for quite a few years now. With the men

away at work more than they're here, we're vulnerable. You'd be surprised how many shady characters wander by looking for a place to squat with their tent or a bedroll, or even less savory purposes. That was why Daphne and I were so surprised when you appeared out of nowhere."

Chan couldn't help being taken back a little. "You folks act as if you own the mountain."

"Well, we do. Or at least Samuel does. Back in colonial times some ancestor of his laid claim to the plot of land that includes the mountain and got title."

Once the gate was open, Nicolette started rolling again, but then Chan spotted something attached to a post set just beyond the guardhouse.

"Wait!" As she stopped again he stared at the marker wired to the post. "What is that?"

"The little sigil?" she said. "We have them posted on all the corners of the property."

"How many corner posts?"

She got rolling again. "Seven. Why?"

And then they cleared the gate.

"Whoa!"

Nicolette hit the brakes again. "What now?"

"It feels different out here."

Like being splashed with a bucket of icy water, the malaise was back, far more noticeable at the moment because he'd been free of it for a while.

"Different how?"

"That peaceful, welcoming feeling is gone, replaced by…the opposite."

She smiled. "Well, you are a tairongo, after all, but even a tairongo can't sense the Mountain outside the fence."

"The seven-sided fence."

"Exactly."

"The area where I was transported from New Jersey also had seven sides."

"Well, it would, wouldn't it."

"Why do you say that?"

"Because seven sides makes a powerful shape."

She said it so matter-of-factly that he couldn't come up with a response.

"The Mountain's aura stays inside the fence," she added. "And so do we—as much as we can."

When they reached the highway she turned left. A sign told Chan they were on 23 East.

Feeling suddenly exhausted and overwhelmed, he slumped in the seat and let his head loll back. "I don't understand any of this."

"It's really very simple," Nicolette said. "We need you and the Mountain brought you to us."

He wanted to shout, *How can a giant mound of rock do anything at all, let alone transport me a hundred-some miles in an instant?* But he didn't. Because that was exactly what had happened. He doubted very much her mountain had done it, but *something* had... something connected to these people who lived on the mountain.

"Why do you live there?" he said.

She gave an isn't-it-obvious? shrug. "To raise my son in the presence of the Mountain."

Oh...she had a child.

"How old?"

"Eight."

"Okay. I have to ask the next question: Why raise him in the presence of your mountain?"

"Growing up in the Mountain's presence will help all the children develop into exceptional adults who will eventually change the world."

Okay. Now he got it. These folks were some sort of utopianist cult. Producing children who will change the world... how many cults had been built on that? Well, he supposed that was a lot saner goal than the Heaven's Gate folks waiting to hitch a ride on the Hale-Bopp comet, or those Aum folks spreading sarin around Japan. Right now he might have been writing these folks off as just a bunch of harmless kooks except...

Except he was being driven through the Catskills and had no idea how he'd got here.

Translated, my ass!

Nicolette rambled on about her son and life in the Family. She seemed pretty intelligent and definitely well read. She taught literature to a range of ages; her son was in math class at the moment and would stay with Daphne while she was driving Chan.

Eventually they arrived in Catskill—not only the name of the mountain range, but also the name of a town. When she stopped at the Hertz office, she turned to him and said, "What's your email address?"

"Why do you want—?"

"I'd like to stay in touch."

He couldn't see the harm. He could always ignore an email if he chose. When he told her she simply nodded.

"Aren't you going to write it down?"

She tapped her temple. "It's up here." Then she grabbed his hand before he got out. "Please come back," she said with a smile. "I'll be waiting for you."

What was that? An offer? Enticement? Inducement?

"I'll be thinking about it," he said.

Not entirely untrue, he thought as he waved good-bye. But I've got a whole other shitload to think about on my long drive home.

9

He took the cheapest compact available for a one-way rental—small was okay since he'd be the only person in the car—and hopped on the NY State Thruway south.

Beyond his inexplicable "translation," the thing that bothered him most about this whole affair was all the connections linking up in his brain. Chan's drawing from during his ten-hour blackout showed the septagonal area where Kurt Maez had been putting up bogus signs and moving glyph-encoded markers, an area that somehow "translated" Chan over a hundred miles away into the next state to another septagonal area delimited by identical markers. So… the drawing was related to his blackout which was in turn related to the Atlantic City disaster, which meant the area in the pines and the mountain in the Catskills were also related to the disaster.

Shit!

Everything seemed to lead back to the disaster.

Try as he might, Chan had been unable to learn any more than what the authorities were telling the public. Danni would know, though. DHS was in charge, but the FBI was there as well.

Danielle "Danni" Boudreau…they'd met freshman year at U of P where he'd developed an instant crush on her. They discovered not only were they both fans of the Beatles, who were anything but the rage at the time, but that they even liked the same songs.

They had other things in common, one of which, much to Chan's dismay, was an attraction to the female of the species. That didn't lessen his crush on her, even though he had no illusions of it leading anywhere. He felt what he felt. He had a number of girlfriends through college, and a few while working at the casino, but Danni had always owned a special corner of his heart. Always would.

And damn it, he *had* to speak to her. If she'd remembered something, anything, he had to know. The most he'd gotten during the nine weeks since he'd last seen her was a couple of text messages saying she couldn't talk right now. He grabbed his phone and called her again as he drove. As usual, he was put through to her voicemail. So he left yet another message.

"Please call me, Danni. I'm begging you. I've had some really weird shit happening to me and I'm sure it's connected to what happened in AC. Please call me. *Please.*"

He ended the call and tossed the phone onto the passenger seat. Damn it! Why didn't she pick up, or at least call him back? Nine weeks! What was going—?

The phone rang. *Danni* lit the ID. He snatched it up.

"Danni! Where—?"

"I can't talk to you now, Chan, but I'll bet my weird shit can top yours. Are you home?"

He didn't know how long this trip would take. Three or four hours, he figured.

"I'm on the road. How about my place at seven?"

"See you then."

And then she was gone. But at least she'd called back. He'd actually heard her voice and she sounded all right. But where the hell had she been for nine weeks? At least he'd have a chance to find out tonight.

10

He found Danni waiting for him outside his building. Their hug was a long one, then he pushed her back for a good look. Chan was sure a plastic surgeon could find all sorts of things to fix on her. Maybe her nose didn't turn up enough and could be a little straighter; maybe her mouth was a bit too wide and her chin a little too strong; and maybe her eyebrows needed reshaping. But to Chan she was perfect, especially when a smile dimpled her cheeks. She wore a T-shirt, a vest, and faded jeans. Her dark brown hair was shorter and she'd definitely lost weight since he'd last seen her. She'd never been heavy but now she looked thin.

"I've missed you," she said finally.

"Oh, lady, you have no idea how I've missed you. But how'd you beat me here?"

"I'm close by. I've been assigned to the Bureau's AC team and they put us up in Smithville."

"Really?"

He hid the hurt as he led her to the elevator. She'd been just a dozen or so miles away and hadn't contacted him.

She must have seen something in his face because she said, "I really wanted to get together with you but I've been out of state and incommunicado since the Upwelling. I've been back in Jersey only a few days and my schedule's finally loosening."

"The AC team is...?"

"All the intelligence services are involved: FBI, DIA, CIA, NSA, DHS. They've been especially interested in me: a special agent who was in AC the night it happened. When they found out they yanked me out of Newark and hauled me down to Quantico for in-depth debriefings. I spent endless weeks being shuttled between various agencies before they drafted me for the team."

Once in the apartment he popped the cork on a bottle of prosecco for her. He knew she liked it and he'd stocked in a couple of bottles months ago, thinking he'd see her again soon. At least it was good and cold. He quick-mixed a Jack Daniels Manhattan on the rocks. He'd picked up a taste for them at the casino, and after the day he'd had, prosecco wasn't going to cut it. He debated telling her about his "translation" to the Catskills right away but decided to hold off a bit. Instead he led her out to the balcony to stare at the place where Atlantic City had stood.

An evening mist was filtering in from the ocean and drifting over the ruins.

She said, "Just yesterday I was at the north end of the city, looking in the opposite direction."

"What's new down there?"

"Nothing I'm allowed to tell you."

Her eyes made it clear she had so much to tell him, so much she *wanted* to tell him. And damn, he wanted to know.

"I've seen photos of people heading for the ruins in hazmat suits."

"Carefully vetted photos. They've become a sort of uniform."

"I like the shorter hair." She'd look nice cue-ball bald as far as Chan was concerned. "What *can* you tell me?"

She thought a moment. "Well, we have a pretty good idea of what *didn't* happen, but we still know only a small part of what *did* happen. The experts they've brought in still have no clue as to what caused the devastation."

"The *massive* devastation. We were *there*, Danni. Why don't we remember any of it?"

She shrugged. "I wish I knew."

Their glasses were both empty so he led her back inside where he refilled hers and made himself a second Manhattan. While he was measuring the ingredients, she wandered to the Fu Manchu painting.

She said, "I still say nobody has eyes that green."

"He's allowed. He's fiction."

"Did you ever notice that his eyes seem to follow you?"

He said, "Definitely," just to humor her. He'd lived with that painting for over a year now and had noticed no such thing.

"Obviously we must have evacuated ourselves ahead of the flooding," she said. He seated her at the round, glass-topped coffee table, then sat down opposite her.

"Back to that night: When we returned here, we both had the same hole in our memories. Has anything come back?"

She shook her head. "I don't think so."

"Let's go over it. Tell me what you remember."

She leaned back. "I remember checking in at the Hard Rock on Friday for the weekend, then meeting you guys for lunch at the café. Mac and Aldo had come in together from Philly—"

"And I'd skipped over from the Xìngyùn."

"Yeah. I remember Aldo had this bug about seeing the Pine Barrens, so we hopped in Mac's Rover and rode out the expressway. You directed Mac to take some cross road and we got off on that."

"Right. Route 50."

"If you say so. It was early on a sunny afternoon and I remember turning off that road and heading into the trees and... the next thing I remember it's near midnight and it's just the two of us, both soaked to the skin, and you're driving Mac's car like a madman along some road out in the middle of nowhere."

"Yeah. The Black Horse Pike, with no idea of why or how I got there."

She shook her head. "I didn't know it was called the Black Horse Pike back then but I remember everything that happened after. I remember you turning around and trying to get us back to AC but all the roads were flooded."

"And we were shocked. We had no idea there'd even been a storm."

Danni said, "I now know the water had already started receding by then, but not enough to allow us anywhere near AC. And I remember we had to take the long way round to get here."

"You spent the night here, the two of us glued to the TV trying to find out what happened." He pointed to the balcony.

"And then at first light we went out there and saw for ourselves,"

They both sat silent with the memory of the horror of that moment...

Chan shook it off. "So you still have no inkling what happened to Mac and Aldo?"

She looked as distressed as he felt. "Not a clue. Did we leave them behind? We never heard from them again, and they were never found. They've just been added to the missing twenty-five thousand."

"I don't remember going back to AC that afternoon, but we must have returned because I found a check from the casino in my pocket for fifteen thousand bucks. I must have won big but I don't remember a bit of it, or even what game I was playing. And your luggage was in the back of Mac's Rover—but nobody else's."

"My luggage with two five-grand banded stacks of hundreds in it," she said. "Which means I must have won big too. So we had to have gone back. But why the *hell* can't I remember? And what about Mac's and Aldo's luggage? Why didn't we have theirs?"

"It's not as if we can check with the Hard Rock. It's as flat as everything else."

"I miss those guys, Chan," she said, slumping back and getting teary.

"Even Aldo?"

A fleeting smile. "Even Aldo. You know, he'd call me every so often, reminding me he was in a personal-injury firm and to remember him if I came across anyone who thought they had something to sue about. Even sent me a stack of his cards."

"Aldo the ambulance chaser. Who'd-a thunk, right?"

"And Mac would always be calling with a hot stock tip I should take advantage of. Like I had discretionary cash at the end of the month, right?"

They sat in silence then. Chan would get those calls too. Mac was never looking for a commission—he was always like, *Call your broker and get in on this.* His family's asset-management firm employed analysts and he was simply trying to share a good thing with his friends.

Finally Danni said, "I told you how, when the Bureau found out I'd been in the city that day, they did a major debriefing down in Quantico. And during all of that, they decided I had some kind of PTSD. So they ran me through their shrinks and the consensus diagnosis is a real mouthful: 'event-specific dissociative amnesia.' It happens after a traumatic event. I assume you're in the same boat. They tell me it's temporary and I'll eventually get it back, but they can't say when."

"I figured it was temporary too, but it's been over two months now. I'm thinking I should try some therapy myself… before my health insurance runs out. Maybe try hypnosis."

"Been there, done that," she said. "The Bureau docs wanted to start me on meds but I'm not cool with drugging myself. They suggested hypnosis and I figured, what could it hurt? But nothing. They say it's buried too deep."

Chan found that hard to buy. "Really? Think about it: What event could be so traumatizing that we'd *both* forget?"

"Isn't it obvious? Something nasty happened to Mac and Aldo in AC—so nasty that our brains decided to hide it from us until we could handle it. And the only thing I can think of nasty enough for that is that some sea predators came in with the tide and got hold of Mac and Aldo and tore them apart and ate them alive right before our eyes."

Chan shuddered as he imagined that. "That's pretty nasty, Danni. Thanks for the image."

"De nada." Her smile flickered then disappeared. "I'm with you, though. Something like that is nasty enough to give us permanent nightmares and PTSD. But is it nasty enough to wipe ten hours from our memories?"

"But what *did* happen during those ten hours, Danni? Where did they go? And where did Mac and Aldo go?"

"I don't think we'll ever know, Chan."

"Never?"

She gave her head a slow shake. "Never." After a pause, she said, "Have you ever heard of someone or something called the Squatter?"

"'The Squatter'? No. Why?"

"I interviewed some poor man who sneaked into the

ruins and went completely bonkers. He kept talking about the Squatter being to blame."

"Come to think of it, it does have a familiar ring." He searched for recognition but couldn't find a link to anything. "Nope. Sorry."

Chan stared down at his second Manhattan and realized it was half gone. If he didn't get some food into him soon...

"Want to order out?" he said.

Danni smiled, obviously glad to put the painful memories aside. "Sure. A pepperoni pizza like we always got would be cool. Pizza, pepperoni, and prosecco: the three Ps...and food of the gods."

"Pepperoni!" He shook his head and laughed. "Still not a proper lesbian."

She gave him a look. "Oh, really? Why don't I get into my hiking boots while you play some MUNA for me?"

"Now, now—"

"Or let's go classic and put on some Indigo Girls."

He shook his head and laughed. "Okay! Point taken!"

"Seriously, gonna take my dyke badge because I'm not a vegan?"

He shook his head again, this time more with dismay. "That word..."

"What? 'Vegan'? Yeah. Makes me shudder too."

"No. You know what I mean."

"'Dyke'? Hey, we took it back. We own it now." She grinned and jabbed a finger at him. "So only *we* can say it."

"You're welcome to it."

"I've told you this before and I'll tell you again: A dyke may be *what* I am, but it's not *who* I am."

"You've said that before but I don't get it."

"All right," she said. "*What* I am consists of all the things I had no choice in: I'm a blue-eyed, brunette female who prefers women over men in bed. I had no choice in any of those things. *Who* I am is what I've chosen to be: a Special Agent in the FBI with a BA in poly-sci from the University of Pennsylvania."

"Okay. Now I've got it."

As he ordered a large pepperoni, he watched her wander

over to his clipping wall. After browsing his selection she gave him a questioning look.

"What?" he said as he hung up, though he knew exactly what.

She gestured to the wall. "You're a clipping service now?"

He poured her some more prosecco. "Sit down. We're now coming to why I had to see you."

11

Using the clippings to bolster his story, Chan told Danni about the disappearing fireproof bodies and how the incidents had to be related. He started with Kurt Maez's bogus signs, how he fled from Chan for no reason, how he died, and the aftermath of that death.

The pepperoni pizza conveniently arrived at the end of the Maez story, but Chan stopped only long enough to pay the delivery guy and refill their glasses. He was rolling and didn't want to lose momentum.

So he showed Danni the printout of this morning's article, the one with the story about how Philip Sirman's body was stolen from the funeral home after a cremation failure.

"Okay," she said, grabbing another slice. "You've got yourself a mystery there."

"Mystery?" he said, surprised by her blasé response. "This is bizarre out the wazoo."

"Last week I would have agreed with you, but after the last couple of days...?" She shook her head. "I can out-bizarre you tenfold."

"Well, I'm listening."

"Sorry. An iron-clad NDA zips my lips."

Damn. He was dying to hear. But then, he hadn't let her in on the big picture yet. So he started enumerating all the connections he'd made that linked Maez and Sirman to the Upwelling. As he rattled on, he realized how flimsy they sounded when he spoke them out loud.

"Is this another one of your *feelings*?" she said.

"I know you like to have your fun with that, but don't be too quick to disparage my perceptions. I am, after all, a tairongo."

"A *what*? What's that?"

"Not sure, but someone called me that earlier today. And that's where the story gets even weirder. I mean, we're about to take a hard left turn into *The Twilight Zone*."

Her smile was dubious. "Been there, done that. But I'm all ears. Make it good."

She lost that smile long before he finished his tale about his trip to Alberta, New York.

"Are you sure you didn't fall into some sort of fugue state?"

"Danni, I managed to walk into that plot of woods, crawl out of the cave I found myself in, walk down the hill, and enter these folks' compound in less than half an hour. At no point did I lose consciousness."

"But..." She waved a hand. "But..."

"Yeah, I know. Impossible."

She pulled out her phone. "Just give me a second here..." Tap-tap-tap. "Okay. I just checked my map. Alberta, New York, is around one hundred eighty miles as the crow flies." She stared at him. "You're telling me you traveled—"

"Was translated."

"Whatever. You went one hundred eighty miles in an instant?"

"Yeah, and I don't recommend it. Took me the whole damn afternoon to drive back from the Catskills in a rental."

She continued staring at him. "You were never a bullshitter..."

"And I'm not one now. And because I'm not, I won't even *try* to explain what happened to me today, because I have no idea. For the time being I'm simply going to accept that it happened and put it on the back burner. I'm more interested in those two fireproof bodies right now and how they connect to AC."

"Well, there's no connection there to find, trust me. In nine weeks of looking, the team has come across no fireproof bodies."

"But that means nothing because you haven't come across *any* bodies at all, have you?"

"Well, no."

"So, then, I think we should look into these two."

"'We'? Just exactly how are 'we' going to do that?"

"We're going to take a run up to Lincroft, NJ, and talk to

Mrs. Sirman. I found her address online."

She made a face. "That article said her husband was just run over by a truck or something. Kind of soon, isn't it?"

"For a nosy computer nerd, most definitely. But for FBI agents investigating a similar body snatch—"

She had both hands waving in the air now. "Ohhhhh, no! No-no-no-no! No way!"

"Please, Danni, I've got to get some personal info on this Sirman guy. He's gotta be connected to Maez and Maez is somehow connected to our memory blank spot which is definitely connected to what happened to AC. Consider it part of your investigation."

"No fucking way, Chan!"

It took a while to convince her—he probably would have failed if he hadn't had the false courage of the Manhattans to bolster him and if she hadn't finished the bottle of prosecco. Allowing him to pose as a fellow agent was absolutely out of the question, but she finally agreed to a compromise.

"Here's what I can do," she said. "I can accompany you to the widow's home and flash my badge and give her a story about looking into a link between the two stolen corpses. That's going plenty far out on a limb for me but nothing I can't massage into a legitimate inquiry should any questions be raised. You can be a 'consultant' to the Bureau. Everybody and his mother is outsourcing these days so that should slide right on by."

"Great!" Chan knew he could make this work. "When can we go? Tomorrow, maybe?" He wanted to get on this ASAP.

"Yeah, why not? Get it over with. But first I've got to see if I can get the morning off. Can I use your laptop?"

He stepped to the desk and opened it for her.

He stood back but watched her keystrokes as she logged in. He was a little drunk but that didn't impair his ability to pick out and memorize the keys she tapped. Same screenname as before but new password. Good thing he'd watched.

"Oops," she said. "They want a second verification because it's a new computer."

Her phone hummed with a text and she tapped in the verification code.

"Let's see..." she said when she was in. "They're finally giving me some personal days, but only one of the team is allowed off at a time. I won't be able to get free if someone's already out. Nope. Clear. Let me take myself off the schedule for tomorrow morning... there. Done." She logged out and leaned back. "Lincroft here we come. Where is that, by the way?"

"Monmouth County. Now, I have one more favor. Can you follow me to the airport so I can return my—?"

"Drive? As in Get Behind a Wheel? Are you out of your mind? You've had three of those Jack Daniels thingies and I've had way too much prosecco. I'm not used to drinking anymore. No way, Jose. You're staying right here for the rest of the night, and so am I."

"Fine with me," he said. Wouldn't be the first time. "I'll take the couch, as usual."

"Yes, you will. I'm beat, by the way."

He gave her shoulder a gentle squeeze. "You hit the hay. I'll clean up."

"You're a love."

She pecked him on the cheek and headed for the bedroom.

Good. He wanted her out of the way. To kill the time until she fell asleep, he checked messages and found an email with "It's Nicolette" for its subject line. The body of the message was one line: "When are you coming back? I'm waiting."

Was that a personal message or was she taking direction from Samuel? He didn't reply, mainly because he didn't have an answer yet.

12

Chan cracked the bedroom door and heard Danni's gentle snoring. Excellent. He hurried to his laptop and punched in her screen name and password. As he'd hoped, the site recognized the computer from her earlier log-in and didn't ask for further verification.

He'd had her old log-in info since her last overnight here but hadn't had the nerve to use it. His fear was that if he tried to get in while she was already on, or vice versa, he'd be in deep shit with the feds. But with her sound asleep—not a problem.

Okay, he was in. He had no desire to hack the FBI's system—he wasn't crazy—but he wanted to search its files. He knew Danni was too much of a straight-arrow to use the Bureau's system to look into everyday people who weren't suspected of any crime, but Chan felt he needed a leg up on Mrs. Sirman and her late husband if he was going to get anything useful out of tomorrow's visit.

Okay…first thing to do: search *Philip Sirman*…not a common name so maybe—

Holy crap. They had a file on him—combined with his wife. Chan opened it and was stopped cold by the header about an investigation into the abduction of an infant girl.

Holy shit! Their child had been stolen!

He scanned down. Their day-old daughter disappeared from the hospital nursery seven years ago. The Bureau turned the hospital upside down, watched all the CCTV footage for miles around, interviewed all the staff, all the visitors, all acquaintances of the Sirmans, but the child was never seen again. No ransom call, but apparently that wasn't unusual. The investigators figured the baby was taken either to be sold to a childless couple or raised by the abductor herself.

That poor woman. Her child stolen, then her husband killed and his body stolen. Talk about the shitty end of the stick. He'd have to walk on eggshells with her tomorrow.

He put the shock aside and searched *Kurt Maez*, another uncommon name. Once again, to his shock, he found a pre-existing file on him and his wife. What were the odds the FBI had investigated both couples? Wait…could it be? The anticipation as he clicked to open the file was almost unbearable. And as soon as he did, it leaped out at him, right at the top:

Investigation into the abduction Baby Boy Maez

Four years ago…taken from the nursery of a hospital in Enid, Oklahoma…

Chan bolted from the chair and staggered around the room. *OhGodohGodohGodohGod!* He couldn't stay still. This was big—beyond big. This was huge. This was fucking *monstrous!*

Both men had had a child abducted. The body of neither man would burn. Both bodies had been stolen.

They were connected. Oh, God, were they *ever* connected!

So many parallels in their lives. Only their deaths diverged. A more paranoid type might think they could be murder victims, but their accidents weren't sneaky hit-and-run affairs. Chan had been an eyewitness to Maez's demise, he and hadn't the slightest doubt it was accidental. Sirman's, too, seemed cut and dried: the driver who hit him had a suspended license, was confirmed DUI, and had been taken into custody.

Chan was satisfied the deaths were accidental and unrelated. But the theft of their bodies… that was most certainly a conspiracy. Someone didn't want a post-mortem performed on either of those bodies.

He went back to the laptop and the files. Why didn't the Bureau see the parallels? Chan knew he had a high IQ but was hardly a crack investigator like Holmes or Dupin. A little more reading and he had his answer: Nobody had noticed because the parallels hadn't existed back then.

Well, okay, both infants were taken from a hospital nursery on their first day of life, but there it stopped. The abductions took place three years apart at different ends of the country.

Sirman was an accountant with a teacher wife; Maez was a taxi driver, his wife a waitress. Neither of the Sirmans had been farther west than the Rock 'n' Roll Hall of Fame in Cleveland, and neither Maez partner had ever been out of Oklahoma.

The Bureau had no suspect in either case and had found no reasons to connect the two cases. Chan had the benefit of knowing that neither of their bodies would burn and that they'd been stolen. He was *primed* to connect them.

He had to tell Danni.

No, wait. He couldn't do that. Because that would involve telling her that he'd stolen her password, broken into the Bureau's computers under her name, and pried into the lives of crime victims who had come to the FBI for help.

She'd never forgive that kind of betrayal. He'd never see her again. In fact, she'd have a duty to report him.

What a shitbum I am.

"Chan?"

His head snapped up. Danni was coming down the short hall from the bedroom door, dressed in her T-shirt and panties. Any *wow!* factor was blasted away by the possibility that she'd seen the screen. Had she? He slipped a finger toward the power button as she came toward him.

"Just...just doing a final check to see if there's anything new on the disappearance of the Sirman body."

He held the button down but the FBI site stayed lit on the screen.

Come-on-come-on-come-*ON*!

It went black just as she arrived. He stood and she hooked an arm around his.

"Would you come in with me?"

He could tell she was only partially awake and still feeling the prosecco.

"Wh-what?"

She smiled. "You know better than that. I just need a snuggle, like we did the last time I was here."

The last time...the night/morning of the disaster. After hearing nothing of any use on the news networks, and with nothing visible from the balcony, they'd curled up fully clothed on the couch, Danni spooned against his back. Neither had wanted to be alone. He might have slept, he wasn't sure.

But now?

"I've had two very bad days," she said, "and all that talk about what we did before and after the disaster... I've been able to hold it at arm's length but tonight brought it all back. I keep thinking about Mac and Aldo and why don't we know what happened to them. Can we, you know...snuggle?"

"Absolutely."

He followed her in where she lay down with her back to him. He slipped behind her and, when he spooned against her, she pushed back against him, pressing her pantied butt against his pelvis. Immediately he felt himself beginning to respond.

"We were the other way that night," he said. "Let's flip."

So they both turned and now Danni was tight against his back. He preferred the other way but that could get awkward real fast.

"I don't have anyone, you know," she whispered against the back of his neck. "Not for a while now."

"Why not? You're a catch."

"I had someone for a while and thought it was the real deal. We tried moving in together but found ourselves butting heads more and more. We decided we weren't a good fit, so she left. And soon after that, AC happened and I've been dragged all around the Washington Metro area. I haven't had any time to myself let alone time to meet anyone. What about you?"

"A few relationships that didn't get past the fling stage. I guess I'm just waiting for you to decide you're a closet straight."

A faint laugh. "Awww, that's sweet."

"I'll even settle for you coming out as a bi."

"Don't hold your breath. Before I knew for sure, I experimented with some guys and, well... yuck."

Chan was trying to think up a clever response to that when he heard her soft snoring against his back. But sleep was playing it coy with Chan, kept at bay by his dilemma: Somehow he had to let Danni in on what he'd learned. But how?

He'd worry about that in the morning and just try to enjoy the moment. He reveled in the warm pressure of her body against him, and realized that this was the closest he had ever come to happy. Not all the way to happy, but probably the closest he would ever get.

WEDNESDAY

1

Someone was shaking him awake. Chan forced his eyelids open. Danni, dressed in her jeans again, looked down at him.

"I'm going to run to Smithville for a shower and FBI-appropriate clothes. I left the address on your kitchen counter. Show up in an hour and we'll run your rental to the airport."

And then she was gone.

God, how could she be so bright and chipper when he felt so awful? He dragged himself to the shower, then dressed up a little with a sports jacket over a blue Oxford and khaki slacks.

He stopped at the Wawa on Ventnor for a coffee and a sausage-and-egg Sizzli, and ate it as he made his way to Route 9. The address Danni had left turned out to be a garden apartment complex. She appeared, dressed in a white blouse, a one-button blazer, and straight-leg slacks, and led him on the twenty-minute trip to the airport.

With the car returned, he hopped in the passenger seat of her Volvo.

"Sharp," he said. "You look all business."

"Well, I'll be representing the Bureau, after all. We should take two cars, by the way. After we finish in Lincroft I need to head up to Newark to straighten up my apartment there and gather a few things to bring back to Smithville."

"Yeah, we can do that, I guess. But my car is in the pines—at least I hope it still is. I'll show you where."

The airport exited onto the Atlantic City Expressway and she took that west.

"Hard to believe this was all underwater last time we were together," she said. "It had already started receding by then, but still…"

"Yeah. We couldn't get past Mays Landing."

He directed her onto Route 50 and pointed out the abutment where Kurt Maez ended his life.

"That's where he crashed and burned—or, rather, *didn't* burn."

As they continued on 50, she said, "I remember Mac driving us along here that afternoon."

"Yeah…poor Mac. If we could only remember." He pointed to a side road. "Turn here."

"I remember some of this." As they drove farther into the trees, she added, "But I don't remember any of *this*."

"And nothing's coming back now?"

She shook her head. "Not a thing."

"Damn. I was hoping that being in the woods might trigger something."

He used his phone's GPS to direct her to the vicinity of the septagon, then went the rest of the way on instinct. He was relieved to see his Sentra waiting right where he'd left it. Danni pulled to a stop behind it.

"Yours?" she said with a grin. "You didn't get another sexy little Beemer?"

He sniffed. "Not all of us have government jobs. A lot of us lost our place of employment in the disaster."

"Oh, right. Sorry about that." She pointed to the Rutgers sign. "Is this where you… 'translated'?"

"Yeah. Step out a sec. I want to try something."

He led her to one of the corners of the septagon, the same corner where he'd entered yesterday. He showed Danni the little marker with its glyph.

"This is one of seven at each corner of the plot. Does it look familiar?"

She stared at it, then said, "You know, I get the feeling I've seen it before, but I couldn't tell you where." She looked around.

"The team has been out this way a few times because this is where the flood stopped. But that was before I joined up. I've no memory of ever being here before but it gives me a little déjà-vu feeling."

"Okay, I want you to take a few steps with me into the underbrush here."

He led her three paces into the septagon, feeling that same tingle and temperature drop as he crossed the border, along with the feeling of being watched and the fading of the perpetual malaise from his *xiānzhī* sense.

"Now tell me: Did you feel anything as we stepped in here?"

She frowned. "Feel? Feel how?"

"Like a tingle under the skin."

She shook her head with a baffled expression. "No...not a thing. Did you?"

"Yeah."

"One of your feelings."

"Yeah."

"Sorry. Nothing."

"Nothing to be sorry about. Let's go back onto the fire trail. I want to show you something."

As they reached the middle of the trail, he pointed to all the browned-out undergrowth to the east of the sandy path.

"The salt water from the Upwelling came this far and stopped," he said. "After flowing twenty miles inland, it stopped right here and started receding. Why?"

Danni shrugged. "That's what the team is trying to discover. But it didn't stop just here. The width of the flood was four to six miles. It stopped across a broad front, not just here."

"Okay, granted, but I know, I just *know* it has some significance... that this area of the pines and the Upwelling are related."

She gave him an askance look. "Really? You think those little markers like the one you showed me turned back the tide? Are we talking some kind of magic here?"

Chan sighed, feeling deflated and maybe a little ridiculous.

"You know I don't believe in magic."

"It's another of your feelings, then?"

"More than just a feeling. And we can both scoff at 'magic,' but come up with a better term for me winding up 180 miles away in the blink of an eye."

She pointed back at the septagon. "It happened in there?"

"Yep. Somewhere near the middle."

"Can we send you back in and see if it'll happen again?"

"Oh, no. I don't feature winding up in a cave up in the Catskills again."

"But at least I can be your witness. As it is, people will just think you're bullshitting them or off your rocker."

"You believe me, don't you?" The answer was important to him.

"I believe you'd never lie to me."

"That's a relief."

"But that doesn't mean you haven't gone off your rocker."

"So...you don't believe it happened?"

"I'm having problems with it, yes. I believe that you believe it happened to you, but when you tell someone else about it you're asking them to believe the impossible."

He stared into the septagon. It *was* impossible, wasn't it. But he hadn't had a break with reality. He could account for every minute of yesterday. He'd had to rent a damn car to get back here. It *happened*. Which meant it was possible, just not explainable.

"Okay. I'm going to go back to that spot, but you know damn well nothing will happen this time."

"If it does. I'll drive up and get you."

"You won't have to."

"Why not?"

"Because..."

Because why? He knew what Nicolette would say: The Mountain had already brought you once to meet the Family, so there was no reason to bring you back again.

Chan didn't believe any of that, but what could he say?

"Because I simply know it won't happen again."

He left Danni by her car and waded into the septagon, feeling the changes again. He made his way through the trees to approximately the same spot in the middle where it had happened. And waited.

But no darkness rose to engulf him. After ten minutes of nothing, on a whim, he tried his GPS. He hadn't been able to get an accurate reading on the septagon along its edges. Maybe at its heart…

A set of coordinates popped up right away:

Latitude = 42.305 N
Longitude = -74.291 W
Alberta, NY

"Holy shit!"

He took a screen shot just in case he lost the readings, then hurried back to Danni.

"I'm sorry," she said as he approached. She sounded sincere.

Chan wasn't sorry. Not really. As much he'd like to have someone else witness his translation, and wouldn't mind seeing Nicolette again, he didn't want to go through all that a second time.

"Don't be," he said. "I got something almost as good."

He showed her the readings. As she stared she pressed a hand to her abdomen.

"You okay?"

"I don't know." His voice sounded a bit shaky. "My stomach just did a flip. You got this reading in there?"

"I'm as surprised as you are." He gazed back toward the center, hidden by the intervening trees. "We've got a weird anomaly here, Danni, and it's linked to those disappearing fireproof corpses."

"So why don't we go investigate them?" she said. "Anything to get me away from this place."

"Good idea. It's time we headed north. I'll text you the Lincroft address so you can stick it in Waze if we get separated. Follow me to the Parkway. We're headed for exit 109."

2

Pam answered the door expecting to find Chet the undertaker again—nice enough guy, but was he going to become a pest? Instead she found this suited gal in her mid-twenties or so and a Chinese guy about the same age. Oh, fuck. Jehovah's Witnesses.

"Hey, look," she said. "I already know the answer to life's big questions: We're all fucked."

"I'm sorry?" the gal said. "Are you Pamela Sirman?"

The wandering Witnesses never knew your name, so obviously this pair were selling something besides Jehovah.

"That's me. Who wants to know?"

She held up a little leather folder with a gold badge and a photo-ID card inside. Fuck. How many of those had she seen over the years?

"I'm Agent Danielle Boudreau from the Federal Bureau of Investigation and—"

"FBI?" Pam had to lean against the door as her knees softened. "You've found Julie?"

She was rewarded with a confused look.

"Julie?" the woman said. "I'm sorry, ma'am, I don't know who you mean. We'd just like to ask you a few questions."

Pam was shocked by the intensity of the anger that suddenly replaced her momentary weakness. An old rage blazed to new life with the realization that after all this time the vaunted Federal Bureau of Investigation still knew nothing. No, of course they hadn't discovered anything about Julie. Out of sight, out of mind.

"Questions? You incompetent assholes have *questions*?"

The young woman blinked in shock. "I beg your pardon?"

"I asked what you fuckers *want*? What are you going to waste my time with now?"

Confusion reigned in both their faces.

"Mrs. Sirman," the woman said, "you seem to have a history with the Bureau that I'm not aware of."

"You mean to tell me that after all these years they send two greenhorns to look me up who don't even bother to review the case?"

"We're here about the disappearance of your husband's body yesterday."

"Phil? You mean this isn't about Julie, you want to know about Phil?"

"Yes, ma'am. Philip Sirman."

She felt her anger fading almost as fast as it flared.

"Why's the FBI interested in Phil?"

"May we come in?" she said. "I'll be happy to explain."

Pam pointed to the Chinese guy who hadn't opened his mouth yet.

"What about Bruce Lee there. I didn't see any ID from him."

"He's not an agent. He's one of the outside consultants we're using."

He offered his hand. "Chan Liao," he said in perfect English.

She ignored his hand and left it hanging. She didn't want to get friendly with these two or any other fucking FBI agents. Or their fucking consultants.

"Some sick fucker stole Phil's body. Why's that an FBI matter?"

"Because he's not the only case. May we come in?"

"Oh, shit, I guess so." She backed up a couple of steps to let them in, then pointed to the couch. "You can sit there, but don't get too comfortable. You won't be staying long."

They sat and the Chinese guy—Liao, was it?—took out a small notepad and a pen.

"You mean to tell me," Pam said as she retrieved her coffee cup from the kitchen and dropped into Phil's La-Z-Boy opposite them, "that the higher ups sent you here without warning you about the Dragon Lady?"

The agent—Pam remembered her name was Boudreau—shook her head. "We were told nothing about previous encounters."

Typical. She'd been pretty rough on the agents assigned to Julie's case, venting her mounting frustration as time after time after time they came up empty. But did anyone give these two newbies a heads-up? Uh-uh.

"Okay," she said. "Explain to me: What's the FBI's interest in Phil?"

She could have offered them coffee, but she saw no reason to make them feel welcome. Fuck 'em.

"Well, ma'am," Liao said, "there was—"

"Let's cool it with the 'ma'am' shit, okay? I'm not that much older than you two." She pointed to the agent. "You. How old are you?"

"Twenty-six." She didn't look comfortable giving personal information. But it was okay to ask others for it, right?

Pam looked at Liao. "And you're about the same, I assume?" When he nodded, she said. "Okay, I'm thirty-two. Not exactly your old Aunt Tilly. So no more 'ma'ams.' But we can keep it formal with 'Mrs. Sirman.' Got it?"

They both nodded, then Liao said, "There was a similar body theft in Atlantic County six weeks ago—stolen from a hospital morgue."

"Both in Jersey. That makes it a State Police case. Where does the FBI come in?"

Oh, yeah, she'd learned the hard way about competing jurisdictions and all that shit.

"Similar cases have been reported in other states. We've been assigned to see if these are isolated incidents or organized into some sort of interstate ring."

Pam found that hard to buy. "A fucking body-snatching ring? For what purpose?"

"That's what we're looking into." Liao hesitated, then said, "If I might ask you, Mrs. Sirman... we're going to be talking to the funeral home at some point, but the news sources carried something about the funeral home being unable to cremate your husband's body? Is there any truth to that?"

"There's a shitload of truth to that. I saw it myself."

"Oh, really?" he said, his eyes alive with interest. "Would you care to elaborate?"

"Well, at first, naturally I'm thinking, What kind of bullshit are these fuckers feeding me here? They had Phil's body outside the oven there, so I told them to show me: Show me how he won't burn. And they do. They slide him in there, turn up the flames, and nothing fucking happens. He's not even scorched."

"Fascinating," Liao said. "So it's not just hearsay. You're an eyewitness."

"Absolutely. Chet—that's the funeral director—was going to send Phil back to the county coroner for an autopsy but his body disappeared overnight. Do you think there's a connection— between him not burning and being snatched?"

"We're going to be looking into that," he said, then quickly added, "But tell me, Mrs. Sirman, had your husband ever expressed any thoughts about cremation?"

Agent Boudreau's phone buzzed before Pam could answer.

"Excuse me," she said and pulled it out to read a text. She rose from the couch and said, "I'm afraid I have a meeting I can't miss."

Liao said, "Really? I need to get some more personal data on Mister Sirman. If it's okay with Mrs. Sirman, I'll stay on a little while longer and catch up to you later with my report."

If Pam had to stay with anyone, she preferred the non-agent than the agent. "Knock yourself out," she told him.

Boudreau turned to Pam. "Before I go, Mrs. Sirman, may I ask who Julie is?"

The rage boiled back. "Yeah, you can ask, but why should I do your work for you? You can go look it up yourself. You fuckers must have a file on her somewhere. But in case you don't, in case you incompetent fucks have lost it or thrown it away, Julie was my daughter who was stolen from the hospital nursery when she was a day old. That was seven years ago—seven fucking years—and you worthless phonies put up a whole lot of smoke and mirrors and investigative bullshit, but you found nothing!"

The young agent looked shocked. Pam didn't know what she expected to hear, but obviously it hadn't been that. "I have no doubt the Bureau still has the file on your daughter, Mrs. Sirman, and I'm sure they did everything they possibly could."

"What do you know of it? You were a teenager then and your future employer was too busy trying to rig elections to devote any real effort to finding my child! No clues, no suspects, *nothing*! And here you are, all this time later, and you've still got nothing! Julie is still missing!"

Earlier on she would have burst into tears after a tirade like that, but Pam was all cried out. She'd been dry for years.

"I assure you I will read through your daughter's file as soon as I get to a computer."

"You do that, Agent Boudreau. Get a firsthand look at what incompetent assholes you're working with."

Boudreau's lips tightened. Obviously she didn't like hearing that, but too fucking bad. She was still idealistic with stars in her eyes. She'd learn. And soon she'd become as jaded as the rest of them. She turned to her consultant. "Can I have a word with you before I go?"

"Sure."

Liao hopped up and followed her outside. Pam watched from the door, wondering about those two. Some sort of bond between them, something that went beyond work. Pretty obvious that he was into her, but as for her... sort of like that movie title but with a gender switch: *She's Just Not That Into You.*

3

"Jesus, I'm sorry about this," Chan told Danni. He felt bad for her. "I had no idea I was leading you into the dragon's den."

"Yeah, well, I'm wearing my big-girl panties, so I can handle it. But we sure as hell walked right into that one. Our focus was on the husband's disappearance. Who could know their daughter had been kidnapped?"

Well, Chan had known. He'd simply had no way to tell her without letting on *how* he knew. But now that that particular cat was out of its bag, he could push to expand her research once she started looking.

"Do you really have a meeting?"

She nodded and showed him a text on her phone from someone named Benigno.

Need you back here ASAP as in immediately. NSA types need to talk right away.

"Sounds urgent," he said. "Do you know what it's about?"

"Could be a couple of things. I've got to get moving."

Which, he gathered, was just fine with Danni. The less involvement she had in this, the better. She'd be more comfortable with simply introducing Chan as an outsourced consultant and leaving.

Chan wanted to milk this visit for all the info he could get. He doubted he'd get a second chance, so he didn't want to rush it.

"I'll stay a while longer. But listen: While you're searching out the Sirman file maybe you can check and see if the Bureau has anything on Kurt Maez."

"Can't hurt. You'll be okay with the Dragon Lady?"

"Considering what she's been through, who can blame her?"

"Yeah, I guess. Good luck."

As Danni drove off he hurried back to the house and found the stone-faced Pamela Sirman waiting for him.

"Thanks for letting me pursue this a little further," he said as she let him in.

"How much further do you want to go?"

She returned to the La-Z-Boy as he resumed his place on the couch.

"Let's go back. Was there any indication of your husband's resistance to fire before the attempted cremation?"

She shrugged. "As far as I know he had a normal childhood up to age nine."

"What happened then?"

"His parents died in a restaurant fire in Toms River. Some idiot brought him in to identify their charred bodies and he never got over a fear of getting burned."

Chan didn't mention the irony of someone being afraid of burning when all the while he was fireproof. Did Phil know?

"No brothers or sisters?"

She shook her head. "An only child and his only relative was his father's spinster sister, Aunt Alice. When he was orphaned he moved out of state to live with her, and then she died just as he graduated high school. She left her house to him so he sold it and came back to Brick Town. We met shortly after that."

"So you never knew him as a child. Do you happen to know where he grew up? The address, I mean?"

She hopped out of her chair. "As a matter of fact, I was just going through his papers and saw his birth certificate."

She ducked into one of the side rooms and returned immediately with a yellowed sheet of paper.

"Born to Joe and Amelia Sirman, 430 Arc Lane, Brick, New Jersey."

Chan made a note of that.

"What use is that?" Pam said. "He moved out at age nine."

"Some primary research. I'm going to knock on a few doors and see if anyone remembers him."

"What good's that going to do?"

How much should he tell her? He didn't see any downside to leveling with her to a certain extent. However, he'd leave out what he knew about Kurt Maez and his child's abduction. He didn't want that getting around yet.

"Here's how I look at it, Mrs. Sirman. Your husband's body was fireproof. The crematorium couldn't touch him. Have you ever heard of anything like that?"

"No way."

"Exactly. But then, less than a day after they establish that his body is fireproof, it's stolen. The two have to be connected. I figure he was either born fireproof or became so along the way. So I want to go back into his past and see if I can find out how it happened. Obviously his parents weren't that way, otherwise they'd have survived the restaurant fire. If I can get a line on how he became fireproof, I can get a line on who would want his body."

"I see. You want to find out who Phil was and what all his connections were."

"Right. And one of those connections can lead us to who stole his body."

"When are you going to start knocking on these doors?"

"I see no reason to delay, so I'm going to start at 430 Arc Lane today."

"Good. I'm coming with you. Because it occurs to me that after nine years of marriage, I don't really know much about Phil's roots either. And I want to find out."

Chan couldn't figure a way to turn her down because, well, she hadn't asked. Just, *I'm coming with you.* How do you say no to that, especially when you'll probably need more input from her?

4

"You made good time," Benigno said as he got into the passenger seat of her car and handed her a note.

Don't say a word, just put your
phone outside on the pavement

She gave him a questioning look but his rapid nodding told her to follow instructions. She'd been in contact with him along the way from Lincroft, and he'd said he wanted to have a private tête-à-tête before she met the NSA people. He didn't think his office was private enough. She wanted to ask why all the cloak-and-dagger stuff, but figured he'd get to that.

When the phone was outside and her driver's door closed again, she said, "What's the skinny?"

He smiled. "'The skinny'? Haven't heard that one in a while. Sorry for the drama but we're dealing with NSA and they've got big ears."

She understood. "Got it."

"Okay, here's the deal. This morning I get a call from the Black Box that the Troika is on its way. They will stop at Wharton State Psychiatric Center to see Pastor Seward and view your encounter with him yesterday. Just in time, too."

"What's that mean?"

"His doc is transferring Seward to a New York facility—the Creighton Institute for the Criminally Insane up in Rathburg on Hudson. Wharton doesn't have the staff to manage him. And then I'm told the Troika is coming to Brigantine and I should make Special Agent Boudreau available for an interview."

Danni had been interviewed at NSA Black Box headquarters

at Fort Meade, Maryland, last month, but it had seemed like a perfunctory encounter.

"I'm fine with that," she said. "But what is 'the Troika'?"

"That's what they like to call themselves. A sister, a brother, and a cousin, all with Russian names but born and raised in the US. They are full-bore conspiracy nuts who are considered whacko pests and have been the joke of the intelligence community because their ideas are so far out there."

"So I rushed down here to meet some nut cases?"

"Yeah, well, when the deputy director's office calls and says have Boudreau available, I make her available."

The deputy director's office? Okay, that was serious.

"Now," he added, "the reason I wanted this private little meeting is to give you a heads-up because of the rumors about them."

"Such as?"

"They're as ruthless and reckless as they are crazy. All three are in their mid-thirties. The siblings' father was a major ufologist, i.e., aliens-in-flying-saucers nut. Word is that Zina, the sister and their leader, seduced Senator Howland of the Senate Intelligence Committee and made sure they did their boinking at her place where a nanny cam recorded all the goings on. She then blackmailed him into finagling funding for her group's own department in NSA's Research Directorate. Officially they are Department R3A, but like to refer to themselves as the Troika. They were pretty much shunned and stonewalled by everyone until the Upwelling, and now suddenly they're NSA's fair-haired boys and girl."

"When do they arrive?"

"They're waiting for you in the meeting room."

Oh, hell. Already?

"The one where you first briefed me?"

"The same. They've already been to Wharton and when they arrived here they viewed my body-cam footage of the cockroach incident. I can safely say they're salivating to meet you."

She felt like she was going on display at a freak show.

"Is there any subject I should avoid?"

Benigno made a face. "Not much point. They're NSA, with access to ECHELON and SIGINT and every other kind of snooping operation, so there ain't much they don't already know about what we do here. The idea is to see what you can learn from them. So let's take you in to meet them."

Danni couldn't explain the anxiety that clung to her as they walked into the library. They found the Troika slouched in three of the chairs in the meeting room. The two males rose as she entered and shook hands as they introduced themselves.

"Ilya Medved," said the big, black-bearded one in the flannel shirt.

The skinny, ponytailed guy all in black smiled and said, "Luka Borisov."

The woman, blue-eyed, shapely, and Slavic-looking, stretched a languid hand from her seat and said, "Zina. Another Borisov, twin to Luka." She was probably a natural blonde but she'd dyed her shoulder-length hair a pinkish purple.

Danni couldn't resist. "Twins? Are you, like, identical twins?"

This earned the expected incredulous looks, and then Zina laughed. "Very good. You had me there for a moment. I think I like you. Sit down and the four of us will have a nice little chat." She directed a pointed look at Benigno. "*Just* the four of us."

Benigno got the message. He looked at Danni and said, "I'll be in my office," then left, closing the door behind him.

"Now," said Zina, "here we are, exactly two months to the day after the Upwelling, and we've got only a little time before we have to catch our return flight. What should we talk about first? So many choices."

From the name and the looks, Danni would have expected a Russian accent, but if anything, she sounded Midwestern—flat A's and all. Zina was really rather pretty. A little old for Danni, but still quite qualified for the *hot* category. She could see how a senator or any other man could be tempted into indiscretions.

"Well," Danni began—

"I know!" Zina said, snapping her fingers as if the idea just hit her. "Why don't you tell us why you visited Pamela Sirman this morning?"

The question shocked her. And, judging from the way Zina had asked it, that was obviously what she'd intended. As her mind raced to fabricate an answer, Benigno's words came back to her:

They're NSA…with access to ECHELON and SIGINT and every other kind of snooping operation…

Better go with the truth.

"Her husband's body couldn't be cremated and was snatched from the funeral home. This was very similar to an incident a month or so ago here in Atlantic County. I was looking for a connection."

"On your own? Because the Bureau is clueless about it." When Danni hesitated to answer, she added, "Never mind. It's obvious you're doing this on your own." Zina nodded at her brother and Ilya. "See that? She came up with the question and is pursuing answers on her own." She beamed at Danni. "Now I'm *sure* I like you!"

If her purpose was to disorient Danni, she'd succeeded. Admirably so.

She fumbled for a reply. "So, NSA has linked up Sirman and Maez as well?"

"We spotted the similarities," said Ilya, smiling though his beard. "NSA has provided logistical support."

Zina said, "Let's move on."

"Wait," Danni said, not ready to drop the subject. "What have you learned?"

"We're playing that close to the vest at the moment. But I suggest you and Mister Liao dig deeper into those two men."

They know about Chan! she thought. Jesus.

"The cockroach incident," Luka said. "They appeared to be of the *Periplaneta americana* species."

"You could tell?"

"Well, I'm ninety-seven percent sure. They're omnivores usually found indoors but can thrive outside in warm weather. That must have been pretty scary. We examined your hazmat suit. Given a little more time they would have chewed their way through the material."

And then started chewing on me, she thought with a shudder.

"Suffice it to say that I don't want to go through that again."

Zina was staring at her. "Can you give us any reason why they singled you out?"

"No, I—"

"Could it be because 'the Squatter touched you'?" Zina said.

"Who or what is the Squatter?"

"I wish I knew. I never heard the term before except associated with urban blight."

"I've never heard of it either," Ilya said, "and I keep a close eye on these things."

"Although," Luka added, "it might be related to other matters we've been investigating."

Danni said, "We're not talking aliens and UFOs and *X-Files* stuff here are we?"

All three of them laughed.

"We wish," Zina said. "At least we'd have the possibility of finding solid evidence. What we're chasing is far more amorphous. We watched your encounter with the pastor. Now *there's* a handsome fellow, right?"

Ilya was rubbing his beard. "Chewed off and ate his own lips. That's a new one."

Zina looked annoyed at the interruption. "We heard him say you'd been touched by the Squatter. Tell me: Have you ever heard the term 'touched by the Otherness'?"

Jarred by the abrupt change of subject, Danni shook her head. "No. Never."

"Here's our conundrum," Zina said. "Those cockroaches obviously had it in for you. And Pastor Seward, by all accounts a pacifist his entire life, wanted to kill you."

Danni shuddered with the memory of his cry of *Die, Squatter! Die!* as he attacked her.

All three were staring at her.

"What have you done to deserve this animosity, Agent Boudreau?"

Good question.

"I wish I knew."

"Could it be lost in that memory hole of yours?"

No surprise that they knew about that.

"That's what I'm afraid of."

Luka said, "I've been through all the tests the FBI, DHS, CIA, and our own NSA ran on you, and read all the consultant reports. I know of ways to break through your memory block but the substances needed are illegal and not without risks."

Was he offering or simply stating a fact? No matter.

"I'm not about to take illegal substances, with or without risk."

"Totally understandable," he said.

Remembering Benigno's directive to see what she could learn from them, she said, "Obviously you know more than I do. Maybe if you tell me what you think is going on, it might trigger—"

"Memories?" Luka said. "We don't want to color them with our theories."

Zina glanced at her phone. "We've got to move or we'll miss our flight." She leaned close to Danni. "It's obvious there's something much bigger going on here than hungry cockroaches and a preacher going nuts. Maybe even bigger than the destruction of a city—which is already a humongous thing. You somehow got yourself involved that night. I don't know if there's any such thing as the Squatter or whether it touched you or not, but *something* touched you—marked you, maybe—and we're determined to find out what, because that 'what' is going to answer a lot of questions."

"I'm all for answering questions," she said. "I've got plenty myself."

"Good. We're not through with you and you're not through with us. I think you know that we'll be keeping watch over you. We'll meet again, Agent Boudreau. Count on it."

With that she rose and waited while Luka and Ilya said good-bye. Then she pressed a business card into Danni's hand.

"If any memories return, you call this number right away. And this meeting? It never happened. Don't say a word about what we discussed, even to your boss here. Because we'll know."

And then the Troika was gone.

Danni checked out the card. *R3A* dominated the center in

big block letters. Much smaller was "Zina" in the bottom left corner and a phone number bottom right.

So what was she expected to do—drop the Sirman-Maez thing? Like hell. If NSA was interested, so was she.

5

Home sweet home, Pam thought as they took Exit 89 off the Parkway. *Not.*

They arrived in Brick around twelve thirty. The drive had been only thirty minutes or so, but they got a late start because she'd made Liao cool his heels while she showered and gathered up all of Phil's personal papers to bring along. During the trip south she decided Liao wasn't a bad guy—a little nerdy maybe, but not in an obnoxious way. She guessed she warmed to him because he wasn't real FBI—merely an independent contractor.

He'd quizzed her along the way.

"Tell me about your marriage, Mrs. Sirman."

How do you tell someone about a marriage? Where to begin?

"Well, we met in college. Rutgers. He was an accounting major, I was going for a teaching certificate. Having Brick Town in common gave us something to talk about at first, and that led to going out together, and before long we were inseparable. After graduation we stayed together. He had this big nest egg from the sale of his folks' home and his Aunt Alice's home, and he wanted to get married. So we did. He got his CPA and an accounting job, I was substitute teaching, waiting for a full-time position to open, when I got pregnant with Julie. The pregnancy went fine, I had an uncomplicated full-term delivery, and Julie was perfect. You could look at us on the day of Julie's birth and say our lives were storybook perfect, couldn't be better."

She paused as a pressure built in her chest as it always did when she talked about this.

Liao must have thought she was waiting for a response because he said, "It does sound perfect, Mrs. Sirman."

She pushed on, saying, "Of course, just when things couldn't be better is when the shit hits the fucking fan. The nurses took Julie away for a routine newborn exam by the pediatrician on call, and that was the last I ever saw of her. Phil had stayed overnight in the room with baby and me and we were both waiting for Julie to be returned but she never came. When we asked if there was a problem, everyone was shocked she wasn't with me. Two nurses were on, and each thought the other had returned Julie to my room. Security came, the police came, the FBI kidnapping unit was called in, but no one could find a trace of her. The hospital had CCTV all over the place but not a single camera picked up a thing."

"I'm so sorry, Mrs. Sirman. That must have been awful beyond imagining."

"You know what else is awful?" she said. "You calling me 'Mrs. Sirman' all the time."

"But you said—"

"I know what I said, but it's getting on my nerves, so switch to Pam, okay?"

"Sure. And I'm Chan."

"Chan is your first name? I thought it was a surname."

"It is. I'll refer you to my parents who, by the way, tried calling me 'Chuck' for years."

"Oh, no."

"Oh, yes. They were immigrants in love with America and desperate to have me accepted as American. Thankfully, it didn't stick, because I wouldn't allow it to. *Hated* the name. Anyway, back to your marriage?"

Yes...her marriage...

"Phil and I were zombies for years as we waited for a break in the search for Julie. I stopped looking for a teaching job, he dropped out of accounting and took up carpentry, saying he couldn't think straight anymore and needed to do something with his hands. Phil changed, I changed. We drifted apart. Lived in the same house, slept in the same bed, but something had died inside us. I knew he was depressed, and so was I. But that's enough on that. I tried to feel bad for him when he died but he was just sleepwalking though life. Maybe he wanted to

die. And, let's face it, he was no longer the love of my life. Julie—
or at least my brief memory of her—had replaced him."

To get off the subject of her marriage, Pam tried to get Chan
to talk about himself. He revealed that most of his education was
in computers but said the sort of organized thinking required
for programming worked well for him as an investigative
researcher—whatever that was.

And now they were cruising Brick Township, a mostly
blue-collar burg on Barnegat Bay. After spending most of her
life here, she knew her way around, and directed him to Arc
Lane. Phil had left town at age nine, but even if he'd stayed, she
probably never would have met him here. She'd grown up on
the northern side of town, and their different neighborhoods
meant different high schools.

Arc Lane was indeed an arc—a short one connecting two
longer streets—with three houses on each side. Number 430
turned out to be a three-bedroom ranch on a quarter acre lot,
just like the five other lots on Arc Lane.

"How are you going to work this?" she said as Chan parked
by the curb in front of the house.

"I guess I'll just ring the doorbell and ask if they remember
the Sirmans. And if so, I'll ask about little Philip."

Pam had problems with that. First off, she was a Bricktowner
and she knew Bricktowners. A young stranger appearing
on the doorstep asking personal questions about one of their
neighbors... uh-uh. Not gonna fly. Second, he was a foreign-
looking stranger. That was DOA.

But she couldn't come right out and tell him this.

"Why don't you let me do the talking? I can get us a lot
further playing the widow card than you can with whatever
story you were going to try to sell them."

He looked at her. "You'd do that?"

"I told you: I want to find out more about Phil too."

"Okay, then. Let's do it your way."

She'd brought along a manila envelope stuffed with all
Phil's personal papers, and she took that with her as she led
Chan to the door. An older man answered her ring. He was
balding, needed a shave, and had reading glasses hanging on

a lanyard from his neck. He wore a gray sweat suit and worn slippers. The retiree uniform.

Putting on her nicest smile, Pam said, "Hi, sir. May I ask how long you've lived here?"

His gaze was fixed on Chan, who was standing behind and to her right. Probably wondering if he was going to pull some kung fu on him. But he didn't hesitate. "Bought it in 1974."

"Excellent. Well, then, do you...?"

Wait a sec. That wasn't right. Couldn't be. Phil was born well after that, like her. These people couldn't have lived here since '74.

"Do I what?" the man said.

"Well, I'm confused. You see my husband died last week and—"

"My condolences," he said. "Sorry to hear that."

"So was I," she said, fishing in her envelope. "But you see, I'm traveling down memory lane, so to speak, and I wanted to visit the place where he was born, and his birth certificate gives this address."

She pulled it out of the envelope and handed it to him. He lifted his reading glasses for a look, then handed it back.

"Gotta be a typo. My father built this place in 1962, then sold it to me when he moved to Florida in '74. I've been here ever since."

Okay. That pretty much settled that. This wasn't Phil's boyhood home. She looked around. Which one was?

Chan said, "Which was the Sirman house then?"

"'Sermon'? You talking some church thing?"

"No," Pam said. "Sirman—S-I-R-M-A-N."

He shook his head. "Never heard of them."

"Joe and Amelia Sirman. They were killed in that restaurant fire in Toms River."

"The Bernardo's fire? I remember that. A bad one. If anybody in this neighborhood died in that I'd know about it. We'd all know about it. That birth certificate's all screwed up."

"I'm thinking you're right," Pam said. "Thank you for your time."

Chan looked like he wanted to say more but Pam dragged him away.

"We weren't going to get any more out of him," she said once they were back in the car.

"Well, he could be a crank or he could have dementia. I mean, how can a birth certificate be that wrong?"

"We'll try somebody else."

Only five other houses remained on Arc Lane. No one was home at the first one they tried; at the second they found an elderly woman who had lived there for forty years. She remembered the Bernardo's fire but had never heard of the Sirmans. So, back to the car again.

Chan started the engine. "If you can guide me over to Brick Hospital, we can check out this birth certificate at the source. They should have been computerized somewhat back then, so it shouldn't be a big deal for them to look up Phil's birth and give us his folks' right address."

Pam had another idea with a more immediate solution.

"Let me look up the Bernardo's fire. I was just nine years old then myself, so I don't remember much about it. I do remember driving down Hooper Avenue with my dad and passing the blackened ruins. They impressed me."

She DuckDucked Bernardo's fire in Toms River on her phone and a slew of hits appeared. With growing anxiety she scanned through three of them in quick succession.

"What's wrong?" Chan said.

Obviously her malaise was showing.

"Yeah, there was a kitchen fire, and yeah, it destroyed the place, but everywhere I look they talk about how it's such a damn good thing the fire happened on a Monday when the place was closed, otherwise people would have been hurt."

His expression went slack. "No casualties?"

She shook her head. "Nope. Not a one. Unless you count a minor burn on a volunteer fireman." She dropped her phone onto her lap. "What the fuck? He totally lied about his parents dying in that fire."

"Maybe he was mistaken about which fire," Chan said. "Maybe it was another fire."

"He was pretty specific about being nine years old and having to identify his parents' 'charred remains.' That's how he always referred to them: 'charred remains.' And there was only one bad restaurant fire that year: Bernardo's. So he didn't make any mistake. Was his whole life a fucking lie?"

This was beginning to creep her out—totally creep her out.

"Let's not go jumping too far ahead here," Chan said. "We'll go to the hospital and check the birth records. They may have a different address. We'll check that one out and, who knows? We'll straighten out this whole mess."

"You're a real optimist, aren't you."

"Not usually. I just like to be armed with as many facts as possible before I draw a conclusion. And that birth certificate is an important piece of the puzzle." He put the car in gear. "Which way to the hospital?"

Brick Hospital had become Ocean Medical Center when she'd last been here after her father suffered his fatal stroke. That had been shortly after her wedding. Its title now was a real mouthful: Hackensack Meridian Health Ocean Medical Center. Seemed they'd added yet another building since then.

She and Chan found their way to medical records where a heavyset, sixtyish woman greeted them from behind the counter.

"I have a faulty birth certificate here," Pam said, handing it to her. "My husband died last week and I've been revisiting his past and found out that this is all wrong."

"I'm so sorry to hear that." The woman stared at the certificate a second, then said, "In what way is it wrong?"

"The parents, Joe and Amelia Sirman, never lived at that address."

"How odd. Well, we've digitized all those records so we should be able to straighten this out in two shakes of a lamb's tail."

Chan looked at Pam as the woman turned away and mouthed *lamb's tail?*

Pam could only shrug.

The woman stood before a terminal and did a lot of keyboarding before returning to the counter. Her troubled expression triggered a sour feeling in Pam's stomach.

"This is strange. We have no record of a Philip Sirman being born here. In fact, we have no record of an Amelia Sirman being admitted to maternity or any other department. Ever. I'd have to say that this birth certificate is a fake."

Through the roaring in her ears Pam heard the woman ask permission to copy the certificate so she could bring it up with the hospital administration because it deserved to be investigated blah-blah-blah. She absently gave her the go ahead.

What the fuck was going on?

When the certificate was returned, she walked back out to the parking garage in a daze. Chan guided her to the car and even held the door for her.

"Phil's whole life was a pack of fucking lies," she said. "Or are you still going to play the optimist?"

Chan looked shocked himself. "Not anymore. A guy named Schopenhauer once said, 'A pessimist is an optimist in full possession of the facts.' These facts don't lead to a good place, because we haven't been able to verify a single thing about his life. It's as if he didn't exist. But obviously he did. So the question is, Who was Philip Sirman? Where did he come from? Who were his real parents? And why did he lie about everything?"

"Wouldn't a better question be, *What* was Phil Sirman?"

Chan frowned. "I don't under—"

"His body wouldn't burn! I saw it in the flames and it would… not… *burn!* So I've got to wonder if he was even fucking human."

She didn't quite believe she'd just said that, but there it was, out there squirming on the dashboard for all to see and think about.

"But you lived with him for—how many years?"

"Nine. And knew him even longer. I wish I could tell you that now, as I look back, I remember some things that I never could explain. You know, clues that he was, you know, *off*. But nope. Nothing. Not one fucking hint that he was any different from any other average white American male. He drank Coors Light, rooted for the Eagles in the winter and the Phillies—of course—in the summer. He got T-boned by a truck and died on the spot. Only one problem…"

Chan chimed in with, "His body won't burn."

"Yeah, that, and the fact that everything he told me about himself was a fucking lie."

"And you never suspected?"

She could only shake her head. "I never had reason to. According to him, his spinster Aunt Alice had been his last living relative. With her gone, he had no family left, so there was no one for us to visit. What reason did we have to go visit the house where he and his folks used to live—where he *said* they'd lived? As for me, my mother died of breast cancer when I was eight. My dad died shortly after we were married. This is the first time I've been back to Brick Town since. I never noticed discrepancies in the life history he told me because none had a chance to present themselves. And let me tell you, he was a damn good liar."

"Or maybe he believed everything he told you."

The possibility jolted her. "You think that's possible?"

"Well, people have been known to concoct detailed fantasy lives for themselves that became more real to them than, well, their real lives."

"You're saying he might have thought his lies were true?"

"I'm saying it's a possibility, but that doesn't mean it's a likely probability."

An awful thought struck her like a blow.

"Can you do me a favor?" she said.

"Sure. What?"

"Drive me to Herbertsville?"

"Glad to, but I have no idea where that is."

"It's the northern section of Brick. I'll guide you."

It took less than ten minutes to reach a Dutch colonial house on a tree-lined street.

She had him stop in front and told him, "Here's where I grew up. Stay in the car. This should only take a minute."

As she hurried up the front walk, she noticed that the current owners had augmented her father's sparse landscaping, adding new shrubs and an ornamental tree. She looked up at the dormer where little Pamela Gunning used to sit in the sun on the window box and read her *Little House* books. That was before she evolved into Potty-mouth Pam after Mom died.

Pam recognized the woman who answered the door but couldn't remember her name.

"Hi," Pam said. "Do you remember me?"

The woman frowned. "No..." she said slowly. "I don't think so."

Please-please-please!

"You bought this house from me. I was the seller."

She broke into a smile. "Oh, yes. Of course. Gunning wasn't it?"

Relief flooded her.

"Yes. That was my maiden name."

"Well, it's been a long time and you've changed."

Oh yeah, she thought. You could say I've been through a bit of shit.

"I...I was passing by and just wondered how you like the house."

"Really? Isn't that nice. We made some changes but we love the place. Would you like to come in and look at what we've done?"

"Yes, I'd love to but I'm pressed for time. I'm just glad to know you like it."

How easy the lies come, she thought as she all but ran back to the car.

6

Chan checked his messages while Pam talked to a lady at the front door.

Another email from Nicolette asking again when he was coming back. He really wouldn't mind seeing her again, but going back was a huge step.

He found a text from Danni.

Chan we have to talk ASAP. I checked the Sirman file and everything she said is true. But then I found we already have a file on your guy Maez and you won't believe what I found. I still don't believe it myself. Call me call me call me!!!

Chan was way ahead of her but couldn't tell her that. He tapped in a quick message…

I'm with Mrs. Sirman now and can't talk. Will callASAP.

…and sent it off just as Pam arrived back at the car.

"Take me home, Chan. I've had enough for one day."

He did as he was bid and got the car rolling.

"What was that all about?" he said.

"Just checking to see if I was real."

"Seriously?"

"Very seriously. When you said Phil might have truly believed all the bullshit he spun for me, I began thinking: What if everything I believe about myself is a lie? This stop here was my attempt at a little reality check."

"And did it work?"

"Yes, it did. You see, when my father died, the house passed to me. I'd recently married Phil, and we already had our own place, so I put it on the market. That woman remembered me as the seller. Which means my memories are real."

"That must be reassuring, what with everything surrounding Phil being so unreal."

He noticed her folding her arms across her chest. Despite the warmth of the day, she looked like she was feeling a chill.

"You all right?"

"Just thinking. What if..." she began and then her voice trailed off as if her train of thought had dissolved. She tried again. "I know this will sound far out, but I'm making it up as I go along. So...what if Phil was some sort of android created by a secret government agency and programmed with a bunch of memories that he thought were real?"

"That's a big *what if*, don't you think?"

"But it would explain why Phil wouldn't burn—because he's an android. What if these androids were sent out to father children which were then stolen to be raised by the government? And what if this android, after fulfilling its mission, was then killed so there'd be no way to track him back to the government agency?"

She stopped, obviously waiting for Chan to say something, but what could he say to that? She'd segued into Conspiracyland, a place that was too easy to get lost in.

Finally she said, "Well?"

Okay, he'd try to guide her back. But he'd have to be careful.

"I'm not sure what to say. Sounds like something on the Syfy Channel."

"I told you it was far out."

"And typical of the Syfy Channel, it's got holes. The big one for me is how does an android father children? I mean, I'm assuming you and Phil..." He left it hanging.

"Yes, of course we did. We fucked like bunnies. Well, at least until we didn't. And no, I was never with anyone else once I was with Phil. Julie was definitely his baby. So maybe he was a special android that made sperm."

He'd give her that, but...

"Okay, then, why kill him? You run the risk of someone trying to cremate his fireproof body."

"That's why they had to steal Phil's body."

Chan nodded. Any conspiracy theory had to have enough valid points to make it palatable.

"That's a good thought, but why make his body fireproof in the first place? It serves no practical purpose unless he's a firefighter, and it risks discovery, especially if you plan to murder him."

"Maybe there's a purpose to it that we don't know."

But Chan wasn't finished. "Another thing is why steal the child? That's risky as all hell. Why not make you do all the work of raising her?"

"But that won't work for them if they want to raise her a certain way, train her to be a super assassin or something."

"Now you're retreading *La Femme Nikita*. But here's another plot hole: Why do they need this android to father children they can steal? If they're that good at snatching infants, they can do it any day of the week, because babies are being born all the time."

She fluttered her hands in the air. "I don't know! I told you this was coming off the top off my head. I haven't thought it through. But what if they wanted a special kind of kid they could fill with experimental drugs?"

Suddenly she retched.

"What's the matter?"

"I'm making myself sick here. These are my worst nightmares!"

He reached over and patted her arm. He needed to reel her back in to reality.

"You shouldn't go upsetting yourself about Julie. You can pretty much count on her being with a loving couple desperate for a child they can raise as their own and lavish with love and kindness."

He was doing what he could to ease her pain by offering a best-case scenario, one that he hoped was true himself.

"I tell myself that too," she said. "And then I think, What will I do if I ever find her?"

"You'd have to identify her first. You'll never recognize her so you'll have to get a DNA—"

"Oh, I'll know her. I know my daughter."

"But how? She'll look nothing like her newborn self, so—"

"She had a birthmark." She held up her left middle and ring fingers. "A port-wine stain right here."

Chan was baffled. "I have no idea what you mean."

"It's a reddish area on these two fingers. Looks like a wine stain left on a white tablecloth. If she had to have a birthmark, I'm glad that's what she got and where she got it. They can be on the face and I wouldn't want my child to have to grow up with that. But if I saw a little seven-year-old girl with that today, I'd be pretty fucking sure she was mine." She sighed. "But what do I do then?"

"If there's a DNA match, you take her home with you, of course."

"But would that be the best thing to do... for Julie, I mean?"

"They stole her. They have no right to her."

"But what if they *didn't* steal her? What if they thought they got her from an unwed mom through a legit adoption? What do I do then?"

"She's *your* baby, Pam."

"You're looking only at my side of it, and I appreciate that, but I've got to think about Julie, or whatever they've named her. As far as she's concerned, that couple are her real parents. They've been Mommy and Daddy for as long as she's been alive. For all her seven years she's never known anybody else. And here I come along and rip her away from the two most important people in her life. What does that do to a child—*my* child? What kind of harm does that cause? Do they ever get over that kind of life disruption? I want my child back, but I don't want to damage her in the process. And if that couple is innocent, imagine how devastated they'll be losing their only child? Do you understand where I'm coming from?"

Yeah, he did. And he was amazed by her empathy for everyone involved.

"You called yourself 'the Dragon Lady' earlier. But you've got to be the most compassionate dragon anyone's ever met."

She actually blushed. "Bullshit. I'm a foul-mouthed bitch on wheels, and don't you forget it."

"You just made that pretty hard."

She lifted her envelope of Phil's papers off the floor and said, "I might as well throw this out. It's all lies anyway."

"Not so fast. We know he went to Rutgers, right? I mean you were there with him, so we know that's not a lie. What else have you got?"

She looked through. "Here's a baptismal certificate. Gotta be bogus. Here's a high school diploma—Cairo-Durham High, wherever that is. Someplace in New York, I gather."

"Why New York?"

"That's where his supposed Aunt Alice lived, who he supposedly moved in with after the fictitious death of his fictitious parents."

"They have websites with high school yearbooks online. Why don't you see if you can find that one?"

"Ooookay." She began tapping her phone. "Cairo-Durham High...and the diploma says his graduation year is the same as mine. Let's see...well, damn me, here it is. And here are the photos. Let me flip to the S's...nope. No Sirman, Philip or otherwise."

"Try the index, just in case he missed the photo shoot."

She laughed. "You really are an optimist. Okay, back to the index and... nope. No Sirman. Well, fuck it all. I'll bet even Aunt Alice's town was made up. All that talk about growing up in ski country."

An alert dinged in Chan's brain. Not an alarm, just a sudden desire to hear more.

"I take it we're not talking Vermont?"

"No. Catskills. Talked about us going on ski trips to Wyndham Mountain and Hunter Mountain, but he knew how I hate the cold. No way I'm going skiing."

Now an alarm sounded.

"Did he say what town he grew up in?"

"Yeah, once or twice. He never talked about Aunt Alice much—probably because she didn't exist. Yeah..." She snapped her fingers. "What was the name? Sounded like it should be in Canada."

The alarm was screaming. "Alberta?"

"That's it! Alberta, New York."

"Holeee crap!"

The car wobbled but Chan managed to keep it on the road.

"What's wrong? You okay?"

"Yeah. Fine." What to say? "Alberta, New York...you're absolutely sure of that?"

"Yeah. Absolutely. Once you said it, it clicked. What's the big deal?"

"Well, it's just...you won't believe this, but just yesterday I was in the Catskills and I stopped in this two-horse town called Alberta."

"No shit! So it does exist! I was beginning to wonder if that was just another of his lies."

"No, it exists. I may wind up back there."

Chan had been undecided about returning to Alberta, and definitely leaning toward not. But this new piece of info cast all that in a different light. He had some weighty decisions to make.

7

He dropped Pam off. She gave him her cell number and made him promise to keep her informed on the investigation into the disappearance of her husband's body. That wasn't exactly what Chan was after, but if he learned anything, he'd certainly tell her. As soon as he hit the Parkway south, he called Danni. Apparently during the interval between her text and his call she'd changed her mind about discussing the Sirman and Maez files over the phone. She asked him to meet her at her Smithville apartment. He would have preferred a phone conversation because he knew he'd have a harder time faking shock and surprise in person.

For the rest of the drive, he juggled the pros and cons of returning to Alberta. When he reached Danni's parking lot, he pulled out his notebook and began scribbling. He had a visual mind and he worked best when he could lay out his options in black and white. As he finished his diagram—much like how he planned some of his programming—he knew how he'd be responding to Nicolette's email, because he didn't see how he could stay away.

When he showed up at Danni's door she literally grabbed him and pulled him into the apartment.

"Thank God you're here! I've been going crazy waiting for you."

"What is it? All the way here I've been wondering what it could be that you can't discuss on the phone."

Had to appear totally in the dark here. Couldn't give a hint that he had the slightest clue as to what was coming.

"Okay, okay." She sounded almost breathless as the words tumbled out of her. "I looked up the Julie Sirman kidnapping file, just like the Dragon Lady said, and it's just like she told us: Day-old baby abducted from the hospital nursery and no leads on her in seven years. But after that, I took your suggestion to see if the Bureau had anything on Kurt Maez, and it did. Nothing about his death and disappearance, but lots about—wait for it: the kidnapping of his infant son!"

Chan dropped his jaw and stared for a few heartbeats, then forced a laugh. "You bitch! You almost had me there!"

"Chan, I shit you not. This is *not* a joke. Kurt Maez's one-day-old son was abducted from the nursery of a hospital in Enid, Oklahoma, exactly like the Sirman baby."

Another jaw drop. "You mean this is for real?" He violently shook his head. "No. No way. I can't believe this. It's too much. Prove it."

"All right, I will."

As she sat down at her laptop and began the log-in process, he glanced around her apartment. Obviously a furnished rental, with hand-me-down furniture and indifferent landscape prints on the painted walls. Except for her Jackson Pollock print. She'd had that in her dorm room at U of P and he was sure she'd imported it from her Newark apartment to keep her company during her stay down here.

Finally she popped out of the chair and pointed for him to sit.

"Read it and blow your mind."

He read it through, although he already knew what it would tell him. When he finished he leaned back and looked at her.

"My God! This is incredible! Two men, both fireproof, both with kidnapped infants and kidnapped corpses!"

Danni was nodding excitedly. "Can you spell *'conspiracy'*?"

"I sure can, but one that goes deeper and wider than we can imagine."

"What do you mean?"

"Pam and I took a trip—"

"'Pam'? The Dragon Lady is 'Pam' now?"

"She's not a dragon lady, she's had her daughter stolen and her husband killed, and nowhere to point the finger, so she's mad at the world."

A slow smile from Danni. "Sigmund Liao has her all psychoanalyzed, I see."

"She may have been rough on you, but you need to cut her a break." He wondered at his sudden, protective feelings toward Pam. "Especially when you realize that today she had another serving of steaming feces handed to her: We learned that everything she thought she knew about her husband is false. Everything he told her about his life before they met in college is total fabrication. His birth certificate is bogus, his parents never died the way he said they did, he's not in the yearbook of the high school from which he has a certificate. It goes on and on."

"Nothing is true?"

"Nothing. So that brings up a major question: Why didn't the FBI uncover any of this when they were investigating his daughter's kidnapping?"

"I just read the file a few hours ago and they checked him for a criminal record, and he has none. They interviewed people at his accounting firm and even some of his college professors, and all gave glowing reports. A stable, hardworking, honest guy. They saw no reason to go back further in his life—"

"If they'd done that they'd have found a pack of lies."

"I have to agree with them stopping where they did. Easy to Monday-morning quarterback when you find out later something's wrong, but he was never a person of interest. Every moment of his existence during the time before, after, and when the baby disappeared was accounted for by either his wife or CCTV, so his investigation was routine."

"I'm guessing the people behind this were counting on that."

"'The people behind this'? Who do you mean?"

"The people who created a bogus identity for him."

"We call it a 'legend.'"

"Okay, then, a legend. But they also created a bogus body for him."

"You mean one that won't burn."

"Right. Pam came up with this wild scenario that he was an android of some sort who was supposed to impregnate women so that the people running him could steal the babies.

It's farfetched as all get out, but the fact remains that we have two guys whose bodies wouldn't burn and who were snatched away before they could be autopsied. I'd say we definitely have a conspiracy here."

"One that I have to bring to the attention of my boss."

Oh, hell. He'd been dreading this, because he'd known as soon as Danni found out, she'd be raising an alarm. But maybe he could slow her down.

"How are you going to explain your path to making the connection?"

"Welllll...I was thinking of borrowing some of your research and telling a few little white lies."

He'd figured as much. "Such as?"

"I thought I might say that I'd heard on the news about Philip Sirman's body being stolen and thought the name sounded familiar—something crime related. So I looked him up and when I saw the kidnapping investigation I knew why I recognized the name."

"Will they buy that?"

She shrugged. "There are a hundred legitimate reasons why I might have seen 'Sirman' mentioned in passing. From there it might get a little shaky. I'll tell them that the news story about the body snatching also mentioned how they couldn't cremate his corpse. Now that struck me as really, really odd, so I did a news search for stories about other stolen corpses and other fireproof bodies."

"You'll want to do those for real, just so they're in your search history to cover all your bases."

"Good thought. I'll do that right away. Then I can legitimately say I came across Kurt Maez, 'miraculously' undamaged after his car fire, whose body was also stolen. After that, it was only natural to check and see if we had any sort of file on Maez and, lo and behold, I find out his son was also the victim of an infant kidnapping. And there we have it. What are the odds of those sequences of events happening twice by pure chance?"

"Zilch."

"Exactly. So it's a conspiracy until proven otherwise. Slam, bam, thank you, Chan."

He had to admit she'd concocted a believable scenario.

"I think they'll buy it."

"I'm not terribly worried about that. I mean, let's face it, the parallels between Maez and Sirman are so striking, I can't see them giving a second thought as to how I came across them. They'll immediately want to investigate what's behind them. And I'll do my damnedest to get myself attached to the investigation."

"You think they'll take you off the Atlantic City team?"

"They'll owe me a spot because it was my analytical skills that brought it all to light."

Chan cleared his throat, loudly and very pointedly.

She laughed. "Okay, okay. You got the ball rolling. But the thing is, with what you just told me about Sirman's bogus history, I'll make sure they do a deep dive into his whole past." She grinned and rubbed her hands together. "This is so exciting!"

He was glad for that. Anything to help Danni. Except...

"Can I ask you a favor?"

"Anything."

"Hold off for a while?"

She frowned, her expression troubled. "Why?"

"Because I came across another revelation from Pam about her husband. Guess where Philip Sirman says he grew up." He didn't wait for her to guess. "Alberta, New York."

"No! That place in the Catskills you were transported to?"

"One and the same."

She sat down. "Wait. If this guy told nothing but lies about his past, this could be just one more."

Chan nodded. "Right. Could be. But of all the small towns in the US he could have chosen, why choose Alberta? Why choose the place where I landed when I was translated from that area of the Pinelands—the area that Sirman's fellow fireproof dead man, also father of a kidnapped infant, was warning everyone away from?"

"You think Sirman was really from Alberta?"

"I do. And it kind of makes sense because all the weirdness I've encountered triangulates on Alberta, New York. Where did the Upwelling stop moving inland? At the septagon in the Pinelands. Why was that?"

"We don't know."

"Okay then, what's the last place we both remember that Friday afternoon?"

"The pinelands."

"Right. Our memory loss began there. The next ten hours are a blank. I don't know what triggered the amnesia, but I do know from personal experience that the septagon is definitely connected to Alberta. So as far as I'm concerned, that forges a connection between Alberta and the Upwelling. And the Upwelling is, as we both know, related to the holes in our memories, because it was during the Upwelling that those holes appeared."

Danni was sporting one of her askance looks. "That train of links is tenuous at best, and I'm being generous."

He pulled out his notebook and showed her his scribbles.

"Here it is in black and white."

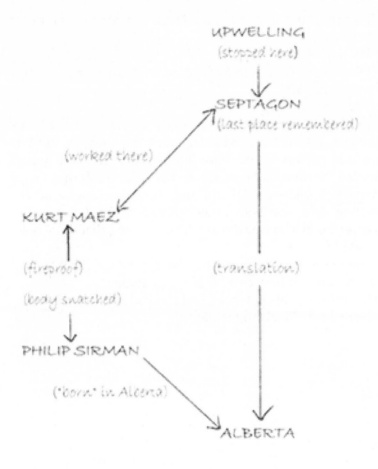

"You can't tell me you don't sense a connection."

She sighed. "I do. The logical part of me rebels at it, but there's another part that tells me to go with it. But why hold off the Bureau's involvement? What do you think that will accomplish?"

"They'll come storming into Alberta investigating Sirman's background, poking and prodding anyone who may have known him. Their very presence could shake up everything. I don't know how the people on that mountain will react when they know the Feds are sniffing around. I'm not even sure yet what I'm looking for, but they may all very well shut down and then I won't learn anything."

"Well, if you don't know what you're looking for, how are you going to know where to look?"

"I'll know it when I see it. I have an in with the mountain community, so I'm going to go."

She stared at him for a moment. "How are you going to work that? Just waltz in and join them?"

"Well, first off, they *want* me back. You and Mac and Aldo have always made fun of my 'feelings' and—"

"We're just ribbing you, Chan. There's no ridicule there, at least not on my part. Just having a bit of fun with a friend. Mac and Aldo can't speak for themselves anymore, but I'm sure they felt the same."

"I'm not saying I have some sort of psychic power. I don't. All I'm saying is that I just happen to be sensitive to things that most people don't even notice."

"I can buy that," Danni said, "though I will confess that I can't always buy into your feelings themselves."

"That's okay. I can't always either. But these people up in Alberta apparently take this sort of stuff very seriously. They even have a name for people like me: tairongo."

"You said that word before. What language is that?"

"No idea. But that's how they think of me. I won't have to infiltrate them and worm my way into their confidence. They want me there and they'll welcome me."

"But what do you hope to get out of this?"

"My memory, goddamn it!" His frustration at being unable to remember that night no matter what he tried boiled over for an instant. He clamped an immediate lid on it. "Sorry. Didn't mean to shout. It's just that this ten-hour hole isn't only in my memory, it's in my life—*our* lives, because you were with me that night. So if I'm successful, we'll both come out ahead."

Danni's expression telegraphed what she thought of his chances for success, but she said, "I didn't realize how much this means to you. And I guess if I'd been allowed more time to think about it, I'd be more into it myself."

"You haven't been out of work. I've had a ton of empty hours to obsess on this."

"If I do hold off, how much time do you think you'll need?"

"Can you give me till Monday? I figure if I'm not getting anywhere by then, extra days won't make any difference."

"Okay. It's gonna kill me to keep this to myself, but I can hold off till Monday."

Yes!

"Thanks, Danni. I'll keep you informed."

"You'd better. And you'd better be careful. You don't know anything about this Family."

"It's got mothers with happy-looking children running all over the place, so how bad can it be?"

"Well, FYI: The Manson Family had women and kids living at the Spahn Ranch while they were plotting a string of murders in the hope of starting a race war."

Well, damn. No, he had not known that.

"Thanks so much for those comforting words, Agent Boudreau."

"Just a friendly heads-up. Is it a religious group? A cult? Are they waiting for a saucer?"

"I'm not sure what they're about but they seem to think they're communicating with their mountain."

She frowned. "With the mountain...like it's alive?"

"I guess so. When I was translated up there I wound up inside the mountain, but nothing or no one communicated with me. They're led by a guy named Samuel."

"Last name?"

"Damned if I know. No one ever said it."

"Too bad. I could check to see if the Bureau's got a file on him like we found on Sirman and Maez."

"I'll get back to you on that when I find out."

"When do you leave?"

"First thing tomorrow."

He'd email Nicolette tonight to let her know he was coming.

"Well, then, we should go out for a farewell dinner. What are you in the mood for?"

"Something Asian but not Chinese."

He hadn't found a restaurant yet that could hold a candle to his mother's Longjiang and Manchu cuisine.

"A guy named Chan Liao? Imagine that." She grinned.

"Can't interest you in some egg foo yung?"

"Let's not go there. It's just that I have a feeling I won't see anything the least bit exotic on my plate up on that mountain."

"I spotted a Thai place on Route Nine. But it's my treat."

She headed for the door and he followed.

"Considering my ongoing lack of income, I won't argue." As they passed the Pollock print, he stopped and said, "Does this follow you everywhere?"

"Pretty much. It speaks to me, Chan. You know that."

He did know. But it didn't say a damn thing to him. A bunch of sloppy white swirls moving in from the edges of the canvas, crowding a central black crevasse. Left him cold. But he knew Danni's feeling.

"Chaos, right?"

"Chaos everywhere. And it's my job to make order out of chaos. And right now that means the chaos of what happened to AC. And the title of this baby makes it more meaningful than ever. You remember it?"

For the life of him, he couldn't. Something about this painting made him want to forget it.

"Nope."

"*The Deep*. Since the night of the Upwelling, I can't look at this without thinking of the Sohm Abyss."

"The source of the Upwelling?"

"Uh-huh."

Now *that* was a creepy thought.

THURSDAY

1

When Chan left early the next morning, Nicolette had yet to respond to his email of the night before. He didn't let that deter him. He figured he'd pass the time on the monotonous four-hour ride by blasting the song collection on his phone through his car radio, and that was fine for a while. But then a thought that had flashed through his mind just as he'd been drifting off to sleep last night sneaked up on him again.

All those children he'd seen running around the community—they all seemed to have mothers, but could that possibly be where the Sirman and Maez children had wound up? Were Philip Sirman and Kurt Maez connected to the Family? They'd both had children abducted and never seen again. But would they aid in the abduction of their own children to be raised by the Family? Could they be so heartless that they'd do that to their wives? It seemed farfetched—*too* farfetched. But the thought wouldn't go away and nagged him all the way up the Parkway and onto the New York State Thruway.

When he stopped for a quick lunch in Saugerties he checked his email and found an enthusiastic response from Nicolette. She'd tell Samuel to expect him.

Okay. The game was afoot.

He bought two chili dogs to go from a place called Dallas Hot Wieners. He ate them in the car and burped the rest of the way up Route 23.

When he arrived in Alberta he missed the road that led up to the Family and had to double back. He stopped at the lowered red-and-white-striped gate pole. The armed security man who stepped out of the guardhouse wasn't the same one he'd passed Tuesday on his way out. He wore a similar gray outfit but this fellow was African-American.

"You have business here?" he said.

"Samuel's expecting me, I believe. Chan Liao."

The guard whipped out a cellphone as he returned to the guardhouse. Half a minute later he stepped back out, a bright smile lighting his dark face as he approached the car.

"You're the new tairongo?" he said, sticking out his hand. "Why didn't you say so?"

Tairongo...would he ever get used to that weird word? And since he had no idea what the future held for him, he didn't want to commit to anything. At least not yet.

He gripped the proffered hand and gave a drawn-out, "Welllll..."

"Your name's Chan, right? I'm Henry. Welcome. Samuel will meet you at the fort. You know where you're going?"

"Yep. Been here before."

Henry stepped back into the guardhouse. The gate swung up and he waved Chan through.

Well...things were off to a friendly enough beginning.

As soon as he cleared the gate he felt that welcoming sense of peace he'd experienced during his brief interlude here on Tuesday.

Yeah, the tairongo was back.

He drove up the steep incline through the trees to the plateau where he found everything pretty much the same as he'd left it two days ago. The small, rustic houses were arranged in a semicircle facing up the slope where the stone fortress backed against the mountain. Children frolicked in the central playground area while their mothers looked on.

He couldn't help wondering again if seven-year-old Julie Sirman might be among them. She wouldn't have that name, of course. But she'd still have the port-wine stain Pam had described on her fingers. That would be a clue. He vowed to keep watch on all the hands of little girls he ran into around here. He knew the odds of Julie Sirman living in this community were somewhere in the neighborhood of zero, but what could it hurt to look?

He headed straight for the castle-like fort. As he neared he saw a smiling dark-haired woman standing outside the big wooden door at the entrance. Nicolette. A welcoming committee of one, but a very attractive one.

He spotted three vans parked off to the side—all GMC Savanas—and pulled his Sentra in next to them. A UPS driver was unloading packages near the front door. As Chan got out and began to stretch, Nicolette walked up and hugged him. Not tight enough to start him reading too much into it, but definitely warm and welcoming.

"We're so glad you came back to us!"

He'd rehearsed a number of responses on the way up. None of them entirely true, but none entirely false either.

"Well, I'm glad to be back." Not the least because of this particular woman.

Had she done herself up a little? She definitely looked more put together than last time. For him? He'd caught her and her friend off guard when he'd strolled in from the woods unannounced and unexpected on Tuesday.

"Come inside. Samuel is waiting for you."

She led him through the fortress's big oak door to the large, windowless great hall with its long tables. Samuel waited at one of the smaller side tables. He rose and offered his hand.

"Delighted you came back."

"Well, to tell you the truth, I'm a bit at loose ends at the moment." Here was another one of his prepared responses. "I ran the computer network in a casino that was destroyed in the Atlantic City Upwelling. Not only is my workplace gone along with all my friends there, but so are the people who owned and ran it. So I've got nothing to tie me down anywhere."

"I hate to quote a cliché, but I'm sure you've heard the expression, 'When one door closes, another opens.' We hope you will see us as that other door."

"I hope so too."

Again, just like last time, no interest in the AC disaster. Every single other person he'd ever mentioned it to wanted to know more, wanted any details he could supply because the government was supplying so few. But these folks... no questions about how he happened to survive when 25,000 died.

Samuel indicated a chair. "Please, have a seat. Are you hungry?"

"No, I had lunch on the road."

When the three of them were seated, Samuel said, "Now that you've had a little time to mull what happened to you the other day, I'm sure you have some questions."

"I'm still having a problem accepting the reality of stepping into the woods in South Jersey and walking out of a cave in the Catskill Mountains seconds later."

Nicolette cocked her head. "'Accepting'? It happened. To you. Unless you think your mind played a trick on you."

"I guess 'accepting' wasn't the right word. 'Processing' is probably more like it. That sort of thing doesn't happen in my life."

Samuel's broad face lit with a smile. "The Mountain wanted us to meet you, so it brought you here."

"You keep talking of the mountain as if it's alive. Mountains aren't alive."

"This one is," Nicolette said. "When I drove you out the gate the other day, you told me you felt an immediate difference—you didn't feel the Mountain anymore."

"A feeling I'd been having suddenly stopped, replaced by another, but that didn't mean it had anything to do with your mountain."

"And when you returned to the Mountain today, did that feeling return as well?"

"Yes, but—"

She grinned. "See? The Mountain welcomed you back."

Well, damn. He had indeed felt welcome.

Chan looked at Samuel, then at Nicolette. "But neither of you feel anything when you go in and out?"

"We're not tairongos," she said, as if that explained everything.

"Okay...about that: You say I'm this 'tairongo,' so I guess my biggest question has to be about what you expect of me."

"Ah!" said Samuel with a clap of his hands. "That's easy: Just be yourself. You've shown yourself to be attuned to the Mountain, so we will depend on you to monitor the mood of the cosmos, which you will perceive as soon as you step outside the gate."

Whoa. "Mood of the cosmos?"

"Yes. Our purpose is to serve the Mountain. To do that we must know what is going on beyond our gate."

He shook his head. "This isn't making a whole lot of sense to me."

Samuel laughed. "I'm sure it isn't, but it will once you join us."

Chan wasn't so sure about that.

"So that's all I'd do? Hang around and interpret the moods of… the cosmos?"

Damn, he had a hard time even thinking that, let alone saying it out loud.

"You're thinking that sounds dull?" Nicolette said with a sly smile.

"Doesn't it?"

Samuel said, "It sounds excruciatingly dull. But that's not the only duty of a tairongo. You'd be intimately involved in the day-to-day running of the Family. You'd be part of something."

Chan tried hard to keep his deep skepticism about that from his face and tone.

"I don't know…"

"There would be a quid pro quo, of course," Samuel said. "We know what you'd be doing for us. What could we do for you?"

Well, he couldn't very well say, You can tell me the connection between this place and the Atlantic City Upwelling. And after he knew that, maybe they could answer another question: What happened to Mac and Aldo?

But realistically he could ask for something seemingly small scale, something that appeared inconsequential in the larger scheme of things, but hugely important to him.

"I have a hole in my life."

Nicolette brightened immediately. "We can fill it! With love and kindness!"

"It's not that kind of hole." Although love and kindness were sadly missing from his life these days. "It's a hole in my memory."

"Amnesia?" Samuel said. "You've lost your past?"

"Just ten hours of it. It occurred during the Atlantic City Upwelling. I was there that day. But from early afternoon to almost midnight is a blank."

"I'm familiar with the story. I know the city was mysteriously destroyed, but we don't follow the outside world closely here. Have they figured out yet what happened to it?"

Chan shook his head slowly. "They still have no idea."

"But it's been—what?—it must be two months now."

"Almost nine weeks now. Do you think anyone here can help jog the memories back into my consciousness?"

A careful shrug. "Perhaps. The First is very wise. He knows many things that are far from common knowledge. Forgotten things. Perhaps he can help. I make no promises—"

"I'm not asking for any and I don't expect any."

"—but I will tell him about it and ask him to work on it for you."

A ray of hope? Nah. Don't get your hopes up. But Chan wouldn't turn it down.

"That's all I can ask."

"If I may quote another cliché: Be careful what you wish for. These memories might have fled for a very good reason."

"I lost two old friends that night. I need to know what happened to them."

"I sympathize, Chan. But be aware you might very well uncover something you wish had remained hidden. You may have witnessed something that is too painful to remember."

He sighed. "Yeah, I know."

Danni's words from the other night came back to him. *Isn't it obvious? Something nasty happened to Mac and Aldo in AC, so nasty that our brains decided to hide it from us until we could handle it.*

"Or it could be even worse."

Uh-oh. He didn't like the sound of that.

"Like what?"

"Like...well, you might have *done* something in those hours that's too painful to remember."

Oh, hell. He hadn't thought of that. What if he'd committed

a crime or some sort of atrocity that he couldn't face? Damn, why couldn't he remember? He'd risk anything, even shame and self-loathing, if he could only get those hours back. He was sick of guessing. He needed to *know*.

"I'll let you know what the First says," Samuel said. "Don't expect an answer right away. The solution might not be readily at hand. And, of course, the First has to accept you."

"Accept me?"

He'd thought acceptance here was a given...that it was up to him to decide whether or not to stay.

"Yes. He has to be sure that you're conscientious and reliable. Just because you've been gifted with tairongo abilities doesn't guarantee that you'll be a good fit. You'll be an integral part of this community. We'll have to be sure we can trust you. In the meantime, I'd like to invite you to dine with us tonight."

"Well...thank you."

He'd kind of taken it for granted that they'd be supplying room and board.

"We all meet right here at six and sup at the big central table. That will give you time to settle yourself at Cliff House."

"Cliff House?"

"It's a local B and B."

"But I thought—"

"You'd be staying here? I'm sorry about that, but I'm afraid you can't stay on the Mountain until the First has accepted you. But we have an account at Cliff House, which is just down the road apiece. Less than a mile away. I reserved you a room this morning when Nicolette told me you were coming. Ian Carroll and his sister Erica run it. Nice people. They're expecting you. And now I have a meeting with the First." He rose and extended his hand. "Why don't you get settled in and we'll meet you back here at six."

I guess I'm being dismissed for now, Chan thought as they shook hands.

Samuel walked off toward the rear of the great hall while Nicolette walked him back outside.

He said, "Well, that was abrupt."

"Yeah," Nicolette said. "Samuel can be that way. He used

to be some high-powered executive before he started the community."

"Really? For what company?"

She shrugged. "I don't remember...or even remember if I ever knew or cared to know. Some sort of research company... something scientific. All before my time here. I hear he sold it for a ton of money that he uses to keep us going."

Interesting...

"Does he have a last name?"

"Lamm—with two Ms."

"Samuel Lamm. I'll have to look him up."

Wikipedia might have something on him.

"See you tonight?" she said as he opened his car door.

"Definitely."

Most definitely.

Downhill at the gate, Henry was still on duty. Chan again noticed the little plaque on the post. Nicolette had said the property had seven corners. This would mean the gate here was on the southern corner. Kurt had told him the plaques around the pinelands septagon had been posted by "eggheads" from Rutgers. That turned out to be a complete fabrication. So what were they... really?

Before the smiling Henry could wave him through, Chan pulled the car over and walked to the guardhouse.

"Can I ask you a question or two?" he said.

"Sure. Shoot."

"This fence...does it run all the way around the mountain?"

"Indeed it does."

"That's a helluva lot of chain links."

"You bet."

"But what about animals? You must have tons of game up here, what with the whole mountain posted for no hunting."

"The little guys can climb over or burrow under. The deer and such have to stay put. But I look at it as doing them a favor. Inside the fence they're safe. Outside they can get shot by hunters or wind up roadkill."

Chan pointed to the plaque. "And what about that? Nicolette told me you have one posted on each of the seven corners of the property. Why's that?"

"The sigils? I have no idea."

"It's not some sort of religious thing?"

Henry chuckled. "Naw. Samuel says we must keep them on the corners for the safety of the Mountain."

For the safety of the Mountain...that baffled Chan.

"I don't understand."

Henry shrugged. "That makes two of us. But Samuel calls the shots. We keep an eye on them to make sure the sigils remain on the corners and nobody sneaks in and takes one for a souvenir."

"Whoa. That's a lot of ground to cover."

"It sure was, but Samuel brought us some help." He motioned Chan into the guardhouse where he pointed to a four-propeller contraption charging on a corner table. "Our eye in the sky."

"A drone! How cool!"

Henry beamed with pride. "We can patrol the whole perimeter without leaving the guardhouse here."

"You folks really take your privacy seriously."

"I guess. We have a lot of women and kids to protect. Like that gate there."

Chan saw that the striped steel pole didn't just hang in the air, it rested in a slot in the top of a concrete support.

"It's solid steel," Henry said. "A car might ram its way through, but it would take a few good hits and probably do a lot of damage to the car. As for the drone here, in the night hours we sort of have to keep our fingers crossed. It's got a low-light, night-vision camera, but you still can't make out much detail. At least we can spot someone who's on the wrong side of the fence and we can make sure the sigils are still in place."

"They're that important?"

"Well, Samuel's always had us keep an eye on them, but that wasn't all that often when I started out here, because we had to do it on foot. Then we got the drones and we were able to patrol the entire perimeter twice a day with them. Hang on a sec."

He stepped to the door and pressed a button on a console affixed to the wall beside it. Outside, the gate swung up and he waved the UPS truck out. When it passed through, he pressed the button again to lower the gate.

"Anyway," he said, returning to Chan and the drone, "the twice-a-day patrols were the routine for the last couple of years, but then a couple of months ago he shows up and says he wants six patrols a day at random intervals. And to keep it random he gave us this die with only twos, threes, and fours on the sides. We roll it to decide the interval. He says nowadays we have to keep an extra-close watch on the sigils."

"What brought that on?"

"No idea. But if Samuel wants it, we do our damnedest to make it happen."

Chan left with the distinct impression that not only did Henry know a lot more about the sigils than he was letting on, he knew what had sparked Samuel's sudden concern over security. Had the Family been threatened?

2

Samuel climbed the steps to the upper level. The door locked automatically behind him as he stepped left into the surveillance room. The First stood before a bank of monitor screens. Only one was lit; its feed came from the great hall directly below. The walls here were otherwise bare except for the large black resetter, looking like a twisted ankh, mounted on the near wall. He pressed a hand against its cold surface as he passed.

"The new tairongo is here," he said.

The First peered at him from under the prominent ridge of his sloping brow. "What do you think of him?"

"I'm not entirely convinced he is right for us. He has the gift, of that I am sure. He's kind, he's gentle, and he's very intelligent."

"In other words, a good man."

"Yes. I believe so."

"Then what's the problem?"

"I sense he is holding something back... hiding something."

"I had the same feeling as I watched him," the First said in his rumbling voice. "I sensed another agenda in him."

During the rewiring to accommodate the outside electricity source, the great hall had been fitted with sophisticated audio-visual monitoring equipment. The First lived in seclusion and this allowed him to keep track of what was going on in the Family.

"We need a tairongo, now more than ever. The Atlantic City incident leaves us little leeway. But there is an unresolved issue in him that we must assess before we allow him into our ranks."

"Our *thinning* ranks," the First said. "We have lost two Enhanced in the weeks since the Atlantic City debacle. That is unprecedented."

"Those deaths have no relation to Atlantic City," Samuel said. "Nor even to each other, for that matter. Random incidents."

The First grunted. "Random incidents that could have sparked serious consequences had either of them been autopsied."

"The differences from unenhanced humans are subtle. It's highly unlikely a run-of-the-mill medical examiner would even pick them up. But the mystery remains: Where are their bodies?"

"I remain deeply disturbed by this situation," said the First. "On the surface, it appears to work to our advantage that someone spirited their remains away before anyone could take a scalpel to them. But the question is *why*? Of all the bodies in morgues and mortuaries around the county, why those two bodies? Why our two dead Enhanced?"

"More important to my mind is *who*? But since we don't know and have no way of finding out, let me return to the matter of the tairango's other agenda that you mentioned. I believe it might be his quest for his lost memory."

"Yes, I heard you tell him you would approach me for restoration."

"Merely a delaying tactic."

"Dare we return it to him?"

Samuel shook his head. "I'm hesitant. At least not so soon after the devastation. The truth might crush him. And then he'll be of no use to us. Nor to anyone else, including himself. I can use the possibility of restoration like a carrot. That is, if we decide he's right for us."

"We can always give him a trial run and see if we can trust him not to become too curious. If he does become too inquisitive, we'll send him on his way."

Samuel said, "If he's at all intelligent, he will have questions. But even if he does, where is he going to find answers? The children know nothing, and the Enhanced would never share with an outsider."

The First stepped to a side counter and grabbed an open bottle of Perrier. He had a short, squat body with broad, powerful shoulders.

"Was it my imagination," he said after a sip, "or is there an attraction between the tairongo and the Enhanced who was sitting with you."

Samuel nodded. "Nicolette. Yes, I noticed that too. The Enhanced are human, after all. Well, mostly so. They have normal human desires and needs—toned down, of course, but still present. And different personalities. Nicolette happens to be more adventurous than most."

"You're the Enhanced expert. Should we discourage her?"

This was what Samuel liked about the First. He was knowledgeable and intelligent enough to know what he didn't know. He knew Samuel knew the Enhanced better than anyone, and deferred to him on that subject.

"I think we should turn a blind eye and let nature, as it were, take its course. Who knows? We might learn something important about him."

3

Cliff House looked like it had once been a barn. Chan would never have taken it for a B & B and might have passed it had he not spotted the sign at the last moment. He just barely made the turn into the gravel driveway.

He parked by the side door with the *Welcome* sign. As he removed his carry-on bag from the back seat, he looked around for a cliff. The place faced a steep wall of the mountain across the street. Maybe they meant that. Or maybe they got a deal on a used sign.

He turned to find a middle-aged man in a full-length, tie-dyed kaftan standing in the doorway. He wore his light-brown hair in a ponytail.

"Cheers, mate," he said in a soft English accent. "You must be Mister Liao, the guest from the mountain."

"That's me. And you must be Ian."

"One and the same." He offered a limp hand which Chan gave a quick shake. "Follow me."

Ian's kaftan fluttered around him and his clogs clip-clopped on the hardwood floor as he led Chan down a short hallway to a desk where a woman—also middle-aged—stood waiting.

"Good afternoon," she said, smiling. "Welcome to Cliff House. I'm Erica."

Chan could see the family resemblance in their faces but there the resemblance ended. Where Ian was all flowy and airy and looked like a refugee from a sixties commune, Erica looked totally put together in tailored slacks, a tight, long-sleeve blouse buttoned up to the throat, and a tightly buttoned vest. Even her gray-streaked hair was tight—wound into a bun at the back.

And her grip was definitely tighter than Ian's.

She pushed an index card and a pen across the desktop, saying, "We need to get some routine paperwork sorted. Just your name and contact info: address, email, cell number—that sort of thing. Innkeeper stuff."

"No problem," Chan said and began writing.

"You're our only guest at the moment," Erica said.

"This is our slow season," Ian added. "It'll pick up next month when the leaf peepers start showing up, and gets absolutely bonkers during ski season. But I tell you, if the winters keep getting much bloody warmer, there won't be a ski season before long."

Erica said, "We serve breakfast between six and ten, but since you're the only guest, Ian will heat up the skillet whenever you want."

Ian pointed to the right. "I'm planning on eggs benedict tomorrow. We serve it right in that room over there. It gets lots of sun in the morning. And..." he said with a flourish, "...that's also where I share a bottle or two of wine every night with our guests." He aimed the point at Chan. "Which would be you. What do you prefer: red or white?"

"The kind with alcohol," Chan said.

Ian laughed. "My kind of man!"

Somehow I doubt that, Chan thought.

Ian added, "That will be a good time to discuss your dinner options around here. You'll have to drive to Wyndham but that's only three miles down the road."

"Thanks. Maybe tomorrow. But I'm set for tonight."

"Where, if I might ask?"

"On the mountain. They've invited me to dinner up there."

His eyebrows rose. "Oh, really? Are you a member of...what do they call it... the Family?"

"No. As a matter of fact, I didn't know they existed until two days ago."

"Really? How unusual."

"How so?"

"Well, every so often they have contractors up there for installations and service and renovations and the like. Most of them stay here for the convenience. But those folks on the hill never feed them a thing."

"I suppose I should feel honored then. Where is my room?"

"I'll show you. We're giving you a rear room on the second floor. They're the quietest."

He led Chan toward the stairs but stopped along the way to point through a doorway.

"This is our great room."

It had a high ceiling all the way to the rafters and a dozen or so well-stuffed chairs scattered about before a huge stone fireplace against the outer wall.

"I'll bet it's popular in the winter."

"Can't find a seat."

In the upstairs hall he pointed out the bathroom on their way to a spacious antique-furnished room—no closets but two wardrobes—and a king-size bed.

"I let you get sorted," Ian said. "Remember: wine at five."

"Got it."

As soon as the door closed, Chan flopped back on the bed. Nice and firm. Resisting the urge to nap, he pulled out his phone and texted Danni.

Made it. See if your people have a
file anywhere on a Samuel Lamm.

With that sent off, he opened the browser, accessed Wikipedia, and searched for the name. He found a short article. It gave Lamm's birth year as 1956, which meant he was his pushing seventy. He looked pretty damn good for his age. Apparently he'd been born right here in Alberta. He earned a BS in Biology at Columbia U and an MBA at Stanford. The article didn't say where he got the money, but at age twenty-five he bought controlling interest in a small Tahitian bioengineering firm called TonaTech, moved it to Delaware, and entered the GMO market. Under his guidance they quickly came up with uniquely modified strains of wheat and rice and other crops that were remarkably drought resistant. TonaTech became a darling among the biotech firms and its IPO went through the roof. Fourteen years ago he sold the whole shebang and walked away a multibillionaire. He retired to his old home town, Alberta, NY, where he lives in seclusion.

Well, not exactly seclusion, Chan thought.

He scrolled down farther and found nothing more. That's it? Not just short—downright sketchy, to Chan's mind. You'd think a billionaire former CEO of a biotech firm beloved by Wall Street would rate more than that. Unless...

What if there *was* no more than that? Lamm and Sirman... both supposedly born in Alberta, New York. Sirman's biography had proved to be a tissue of lies. Could Lamm's be the same? Because if his past was as fictional as Sirman's, it would explain the sketchy Wikipedia piece.

If only he could find a connection between Lamm and Philip Sirman. Chan didn't know the details of Kurt Maez's biography, but he had a feeling it would be equally bogus, so a Lamm-Maez connection would be almost as good.

This was where the FBI's direct involvement would have come in handy. They could do what Danni had called a deep dive into Lamm's background, and even Kurt Maez's. But he still didn't want them involved yet, so he'd have to work with Danni's limited access.

He closed his eyes. Anticipation of this trip and of infiltrating the Family had made sleep difficult last night. A nap would be good.

4

His phone woke him. Danni calling. The display read 4:32. Already? He must have needed that nap.

"Hey, Danni. How goes it?"

"As well as can be expected, seeing as I'm still on the AC team instead of looking into another matter that has caught my interest."

He laughed. "I get it, I get it! I know you're impatient but it's only till Monday. Is that fellow I mentioned a person of interest in anything?"

He was being circumspect because he didn't know how well sound traveled in this former barn. Ian was definitely nosy. Erica might be as well. He didn't know how close they were to Samuel and the Family.

"Good news and bad news. I googled him, and then his company. The good news is that it looks like everything at TonaTech was clean and above board."

"I'm more interested in the bad news."

"The bad news is that it looks like everything at TonaTech was clean and above board and so we have nothing on him."

Well, damn.

He told her about being put up at a B&B rather than staying on the mountain.

"How inconvenient. And after they asked you back and all. That really limits your contact with the members. Do you think that's the reason?"

"Could be. They seem pretty insular in general, however. The innkeeper here told me they don't let any outsiders stay up there. He seemed almost shocked when I said they'd invited me back to join the Family dinner tonight."

"Okay. That's something, then."

"I guess. I'm playing this entirely by ear. I mentioned my memory loss to Samuel at our brief meeting today. He said the Family's elder might know a way to get it back."

"Well, if he comes up with something that works, get an extra dose for me. Okay, gotta run. Let me know how it goes tonight."

"Will do."

Chan debated unpacking the clothes he'd brought along and decided to leave everything in the carry-on for now. He grabbed his travel kit and ambled down the hall to freshen up. When he finished and stepped back into the hall, he heard Ian's and Erica's voices echoing up from the first floor.

"—still, they did invite him to dinner," Erica said.

"From the sound of it, it almost seems as if they're courting him."

"Whatever for?"

"That's what I want to know. If he doesn't show up for the wine hour, you go knock him up."

Chan heard a smile in Erica's voice as she said, "Going to exercise your interrogation skills?"

"You know me, pet. Once I get someone talking about themselves, you can't shut them up."

Chan tiptoed back to the room. He'd definitely be attending the wine hour tonight.

5

Chan showed up at five oh five.

Ian grinned. "Ah! It appears you're a punctual bloke. Excellent. Any problem with a cabernet? I might be able to scare up another sort of bevvy if you prefer."

Chan doubted Ian would have the makings of a Manhattan, so he didn't bother asking.

"Cab is fine. Where's Erica?"

"My sister is a teetotaler, I'm afraid." He lowered his voice. "Had a problem with the stuff, if you know what I mean. I do my best to compensate for her lack of consumption."

He popped the cork and then began to pour, filling each glass to within an inch of the top.

"Wow. Generous pour."

"Well, it's just the two of us. So..." He raised his glass. "Cheers, mate."

"Cheers right back at you."

He sipped. Nice flavor. He'd been a beer drinker until he'd gone to work at the casino. With the sedentary nature of his job, he began to put on weight with the lagers, so he switched to wine. His knowledge base about the varietal regions was small but growing.

"Can I ask you about your accent?" he said. "I can't place it."

Ian smiled. "That's because you probably haven't heard it much. It's Northumberland—way up north. I was born in a tiny village called Carham on Tweed. Another mile north across the river and I'd be a Scot."

"Reminds me of where my folks came from: Heilongjiang Province in the very north of China. Cross the river there and you're in Russia."

Ian leaned back and crossed his legs. "So now we know where I'm from and your folks are from. How about you, Mister Liao?"

"Chan, please. Born in Cincinnati, but now I live in New Jersey in a town called Margate. Right south of Atlantic City."

Chan had made sure to drop that particular place name. It had the expected effect.

Ian bolted upright. "Atlantic City? Bloody hell! Were you there for the Upwelling?"

Chan nodded. "I was. I used to work at a casino that no longer exists. He sipped the cab. "Hey, this is good. Where—?"

"Forget the bloody wine. What happened? I've tried my damnedest to find out and everyone's lips are sealed up tight as a nun's twat."

"From what I can gather, nobody knows. It remains a complete mystery."

"But surely not to you if you were there."

Chan shrugged helplessly. "I wish I could tell you more."

"Are you sworn to silence or something?"

He didn't want to bring up the memory loss—he wasn't the sharing type to begin with—but he had a feeling Ian would never get off the subject if he didn't.

"The truth is, I can't remember what happened that night. It's all a blank."

"Were you pissed?"

"Well, I'm not happy about it."

Ian laughed. "No, I mean drunk."

"Oh, right. No, I wish. Ten hours missing. I've been told it's..." He groped for the term Danni had used. "It's known as event-specific dissociative amnesia."

"Crikey. That sounds serious. Is it because of what you saw?"

"I don't know what I saw. That's the problem."

"Yes, of course. Stupid question."

"Samuel says that maybe the elder up on the mountain can help, but I have my doubts."

"What you don't remember must have been pretty awful."

"Well, I suppose you've seen the drone footage. The city's gone. There's nothing left."

They sipped in silence for a few heartbeats, then Ian said, "Does what happened down there have anything to do with why you're up here visiting the mountain?" He suddenly frowned. "Wait a minute. You worked in a casino. Samuel's not planning on bringing gambling up here, is he?"

Chan almost laughed in his face. "No way. At least not that I know of."

"Then why are you up here—if you don't mind my asking?"

I do mind, Chan thought. This is one nosy guy.

"I'm just...consulting."

"On what?"

"Oh, this and that."

That ought to frustrate him.

"Okay," Ian said, nodding. "No telling tales out of school. I can appreciate that, one hundred percent."

"I'm the proverbial inscrutable Oriental."

"I thought we were supposed to refer to you as Asians."

He shrugged. "Somehow it doesn't have the same sinister ring."

"Well, whatever. You said earlier that you hadn't even heard of these folks until two days ago. How did you make the connection? Because I've got to tell you, they don't get out much."

"A chance encounter in New Jersey."

Close enough to the truth.

"New Jersey? Of all places. What do you know of them?"

"Next to nothing. Care to enlighten me?"

Chan sipped his wine and waited, figuring he'd take a turn now at pumping for information.

Ian shrugged. "I'll be glad to tell you all I know...which is next to nothing. Nobody knows anything about them. The Lamm family goes back forever around here, apparently. Back in colonial times some ancestor of Samuel's laid claim to a big tract of land that included the mountain and the old fortress that was on it."

"It's still there," Chan said.

"Is it now? Some say we Brits built it, some say it's even older."

"I've been in it, and I'm no expert, but it doesn't look like anything the indigenous folks knew how to build."

"Well, we'll probably never know because I can't see those people up there letting some archeologist types poke around on their mountain. Erica and I have been here only a few years but I talk to the locals a lot and they tell me that the Lamm land had always been fenced and posted for no hunting and no trespassing, but a dozen or so years ago they put up an entirely new fence and started building housing up there."

"Are they some sort of cult?" Chan said. "They told me that they 'serve the Mountain,' but I have no idea what that means."

"Neither do I." Ian leaned forward, suddenly intense. "Who do *you* serve?"

The question took Chan aback. "What do you mean?"

"Well, as the song goes, we all gotta serve somebody."

The reply seemed important to Ian, but Chan had no answer for him.

"I'm afraid I have no idea what you're talking about. I don't serve anyone, least of all a mountain."

Now he leaned back, suddenly affable Ian again. "Well, be that as it may, they're up to something, those people."

"Like what?"

"How the bloody hell should I know? When Erica and I first took over this place, I tried to drive up there for a neighborly visit and was turned away by a guard—an *armed* guard."

Ian drained his glass. Chan wasn't far behind, so his host refilled both glasses to their original levels.

Chan said, "There doesn't seem to be any bad blood between you. I mean, they seem to send you business."

"Yes. Samuel came down and opened an account. Had no idea I'd been turned away by his guard, but didn't apologize. He explained that over the years the mountain had become a popular hunting and camping spot, despite the old fence and all the no-trespassing signs. He was settling men and women with children up there and he made the move for safety reasons. That's probably true, but I'm pretty sure it had more to do with privacy. Really, what's going on up there? In my darker moments I imagine Roman-style orgies."

Chan couldn't help making a disgusted face. "What? With kids?"

"Oh, bloody hell! Of course not. It's just that the women seem to far outnumber the men."

"Women who seem devoted to their children. I've been there twice and they've got a playground that's always full of kids with their mothers standing watch."

"Yes…about those kids. I've got questions about them. The UPS guy who delivers here delivers up there as well, and I pick his brain whenever I can. Anyway, he says he's seen kids ranging from infants to pre-teens."

"I haven't seen any infants," Chan said, "but I've seen a range of ages. So what?"

"Well, think about it: Infants mean pregnancies, but the women don't go to any doctors around here. Do they have their own doctor up there? Do they deliver up there?"

What was it with this guy? Why was he so obsessed with Samuel's community?

"Well, Ian, women all over the world, including the US and UK, deliver their babies without an obstetrician. When my parents emigrated from Heilongjiang they had never heard of an OB doctor. I was delivered by a Chinatown midwife. You *have* heard of midwives, haven't you?"

"Of course I've heard of midwives. And they're just fine for an uncomplicated delivery. But it just seems so primitive—no offense intended, of course."

"None taken."

"It's just that I've got a feeling they have plans for those kids."

"Plans?" The way he said it gave Chan an uneasy feeling. "Like what?"

"Who knows? They're born up there, live up there, go to school up there. Occasionally a mother will bring one down to the general store to buy some goodies, but with the delivery trucks going in and out all the time, I think they do most of their shopping online."

Chan imagined Ian peering through a pair of field glasses from behind a tree.

"Sounds like you keep close watch on the place."

"Bollocks! I do no such thing. Just curious, is all. Their secretiveness creates this itch I want to scratch." He leaned closer. "So keep your eyes and ears open tonight. I want a full report in the morning."

Not gonna happen, Chan thought, but forced a laugh.

"Am I your spy now?"

He waved a hand. "Well, I wouldn't go so far as to say that. But as I told you, you're the only one I've known—or ever heard of, for that matter—who's been invited up there for dinner. So you can at least tell me what they serve."

"That I can do." Chan rose. "And speaking of dinner, I'd better get going."

Ian held up the bottle. "Still some left."

"You finish it. I don't know what they'll be serving with dinner."

"For all we know, they have a still up there. Maybe those women will get you drunk on moonshine and have their way with you."

"I can only hope," Chan said, thinking of Nicolette.

6

Ian watched from the breakfast room window as Liao made a left onto the highway. He hurried down the hall to his room where he pulled the foot locker from under the bed. He kept the only key on his key ring, attached by a small chain to one of the belt loops on his trousers.

After propping up the lid he began sorting through the contents. Because he hadn't known what he'd be dealing with when he moved up here, he'd come prepared for pretty much any eventuality. Which meant he was grossly over-prepared, because for years now he'd done little more than watch and wait.

He removed his trusty old Webley Mk VI .38/200 revolver and laid it on the carpet. Then he moved the two blocks of Semtex aside and placed them atop the remote-controlled detonators' lead-lined box, revealing his stock of drugs. He had small packets of cocaine and heroin along with chloral hydrate—the active ingredient in the classic Mickey Finn cocktail—plus scopolamine and Pentothal for interrogation enhancement, and even some sodium cyanide in case something lethal was called for.

He turned to call Erica but found her standing in the doorway.

"Oh, hello, pet. I assume you were listening to our guest a little while ago."

She smiled and dropped into the desk chair. "Of course. Do you think he's telling the truth, or just trying to avoid talking about what he saw in Atlantic City?"

"Oh, I think he was giving it straight. He seems genuinely put out about it. The irony is him thinking Samuel is going to somehow bring back those memories."

Erica's smile broadened. "The very *height* of irony. I mean, considering Samuel is the one most likely to have suppressed them."

"But the question is why? What doesn't he want our Chinese friend to remember? What did he see in Atlantic City that Samuel doesn't want him talking about?"

Erica said, "That might be why he brought him up here...to have him close where he can keep an eye on him."

"But what pretense did he use to get him here? It's not as if they go out recruiting new members."

"Maybe he's here to replace the strange one."

The strange one...

Ian considered that. The mountain Family was unfailingly insular except for one older fellow named Lorenzo who showed up every morning at the general store for a cup of coffee. He'd sit on the bench outside on nice days, or at one of the two tiny inside tables when snow or cold or rain made that impractical. Just sit and not speak to anyone as he sipped his coffee. When finished he'd drive back up to the mountain. He showed up in all sorts of weather. Only in the worst blizzards, when the roads were impassable, would he stay home. And then one day last year he stopped coming and was never seen again.

"You always thought he was a sensitive, didn't you, pet. Leaving the mountain every day to gauge the cosmic temperament."

"I still think so."

"But if Liao is his replacement, they've taken their own sweet time finding him."

Erica pulled out a pack of cigarettes. "Sensitives are rare. And they don't wear signs around their necks. It's probably taken them this long to find him. And don't worry. I'm not going to light up. Sometimes it comforts me to hold one."

She damned well better not light up in his room. This was a recurrent battle. She'd stopped drinking but replaced it with smoking. He couldn't stand the stink. Fortunately her lighter hadn't made an appearance.

Ian acted as the face of Cliff House while his sister minded the business side. Though he hadn't been stationed here to run a profit center for the Order, he was expected to make some sort of go of it while he kept up his surveillance of the mountain and its occupants. So Ian did his best to charm the guests and garner favorable reviews on Yelp and the like, while Erica used her business skills to keep costs under control.

He said, "Well, if it's true that he is a sensitive, that gives them another reason, in addition to making sure his suppressed memories stay suppressed, to want him to stay around."

"Those memories sound like something your people should know about."

"Yes, dear sister." She had such a talent for stating the obvious. "They might be game changing. There must be a way to counter the block."

"Is that why your precious goody box is open?"

"Yes. I've a panoply of potions for all occasions except restoring memories."

"Maybe it's time you called in outside help. Doesn't your boys club have troubleshooters for this sort of thing?"

*Boys club...*it would always rankle Erica that the Order allowed no women. She had a right to her vitriol, he supposed. She shared their goals and had proved herself quite an asset in this little operation. But rules were rules, and all that.

As for outside help, Ian wanted to handle this himself—if he could.

"You know very well, pet, that the troubleshooters are called Actuators and I think I'll first call *on* one of them—for advice only, at this point. They always seem to have a repertoire of solutions for arcane problems such as this. I'll ring them up." He pulled out his phone. "As a matter of fact, I'm going to do that right now."

Erica rose and headed for the doorway. "You do that while I step out to indulge in a fag."

Dear, dear Erica. Would she ever quit those things?

The nearest Actuator was assigned to the Manhattan Lodge. Ian had the number in his phone's memory. He'd frame a carefully worded request—you never knew who was listening these days—and the Actuator would know just the thing to get this sorted.

7

Chan guessed Henry's shift was over because a different guard stopped him at the gate on this trip. He recognized this fellow as the same who passed Nicolette and him through on their way out Tuesday.

"You're the tairongo, right?" he said, peering at Chan.

"That would be me."

He smiled. "I was told to expect you. Head straight on up to the fortress."

Chan waved and drove on. He parked in the same spot as this afternoon, but this time he found no attractive woman waiting for him. He stepped through the front door of the fortress into a bustle of activity and the clamor of children's voices. They all quieted and stared when he entered. Some pointed his way. A stranger. The effect was eerie. A half dozen or so boys of varying ages and skin tones were clustered near a round table to the right of the big banquet table, and an equal number of girls near another table to the left. Some of the adult women were seated at the banquet table and some were serving.

He spotted a smiling Nicolette approaching, holding out her hand.

"Come with me. We've saved you a spot near the head of the table. Samuel should be down any minute."

As she took his hand and led him, the kids went back to whatever they'd been up to before he arrived.

"Are boys and girls segregated here?"

"Yes. As much as possible without being Draconian about it."

"Any reason? Is it a religious thing?"

He prepared himself for a reply like, *The Mountain wants it that way,* or some such nonsense. But instead...

"No. It's just that the old adage, 'Familiarity breeds contempt,' is too true. We don't want them to get too used to each other. We think it's better to preserve a little mystery between the sexes."

"But surely—oh, wait. Seeing them all gathered together like this, I unconsciously thought of them as brothers and sisters, or at least cousins. But they're not, are they."

She shook her head. "Not in the least. No blood relationship at all. So the last thing we want them to do is start thinking of each other as siblings." She patted the back of a chair near the head of the table. "Have a seat and I'll get us some food. I'm not on the service detail tonight, but I'm happy to wait on you."

"You don't have to. I'll come along and—"

"No-no-no." She pushed him down onto the seat. "You're our guest tonight. When you join us, you'll have to share duties, but right now you get the royal treatment. And besides, the kitchen is always a madhouse."

He watched her bustle away. She looked as good from the rear as she did from the front.

... the last thing we want them to do is start thinking of each other as siblings...

An odd thing to say. He wondered what she meant.

He checked out the table. A knife, fork, and spoon—ordinary tableware—lay on a folded napkin before him on the white tablecloth. And beyond the place setting, two open bottles of wine, a red and a white. He lifted the red and checked out the label: *Lamm and Lyon Vineyard,* Sonoma Valley. Whoa. Samuel had his own vineyard? Well, why not? With a couple of billion to his name, he could afford it.

He looked up to see a boy staring at him from the other side of the table—*really* staring. He guessed his age at about eight.

"I saw you with my mother," he said.

Chan put the wine bottle down. "Oh? Is Nicolette your mother?"

A nod, then, "Are you Chinese?"

He smiled. "I'm American but my mother and father were born in China."

"I can speak Chinese."

That threw him for a second. According to Ian they were all home schooled. He'd have thought the parents would have their hands full with the basics of readin', writin', and 'rithmatic.

"Can you now?" He stood and gave a little bow. "Wǒ jiào Chan."

The boy returned the bow. "Wǒ jiào Wayne. Hěn gāo xìng jiàn dào nǒ."

Chan was totally wowed. Something weird about this kid. Yeah, he was charming, and smart as all hell, but Chan sensed something... *off.* He'd just returned Wayne's *Nice to meet you* greeting when Nicolette returned with two steaming plates.

"I see you've met my son."

"He's something of a wonder." In a number of ways. "He speaks Chinese?"

"They're all learning Spanish, but some of the kids are learning Chinese, some Japanese, some Russian."

"I gotta go eat," Wayne said as he moved off toward the boys' table. "Húi tóu jiàn!"

"What did he say?" Nicolette said. "I don't know Chinese."

"'See you later.' I'm impressed."

"That's nothing," Nicolette said. "Wait till you taste the pot roast."

Chan laughed as he sat. "No, seriously. How old is he? Eight?"

"You nailed it."

"And you're teaching him Chinese?"

"Not me. Naomi. She calls it 'simplified Chinese.'"

"Still and all, any kind of Chinese is difficult for a westerner."

"Eat," she said, digging into her meal. "This is a real Mommy Meal. Taste the pot roast, I mean it."

Pot roast, peas, and mashed potatoes topped with brown gravy.

Maybe your mommy, Chan thought. Not mine.

He cut off a piece of pot roast and forked it into his mouth: tender, juicy, and flavorful.

"Hey, pretty good. In fact, *very* good."

"Told you. Anyway, these foreign languages are a way of making the kids aware that there's a lot of world out there that they're not seeing but eventually will. Right now, though, they're as sheltered as can be. We filter a lot of what they see and hear."

"No computers?"

"Can't escape computers. They've revolutionized home schooling. But no Internet—at least for them."

"No smartphones?"

"Adults only. No phones at all for the kids." She shrugged. "Who're they gonna call?"

Good question, he guessed.

"By the way, have you noticed the children sort of staring at you?"

"I thought it was because I was a new face."

"Well, you *are* a new face," said a male voice. "And we don't see many around here."

Samuel had arrived.

"We were talking about the children," Chan said.

Samuel smiled warmly. "The Family is all about our children."

"But segregating them—"

"Oh, it's not as strict as you might be thinking," Nicolette said. "When I have duties, Wayne will often stay with Daphne and her daughter Lexie, and vice versa."

"But in the long run, won't that simply increase the attraction?"

Samuel's smile widened. "Oh, we're counting on that." He indicated the wine bottles. "Try the wines. I think you'll like the red. It's an excellent Bordeaux blend. I can't sell it as a 'Bordeaux,' of course, since it was grown, aged, and bottled in California, but we use the same blend of grapes."

Chan pointed to the label. "Who's Lyon?"

"My vintner and managing partner in the vineyard. He happens to be from Lyon, so the name was irresistible."

Chan noticed that Samuel was served exactly the same meal as he and Nicolette. He leaned toward her and lowered his voice.

"So…no choice on the menu?"

"Not with these group dinners. We prepare our own meals at home most of the time. But for these gatherings, it's more expedient to say, 'This is what we're serving, sorry if it's not your fave.'"

Made sense.

Chan hadn't tasted enough wines from Bordeaux to make a knowledgeable comparison to Samuel's blend, but had to admit he liked it better than the cabernet Ian had poured him earlier.

As Samuel blathered on about wines, Chan leaned back and took in the people around him. They seemed generally friendly and happy, or at least content, for the most part. He realized he had a chance to find happiness—real happiness here. And it wouldn't necessarily mean warehousing his computer skills. He could teach these kids programming, which was more than just a useful and practical skill, it was an approach to critical thinking and problem solving. But it would mean giving up the luxury life he'd been fast becoming used to.

Well, so what? That life, though exciting in its way, involved spending every minute wading through a miasma of doom. A miasma that for some unfathomable reason, could not follow him here. If he wanted to be free of that, he could stay here.

As he looked around, something else occurred to him.

"Where are all the men?" he said.

That pretty well stopped the conversation at his end of the table.

Samuel gestured around him. "There's two of us right here, and—" He pointed to the end of the table where Henry sat with an Asian—"two down the other end there."

"I can see that, but though the children seem equally divided, the adult women outnumber the men four to one. Where are all the husbands or partners or fathers or whatever they are?"

"Well, as you know," Nicolette said, "mine is deceased. Others are off working."

Samuel said, "The Mountain may be a beautiful and bucolic setting to raise a family, but there's not much in the way of work in these parts. Some of the men have to travel far afield to find the work they want. The structure of the Family allows them that freedom. But as a result, some of them can get home only sporadically."

"The thing that is most important to us," Nicolette added,

"the thing we've all agreed on, man and woman, mother and father, is to raise our children in the presence of the Mountain. We're all prepared to make sacrifices for that."

"'The presence of the Mountain'…why is that so important?"

Samuel said, "Surely you, as a tairongo, must have noticed."

He had. Of course, he had. He was feeling it now. But *what* was he feeling?

"You mean the…" He searched for the word. "Well, for want of a better word, the *serenity* within your fence?"

"Exactly!"

"But does that come from the mountain or from the fence blocking out the rest of the world?"

"I'm not a tairongo, so I can't say for sure, but a little of both, I imagine."

No denying the difference around the mountain. He was convinced the fence was the reason, but how did it accomplish that?

"What's so special about your fence?" he said.

Samuel didn't hesitate. "The sigils at the seven corners—they're the key. And I already know your next question so I'll answer it right off: No, we don't know how that works. They've been handed down to us for many, many generations. All we know is that if you plot out an equilateral septagon and place one of the sigils at every corner, it happens."

"And that's why we want to raise our children within that boundary," Nicolette said.

Samuel added, "These children are extraordinary, as are their mothers and fathers. Spending their formative years here will make them even more extraordinary. And when they mate and move away to have children of their own, those children—the grandchildren of people like Nicolette here—will change the world."

Utopianism again.

"Change it how?" Chan said.

Nicolette's smile was beatific. "Only the Mountain knows."

"But we need a tairongo to help us preserve the serenity here."

That seemed a huge responsibility.

"What would you expect of me?"

"Simplicity itself: You merely venture out beyond the fence every day and take the temperature of the cosmos."

That was what he'd said this afternoon.

"I still don't—"

"Tell us what you feel out there. Is it just another day of cosmic doom and gloom, or do you sense something different, something brewing, something more ominous than usual?"

The words were vague but somehow Chan knew exactly what he was talking about.

"And if I do?"

"You tell us so we can be prepared."

"'Prepared' how?"

"Leave that to us," he said, nodding to Nicolette who nodded back. "We simply want a heads-up."

Dinner was finished quickly, followed by fresh fruit and homemade ice cream, and then Nicolette was guiding him around the table and introducing him to the other parents. And the children as well. They all seemed a little off, but he couldn't put his finger on exactly how. Chan made an effort to see if any of the girls who'd be Pam's daughter's age had a port-wine stain, but didn't spot one.

And then he was back at the table with Samuel who stood and extended his hand.

"I have to consult with the First. But I hope you enjoyed your dinner and I hope we went a ways toward convincing you to join us. These are good people and you can have a good life here."

Chan felt himself wavering. He'd come here for another purpose, but found himself agreeing with Samuel. Yes, he *could* have a good life here, a happy one, but…

"I can't commit yet, but I'm definitely leaning your way. Any glimmer of hope for my memory?"

He laughed. "Well, no, not yet. It's only been a few hours since you brought it up."

Only a few hours? Yes, of course it was. It seemed like days ago.

Samuel invited him to another community dinner they

were holding tomorrow night, and he accepted. The food was good, and the company pleasant, and he didn't have any other offers, so why not?

After they said their good-byes, he looked around for Nicolette. He wandered around the emptying hall but didn't see her. Where could she have gone?

Disappointed, he headed for his car. As he started the engine, he jumped when he heard her voice behind him.

"Can I come back with you?"

He turned and saw no one, then spotted her on the floor behind the front passenger seat.

He laughed. "You scared me! What are you doing down there?"

"Being discreet. Well, can I?"

"Come back where?" Did she want to escape the community?

"To the B and B."

"What for?"

"To spend the night, silly."

"Where's Wayne?"

"Staying with Daphne. Would you rather not?"

A genuine attraction or another inducement to stay? He thought about that for a second, and only for a second, and decided he didn't care.

"Oh, I'd very much rather."

"Then what are we waiting for?"

Chan coasted to the entrance where the guard raised the gate and waved them past from the doorway of his shelter.

And as soon Chan was through, it hit him again. Or left him rather. Good-bye peace and tranquility, hello doom and gloom. This was what they expected their tairongo to do every day: step outside the boundary and "take the temperature of the cosmos," as Samuel had put it. Well, he could do that. No biggie, as long as he could return to the serenity inside.

So what was the temperature today? Same as ever: cold indifference with a soupçon of maliciousness.

He shook it off. He had an attractive and willing woman crouched behind him. That was what he should be concentrating on.

At Cliff House he helped her from the back seat and escorted her inside and up to his bedroom where she kissed him immediately and they began undressing each other with frantic haste. It had been a long time for him and he sensed it might have been even longer for her.

FRIDAY

1

They slept in and, after a bout of morning sex—much less frantic than last night's—Chan and Nicolette lay in an exhausted tangle of limbs. Though Chan had had his fair share of sexual encounters during college and after, he'd never encountered a woman as enthusiastic and uninhibited as Nicolette. She had small firm breasts which were perfect for her slight build. And she liked to be on top where she could control the pace, which was fine with Chan.

"That was nice," she said, snuggling closer against him.

"Nice? That was super. And not the way I expected last night to end, or today to begin."

"Well, I'll have you know that I began planning this as soon as I knew you were coming to dinner."

"And you assumed I'd just go along?"

"First, you returned—that means you're interested in us. Two, you returned alone; if you had a partner, you'd have brought her along for a look. And three..." She gave him a sly grin. "I've caught you looking at me, checking me out. My only assumption was that you liked what you were seeing, even if it was an old bag."

He laughed and hugged her close. "You're a riot. And come on, we're not that far apart in age and I very much liked what I was seeing. Plus, I find you charming and smart and I love your accent, so what's not to like?"

"I wanted to have you before Daphne started making her moves."

"Daphne? Doesn't she have a husband?"

"Yes, but he's away a lot. Lots of horny women up there, Chan. As tairongo you can have your pick."

He nuzzled her neck. "But I like you."

"I'm not greedy. I'm willing to share."

"Share? That's very, um, liberated."

"As you should have guessed by now, we're not too conventional in our attitudes."

Was Ian's remark about orgies up on the mountain more than just a fantasy?

Suddenly she levered up in bed and sniffed the air. "Is that bacon? Yes! Someone's cooking bacon."

"That would be our innkeeper, Ian."

"Let's go. I'm famished."

Chan had to admit he'd worked up a fair appetite himself, so they gathered their scattered clothing and got dressed. He led her down to the first floor and the kitchen.

"Good morning!" Ian said from around the corner. "Not an early riser, are you, mate. I thought the smell of Canadian bacon on the grill might entice you down."

"I brought a guest for breakfast, Ian. Is that okay?"

"No problem. I was expecting that."

"Oh?"

"Yes. We guessed either you're a terribly restless sleeper or you had company." He stepped out for a look. "And you are?"

"This is Nicolette," Chan said.

Ian gave a little bow. "Nice to meet you, pet."

"The pleasure is all mine."

"Oh, zee mademoiselle eez Fronch?" he said in a terrible accent. "Ah would shake hands wiz you but zay air tres greasy at zee moment. Zee Hollandaise eez done and Ah weel start poaching zee oeufs now. Have a seat in zee salon de petit déjeuner and Erica will bring zee café and zee juice."

As they seated themselves in the sunny room, Nicolette said, "I don't sound like that, do I?"

Chan laughed. "Please, God, no."

The coffee was delicious and the eggs benedict superb. They ate while Ian—sans the faux accent, thankfully—hovered over them, babbling about how they'd never had anyone from the mountain at the inn before and peppering Nicolette with questions until she said she had to get back home to her son.

"I don't want Daphne to have to make him lunch too."

Chan had been hoping for another tumble under the covers before returning her, but that was not to be.

As they left, Nicolette called Daphne to let her know she was coming, then resumed her place crouched behind Chan's front seat. Henry was on duty at the gate. He saw Chan coming and waved him through with a smile.

Chan couldn't suppress an "Aaaaah," as he passed the boundary.

"What was that about?" Nicolette said from the rear.

"It feels good to be back here."

"You can really tell the difference between out there and in here?"

"Oh, absolutely. Out there it's like a cold, drafty bedroom on a January night with no blanket on the bed. Passing that gate is like slipping into a heated bed under a thick down comforter."

"Well, then, you've got to stay."

"I think you might be right."

And if staying meant more nights like last night, well…

The playground was deserted when they passed, and no one was around the fort when he parked.

"Where is everybody?" he said.

"Morning classes are over and the kids are back home for lunch. Let's head down to Daphne's to pick up Wayne. Come on and see how we live."

She exited the car and they walked together across the open area.

"Do you really think we're fooling anyone?"

"Not a soul."

"Then why—?"

"The ducking and hiding? I prefer not to be blatant in front of the children. That's why we're not holding hands."

"I get it. No PDAs. Can we do this again? Hope-hope-hope."

"So, you like old-lady sex?"

They'd already addressed that, so he played along.

"Absolutely. I guess that makes you a cougar."

"You'd better believe it. You're back for dinner, so how about a replay tonight?"

He'd been hoping for that. He really liked this woman.

"You are on."

She knocked on the door of one of the cottages and a grinning Daphne answered.

"Wow. You two look..."

"Sated?" Nicolette said.

Nodding, "Yeah, that'll do. Come on in. I'd show you around but the place is a mess. This was art class morning. I'll get Wayne."

"She teaches art and art history," Nicolette said as Daphne exited, calling for Wayne.

Chan took in the carpeted living room, done up with nondescript furniture that might well have come from Ikea. The fold-out couch was still folded out with rumpled sheets and a blanket on the mattress. All in all, he might have been in any living room in Anywhere, USA, except for the strange abstract paintings on the walls. He stepped up to the nearest for a closer look. It seemed to depict a wide open plain of bright orange, but smooth like a floor, with strange, asymmetrical shapes popping up at odd intervals and equally strange shapes floating through the dark gray sky.

"Who's the artist?" he said when Daphne returned with Wayne in tow.

"Lexie."

"Your daughter? They're extraordinary. How old is she?"

"Seven." She called toward the rear of the bungalow. "Lexie! Someone wants to meet you."

Chan experienced an immediate surge of anxiety at the sight of the little red-haired girl who ran through the doorway and up to her mother, but he had no idea why. Like the other kids on the mountain, she seemed a little *off.* He'd seen her before, but where? He didn't recognize her from the girls' table last night. Was she familiar because that wild red hair made her look like Orphan Annie?

"Hello, Lexie. I don't remember seeing you at dinner last night."

"I saw you," she said.

Okay, maybe he had seen her and it had registered only

subconsciously. That would explain the recognition.

"I love your paintings. Where do you get the ideas for them?"

"I paint what I see," she said with a matter-off-fact shrug.

I paint what I see? What a strange answer.

"I don't understand."

Another shrug—this time conveying a that's-your-problem attitude. She seemed a lot older than seven.

"Which is your favorite?"

"The one I'm doing now."

Daphne laughed. "She always says that. Well, go get it and show us." As she ran off, Daphne said, "She uses acrylic so it's dry by now."

Lexie returned with her latest and held it up for viewing. Chan started to take in the art but his attention was drawn to the mottled pink birthmark on the child's left middle and ring fingers where she held the board.

And then he realized why she looked so familiar: Lexie was the spitting image of Pam Sirman.

2

Somewhere around midday, two nondescript packages had arrived at Cliff House by messenger from New York. One held a small vial of liquid, bubble-wrapped to such a degree that it appeared insulated from any injury short of exposure to the Hadron collider. The second contained a thumb drive with an encrypted file. Ian had the key and ran the file through the decryption process. He now had it on the screen, with Erica leaning over his shoulder to read it along with him.

The file contained instructions on how to use the contents of the vial. Its unsigned author was terribly long-winded and appeared to be congenitally unable to get to the point.

"My eyes are glazing over," Ian said, leaning back. "Do you know what he's talking about?"

He knew Erica had a knack for cutting through the fat and getting to the meat with these things.

"I think so," she said, straightening. "What it boils down to is that he's sent a cocktail of hallucinogens, a witch's brew that will break down any blockades that have been set up within Liao and let the repressed memories resurface. He says he sent three ounces, but one-third that amount has proved quite sufficient in the past. It's colorless, odorless, and has a mild, fruity flavor. Coffee or any cocktail made with fruit juice or fruity liquor or even red vermouth will mask it nicely. It causes drowsiness and the subject is out within half an hour."

"Brilliant! The question is... well, you've met the fellow, Erica. Do you think he'd trust us if we offered it to him as a cure for—what did he call it?"

"'Event-specific dissociative amnesia,' if I recall correctly."

"Yes. That. Or do we sneak it into a drink?"

"Wait now. You're getting ahead—"

"Either way, we need to get it into him tonight. After that, I simply have to convince him that I am the person, or at least one of the people, with whom he should share these newly recovered memories."

She slapped him on the shoulder. "Would you bloody stop yammering and listen! It's not so easy. That's what all the blather is about in the instructions. The hallucinogens will put him into a delirious state where he relives the missing hours—*hour by hour.*"

That didn't sound good. What had Liao told him…?

"Bloody hell! He said he lost ten hours! Does that mean it will take him ten hours to get it all back?"

"Unless I'm reading this wrong, and I'm not."

No, Erica didn't read things wrong.

"That means we need a ten-hour window to get this done."

"Yes," she said. "That's the bad news."

"There's good news?"

She pointed to the screen. "Well, according to this, he'll be muttering the whole way through. We can set up a recorder and that should give us a fair idea of what happened during those ten hours whether he decides to confide in you or not."

"Okay, then, it's plain we can't be up front with him about this, so we'll have to resort to slipping him a spiked drink."

"I don't think it will take much coaxing to get an after-dinner bevvy into him. And then we start a recorder going."

"Or even better…we can be there at his bedside—me with the recorder and you with your trusty steno pad—to catch it all on the fly, as if were. That way we won't have to lose another ten hours listening to the recording. You still remember your stenographer skills, don't you, pet?"

"There's no call for them these days, so I'm no doubt rusty, but it's like riding a bike: not something you forget."

"Then we'll get this into him ASAP." He held up the red-stoppered test tube of clear fluid which, for all appearances, might be plain tap water. "Tonight, if at all possible."

3

Chan was pretty sure he'd done an adequate job of hiding his shock at Daphne's. He'd made a show of admiring the painting, all the while trying to get a better look at the child's fingers. Not that he needed it. That one glimpse, added to Lexie's resemblance to Pam, had been plenty.

When he and Nicolette and Wayne left Daphne's, Nicolette led him down to her place to show him what it was like while she made Wayne lunch. He made it as far as the front door and realized he couldn't put off calling Danni a moment longer. She had to know about this.

"Oh, wait a minute," he'd said. "I just remembered I have some business to tie up with my former job before the weekend. I need to go back to get some papers from my bag, so I'll have to take a raincheck on the tour. But I'll see you tonight, right?"

"Oh, *so* right," she said with a smile.

He'd rushed back to the highway and started toward Cliff House when he remembered that Ian had big ears. He needed absolute privacy for the call he was about to make. So he drove along Route 23 and pulled into the parking area alongside the general store. His phone showed him a strong signal, but he hesitated.

Was it possible, *really* possible that he'd found Pam's kidnapped baby? Yeah, it was. Philip Sirman had told Pam he'd been raised in Alberta, NY, so was it such a terrible stretch that his child should be found in Alberta?

What Chan found a more difficult stretch was believing that Philip had been involved in the abduction of his own child. He'd never met him, but how could he do that to Pam? What kind of man could do that to his wife? He found the cold, calculating cruelty involved completely alien. He couldn't imagine inflicting that level of pain on another person.

The question now: How would Danni react? Would she reject the possibility out of hand? Maybe if he laid it out for her piecemeal...

He punched in her number and prayed she wasn't on one of her team's hazmat-suited excursions into the AC ruins—the kind where she'd said they weren't allowed to take their phones.

Thank God, she answered. He rushed through the greetings and niceties, and then, of course, she asked him how things were going up here.

"That's what I'm calling about. I met a little girl today who is the spitting image of Pamela Sirman."

"What? You didn't tell me you'd be up there looking for her child. Are you? Because if you are, it's a proven fact you can develop a tendency to see what you want to see."

"I'm sure that's true, but do you happen to remember when Pam's newborn was abducted?"

"Seven years ago, I believe. I can check—"

"No, it was seven. I remember her telling me. This little girl just happens to be seven."

"Like I told you—"

"Pam also told me her child had a birthmark called a 'port-wine stain' on the left middle and ring fingers. I saw that hand just moments ago: No doubt about it, this seven-year-old, red-haired girl has a port-wine stain on the left middle and ring fingers, just as Pam described it."

Silence. Chan let it ride to allow this bombshell to sink in. Finally, she spoke.

"You never told me about this birthmark."

"I saw no reason to because I never thought the information would matter. The chances against my coming across her missing little girl up here were astronomical."

"And yet..."

"Yeah. I hear you. But just to set the record straight, I didn't come up here looking for little Julie. I came up here looking to get my memory back. But I found Julie instead."

"She was a newborn when she went missing. You can't be

sure—no one can be sure without DNA."

"That's why I'm calling you. I'll work on getting a sample from the child—they call her 'Lexie,' by the way. Can you check to see if you've got Pam's DNA on file?"

"I'm sure we do, but I don't want to use it."

"Why not?"

"Because if the child's no relation to Pam, my superiors here are going to want to know what the hell an agent on the AC team is doing wasting resources, and I don't want to have to tell them that I've inserted myself into the Baby Sirman case without informing them."

"But if she *is* related?"

"Then I've solved a cold case and made the Bureau look brilliant and doggedly committed at a time when its image very badly needs burnishing."

"So what's the solution? Drive up to Pam's and get a fresh sample from her?"

"Exactly. And happy to do it."

That was good news. He sensed Danni hadn't bought the mother-daughter relationship yet, but she was certainly an interested customer.

"Today?"

"No, not today, I'm afraid. They've got me tied up till late. But I've got the weekend free so I can be on her doorstep first thing tomorrow morning and then head up to—what's it called?"

"Alberta."

"Okay, I can come up there—"

"You know the way?"

"Sure. Both my folks grew up in the Albany area. Been to Upstate New York many times to visit my grandparents."

"I thought you were a Jersey girl."

"I am. Born and bred. My folks moved to Cherry Hill before they had me. Anyway, I'll drive up, get the child's sample from you, and then hand-deliver both to a lab on Monday morning for a parental DNA match."

He would have preferred sooner, but the weekend was getting in the way. He had a question, though...

"Getting a DNA sample from Lexie might prove more easily

said than done. Any suggestions?"

"Hair is the most obvious, but the strands have to include the root. Something like clippings from a haircut won't do it. You need nuclear DNA for a good match and there's none in the shaft, only the root."

"So, unless she gets into a hair-pulling fight with another girl, I'm out of luck?"

"Something that's been in her mouth would be ideal."

"Like chewing gum?"

"That would be perfect. Do you know they extracted the entire genome of an ancient woman from a piece of six-thousand-year-old chewing gum?"

"I had no idea they had Chiclets back then."

"Actually it was pitch from a birch tree."

"Just full of arcane info, aren't you."

"Most people would call it useless, but in my field it's just the opposite."

"Birch pitch chewing gum...I don't know if they sell that around here."

"Amazon probably has it. Seriously though, you really think you might have stumbled across the Sirman baby?"

"Yeah, I do. And it's got me totally weirded out."

"That's because it's monstrous."

"She's not being mistreated in the least. As a matter of fact, she's developing into quite the artist. I can't believe Daphne—"

"Who's Daphne?"

"Her mother—or maybe just the woman who's pretending to be her mother. But she seems like a sweet, gentle person. Maybe she doesn't know."

"Know what? We don't know yet if there's anything to know. We have to establish that the child is Pam's daughter first. Let's not get ahead of ourselves here."

"Right-right-right." He'd already established the child's identity in his mind as Julie, and the only way he was going to disestablish that was through a negative DNA match. "But if it *is* Julie Sirman..."

"Then we have to face the possibility that if one of those kids was snatched as an infant, how many others were as well?

How many kids have you seen there?"

"Twenty maybe, ranging from toddler to twelve, I'd say. My God, if they were all—"

"Again, you're leaping ahead."

"Sorry, sorry. You're the pro at this. I'm a rank amateur. I'm glad I have you along. See you tomorrow then?"

"I'll stay in touch along the way."

Chan ended the call and slumped back in the seat. She was right, of course. He couldn't go off half-cocked on this. And what did that expression mean, anyway? Never mind. Keeping a clear head was the key. Approach it just like he would a programming problem: calm and rational and analytical... until he had proof that this shit was real, *then* get royally pissed.

Proof...how was he going to get it? Danni had said a hair sample had to have the root. Lexie had longish hair, so her hairbrush would be a good source. But how to get to it? Another source was something that had been in her mouth. So what was Chan to do? Steal her toothbrush? Go through the household garbage?

To do any of that, he had to get into Daphne's house first. His burglary skills were nonexistent, so how would he manage that?

And then the solution hit him. He'd have to work out the details, but he knew how to be welcomed into Lexie's home.

4

Somewhere along the way Nicolette had mentioned that the kids were in school until three p.m. and so he timed his arrival at the mountain for shortly after. He parked by the fort just in time to see a group of girls exiting and fanning out toward their respective homes. He spotted Lexie's red hair and waited for her to get well ahead of him. As she moved away he took the piece of gum he'd been chewing and placed it onto the stick's foil wrapper, folded it, and shoved it into the side pocket of his jacket. Then he walked toward her home. Daphne answered his knock.

"Chan!" she said, smiling. "The tairongo knocking on my door. To what do I owe this honor?"

"Perhaps not such an honor, since I come not as a tairongo but as an art collector."

Now a frown. "Really? You mean Lexie...?"

"I can't get her paintings out of my head. If they're for sale, I want to buy one."

Her face lit as she swung the door wide. "Really? Well, come in, come in. I don't know if she'll want to part with any of them, but I'll go get her."

She returned with the beaming child. "You want to buy one of my paintings? Really?"

He sat on one of the chairs to put his eyes at the same level as hers.

"I do. Very much. I think you're very talented." All true. "And I think one day you might be a famous artist." Not so true, but certainly not impossible. "But even if you don't become famous, I can't believe this is the work of a seven-year-old girl, so I want one of your paintings for my wall." Totally true. "Which ones are for sale?"

Her smile widened and he saw one of her bottom front teeth had fallen out. He wondered if they had the tooth fairy up here on the mountain. She looked questioningly at her mother.

"Do you want to sell any, honey?"

"I don't know." She turned back to Chan. "Which one do you like?"

"That's just the problem. I like them all." More truth. To Daphne he said, "Could we possibly take them off the wall and line them up on the couch?"

"I'm sure we can do that," she said.

So Daphne took the nearest painting off its nail and handed it to Lexie, who then set it upright on the couch seat, leaning against the backrest. They went around the room doing this until all five paintings were set up side by side. Each measured only eight inches wide so they fit comfortably.

Chan moved back to the far side of the coffee table for perspective. He already knew which one he wanted. All this rigmarole was purely for show.

"Do they have names?" he said.

Lexie shook her head.

"No names? Well, which was the first of these you painted?"

She pointed to the second from the left.

"Okay, Lexie, we're going to call that 'Number One.'" He leaned forward. "Now… let me take a good look at that."

He'd been waiting for the right moment to bring out the gum and figured this might be it. So, as he studied the painting he pulled a pack of Big Red from his pocket, unwrapped a stick, and slipped it into his mouth. Shoving the empty wrappers in his pocket, he offered Daphne the pack but she shook her head.

"How about Lexie?" he said. "Can she have a piece?"

"Can I Mom?"

"Well…we don't usually…"

"It's sugar free," Chan added.

"Pleeeeease?"

Daphne shrugged. "Sure. Go ahead. Why not? It's not every day she gets to sell a painting."

He pulled off the outer sleeve and partially unwrapped the foil from the stick to allow her to pull it free without him touching it. The local general store carried the usual mint gum but he'd wanted Big Red and had to travel to Wyndham for it. He dropped the empty wrappers on the coffee table and went back to making a show of studying the painting while he watched Lexie out of the corner of his eye, waiting for the anticipated reaction. He prayed she wouldn't disappoint him.

She shoved the gum into her mouth and started chewing, quickly at first, then she slowed and stopped as she made a face.

"Yuck! This burns!"

Chan grabbed the foil from the table and held it out. "I'm sorry. Here, spit it out."

She spit the partially chewed wad onto the foil which Chan quickly folded over and slipped into his pocket.

"Here, I'll take that," Daphne said. "You don't need that sitting in your pocket."

Chan was ready for that and had already switched Lexie's wrapped-up gum for his own from earlier. He handed that to Daphne, along with the empty wrappers from a moment before, and she ducked into the kitchen to throw them all away.

Chan couldn't help a tiny fist pump. Got it!

"Sorry, Lexie," he said again. "I'm so used to Big Red that I forgot it's too spicy for some people."

"It's okay," she said, wiping her mouth.

Chan continued his charade of trying to make up his mind until finally he pointed to the one they'd dubbed 'Number 3' and said, "I want that one. How much is it?"

Lexie looked at her mother who said, "What do you think, honey?"

"I don't know," she said, hand on chin. "If I become famous it could be worth a lot later. You know—like van Gogh."

Chan had to laugh. "You're gonna be another van Gogh?"

"You never know." She smiled. "Hey, that rhymes."

"Okay, let's get serious. I'll give you fifty dollars."

She struck the hand-on-chin pose again. "Hmmm."

"All right, all right!" he cried, winking at Daphne. "I'll make it a hundred, but that's as high as I can go." He pulled out the five twenties he'd withdrawn from an ATM in Wyndham and held them up. "One hundred dollars: Take it or leave it."

"Well," she said slowly as she stared at the bills, "van Gogh never sold a painting while he was alive, so I guess I'm ahead of him already."

Daphne said, "Take the money and give him the painting, honey."

They made the exchange and then Daphne gathered Lexie into her arms for a big, tight, motherly hug.

"I'm so proud of you! You sold a painting! My little girl is a professional artist at age seven!"

Your little girl? Chan thought. We'll see about that.

Yet he couldn't deny the love Daphne had for the child.

"Doesn't the buyer get a hug?" Chan said.

She gave him a sidelong look. "I don't think so."

"Okay, then. How does it feel to be rich?"

Lexie shrugged. "I wouldn't say 'rich,' exactly. More like comfortably well-off at the moment. I'm gonna put these in a safe place. Oh, wait. Mom. Do I owe you a commission?"

Daphne laughed. "No. That's all yours."

"'Commission'?" Chan said. "Where did you learn about commissions?"

"I'm a voracious reader."

Voracious?

As Lexie left the room, Daphne approached and held out her hand. "Are you sure you want to spend that much?"

"I truly like it. But can I ask: Is she always like that? I mean, I felt I was talking to a forty-year-old."

Daphne laughed. "I think she was born forty. We had her tested and her IQ came in at one-eighty-two."

An IQ of 182? Holy crap.

"And about that hug you didn't get," she added. "Don't take it personally. She's like a cat: One moment affectionate, the other aloof as can be. Aloof seems to be her default attitude."

"I just hope I haven't ruined painting for her."

"How do you mean?"

"I want her to go on expressing herself freely without thinking about whether or not someone will buy it."

Daphne laughed. "I don't think that will be a problem. I

can't stop her from painting." She looked into his eyes. "You're a good man, Chan."

He stepped outside with his painting and stood in the bright afternoon sun for a moment after the front door closed behind him. He checked the wrapped gum wad in his pocket. He had little doubt that Lexie was Pam's daughter, and he'd just moved one step closer to proving it.

So why did he feel like such a shit?

Simple: Because if what he was putting in motion stayed its course, he was going to break up that happy, loving little family in there.

Not liking himself at that moment, he walked farther on to Nicolette's place. Was Wayne also a stolen child? What about all the other kids here? With that thought in his head, he didn't know if he could go to another Family dinner here, or spend another night under the covers with Nicolette.

He decided not to try. Until he'd answered the questions of Lexie's maternity and who knew about it, he'd have to keep everything here at arm's length. But that would mean staying outside the mountain's snug, safe-haven boundary. Well, he'd lived his entire life in the menacing outlands. He could live there a little longer.

But how to get out of tonight? He didn't want to be a no show. That was a low-rent move. And if it should turn out he was wrong about all this, he'd only screw himself by offending Nicolette.

Maybe he should resort to his old standby as a kid when he didn't want to go to school: play sick.

When she answered his knock, he showed her the painting.

"I just bought this from Lexie."

"Really? That's wonderful. Come in."

"I'd better not. My stomach's in an uproar."

She looked concerned. "What, the eggs benedict?"

"I think more like the slice of sausage pizza I had in Wyndham." He'd passed a pizza place called Neapolis when he'd gone to get the gum. He hadn't gone in but it made a good scapegoat. "It's not sitting well at all. I think I'm going to skip dinner and just crash until tomorrow."

She pouted. "No after-dinner frolic?"

"I'd be no fun tonight. Give my regrets to Samuel, would you?"

"Sure. Feel better, okay?"

"I should be good as new tomorrow."

He walked back to the car feeling like even more of a heel. Nicolette didn't deserve to be lied to.

Damn. What a mess.

5

Ian heard a car on the gravel outside and peeked through the window.

"He's back," he called to Erica.

"See if you can learn his plans for the night."

Liao came in, looking glum.

"Where is zee lovely mademoiselle?" Ian said.

Chan smiled and pointed at him. "Inspector Clouseau, right?"

"No, dear boy, that was Sherlock Holmes."

"Right. How could I miss that?"

"Going back to the mountain for dinner again?"

"They invited me but I don't feel up to it. I'm just going to veg out."

"Can I tempt you with cherry pie, later? It's in the oven as we speak."

"That sounds great."

"I'll have Erica knock you up in a few minutes when it's ready."

Liao smiled again. "You've got to be careful with that expression in the US."

"Blimey, I had no idea."

Which was a complete lie. Ian knew the American interpretation of the expression, but had always found it a good ice breaker.

Liao said, "I need a little plastic bag, a Ziploc or something along that line. Can you help me out?"

"Whatever for?"

"Oh, just something I want to keep safe."

Now there was an evasive answer if he'd ever heard one.

"I'm not prying, mate. I just want to know what size to get you."

"Oh, small is fine. Even one of those snack baggies will do."

Ian got him a resealable clear snack bag that seemed to be just the ticket.

With Liao off to his room, Ian found Erica at the front desk. He lowered his voice and said, "Any new guests on the horizon for today, pet?"

She shook her head. "Not a one. Slow as can be."

"Brilliant. We'll have him all to ourselves tonight. You knock him up in about ten minutes. I'll have an ounce of the witch's brew ready to spike whatever he chooses to drink."

He set the table in the breakfast room, got the hallucinogen cocktail ready, then took the pie from the oven. As he heard Erica leading Liao down from the second floor, he began singing:

Can she bake a cherry pie,
my boy Willie?
Can she bake a cherry pie,
Willie won't you tell me now?
She can bake a cherry pie,
Quick's a cat can wink his eye.
But she's too young to be
Taken from her mother.

"I've always heard that song as 'Billy Boy,'" Liao said as he entered.

"You Yanks steal everything from us, especially our folk songs. It's 'My Boy Willie.' That's the proper title." He gestured to the pie in the center of the table. "How does it look?"

Liao nodded approvingly. "Scrumpdiddilyumptious...or is that another stolen word?"

"Stolen from Roald Dahl who, you'll be shocked to know—"

"Is a Brit. I'm familiar with *Willie Wonka*."

"I see you've had a classical education. What are you drinking?"

"With cherry pie? Coffee, I'd think."

"Cream, sugar, what?"

"Both, please."

"Coming right up. Erica, pet, would you do the honors with the pie?"

Ian hurried to the kitchen. He could hear the murmur of small talk from the breakfast room as he put a dark roast K-cup in the Keurig. He added the witch's brew to the empty cup and watched it fill with fresh coffee. He already had a tea pot ready and waiting under a cozy for him and Erica. He put the coffee, tea, cream and sugar on a tray and deposited it next to the pie.

"Eat up," Ian said.

He and Erica watched avidly as Chan added cream and sugar to his coffee, sipped, then tore into the pie.

"Hot cherry pie—delicious! Tastes like you made it from scratch."

"I did. Seconds await, of both pie and coffee. It takes just a second to pop another K-cup in the Keurig. We've named her Katy, by the way."

He looked up and smiled. "Katy Keurig? I get it."

"Good for you. You'd be surprised how many people don't."

Liao must have been hungry. He had seconds of both pie and coffee. They were only a few minutes into their post-prandial chit-chat when he covered a yawn.

"You know what? I think I'll hit the sack. I'm beat."

Ian immediately began clearing the table. Didn't want to delay Liao a second more than necessary.

After he was upstairs, Ian prepared for the long night ahead. He pulled out his digital recorder and inserted fresh batteries, then stuck a backup pair in his shirt pocket. He rejoined Erica and her steno pad in the breakfast room where they sat and waited. They gave Liao half an hour or so, then Ian knocked lightly on his door. Receiving no answer, he peeked in and saw him on the bed, fully dressed, muttering in his sleep.

"I think it's begun," he whispered.

As planned, Erica turned off Liao's phone—didn't want any interruptions here—while Ian pulled up two chairs beside the bed. He noticed a small abstract painting propped on the dresser. Interesting. He wondered where he'd got it. Out of curiosity he checked the drawers and found the snack bag Liao had asked for earlier. It held what looked like a wad of partially chewed gum. Bloody weird.

Show time. He and Erica settled down to listen as the memories of Liao's missing hours were returned to their rightful owner.

LOST HOURS REDUX

1

For Chan Liao a weekend at a casino-hotel was a busman's holiday, but he didn't mind. The camaraderie was the important thing. His buddies had decided on the Hard Rock Hotel as the destination for their latest semi-annual reunion. They always wound up in AC. They could have chosen a Philly hotel, but Mac and Aldo liked to gamble, and the selection of restaurants at the casinos throughout the city could not be beat.

He left his office at the Xìngyùn Casino early, something he didn't usually do on a Friday, but the post-NBA and -NHL playoff period in late June was a relatively slow time for online betting. Besides, his vacation days were piling up and the casino had a policy of use them or lose them. Thanks in part to Chan's computer skills, the Xìngyùn had become a rip-roaring success. The Borgata's revenues still led them all, but Xìngyùn had taken over as the most profitable of all the casinos along the Atlantic City Boardwalk.

The supposed doyens of New Jersey gambling had said that while using such an obscure foreign word for a name—with the Chinese characters 幸运 beneath, no less—might attract Asian gamblers, too many other ethnic groups would find it off-putting. Well, a casino named "Lucky" certainly appealed to Asians, but no one else seemed put off in the least. The gaming floors stayed crowded day and night.

He strolled the two blocks from the Xìngyùn to the Hard Rock—formerly the Trump Taj Mahal—and made his way to the café just inside the entrance. There he found his three college buddies waiting at the bar. The four of them had bonded during their years at U of P and stayed in contact during the four years since. They made an odd quartet.

A burly bear of a guy, James McIntyre had always been the rich boy of the crew. His father ran Prothaid Capital, an enormously successful Philadelphia-based asset-management firm. Unlike the rest of them, Mac had always had plenty of money to spend during his college years, and was unfailingly generous, often picking up the tab for the four of them when they were out together. He'd joined the family firm right out of school.

Aldo Marchesi was a good-natured bundle of energy, a ferret with an easy laugh who always had an angle. Back in the day, whatever you were in the market for, Aldo knew where you could get a better deal. Everything was a negotiation with him and so no one was surprised when he entered Temple Law School after graduation. He'd recently become a new member of the firm of Seidman and Associates—a personal-injury firm whose ads were a constant presence on the Philly TV shows, and a constant inspiration to needle Aldo.

Danielle Boudreau…Danni, Danni, Danni…he still had a thing for her. All four of them had been close, but Chan and Danni had bonded—in a purely platonic way, much to his dismay. Still, he cherished his time with her. She surprised the hell out of everyone when she joined the FBI. No one had seen that coming. She'd never given a really satisfactory answer as to why. "It's just something I want to do" was undoubtedly true, but was sorely lacking in details. Chan had finally gotten it out of her when he quizzed her about the Pollock print she'd had hanging in her room since day one.

Today she looked perfectly comfortable in an untucked white Oxford button-down shirt over faded skinny jeans.

Mac and Aldo had known each other since they were in Huggies and had driven in from Philly together. Mac, flush as always, had rented a luxury two-bedroom suite that he and Aldo were sharing. They'd been roomies in college and were well suited to each other. Mac was a laid-back, easygoing guy, maybe a little on the passive side, who tended to be content to follow the lead of his more aggressive, energetic pal. With Aldo on the scene, there was no sitting around contemplating your navel. No sitting and no contemplating *anything*.

Danni, a Special Agent in the FBI's Newark field office, had driven down on her own and taken a room on the same floor. Chan lived only half a dozen miles south in Margate, so he figured he'd commute.

"Mister Roboto!" Aldo shouted when he spotted Chan approaching. "He made it!"

Chan had been unable to resist the nerd appeal of Penn's robot club and had joined as a freshman. Eventually he took a first-place design award. Aldo, who seemed to have his own name for almost everyone, dubbed him "Mister Roboto" and had never let it go.

Embraces all around—quick ones for Mac and Aldo, an extra tight, extended hug for Danni—then they found seats at a table where he made sure he wound up next to Danni.

"I'm running a tab," Mac said. "Danni's got a hurricane coming."

"A girly drink," she said, fluttering her long lashes.

"You still down with the JD Manhattans?"

Chan tended to wind up napping if he started drinking this early in the day, and now was definitely too early for the hard stuff.

"I am, but I'll just take a Stella for now."

"Danni took the liberty of ordering lunch for you," Aldo said.

Danni nudged him with an elbow. "Pork egg foo yung, right?"

Yeah, like the Hard Rock Café had Chinese food. But Chan laughed along with everyone else and said, "I hope you made mine a double."

He'd never live down the time in freshman year when they went to a Chinese restaurant on 10th Street and Danni ordered egg foo yung. He'd made the mistake of mansplaining how it wasn't a true Chinese dish.

Today he'd already planned on a pulled pork sandwich. Danni ordered the Bangkok shrimp appetizer for her entrée.

As the nacho platter Mac had ordered for the table arrived, he turned to Danni. "How's the world of law enforcement going?"

A shrug. "Still a boys' club. Always will be. Took a while but word finally got around that I'm a dyke."

Chan cringed. "I hate when you call yourself that." He'd never found her the least bit dykey.

"It's our word now."

"So you've said."

Aldo said, "So does that mean I can't use it?"

She jabbed a finger at him, but she was smiling as she said, "Especially you. Don't even think about it, buddy boy."

He raised protective hands. "Wouldn't dare."

"At least she's doing something in the world," Mac said. "I'm just making money."

"And lots of it," Aldo said.

"Yeah, but what am I accomplishing? I move money from this guy's pocket to that guy's pocket and take a cut as it passes by."

Mac's self-assessment gave Chan a twinge of discomfort. What was he doing but facilitating the transfer of money out of players' pockets and into the casino's? Hardly making the world a better place.

"Don't feel too bad," Aldo said. "You've heard of bowling for dollars? I'm suing for sleazeballs." He shook his head. "I've got the kind of clientele that if they happen to see a bus accident, they hop on board and pretend they're hurt. You wouldn't believe how the idea of a big settlement can bring out the worst in people."

"You can practice other kinds of law," Danni said.

"One day I will. But Seidman's raking it in. Once I pay off the education loans and build up a nest egg, I'll be looking for something else, trust me." He turned to Chan. "How's the casino biz?"

"Better than ever—if you're a casino."

He leaned forward. "So tell me. You work their computers. Is it true you can program them to kill off a player's winning streak?"

Chan laughed. "Yeah, in some games I suppose you could, but it's idiotic to risk it. If you get caught, the fines are enormous. And when you come down to it, the odds are already legally stacked in the house's favor. They don't need dirty tricks. Yeah, a player might get a lucky streak going, but the house knows that if you play long enough, they're gonna win. It's simple math."

"I always hated math," he said and turned to Danni. "How's the love life, babe?"

She made a sour face. "Terrible. Yours?"

"Worse. But Mac here's getting serious."

Everyone had questions about that and Mac was indeed getting serious. The food arrived then and they all chowed down before getting to Chan's love life, which happened to be non-existent at the moment.

"So," Chan said to Mac and Aldo after a few bites, "I hear you two are rooming together for the weekend. Just like old times."

"Yeah," Aldo said after swallowing some of his steak burger. "But what do I do if I get lucky? How do I let you guys know not to bother me?"

"I brought an extra belt," Mac said. "You can use that to tie around the doorknob like we used to do in the old days, although the suite gives us each our own bedroom with its own door."

"Yeah, but I need something to warn Danni away in case she comes looking to cash in her Aldo Airlines frequent flyer miles."

"I sold those to this drag queen I know," Danni said. "He'll be by tonight to collect. But what do I do if *I* get lucky?"

Aldo put on a lascivious grin. "If you get lucky, I wanna watch."

"Really? Well, okay, I guess that could be arranged."

His smile broadened. "Really?"

"Absolutely. You prefer Timex or Seiko?"

That broke up the table. Aldo laughed the hardest. "Walked right into that!"

As they ate, Danni leaned closer to Chan. "You know, if you happen to be overserved tonight, my room has two queen-sized."

"Thanks. Good to know. I might take you up on that."

Chan decided then and there that at least one night this

weekend he'd arrange to be overserved. Or at least appear that way. Not that anything could possibly happen, but he liked the idea of spending a night in the same room with her. Even in separate beds it promised more intimacy than he'd shared in too long.

"Hey, you know," Aldo said as he pushed his empty plate away, "I was thinking on the way here—"

"I could smell the wood burning," Mac said. "Had to open a window."

"That was a fart, pal. Anyway, we were driving along the AC Expressway and I'm looking at all these woods on either side—"

"The Jersey Pine Barrens," Chan said.

"Yeah, I know. But I was thinking it's got to be an interesting place. How many times have I driven through and never stopped off to see what it's like in there?"

"Unless I've had you wrong all these years," Danni said, "you never struck me as the camping-out type."

Aldo grinned. "Oh, you got that right. But I'm talking about driving through in the comfort of a big four-wheel drive vee-hickle like Mac's Land Rover. Maybe we'll find one of the lost towns or maybe we'll see some Pineys."

"As long as we don't get lost," Chan said. "There's lots of stories of hunters going in there and never being seen again."

"That's because of the Jersey Devil," Aldo said.

"Lost towns and inbred Pineys." Mac shook his head. "Sounds like a major snooze—"

"Not if they've got three eyes," Aldo said.

"—but the Jersey Devil—now that would be worth a look."

Chan could have told them that the tales of Piney inbreeding were way overstated, but that would risk another mansplaining charge, so he kept mum.

"Then let's do it!" Aldo said.

Danni made a face. "Really?"

"Well, it's something different. Better than sitting by the pool. And we've got all weekend to lose money at the tables. Come on. We blow a few hours and have some laughs, then we come back and start drinking."

Danni still didn't look too enthused. "There won't be any drinking if we get lost out there and are never seen again. You know, like those hunters Chan mentioned."

"Are you kidding?" Mac said. "My Rover's loaded. It's got compasses and GPSes and interactive maps. I couldn't get lost in that thing if I tried."

Chan nudged her. "What the heck? It could be fun. We're all here to spend time together, right?"

She shrugged. "Okay. Sure. Count me in."

Aldo pumped a fist. "Yes! Pine Barrens, here we come!"

2

After making their way to the garage at the rear of the casino and settling themselves in the Land Rover—Mac driving, Aldo shotgun, Chan and Danni in the back—he drove them through town and out along the Expressway. But once they were rolling, it soon became clear that he had no idea where to go. So it fell to Chan, as the local yokel, to direct them.

Well, Chan was a pinelands virgin himself, no less so than anyone else in the car, but he could put on a good show. He leaned forward over the center console and thrust his head between the two front bucket seats.

"Okay, Mac, let's see this interactive map you were talking about."

Mac hit a button and a screen lit in the middle of the dashboard. Chan had him keep widening the view until he could see past Mays Landing. The areas to both sides of the Expressway were crisscrossed with the thin lines of streets. But as it passed through Hamilton Township, the lines began thinning until they disappeared. The area to the south of the Expressway and west of Route 50 was all green, with not a street line in sight. A sure sign of no human habitation, or at least very little.

"Okay, let's try getting off at Route 50 up ahead."

Mac did and Chan directed him south toward Mays Landing.

"Keep an eye out for a rural road on the right. If we head west from here we'll be in a section of the Pine Barrens."

"There!" Aldo said a few seconds later, pointing ahead to the right. "No street sign. Looks like a possibility."

Mac made the turn onto cracked and crumbling asphalt

and they headed west into a landscape dominated by forty-foot scrub pines.

Danni gestured through the trees on the side of the road. "There's a house back there."

Chan spotted a ramshackle ranch with cracked and faded asbestos siding set way back from the road.

"Yeah. Some loner types, I imagine. We haven't completely left civilization yet."

"You think they might be Pineys?" Aldo said.

Chan shrugged. "Maybe. If you're born and bred in the pinelands, you're automatically a Piney. People born and raised along the beaches around here call themselves 'Clamdiggers.'"

"Sort of like Conchs down in the Keys," Danni said.

He noticed she used the proper pronunciation: *Conks.*

A little farther on, Mac said, "Well, the pavement wasn't much to begin with, but it just disappeared. We're on a dirt road now."

The occasional houses had disappeared too as the road further deteriorated from packed dirt to sand. The pine branches met over the road, forming a tree tunnel.

"We've still got pretty good traction," Mac said, "but I'm going to start four-wheeling just in case."

"Glad to hear it," Danni muttered. "I wouldn't want to get stuck out here." She rubbed her arms. "Hey, Mac, can we ease back on the air conditioning?"

He said sure and made an adjustment.

"You cold?" Chan said.

"More like a case of the creeps. It's so *lonely* in here."

Chan knew what she meant.

Rutted sandy paths started branching off right and left.

"Choose one of the fire trails and take it," Chan said.

"Gotcha." Mac took the next one off to the left.

Aldo twisted in his seat. "Fire trails?"

"Yeah. When you live near the Barrens you hear about fires all the time. Some are from lightning, some from careless campers—"

"And some from assholes smokers flipping a butt out the window, I'll bet" Aldo said.

Chan nodded. "For sure. Anyway, the trails let the fire trucks reach the flames."

Mac was following a pair of sandy ruts. The fire trails branched off, crisscrossing with no sane pattern, and Mac turned left onto one, then right onto another, taking them deeper and deeper into the pines.

"Are we lost?" Danni said, leaning forward and looking around.

Chan knew what concerned her. Every fire trail looked like every other, and the trees were all monotonously uniform. Every hundred feet they traveled looked exactly like the previous hundred feet and doubtlessly would look like the next hundred.

"That depends on what you mean by 'lost,'" Mac said.

She rolled her eyes. "I don't need some Bill Clinton parsing. Are we l-o-s-t?"

"Well, if by 'lost' you mean do I know where we are, the answer is no. If by 'lost' you mean do I know my way out of here, the answer is also no."

"I thought Aldo was the lawyer," Chan said.

"But in truth, my dear Danielle," Mac continued, "we are never lost as long as the map and the GPS are working. And I can assure you that they are working just fine."

She leaned back, looking relieved. "You could have said that in the first place."

He laughed. "And pass up a chance to torment one of my favorite people?"

Chan knew Danni was a bit of a control freak. Not to the point where she and only she had to be calling the shots. She was perfectly willing to relinquish the reins to someone else, but only if she thought they had matters in hand and could manage them.

Mac made a couple more random turns and was driving along a straightaway when Aldo slapped the dashboard. "Whoa! Slow down! Stop!" Mac hit the brakes. "Did I just see…? Back up, will you?" Mac reversed. "Yeah. Take a look. Guys, what do you make of that?"

The four of them peered out the right-side windows at a little ceramic rectangle about the size of a playing card affixed to a slim tree growing a foot or so off the trail at the corner of another branching trail.

"I thought it was a mile marker as we went past," Aldo said, "and it hit me right away: a mile marker out here? I mean, what for, right? But obviously it's not."

"No, it's certainly not," Danni said. "But what is it?"

Aldo opened his door and stepped out and Chan followed. Mac and Danni joined them at the tree. The weathered, buff-colored plaque had a small hole near the top through which someone had threaded a strand of copper-colored wire and twist-tied it through the trunk of a young pine tree. Its ceramic-like material carried a slight glaze and was decorated with an odd black symbol.

Aldo lifted it by its lower edge and angled it this way and that. The sunlight glinted strangely off its glaze.

"Anybody ever see anything like this?"

Three shaking heads, with Chan saying, "Some sort of glyph."

"And what, pray tell, is a glyph?" Aldo said.

"A kind of symbol."

"Then why not just call it a symbol?"

Yeah...why not? Why had he called it a glyph? And then he knew.

"Because it has an ancient feel to it, don't you think?"

Danni was nodding. "Yeah. I can see that."

Chan added, "The Mayans wrote in glyphs—carved them in stone. This could have been part of a message at some time."

Aldo angled it back and forth again. "And somebody just hung it here?"

Mac leaned closer. "Hey, check out the wire. What kind of metal is that?"

"Looks like copper," Aldo said.

"Copper would turn green after being outside like this.

Someone drilled a hole through the trunk to hang it."

"But what's it mean?" Danni said. "Some sort of arcane mystical symbol to ward off evil or the like?"

Chan said, "Let's use Occam's Razor here, shall we?"

Mac gave him a sideways look. "Meaning?"

"The simplest answer to a question is usually the correct one. I'm guessing it's just some piney folk art. Kind of cool though, isn't it?"

Aldo hadn't taken his eyes off it. "Very cool. But I like Danni's explanation better: an arcane mystical symbol to ward off evil. I could use one of these."

He began trying to untwist the wire. The sight of that shot a bolt of warning through Chan.

"Whoa-whoa!" he said, putting a hand on Aldo's. "What're you doing?"

"Taking it."

"But it's not yours. Somebody went to the trouble of hanging it here. You ought to leave it."

"Screw that. I'm going to hang this in my office."

"It's not yours, Aldo," Danni said. "Chan's right: leave it."

"You always think Chan's right. And let's face it: Who needs to ward off evil more than me? I work for Philadelphia's premier ambulance chaser, don't forget."

"It doesn't feel right, Aldo."

"Oh, come on, Danni. Leave the 'feelings' to Chan."

Chan could see that stung Danni. Stung Chan as well. That was Aldo. Sometimes he didn't hear himself and didn't realize how his offhand remarks could have a negative impact. He didn't mean any harm. He was just being Aldo.

"Okay, Aldo," Chan said. "You want a 'feeling'? Here's a 'feeling' for you: No matter what its purpose, whether mile marker or a special plaque meant to ward off evil, it's folk art—some kind of Piney folk art—and you should leave it alone. And the bottom line is, it's not yours."

"Whoever hung it here is probably long dead and won't miss it. And if it's Piney folk art, well, art needs to be seen. Who's seeing it out here? No one. I'll make sure it's put in a spot in my office where people can appreciate it. If I can get the damn thing off!" He turned to Mac. "You wouldn't happen to have wire cutters in that toolbox of your?"

Mac shrugged. "Possible. Take a look."

Aldo lifted the rear hatch and rummaged inside a moment, then returned with a tool held high.

"Got it!" he said with a grin.

It took him two seconds then to snip the wire and pull the plaque free of the tree. At that instant Chan felt a wave of... something. Warning? Alarm? He couldn't put his finger on exactly what had passed through him, but it wasn't good.

"This is wrong, Aldo."

"Enough," he said, pocketing the plaque. "It's done. Let's get moving."

They all returned to the Rover but the feeling of *wrongness* pursued Chan.

Mac had driven only fifty yards to another fire trail branch when Aldo called for a halt again and leaped out. He stepped to another slim pine at the corner.

"Here's another."

"Leave it, Aldo," Danni said.

"No way."

The three of them watched in silence as he snipped the wire. Chan felt a stronger wave of unease as Aldo pulled the plaque free and held it up.

"It's different!" he said.

And so it was.

He stood next to the car looking back and forth at the current tree and the last one. Then he got back in.

"Each of these was posted on a corner," he said. "Go right here and see if there's another at the next corner."

The trail branched off at an oblique angle, maybe 130 degrees. Mac made the turn and they came upon a third plaque at another corner fifty yards on.

"Awright!" Aldo cried and jumped out again.

"This is getting a little crazy," Danni said. "Say something, Mac. He's your buddy."

"I can talk myself blue in the face but you know Aldo when he gets a bug up his butt. He gets tunnel vision. And it's not as if he's hurting anyone."

"He might not be," Chan said as he watched Aldo snip at the third plaque, "but I've got a bad feeling about this."

He grinned. "What? We're in a *Star Wars* movie now?"

"I'm serious. Nothing good is going to come of this."

Aldo removed the third plaque and Chan felt the sense of wrongness heighten further as his friend hurried back to the car and displayed it for them.

"Yet another glyph. I wonder what they mean."

Danni said, "They mean the Piney who made them is going to find you and murder you in your sleep." Her tone was anything but light.

Aldo, oblivious, laughed and said, "Turn here and let's check out the next corner."

Chan noticed that the trail branched off at another oblique angle and it occurred to him that the little plaques or whatever they were might not be stuck on random corners but be set in a pattern. He pulled out his little spiral note pad with its pencil and began sketching the fire trails marked with the plaques.

"What are you doing?" Danni said.

"I think those things might be marking off a plot of land. I want to see what size it is."

"Just don't tell me it forms a pentagram," Mac said. "I don't want to piss off any devil worshippers."

"Well, we're now moving along the third side—so far they're all about equal in length—and I can tell you for sure that if all the angles on the corners remain the same, it won't be square and it won't be a pentagram either."

Another corner, another plaque and Aldo hopped out again.

"You've got to stop this, Mac," Danni said, but Mac only nodded, giving no hint as to whether that meant he agreed or not, only that he'd heard.

As the fourth plaque came free, Chan felt an even greater surge in the sense of *wrong*.

Aldo hopped back in and held up his trophy. "What do you guys think? Gotta be the weirdest glyph yet."

"And the last, I hope," Danni said.

"Onward, Jeeves!" he cried, pointing around yet another turn.

But when they reached the next corner and Aldo started to open the door, Mac kept rolling.

"Hey, yo, stop," Aldo said.

"Uh-uh," Mac said with a shake of his head. "Enough is enough."

"Thank you, God," Danni muttered.

Chan shared her relief but said nothing as he kept drawing.

"Come on, Mac. I want the full set."

"You've got four. That's your set."

He turned the corner and drove along the next leg.

"There's number six up ahead. You gonna stop?"

"Nope. Someone put these here for a reason and I don't want to be pissing off a bunch of Pineys. I can just see them showing up at the Hard Rock with their squirrel guns looking for the city folk who stole all their little plaques, so I want to leave a few."

He took the turn at the sixth plaque, drove to the seventh,

and shortly after that they reached their starting point. Mac
pulled to a stop there.

"Okay, we've come full circle. What've you got, Chan?"

Chan put a finishing touch on his drawing and held it up.

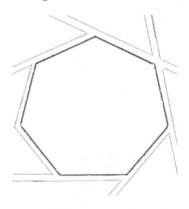

"Well, Mac, you'll be glad to know it's not a pentagram."

"Woo! That's a relief. At least now we don't have to worry
about devil-worshipping Pineys hunting us down.

"No, just the regular kind," Chan added.

He wrote *pinelands* beneath it so he'd remember what it was
if he came across it sometime in the future.

"Seven sides," Danni said, leaning in for a closer look.
"What's that make it? A septagram?"

Chan shrugged. "Kind of reminds me of the Pentagon but
with two extra sides. I guess we could call it a septagon. I don't
think there's any question now that those plaques mark the
corners of a plot of land."

"I guess that means somebody owns it," Danni said.

"Can you own land in the Pinelands?" Chan said. "I don't
know real estate law at all, but I thought it was all protected.

"Obviously somebody *thinks* they own it." Aldo frowned
and held up one of the plaques. "But why mark it with these
weird little glyphs?"

"Their land, their business," Mac said with a shrug. "Think
there's any significance to the seven sides?"

"Seven is a prime number," Chan said. "But so are three and
five, so it beats me. Maybe that's just the way the fire trails run."

"Yeah, but they marked all the corners with these guys," Aldo said. "That's gotta mean *something.*"

The *wrongness* sensation persisted. In fact, Chan felt it gradually increasing, despite no more plaques being removed.

"It means you should put them back," he said.

"Well, that's not gonna happen."

Chan blurted, "What if you released something?"

"Released what?" Danni said.

They were all staring at him. Where had that come from? The words had burst from him, seeming to come directly from his hindbrain, bypassing his cortex, and shooting out his mouth.

"I don't know. It's just a feeling I have."

This elicited good-natured groans all around.

Aldo said, "A get-together wouldn't be complete without at least one of Chan's feelings."

"No, seriously, guys," he said, rushing to explain, "this place felt absolutely fine when we arrived, but now it... doesn't. It feels *wrong.* And the feeling got worse every time you removed a plaque."

"But still," Mac said, his expression a study in dubious, "'*released* something'?"

"Maybe that wasn't the best word."

He was hedging, he knew, because *released* perfectly fit what he was sensing. How else to describe it? A *wrongness* that had been undetectable—at least to him—when they'd arrived had become a very definite... *presence.*

"All right, just bear with me a moment here, okay? What if—I'm just throwing this out, okay—what if those markers, those plaques with their strange little glyphs were set up at those seven corners to..." Oh, shit, they were going to jump down his throat for this, but he had to say it. "What if they're there to *contain* something?"

"What sort of something?" Danni said.

"Something that isn't supposed to be wandering around free. And what if by removing those plaques we released it?"

Aldo grinned. "I think the only thing we released was your imagination, Chan, my man. These here little arts-and-crafts things, decorated with cutesy squiggles, are like the kinds of things we used to make in second grade and bring home to Mom. Do you really think they're being used to lock up an evil spirit or the like in the woods here?"

Okay, when put like that, Chan had to admit it did sound ridiculous. But he felt what he felt, sensed what he sensed. He wasn't a mystical airhead. His day-to-day life was steeped in science. He spent his days with computers—logic machines. If given proper instructions, they gave predictable results every time.

But this was different. Feelings had nothing to do with logic. This was a *feeling*, and not a good one.

But he realized the futility of pressing the issue. He'd said his piece. Aldo was keeping those plaques no matter what anyone said, so why say anything more? He'd already let his feelings be known. Time to drop it.

"Just forget I said anything." He looked at the others. "What say we head back? I could use a good stiff drink."

Oh, yes. After this trip he needed a double.

Aldo clapped his hands. "And after that it's time for some serious steaks and then hit the tables."

Chan joined in the cheers as Mac started the Rover's engine. But instead of putting it in gear he sat and stared at the dashboard.

"How the hell do I get out of here?"

Danni said, "Use that GPS and map you were telling me about."

"I'd love to but the GPS says we're in the Osh region of Kyrgyzstan. Where the fuck is Kyrgyzstan?"

Chan happened to know the answer. "It's the easternmost of all the '-stans.' Right on the Chinese border. I'm pretty sure we're not there. What's the map say?"

"Featureless green."

"I knew it!" Danni said, pounding a fist on her thigh. "I knew we'd get lost."

"It's okay," Chan said as soothingly as he could. This went hand in glove with the *wrongness* he was feeling, but he wasn't going to add that to Danni's distress. "We're just in a poor reception area. All we have to do is backtrack a little until we start getting the signal again." He leaned toward the front. "Hang a U-y, Mac and follow the trail back a ways."

Which Mac did, and after maybe a hundred yards…

"Here we go!" he said. "We're back in Jersey!"

Chan copied the GPS readout into his notebook.

"Why are you doing that?" Danni said.

"In case I want to find the place again."

"And why would you want to do that? I don't know about you, but I'm through with that place."

Chan looked back through the rear window and hoped that place was through with them.

3

The June day was warm so they ambled across the boardwalk from the Hard Rock to the iconic Steel Pier. They passed kiosks selling French fries, funnel cakes, pizza slices, cheesesteaks, and gelato. And then the rides with their screaming passengers: the Ferris wheel and the Wild Mouse and the dive bomber among them. They ordered drinks and sat under the striped awning of the Ocean Reef Oasis at the far end.

"Never been out on the pier before," Danni said, the salty breeze tossing her hair as she sipped her white wine. "Kind of carney."

Chan nodded. "Yeah, this is the Trump version—he rebuilt it in the nineties. Sort of a mini-amusement park. The nice thing is we're *out*side, over the ocean a thousand feet from shore rather than *in*side, don't you think?"

"Definitely. My grandmother once told me she saw the Beatles in the music hall here in 1964."

"The music hall's long gone."

"Was she one of the screamers?" Aldo said.

"Not only screamed, she said she wet her pants."

He laughed. "Now *that's* a fan. They don't have that high-diving horse act out here anymore, either, do they?"

Danni glanced heavenward. "Thank God for that. Sounds cruel."

Chan tuned out the conversation as he sipped his Manhattan and leaned back. He listened instead to the Atlantic Ocean rumbling around the pilings beneath them. And as he sat there he sensed something out in the ocean... something stirring in the deeps. His eyes popped open. He rose and walked to the railing where he gazed out to sea.

He'd grown up in Cincinnati's Chinatown, far from any large body of water—well, he'd seen a couple of Great Lakes on trips to Chicago and Cleveland, but nothing like this—and so the immensity of an ocean always fascinated and frightened him.

More *wrongness* out there, but a different sort of wrongness from what he'd felt in the pinelands. This was subtler, harder to define or pinpoint. Or maybe simply farther away. He couldn't say for sure. But he had no doubt about its presence.

What was the matter with him this afternoon? Everything had been status quo this morning, just the usual background dissonance and malaise from his *xiānzhī* sense. Things had begun to go awry with that trip to the Pine Barrens. He knew in his gut that Aldo should have left those little plaques where they were, but he couldn't say exactly *why* because he didn't know. Just another of his annoying feelings. He'd hoped to leave the *wrongness* behind among the pines but it had followed him back to the city. He could feel it pressing against his spine.

And now this, out in the sea before of him. Clouds were piling up far out on the horizon. Not all along the horizon, just in a limited area straight ahead. What was he sensing out there? Another of his damn *feelings*? He was getting so tired of himself.

Danni came up beside him, swirling her diminished glass of wine.

"At least you're not on your damn phone like those other two," she said.

"Two weeks ago I would have been, what with the NHL and NBA finals raging."

He'd programmed his phone with a backdoor to the Xìngyùn's online sports book and he'd have been checking in a lot. Baseball and golf were the only sports active now and they never attracted the action of the faster-paced games.

"Feeling better since we got back from the woods?" she said.

No sprang to his lips but he bit it back. If he was tired of himself, how must the others feel? Better to pretend that everything was just ducky in Chanville.

He rattled the ice in his near-empty Manhattan glass. "This helped." There, that wasn't a lie. It had helped. Just not enough.

"Great. I was a little worried about you back there. You seemed..."

"Upset?"

"No, I was upset when I thought we were lost. Control-freak Danni doesn't like that sort of thing. No, you looked... I guess *unsettled* is the best word for it."

"I guess I was." Do not mention that you still are. Minimize, minimize, and do *not* mention the ocean. "You know me: sensey-sensey."

"Yeah, but not in a thin-skinned way."

He laughed. "Not with this crew, that's for sure."

"Yeah, a thick skin definitely helps with us. But it makes you interesting, you know. Sets you apart from the hoi polloi. I've said it before: If you were a woman I'd be all over you."

She always managed to say the right thing.

"And you've heard me say how if you liked guys we'd either be engaged by now or you'd have a restraining order against me."

"Maybe I'm not the marrying type."

"Then we'd be engaged to stay eternally unmarried together."

This was familiar repartee and they basked for a moment in the shared intimacy of it. Then Danni said, "The plan is to get dressed for dinner—jackets for the guys, LBD for me—and meet at the lobby bar. From there to the steak place."

"Council Oak, right?"

"Something like that. Five o'clock in the lobby for drinks." She gave his chest a gentle jab. "Be there."

"You got it."

He watched her walk away, then turned back to the Atlantic. He still sensed menace out there. And those clouds had piled higher. Was that where the menace lay? Menace from an ocean? Ridiculous. Wasn't it?

4

The uneasy feelings followed Chan home as he swung by his apartment to shower and dress up a little. They seemed more intense. As he was buttoning up a fresh shirt he stepped out onto his apartment's balcony and was startled by the clouds piled on the horizon. They seemed closer now, or maybe just more massive. Certainly higher.

The anvil top reminded him uncomfortably of a supercell. You didn't grow up in the Midwest without recognizing and respecting and, perhaps, even fearing the supercell. They often stretched to fifty thousand feet with their signature spreading top called an anvil. These were the monsters that brought tornadoes. Chan had seen them over the plains, but never over the ocean. Looking at it gave him a crawling sensation in his gut. But the forecast was for a dry and cloudless night, so maybe it would stay on the horizon.

He did his best to put it out of his mind as he returned to the Hard Rock where he found Mac and Aldo already at the circular lobby bar, drinks in hand. He ordered a JD Manhattan and settled on the stool next to Aldo.

"No sign of Danni?" he said.

Aldo grinned. "Still carrying a torch for her, ay?"

Yeah, he was, but not about to admit that to Aldo.

"I wouldn't say a *torch*..."

"Then what would you call it? I mean, we were all shocked and dismayed when we found out she was playing for the other team, but we moved on. That's life. But you... you're like a puppy dog when she's around."

Was he? He wasn't the type to wear his heart on his sleeve, but was it that obvious he still had a thing for her?

"She's a special person, Aldo. You know that."

"Oh, I do. She's the greatest. It's just—oh, Jesus. There she is."

And indeed, there she was, strolling in from the lobby in her little black dress and her simple string of pearls and her hair pulled back into a tight coil. Mac waved and she smiled and angled toward them. Chan noticed that pretty much every set of male eyes in line of sight, and not a few female eyes, followed her at least part of the way.

"Amazing, isn't it?" Aldo said, keeping his voice low. "Every guy here—well, at the least the straight ones—are lusting after her. But the truth is, not one of them can have her. She's totally beyond their reach. Don't you find that delicious?"

"I don't know about 'delicious'—"

"Except with you it's not lusting, it's *longing.*"

One thing you had to say about Aldo: Despite all his rough edges, he had keen insights into people.

"You find that 'delicious' too?"

"No, that's kind of sad. But tell me: Have you ever seen a woman so alone?"

The statement hit Chan between the eyes. Yeah, Danni was alone. She'd told him many times.

"She's had trouble finding someone."

"They say y'gotta live with the choices you make. Well, you've also gotta live with the choices that were made for you. I don't think it's easy being her."

Chan was struck speechless by this uncharacteristic display of empathy.

Danni arrived then, and as she slid onto the stool next to Chan, Aldo said, "You clean up real good, kid."

She smiled. "Why, thank you, Aldo. That's the nicest thing you've said to me all day."

Chan caught the slight edge on the remark but it went right by their friend.

She ordered a white wine and when they'd finished their drinks they segued toward the front of the casino to their reserved table in the steak house. The maître d' seated Danni across from Chan between Mac and Aldo. Ah, well, if he couldn't be next to her at least he had a prime view.

While they were waiting for their appetizers, Aldo said, "Hey, I got the feeling that earlier this afternoon I made some of you uncomfortable out there in the woods. So I wanted to say I'm sorry if that was the case."

Chan figured Mac had said something, because Aldo tended to be a bit cavalier about the reactions he triggered in others. He and Danni made nice-nice with conciliatory noises.

Aldo reached into his pocket. "And to make it up to you, I'm going to lend—please note, that's *lend*—each of you one of these little markers for good luck at the tables tonight."

He pulled out three of the plaques and, over protests, placed one before each of them.

Across the table, Danni folded her arms across her chest. "I don't want it. I hate to sound like a tight-ass, but it's stolen property and it's not yours to lend or do anything with."

Chan hid a smile. That was Danni in a nutshell: the softness on the outside hiding a core of tempered steel. She didn't let things slide. She knew right from wrong and never blurred the line between.

"Just stick it in your purse for the night and then give it back," he said. "You'll thank me when it's over."

Danni said, "What makes you think they're good luck?"

"I *don't* think," he said. "I *know*. You all know how I suck at gambling, right? If I didn't enjoy the games so much I'd just hand my money to the pit boss as soon as I stepped onto the floor and save us both the trouble. But get this: Earlier, as I'm walking back from the pier on the way to our room, I stop at a five-dollar blackjack table for a quick hand. And guess what? The dealer busts and I win. So I play another and I win again. And then I win a *third* hand. Guys, I've never won three hands in a row in my life. And these things were in my pocket. Gotta be a connection."

An eye roll from Danni. Chan knew she didn't believe in luck. Neither did he, for that matter. As someone who worked in the casino industry, he knew full well that, in the long run, having the odds in your favor trumped luck every time. And the house always arranged the best odds for itself.

"If you were on a roll," she said, "why'd you stop?"

"Hey, if I've got myself a good luck charm, I'm not gonna waste it at a lousy five-buck table. I'm going for the gold, baby! So just do yourself a favor and stick that in your little black purse while you're playing tonight. You can think of an appropriate way to thank me later."

This got a laugh and then the apps arrived, cutting off further debate. As Danni grudgingly stuck the little plaque in her bag, Chan checked his.

If he had time later maybe he'd do an image search and see if he could learn its origin. Until then he'd simply keep it in his pocket.

Luck...right.

5

After finishing their steaks—Chan's bone-in sirloin was done to perfection—and the delicious Barolo that Mac had ordered, nobody had room for dessert, so they wandered back through to the casino area. As they passed the café, Chan noticed a *Special Report from Atlantic City* banner along the bottom of one of the TV screens at the bar. Curious, he wandered over. The sound was off but the closed captioning was on:

The United States Weather Service has issued an alert that offshore buoys are registering an unaccountable rise in the sea level off the Jersey coast, specifically in the waters off Atlantic City. They wish to emphasize that this is not—repeat not—a tsunami since the rise is sustained rather than moving in a wave. It appears to be an upwelling from beyond the continental shelf. If the rise in sea level continues, it could impact the coast with the potential for flooding. We will bring you the latest developments as they occur.

The others had followed him over and caught most of it.

Shit, Chan thought. Something's coming.

"'Potential for flooding'?" Danni said. "That doesn't sound good."

Aldo made a dismissive wave. "Nah. Even a couple of feet of water for a while won't disrupt much here. Mac parked on the third level. What about you guys?"

Danni and Chan were both on the fourth.

"Well, no way it's ever gonna get that high. So let's go win some money and meet back here where you can all lavish me with thanks and praise and buy all my drinks for the rest of the weekend."

"Deal!" Chan said.

He and Danni stood together and watched Mac and Aldo hustle onto the gaming floor.

"Aren't you going?" she said.

"In a minute. I just want to go out and take a look at the ocean."

"I'll go with you. I'm not used to that much food. I could use some fresh air."

He offered his arm and she wound hers through the crook of his elbow as they stepped outside and strolled south of the pier to the railing that overlooked the sand. A dune thickly planted with beach grass swelled before them but the ocean was visible beyond it. The sinking sun lay low behind them but still reflected redly on the ocean.

The feeling of threat was stronger now.

"See anything?" Danni said.

Thankful that she hadn't asked if he *felt* anything, he said, "Looks pretty normal to me." And it did.

"What on Earth is an 'upwelling'? I've never heard of it."

"I have. It's when deep cold ocean water rises to the surface. But I've never heard of it raising sea level."

"Do you think we might flood?"

He shrugged. "Who can say? The city's about seven feet above sea level, so the rise will have to be higher than that before it gets into the streets. Seven feet is a lot. There'd have to be some serious weirdness going on out there if it gets above that."

But wasn't that exactly what he was sensing out there at sea—serious weirdness?

"You're giving me the creeps," she said, tugging on his arm. "Let's go inside."

They wandered onto the buzzing, dinging casino floor.

"What do you feel like playing?" he said.

"I'm going to try blackjack, like Aldo did. See if my little plaque will bring me luck."

"Seriously?"

She laughed. "Kidding! About the luck, that is. I do want to give blackjack a try. What about you?"

"I think I'll wander around and see if anything looks interesting."

He found her a seat at a $10 blackjack table and left her there. He didn't get out on the gaming floor of the Xìngyùn much, at least not physically. However, all his casino's CCTV and NORA feeds were stored on the servers he managed. He knew that someone in the Hard Rock's surveillance bunker was watching him—everyone was subject to one level of scrutiny or another. Chan had no loyalty card for the Hard Rock—nor for the Xìngyùn either, for that matter—so they had no profile on him. He'd be under casual surveillance until he sat down at a table, then scrutiny would increase to make sure he was playing according to the rules.

He stopped at a roulette table, bought $100 worth of chips and dropped a $10 chip on a random number—he chose 22 straight up because that was today's date. Unless the house was cheating—and the fines and risks were too high to try that when the odds were already stacked in your favor—his chance of winning on a single number was two-point-six percent. People thought they had lucky numbers or that certain numbers were "due" to come up, but the odds for any number coming up remained the same every spin.

He watched the ball go around, watched it land on 22.

"Winnah! Winnah! Winnah!"

Hmmm. With the 35-to-1 payout his ten bucks had become three-fifty on his first try. Well, it happened. The table limit was $500 so—why not?—he let it ride.

And again the ball landed on 22.

"Winnah! Winnah! *Big* winnah!"

Whoa. In just a couple of minutes, on two spins, he'd won over twelve thou. That was a bit over the top. No, more than a bit. He couldn't let it ride again because that far exceeded the table limit, and he'd already attracted more attention than he wanted. He worked for a rival casino, after all. He asked the dealer to color up his winnings to the largest denomination chips she had, then walked away, leaving her a $500 chip. As he slipped them into his jacket pocket he felt the plaque from the Pinelands.

Could it be? Could Aldo have been right about it bringing good luck?

Nah. That was stupid. Just to prove him wrong, Chan found his way to the Big Six Wheel and laid one of his original $10 chips on the Joker. The Wheel had the worst odds of any game in any house, and the Joker had the worst on the Wheel. Sure, it offered a 36-to1 payout but the odds gave the house a twenty-four percent edge.

The wheel stopped at the Joker. He grabbed his winnings and made a beeline back to Danni's blackjack table. He won nearly thirteen thousand dollars in ten minutes.

When he arrived he saw people standing behind her. He leaned in and saw the stack of chips before her. He waved for her attention. When she saw him she gave him a wide-eyed grin.

"Chan! I can't lose!"

"Take a break."

"I'm on a roll."

"Trust me, Danni."

She pouted as she gathered her chips and joined him in the aisle.

"I've already doubled my money from one hundred to two hundred. I've never hit a streak like that. "

"Exactly. Did you lose a single game?"

"No. Isn't it amazing?"

"Yes, it's exactly that. A little *too* amazing. Someone's going to think you're counting or cheating."

"Well, I'm not. I don't even know how to count."

Chan jerked a thumb toward the ceiling. "But the eyes in the sky will suspect. And you don't need the hassle."

She knew better than to glance up. "Oh, I'm sure the place is lousy with CCTV, but I was being dealt great hands and even when I wasn't, the dealer was busting. I was *winning!*"

Okay. That wasn't the winning pattern of a counter, so they'd probably let her alone.

"I was winning too," he said. "Twelve grand at roulette on two spins. Here's the thing: We're both carrying one of Aldo's plaques."

"You don't actually think...?" She stared at him. "Oh, that's so not you."

"Let's test it out on the worst odds, okay? And maybe earn you a little money too."

He led her to the wheel and told her to put her total $200 pot on the Joker. She was hesitant but finally relented. She managed to stay outwardly calm when she won $7200, but he could tell she was jumping around in her head.

"I did the same thing a couple of minutes ago," he told her. "It's not natural, Danni."

"You don't really think it's the plaques, do you?"

"I don't want to, but..." He had an idea. "Tell, you what, let's find Mac and Aldo and see how they're doing. If they can't lose either, then something's going on. Have you seen either of them?"

She hadn't. So they each got on their phones—Danni to Mac, Chan to Aldo. Both were on tremendous winning streaks they didn't want to jeopardize, but they finally agreed to meet up at the lobby bar.

"I'm eleven grand ahead," Aldo said when he arrived with a glass of tequila in one hand and a rack of chips in the other. He looked a little woozy. "What's so damn important?"

Mac showed up a minute later with his own rack, $9000 ahead.

Chan said, "Danni and I are way ahead too. It seems the four of us can't lose."

"My little doodads!" He shot the rest of his tequila. "Told you they were good luck!"

Against all his training and education, Chan was becoming a reluctant believer. After all, what were the odds of four people each taking a "charm" to different gaming tables and not being able to lose? Something was up.

Aldo swayed.

"You okay?" Danni said.

He smiled. "Drinks before dinner, drinks and wine with dinner, free drinks at the table." He winked. "When I'm ahead I'm generous with the waitresses and as a result they haven't let my glass go empty."

"Well," Mac said, "I'm going back and hope my baccarat streak continues."

Aldo patted him on the back. "Love you, man. I think I'll go to the room and rest my eyes a bit, then come back down."

"Want me to walk you up?" Chan said.

He laughed. "I haven't had *that* much to drink! Unless of course Danni wants to…"

She grinned and mimicked his slur. "I haven't had *that* much to drink either!"

He laughed and then looked at them. "Hey, I ever tell you how much I love you guys?"

Like every time he had a few too many.

"Never!" they said in unison.

"Well, hey. Here it is: I love you guys. See you later."

As they watched him weave away, Danni said, "You think he'll be all right?"

"I think so. But someone might decide to relieve him of those chips. Maybe we should…"

She nodded. "Yeah, maybe we'd better."

They caught up to him from behind and each took an arm.

"Know what?" Chan said. "We'll both walk you up."

He laughed. "I knew Danni couldn't stay away!"

He seemed to get drunker as the elevator rose. Probably that final dose of tequila working into his bloodstream. They guided him to the big suite at the end of the sixth-floor hallway where he had trouble working his key card. Chan took it from him. But when the door swung in, Aldo started to go with it. Chan had to grab him and half carry him inside.

"Which is yours?" he said as they were faced with two bedroom doors.

Aldo pointed to the right. When they reached the bed, Chan held Aldo upright while Danni pulled down the covers, then let him fall onto the bed like an axed tree. He pulled off his loafers and then Danni tugged the covers over him.

"Safe and sound," she said as they exited the room. "And in for the night, I'm sure."

"Without a doubt. No way he's waking up before morning."

6

Danni said she didn't feel like quitting yet because she'd probably never have a chance like this again. Chan knew he had to quit. A guy from a rival casino running up his winnings... not illegal, but bad form. So he cashed out his chips. He didn't want to be carrying somewhere in excess of twelve thou in bills, so he accepted a check from the casino. As he folded it and stuck it into a side pocket, he felt smooth plastic and pulled out Aldo's room key. He must have slipped it in there when he helped Aldo to his bed.

He showed Danni. "I should take it back up and leave it there."

"Aldo won't be needing it. He's out for the night. We'll be seeing Mac later. Give it to him."

Good thought. He pocketed it and accompanied Danni back to the gaming floor.

Once there he said, "My advice is to play one hand and then move to another table."

"Just one?"

"Yeah. Because if you really can't lose, you're going to cause suspicion if you stay in one spot. If you win one hand and move on, there's no way you can have a confederate at the table and no way you can be counting cards."

"How can anyone count cards with these continuous shuffling machines?"

"I don't think it's possible, especially with the dealer feeding the used cards back into it after every couple of hands. But some people say they can do it."

The lower-limit tables were crowded but seats were available in the high stakes area. These tables used a CSM with a six-deck shoe. He found her an empty seat at a $100-minimum table where the felt informed the players that DEALER MUST HIT SOFT 17'S.

She leaned close. "What's a soft 17?" she whispered.

"A hard seventeen is, say, a ten plus a seven—those cards can add up only to seventeen so that makes it 'hard.' An ace plus a six can add up to a seven or a seventeen, which makes it 'soft.' It gives the dealer a chance to up his total."

Some of the other tables on the floor operated on the dealer-must-stand-on-17 rule. The S17 rule increased the house's edge but that wouldn't matter if she really couldn't lose.

He got her settled, then took up a railbird position behind her. She was dealt a king and a four. The dealer was showing a seven. The odds dictated that she hit on fourteen, but she waved off another card.

"You need to hit on that, honey," said the old guy next to her, looking annoyed. He was showing an ace and a three, adding up to a four or a soft fourteen.

"I don't see why," she said. "He's going to bust. You should hold too."

"Chances are high he's got a hard seventeen or a soft eighteen. Either way he's got to stand and you're gonna lose."

"He'll bust. Wait and see."

"Damn pigeon," he muttered and signaled for a hit. A king came his way, giving him fourteen. He hit again and got a ten.

"Damn you!" he shouted at Danni. "That king should've gone to you!"

Chan was going to step in and say something but Danni remained totally cool. She didn't even look at him as she said, loud and clear, "Stick a sock in it, gramps. You should have held like I told you."

The dealer turned his hole card and now he was showing a seven and a three.

"Watch the fucker pull an ace," the coot muttered.

"You need to bust," Danni told the dealer. "Don't make me look bad."

He smiled and then pulled a five.

"That should have been mine!" the coot cried. It would have given him a nineteen.

With a fifteen hand, the dealer had to hit again. The queen that arrived busted him.

"You should have listened," Danni told her angry neighbor as she collected her winnings and rose.

"Damn pigeon!" the coot said, keeping his head down and toying with his chips. "Good riddance."

Chan couldn't help smiling as they walked away. "'Stick a sock in it, gramps'? My, aren't we snippy tonight."

"Only when provoked. He called me a pigeon. Twice."

"Yeah, well..."

"Okay, what's a pigeon?"

"A player who doesn't know how to play."

She made a *Hmpf!* sound and said, "I know how to play. Plus he said, 'Damn you.' Not nice. Got his just deserts, I'd say."

"I'd say so too. Don't mess with Special Agent Boudreau."

They tried another table where she was dealt blackjack for an instant 3-to-2 payout.

After the third table, where the dealer busted again, she said, "You know... this is kind of boring."

Chan nodded. "Half the fun is not knowing the outcome. Let's face it: When you know you're going to win, you're no longer gambling. Let's cash you out."

"Sure. I'm done here. My hundred bucks has become ten grand. Too much like stealing."

Good old straight-arrow Danni. Uncomfortable with too much of an advantage.

She turned in her chips, wanted cash instead of a check, and wound up stuffing two banded stacks of hundreds into her purse.

"Care to take another look at the ocean?" he said.

"Sure. Why not?"

Chan noticed a change as soon as he stepped out the door. The ocean was louder, the surf sounded... closer. When he saw all the people lined up at the railing and staring out to sea, he knew something was going on. The lights from the boardwalk reflected off the waves, but everything beyond that was featureless black lit by frequent flashes of lightning. When they found a spot at the railing he saw that the surf was indeed closer: The waves were breaking on the dunes and sending streams of water down toward the streets.

"Holy crap!" he said. "We're starting to flood!"

Danni looked angry. "Why haven't they announced anything inside? Don't they know?"

"Oh, they know, all right. They just want to keep people at the tables. That's why casinos don't have any windows and not a single clock anywhere. Your outside world no longer exists. It's only you and the games."

"They need to let people know."

"They will, but they'll wait till the last minute, or until the city orders an evacuation—which isn't likely. Then they'll have no choice."

He stared at the lightning-strobed ocean and realized the supercell he'd seen from his balcony had pushed up to the shore. The weather prediction had been for a clear, cloudless night. What happened? The danger felt closer. Maybe the flood was the danger he'd sensed.

Good try, he thought. He wished it were only the flood. No, something else was out there. Something besides a flood was moving this way.

"Oh, Christ, will you look at that!" Danni said.

Chan followed her point out to sea but saw nothing.

"Wait for it…" she said.

Lightning flashed again and he saw it. "Oh, hell!"

A thick pale funnel cloud swung back and forth over the churning sea. The supercell was living up to its reputation.

"Is that a waterspout?" she said.

"Yeah. They're tornadoes over water. We see a few here now and then."

"Does that mean a bad storm's coming?"

"Not necessarily."

An honest answer, but not exactly predictive in this case. The few waterspouts he'd seen off AC had been ropey, wimpy things. This one had a definite wedge shape, which usually indicated serious destructive power.

More lightning flashed and Danni cried, "Oh, God, there's another!"

Looked like a helluva storm was coming on shore. He stared at the churning water and thought he saw things moving in the surf, but then they were gone.

"Let's go inside."

"You look worried," she said. "Is it about the flood?"

"No, not really." He was more worried about what he sensed coming with the flood. "You guys are all on the sixth floor. No way any flood's going to get that high. An electrical outage would be my only concern, but the casino's got its own generators."

She smiled. "Even if it didn't, I never travel without my Bureau-issued Maglite and nine."

"You brought your gun?"

"It goes where I go. You never know when you'll be called on to help out in a situation. I didn't go through all that Quantico training for nothing."

Chan remembered...especially how at one of their semi-annual gatherings she'd talked about her hand-to-hand combat training and how Aldo, being Aldo, had laughed at the possibility of delicate Danni physically overcoming a guy. She'd challenged him to come at her, which he did, and he'd wound up face-down on the floor, helpless with his arm twisted behind his back.

"So," she said, "if flooding and power failures aren't giving you that look, what has you worried?"

"Something's coming." He hadn't wanted to say that. It slipped out.

She pointed toward the storm. "Damn right. That mess is looking worse and worse. But you're not talking about the storm, are you."

The genie was out of the bottle now. No putting it back, so he had to find a way to deal with it.

"Not only the storm. Something from the other direction as well. Something is coming this way from the pines."

She treated him to her askance look. "'Something'? What kind of 'something'?"

How could he describe what he didn't understand himself?

"Something I can't explain—not won't, *unable* to. You're

giving me that Doubting Thomasina look that I fully sympathize with, but you're also carrying around a stolen plaque in your purse that makes it impossible for you to lose at the gambling tables in there, so don't put up a front that there's nothing in your life you can't explain. I'm going to have to add these plaques to the list of things I can't explain. And don't tell me it's not going on yours."

She sighed. "No, it is. It's already listed. I truly couldn't lose, could I? Even when I played a hand wrong, the dealer busted. How do you explain that?"

"I've no idea."

"But you say something's coming this way from the pines, which is where Aldo took the plaques. Are we talking pissed-off Pineys?"

"I wish. I could explain pissed-off Pineys. I don't know what that something is, but it's not Pineys. And that's not all. Something else is coming."

"Like what?"

"Don't know." He jerked a thumb toward the ocean. "From out there."

She got an annoyed look. "Look, Chan, this is getting out of hand. How many of these 'somethings' are you working on?"

This was why he hated to mention these things. People got annoyed—and rightly so—when he couldn't explain them to their satisfaction. Well, hell, he couldn't explain them to *his* satisfaction either. But he *knew.*

"I told you I felt we released something out in the pines when—"

"Not 'we.' That was Aldo's play. We were against it."

"But we were there, we watched. Let's not split hairs. Blame is not my point. Aldo released something out there in the woods, but now I'm guessing that's not the only thing he released. Something else is coming this way from the other direction."

"Should I be worried?"

"Well…let's just say I don't have a good feeling."

"Okay, but let's just assume these feelings are accurate, and Aldo really did release something, shouldn't that something be grateful?"

"One would think so, but then again, it's not human and, like I said…"

"Yeah, I know. You have a bad feeling." She looked around at the Friday-night crowd on the boardwalk. "Let's get inside. You're giving me the creeps."

They stepped inside and Danni headed for the café bar, saying, "I need a drink."

"I'll sit with you," Chan said, "but I'd better abstain."

"You're going to make me drink alone?"

He shrugged. "I've got a short drive home but I've still got to drive."

"You can Uber or you can stay with me, and I'd prefer the latter. I told you before about the two queens, and I don't feel like being alone tonight."

Tempting…too tempting to turn down. He felt as if he never got enough time with Danni.

"Okay. Sure."

"Yes!" That smile, that smile… "I'm buying."

They found a table, a waitress brought Danni a white wine and Chan another Manhattan.

"Here's to us," she said, raising her glass. "May nothing ever come between us."

Chan could definitely drink to that, but as he reached for his glass, he froze as a wave of malevolence swept through him.

"What's wrong?" she said. "You don't like that toast?"

"It's here." The words came out a croak.

"What's here?"

"The 'something'…the 'something' from the pines.'"

"Here?" She looked around. "Here where?"

Hatred engulfed him and then fear and a bolt of indescribable agony pierced straight through. A scream tore from him as he shot up from his seat and knocked over the table, sending their drinks flying.

"Chan!" Danni cried, but her voice seemed to come from a great distance and he couldn't see her.

A red miasma filled his vision. The agony struck again, and suddenly he was falling. He hit the carpeted floor hard on his back with the world spinning around him. And then Danni was at his side, clutching his shoulders as she called his name.

"Chan! Chan, what in God's name?"

Where was he? He rolled over and got up on his hands and knees. Nausea twisted his gut. He gagged but managed to keep from vomiting. His head was killing him, and he heard a voice mumbling, "...*blood... so much blood... and angry...so angry... and so afraid... terrified... and so cold...*"

He realized it was *his* voice.

Danni hung close by, saying, "Chan, are you all right? What are you talking about?"

He opened his eyes. Danni knelt beside him, an arm over his shoulders. Other bar patrons stood around in a rough circle, staring. Their waitress was asking if he was all right,

No, he was not all right. He was anything but all right. He tried to stand but his knees were wobbly.

"Help me up," he whispered.

"Are you sure?"

"Need to get out of here."

Danni, always stronger than she looked, pulled him to his feet. As he stood wide-legged and swaying, the onlookers began to wander away. Just another Asian who couldn't hold his liquor.

"Let's sit you down."

"Let's not." He noticed the waitress eying him as she uprighted their table. "Do we owe her?"

"I paid her when she brought the drinks."

"Good." He was feeling less ill by the second. "Let's get out of here."

"Where we going?"

"Your room, please."

"Sure." As she guided him toward the South Tower elevators, she added, "What was up with all that talk about blood?"

His mind was blank. "I don't know."

When they finally reached the elevators—damn casinos for always putting them so far from the entrance—they had the cab to themselves, so he leaned against the rear wall. As he closed his eyes, it all filtered back to him, but slowly.

"All of a sudden I was seeing nothing but red. A world of red."

"What were you mad at?"

"Not that kind of red. Blood...I knew it was blood. A world of blood." He remembered the agony. "And pain. But the pain didn't last as long as the blood. The blood stayed, tinged with rage. And fear too. It was overwhelming. I—" He straightened away from the wall as a bolt of terror shot through him. "Oh, my God! Aldo!"

"What about Aldo?"

"It was him! His blood, his agony!"

"Oh, come on, Chan. Aldo's passed out in his room."

He was suddenly terrified for his friend. "I hope you're right." And he prayed he was wrong.

He pulled Aldo's key card from his pocket and held it ready. As soon as the doors opened on six, he dashed to the end of the hall.

"Hey, Chan!" Danni said, following but not running. "This is crazy."

He fumbled the card against the lock, saw the green light, heard the click, and pushed the door open. He stepped in—

—and fell back out with a cry, slamming into Danni and knocking them both to the hallway floor.

"What the fuck—?" Danni began, then saw what Chan had seen.

The suite was painted entirely in blood and decorated with pieces of skin and organs and digits and shreds of muscle and fat strewn all about—*all* about. The centerpiece was Aldo's face, the eyeless, gape-mouthed skin of his face draped over the armrest of one of the chairs.

Danni made a whimpering sound as she backward spider-walked a few steps on her hands and feet, then flipped over and grabbed Chan by the back of his collar and pulled.

Chan felt stuck to the carpet, frozen by the horror of the display. Mercifully the door swung shut on its spring hinges, closing off the abattoir and freeing him from his paralysis. With Danni pulling on him, he regained his feet and followed her back down the hall to a door she opened with her own key. They tumbled into the room where Danni lurched into the bathroom and began to retch while Chan dropped to his knees beside the nearest bed and buried his face in the spread as if praying.

This can't be real...can't be real...can't be...

But a deep part of him knew what he'd seen was all too real. He'd experienced echoes of what had happened down in the lobby bar.

Danni staggered back from the bathroom and slumped on the bed.

"My-God-my-God-my-God! What happened in there?" She began to sob. "Poor Aldo! Who could do something like that?"

"Not 'who'—" Chan began, but Danni wasn't listening.

"What sort of degenerate—was it Pineys? Was it Pineys?"

He gripped her arm. "Danni, no human did that."

"Oh, no!" she said, sitting up. "Don't, Chan. Do *not* start that 'something' shit! It had to be a bunch of Pineys!"

"Danni, my folks ran a Chinese butcher shop. I grew up with a meat cleaver in one hand and a fileting knife in the other. Do you know how long it takes to slaughter and flay and butcher and totally dismember something the size of a human? You and I put Aldo to bed just a little over an hour ago. Trust me, you cannot do what was done to Aldo in that time."

"Then it was a bunch of them."

"Think about that: A bunch of hicks invade the room, hack him to bits—except for his face which they painstakingly flay from his skull in a single flap—and then they all leave that bloodbath without tracking a single drop into the hall. I know because I was lying on that floor and I didn't see one trace of red. Didn't you tell me the Bureau showed you all sorts of crime scene photos while you were at Quantico?"

"Yeah. To desensitize us. Grisly as all hell. I guess it never worked on me, as witness my worship of the porcelain god a moment ago."

"Well, none of those crime scenes involved an old friend. But did any of those photos ever show you anything resembling that room?"

She gave her head a violent shake. "No, but you can*not* expect me to go supernatural on this, Chan."

"How else can we go? It sure as hell wasn't natural."

"But-but-but if we're going to go supernatural and say it was your 'something'—"

"The entity in the woods that Aldo released."

"Whatever. Why would this entity slaughter the guy who freed it?"

Chan had been wondering the same thing. "I don't know. I do know that it's pissed."

"You know this how?" She was calmer, regaining her poise.

"I felt it. The explosion of rage when it attacked Aldo literally bowled me over."

"Is that what happened at the bar?"

"Yes. A frenzied rage, but also fear. It's afraid of something."

"What? Us?"

"Hardly."

"Then what?"

"Not a clue. Maybe there are rules. Maybe you're not supposed to steal the plaques and that's why it came for Aldo."

"Did it take Aldo's plaque?"

"How would I know? And I'm sure as hell not going back in there to find out."

Her hand shot to her mouth. "What if it's collecting the plaques? That means we could be next!"

Chan hadn't thought of that. He watched her run to the closet and pull out her suitcase and fling it on the bed. She threw back the lid and withdrew a 9mm semiautomatic from a side pocket inside. Chan didn't know enough about pistols to tell the model, but it looked like a Glock. A black Maglite appeared from another pocket.

Guns scared him a little but Danni looked perfectly comfortable with it.

"That's loaded?" he said.

"Oh, you bet."

"You really think that will stop it?"

"No idea. But I'd rather have it than not have it. Hey, if it's coming for the plaques, Mac's in danger too."

She was right. Chan pulled out his phone and called him. When he answered, he said, "Hey, Mac. Can you come up to Danni's room? Like right away?"

"Sure. I know the room. And I'm ready. This isn't as much fun as I thought it'd be."

"Great, but hurry. It's important."

"Something up?"

"Yeah. Tell you when you get here." As he ended the call, he turned to Danni. "I think we ought to find a way to return the plaques."

"You mean head into the woods and wire them back onto those trees?"

"No, I mean go back to the spot, toss them out the window, and haul ass out of there."

"Sounds like a plan. But what about Aldo?"

"Yeah, I know. We can't just leave him there. You're the law-enforcement expert here. I was figuring you'd have an answer for that."

"I've been thinking on it. As a law officer I have a duty to report what we found to hotel security and wait around for the local police. We'll be persons of interest because we know him and we'll be expected to answer honestly any and all questions we're asked."

No-no-no! Chan saw about a million reasons why that was a terrible idea.

He said, "I realize we can't leave Aldo in that state all night. But you do realize, don't you, that if we answer everything honestly, the three of us will all end up on a psych ward?"

"Of course I do. Maybe for days. And that will mean we won't be able to return those plaques to the Barrens. Which will give that 'something' plenty of time to find us and do to us what it did to Aldo. Maybe to some innocent bystanders as well. We can't risk that."

"But you said—"

"I was telling you my duty, which is clearly not going to work for us. So we need to improvise. That's why I'm going to suggest the three of us bug the fuck out of here ASAP. On the way out of town we'll buy a burner phone and call in what we found in that room. That way Aldo's remains will be tended to and we can head to the Pines to prevent more deaths—namely ours."

A burner phone…untraceable. This was why he loved her. She'd regrouped mentally and emotionally from the shock of a few minutes ago and was thinking clearly. Chan still had a ways to go before he reached that place.

"After this is over," she added, "I will feel duty-bound to come back here and provide an edited version of what we know."

"Edited how?"

"No 'something.'"

"But how else can you explain what happened to Aldo?"

"I don't have to explain," she said. "That'll be their job."

A knock on the door. Mac entered carrying a full rack of chips.

"What's up?" he said.

"Have a seat and let me take that," Chan said, setting the rack on the dresser.

When Mac dropped into a chair, Chan searched for a way to break the news. How do you tell a guy that his dearest friend had been torn to pieces in their hotel room?

But Danni got right to it: "We've got terrible news, Mac: Aldo is dead."

Mac stared at them, one then the other, back and forth, and then burst out laughing. "Riiiiight! Was this his idea?"

"This is no joke, Mac," Chan said. "Something tore him apart while we were downstairs."

Danni was getting teary again. "It's true, Mac."

"Riiight! A bunch of Pineys came for their little plaques, and when he didn't have them, they killed him. Is that it?"

"No," Chan said. "Forget Pineys. The entity behind the markers, the thing he released did it."

Mac laughed again. "Oh? So now you're upping the ante? Al released some cosmic horror with an unpronounceable name and it killed him? And let me guess—we're next, right?"

Chan nodded. "Yeah. Maybe. Probably. It's pissed, Mac. But—"

"Oh, come on now. I know when someone's gaslighting me. Where is he?"

Danni sobbed. "Aldo is dead! Very, very dead!"

Chan could see the light dawning on Mac that maybe they weren't shitting him. His grin slowly faded. "You're serious? No, you can't be." They both nodded. "Where is he?"

"In the room. We—"

"Show me."

"No," Danni said, shaking her head. "I can't go back there."

Chan held up his hands. "Me neither."

Mac shot to his feet and strode to the door. "All right. I know what's coming. I'll open the door and he'll jump out and try to scare me."

"Can't you just take our word for it?" Chan said.

Mac left without answering. Danni grabbed the door before it could swing shut and held it open. They waited in silence for the inevitable.

It came: A hoarse, guttural, anguished cry from down the hall. Seconds later an ashen-faced Mac slammed into the doorframe, and then tumbled into the room to land on his hands and knees. His head sank to the floor and he stayed there mumbling incoherently for what seemed like a long time.

Finally he raised his head and looked at them. "What... what...?"

"We've got to get out of here, Mac," Danni said.

He struggled to his feet. "No! We've got to report it! Maybe they can catch those guys before—"

"No," Chan said. "We've got to leave."

"And go where? Just drive around in the dark and pray we don't run into them? No fucking way. I'm staying here. Once we report what happened, the place will be crawling with cops and those Pineys won't be able to get near us."

Chan grabbed Mac by his arms and shook him. "Forget fucking Pineys, Mac! Weren't you listening to me before? There *are* no Pineys. It's that thing—"

"What thing? Some creature we supposedly freed from the pines? You're talking crazy now."

Just then Danni and Mac's phones beeped simultaneously with text-message alerts.

Chan waited while they both read. Danni handed hers to him, saying, "You're not registered here so you won't get this."

It read:

ALERT! THE ATLANTIC CITY GOVERNMENT HAS ISSUED A FLOOD WARNING AND IS ADVISING RESIDENTS AND VISITORS TO EVACUATE TO HIGHER GROUND. THIS IS NOT A MANDATORY EVACUATION, THEREFORE THE HARD ROCK CASINO RESORT & SPA WILL BE STAYING OPEN. WE WILL, HOWEVER, BE OFFERING BUS SERVICE TO THE TRANSPORTATION CENTERS ON THE EXPRESSWAY FOR ANY GUEST WHO NEEDS IT.

"That does it for me," Danni said. Her suitcase still lay open, and she began throwing clothes from the dresser drawers into it. "Do what you want, Mac. But give us your plaque. Chan and I are going to return those things to where we got them."

Mac stood there with a tortured expression, then said, "Okay, okay. I'll come with you. I'm sure as hell not staying here alone."

She pulled her black dress off over her head and threw it into the bag, leaving her in a black bra and panties.

"Pardon my undies," she said, "but we haven't got time for social niceties."

Both men stared. Chan tried not to ogle as she slipped back into the jeans and shirt she'd worn earlier.

She stuffed the pistol and Maglite into her shoulder bag, pulled up the handle on her roller suitcase, and said, "Let's go."

They followed her out into the hall where they heard a door slam down the end. Chan saw a man in coveralls step away from Mac and Aldo's room and duck into the stairwell.

"Hey!" he cried, grabbing Mac's arm, "he just came from your room!"

Mac pushed past Chan and sprinted down the hall. Chan followed him, and Danni followed Chan. They burst through the door and pelted down the steps, but as they reached the first landing, a voice from above stopped them.

"All right, everybody freeze or your girlfriend gets a taste of what your friend got."

Chan did a slow turn. The guy in the coveralls stood on the

top step. He had one arm across Danni's chest while his free hand—his bloody hand—held a knife to her throat. He must have waited behind the door for them to rush through. Had he set them up?

Danni dropped her roll-away handle and it clattered to the landing. Her expression showed no fear, only what Chan might describe as concern and concentration.

"Hey, listen," Mac said. "I left close to twenty grand in chips in her room. Take her key and—"

"I'm not interested in your chips, asshole. I want—"

Danni suddenly grabbed his arm, bent at the waist, and twisted. And just as suddenly the guy was tumbling over the railing. With flailing arms he wailed in fear and surprise as he somersaulted through the air to slam against the opposite wall and fall onto the lower staircase. His knife bounced to the next landing and he ended up with his lanky form head-down on the stairs, clutching his right shoulder and groaning.

"Now you've done it! You stupid fucks, now you've really done it!"

Danni had her Glock out and was pushing past Chan and Mac to reach him.

"You killed Aldo!" she said through gritted teeth. Chan had never seen such rage in her face, never could have imagined it possible. "You're gonna pay for that!"

He shook his long brown hair from his face. "Yeah, right. Like I did all that with my little knife." He winced and squeezed his shoulder. "Shit! I think you dislocated it."

"I'll do more than that—"

"You and your asshole friends have already done a fuck-ton more than that, girl. You've condemned this whole city to death."

"What are you talking about?"

"And I didn't kill your friend. He was already way dead when I got there."

He slid his lower body down a few treads so that he was horizontal on the steps, and snaked his good hand toward the breast pocket of his coveralls.

"Don't even think about it!" Danni said.

"Dial it back a little, bitch. I just want to show you something." He pulled out a blood-spattered plaque, the companion to the ones the three of them carried. "I went there for this."

He tossed it to Danni who deftly caught it with her free hand—and screamed, "You killed Aldo for this!"

She still doesn't get it, Chan thought.

The guy shook his head. "Not me, I'm telling you."

Chan said, "It was the thing Aldo released from that spot in the Barrens, wasn't it?"

He gave Chan a funny look. "You know?"

"I've been trying to convince these two that nothing human killed Aldo. It's the thing we released. It's totally pissed, although I don't know why. I mean, we freed it."

"You didn't free a damn thing, pal."

"But those markers…when we removed them…"

"You didn't free it because it was never trapped. It could leave any time. When you removed those markers you removed its protection."

"Is that why it's afraid?"

The guy seemed to be studying Chan. "You're really tuned into this. You must be some sort of closet tairongo."

"Tairongo? What's—?"

"That's not what's important. What's important is that it's been hiding there and you blew its cover."

"Hiding from what?"

He looked around. "I don't know which way the ocean is, but from what's out there."

"In the ocean?"

"Yeah. Trouble is coming. That's why the sea level is rising. Atlantic City is going to be destroyed."

"Why?" said Mac. "Don't tell me because of vice."

The guy made a face. "Vice? You gotta be kidding. It'll be flattened simply because it's in the way." He pointed to the plaque in Danni's hand. "Add that one to the three you guys have."

"What for?" Mac said.

"So you can go back to the Barrens and tie them onto the trees you took them off."

"Fuck that!"

"Well, somebody's gotta do it. You've left me with only one good arm here, so I'm out of the running. You clowns have gotta undo what you did."

Danni said, "We were just on our way out there to toss ours back into that"—she looked at Chan—"what was that? A septagon?"

"Seven corners," the guy said. "Those markers each have to go on a separate corner. Then what's coming will turn back."

Mac fumed. "This is bullshit!"

"Hey, nobody asked you to go out there and mess with things, pal."

"I'm not your pal."

"Damn right, you aren't. What kind of cars you got? Anything good in a flood?"

"Mac has a Land Rover," Danni said.

"That'll do."

Mac shook his head. "I couldn't find that place again in daylight, let alone at night in a storm."

"I can get you there," the guy said, "but my van's in the garage and someone's got to drive it. I can't with this arm." He looked at Danni. "Thanks to you."

She kicked him. "Think about that next time you're planning to hold a knife to a girl's throat."

"Oh, believe me, I will."

"Okay, get up," she told him. "We're going to the garage."

He struggled to his feet and leaned against the wall. He undid a button on the front his coverall, then used his left hand to raise his right forearm. His breath hissed in and out through his teeth as he slipped his hand and wrist into the opening over his abdomen, creating a makeshift sling.

"There. That's a little better. My van's on the fourth level."

"We're leaving your van," Danni said. "Mac will drive us."

"Uh-uh. That's not gonna work. I've got fresh wire to replace what you cut off, and the tools to get the job done. And as soon as we finish up, you're gonna go your way and I'm gonna go mine."

"I thought you couldn't drive," Mac said.

"I can phone for help."

7

The van was a gray GMC Savana that had seen better days. The task of driving it fell to Chan. The guy in the coverall rode shotgun where he could direct them to their destination in the Barrens. Danni seated herself behind him with his knife and her Glock.

"Do you have to sit right behind me?" he said.

"Damn betcha."

"Where's that gun pointed?"

"Right at your back. In case you're wondering, it's a fully loaded Glock Nineteen."

"You sound like you like guns."

"I love them."

"Because they can kill?"

"I've never killed anything. If I get a moth in my house I catch it and throw it outside."

"Then why—?"

"They're beautiful pieces of machinery, especially the autos and semi-autos. Shooting them bores me, but I love to take them apart and put them together again."

Chan couldn't believe this conversation.

"Do you two want to get a room? The hotel has vacancies."

The guy said, "It's just that I was a little worried, but I guess I can assume she knows how to handle her piece. I don't want us hitting a bump and have it go off and splatter my brains all over."

Danni said, "If that happens, we'll just have to call Mister Wolf, won't we, Chan."

The guy barked a nervous laugh and Chan had no idea why. Who was Mr. Wolf? Was he supposed to know?

"You're kind of scary," the guy said. "But I could almost like you. My shoulder would still hold a grudge, though."

"She's FBI," Chan said.

"No shit? Okay, now I feel a little less embarrassed for letting you dislocate my shoulder."

"'Letting' me?" Danni said.

Chan got the van moving toward the down ramp. He passed his BMW on the way. No reason it wouldn't be safe until he returned for it. Down on level three he waited for Mac who'd taken Danni's suitcase to his Land Rover. When the Rover pulled up and flashed its lights, Chan started down to the exit with Mac following.

They'd entered the garage directly from the Hard Rock, so the flooded streets came as something of a shock. Chan had known it was raining and had seen the start of the flooding, but he wasn't prepared for the sight of knee-high water flowing along Virginia Avenue.

"Can this thing handle that level of water?" Chan said.

"Yeah, but not a whole lot higher without stalling. Head for the Expressway. That's higher and the going should be easier there."

"What's your name, by the way?" Chan said.

"Why do you care?"

"Well, it looks like we're going to be stuck in this thing for a while and it's easier than 'Hey, you.'"

"Kurt. You can call me Kurt."

Chan pulled out onto Virginia into a blinding downpour that included ice pellets banging on the roof and bouncing off the hood.

"So loud!" Danni shouted over the din.

He headed toward Atlantic Avenue through the hail and the near-horizontal sheets of lightning-strobed rain. The lightning was manic, the bolts huge, wide, and almost unbearably bright. His usual route home to Margate was via Atlantic but for their purposes now it offered easy access to the Expressway. He found it as flooded as Virginia. And crowded as well. It looked like a lot of people had taken the evacuation alert to heart.

He said, "If the water gets much higher—"

"It will," Kurt said.

"Well, if it does, cars will be stalling out left and right. And that means blocked streets, and when that happens, no one's getting out of the city."

The buildings here were older and rarely higher than two or three stories. The street lights were all on and the traffic signals were still working—for now. If they failed the result would be total gridlock. The occasional pedestrian braving the hail and the falling torrents and the flood and the lightning could wade through the water faster than the van was crawling.

"Probably a good idea to stay out of that water," Kurt said, watching one fellow as he passed the van.

Danni said, "Maybe they've got no other way of getting around."

"That water comes from way, way down deep, and you can be pretty sure it didn't rise to the surface alone. Other things will be coming in with the tide."

"Like what?" Danni said.

He shrugged his good shoulder. "Don't know exactly. And I'll be perfectly happy to get out of here without ever finding out."

Chan noticed groups of pink rose petals floating on the surface.

"Hey, look. A florist shop must have got flooded somewhere."

A pedestrian on their right waded into a cluster of the petals swirling in his path. As he did he started shouting and slapping at his legs where petals had attached themselves. Others attached to his hands and arms where he thrust them into the water. The man screamed as the flesh under the petals began to smolder and smoke.

"Oh, God, what's happening to him?" Danni cried.

It looked like they were secreting some sort of acid. But how was that possible?

"They're burning holes in him!" she said. "We've got to help!"

"Are you crazy?" Kurt said. "That water's a deathtrap."

"Here comes somebody," Chan said.

A guy had hopped out of the side of a minivan and was

sloshing toward the victim of the petals when he tripped and fell into the water. He immediately jumped to his feet, wailing. Visibility through the downpour was blurry, but a flash of lightning revealed that two black, football-sized monstrosities, all teeth and claws, had attached themselves to his arms with their jaws while their pincers ripped at his flesh.

"Oh, my God!" Danni cried. "What are those?"

"Things from the abyss," Kurt said. "Those are small ones. I'm sure bigger ones are on the way."

"Aren't you the optimist," Chan muttered.

"Just sayin'."

"We can't just sit here and watch people die," Danni said.

"We can if we're smart. You leave this car you'll wind up like him."

Just then the would-be rescuer screamed as he fell again and this time he stayed down, thrashing and flailing as more of the things attached themselves. The water around him turned red as his struggles slowed and ultimately stopped.

Chan and Danni could only watch in silent, paralyzed horror. Even Kurt seemed shocked at the ferocity of the attack. Meanwhile the original pedestrian who'd been attacked by the petals had also disappeared beneath the surface.

Kurt cleared his throat and said, "The water's getting deeper and could stall us out. You know your way around this place?"

"AC?" Chan said. "Somewhat."

"Can you find us another route to the Expressway?"

"I don't—"

Lighting hit a CVS in the block ahead, exploding all its windows onto the flood.

"Okay, yeah," Chan said. "Let's try another route. This is only going to get worse here."

He took the next right and started weaving through the side streets. He checked his rearview to make sure Mac was still with him as they passed through a residential neighborhood with some old, dilapidated houses. Street lights showed an old dilapidated man in a poncho standing on his front stoop holding a long fishing pole with a line dangling in the water. The half-empty vodka bottle on the step next to him went a long way toward explaining the scene.

He looked like he was struggling to wind the reel as the bent pole whipped back and forth.

"He's hooked something," Kurt said. "He might not like what he reels in."

"Tell him to cut the line," Danni said.

Suddenly a long, slim black tentacle whipped out of the water, wrapped itself around his legs, and yanked him screaming into the flood, leaving the vodka bottle abandoned in the hail-laced rain.

Danni's voice was shaky as she said, "Get us out of here, Chan."

Eventually he found his way to Bacharach Boulevard which rose out of the flood and led to the Expressway. Okay, at least they wouldn't stall out now. They were passing the convention center on their left and heading up the ramp to the AC-Brigantine Connector when a particularly bright flash of lightning lit the night.

Kurt jerked back from his window. "Holy shit!"

"Don't try anything," Danni warned.

"Check to the right during the next flash."

Chan wasn't moving at any great speed so he kept an eye out in that direction. Lightning flashed again.

"God!" Danni cried.

Chan's mouth went dry. Through the sheets of rain he could make out a thick, pale tornado winding across the flooded marsh areas of the Marina District, heading for the Borgata. The night went dark, but when it lit again, the funnel cloud was right next to the Borgata's main tower, stripping sheets of glass from its mirrored façade. Another flash showed it swirling away from the damaged hotel.

"I think it's coming this way," Danni said.

Kurt had his face pressed against the side window. "That's got to be a mile away. I think we're okay."

Subsequent flashes showed it weaving toward them, but Route 30 stood in its way.

"It's going to hit that highway!" Danni said.

Sure enough, it tore across crowded Route 30, scattering cars and trucks in all directions along with chunks of pavement, rendering it impassable. And then it continued coming their way.

That could be us in a few minutes, Chan thought.

"Maybe you'd better get this thing moving a little faster," Kurt said.

The good thing about the ramp was that it sat high enough to be out of the flood. The bad thing was how its four-foot concrete walls on either side hemmed them in, with traffic ahead and behind.

"Love to," Chan said. "How do you suggest I go about that?"

Kurt could offer nothing.

But at least they were moving. The funnel cloud was still a good half mile or more away. They had some time. They reached the connector and turned toward the Expressway. Almost there. But the trouble with the connector was that it didn't feed directly onto the Expressway; instead it made a 360-degree loop beneath and then over it to feed into the westbound right lane. They lost sight of the tornado as they passed under, but during the temporary reprieve from the constant din of the rain and hail, they could hear it. Tornado survivors tend to describe the sound as like the roar of a passing freight train, and that was exactly the sound that rattled the van as it grew steadily louder.

When they reached the overpass section where they faced due north, a flash of lightning revealed the whirling funnel cloud practically on top of the highway and bearing straight for them.

Danni screamed and so did Chan, and he was pretty sure Kurt did as well, but it might have been lost in the deafening roar of the whirlwind. Then the funnel took a sudden eastward swerve and barreled into the convention center on the far side of the Expressway, tearing off its roof before ripping across the highway a hundred yards to their right. In a repeat of the Route 30 carnage, pieces of cars and trucks and pavement flew in all directions.

And then it moved on, continuing southward into the marshes.

"That was too close!" Danni gasped.

Chan took a few calming breaths as he checked the rearview to assure himself that Mac was okay, then said, "I've had witnessing a real live tornado on my bucket list since I was a teen, but getting caught in one wasn't supposed to be part of the deal."

Lightning lit up the inside of the van as a bolt struck the ruins of the convention center not 200 feet away.

"Anything else we should know about your bucket list?" Kurt said. "Like getting struck by lightning maybe?"

"No. No lightning."

He merged onto the Expressway proper where the cars were bumper to bumper and moving slowly, but at least moving.

As Chan calmed, the thousand questions that had been flooding his brain since their trip to the Barrens this afternoon resurfaced. He glanced at Kurt. Maybe here was a guy who could answer a few.

"I need to know some things, Kurt."

"Like what?"

"Like this thing from the Barrens. You told us we didn't really free it because it was never trapped. You keep calling it 'it.' Doesn't it have a name?"

He smiled. "You've got a real thing for names, don't you. First you want to know mine, now you want its name."

"That's not an answer."

"Okay, the answer is simple: No, it doesn't have a name. It doesn't need one. None of them do."

"'Them'?"

"It's a thing, a consciousness, an entity. There's a number of them out there, some unimaginably vast, others not so much so, all stalking through the multiverse. But there aren't all that many. Not enough so's they need to have names. They know who they are. The only names they might have are the ones little minds like ours have stuck on them. They're few, and in fact their numbers have been slowly diminishing over billions of years."

"They can die?"

"Not really. More like merge. Or maybe 'hostile takeover' is a better way to put it. Occasionally a couple of them will have a falling out and the more powerful one will try to settle it by absorbing the weaker one. That's what happened out there in the infinite a few ages ago. Two of them butted their figurative heads over something or other. It's not possible for our minds to comprehend the reasons behind why these types of beings have a falling out, so don't even try. Whatever happened, the smaller, weaker one tried to avoid being absorbed by going into hiding. It wound up here."

"On Earth?" Chan said.

A nod. "We're talking millions of years ago, which is pretty much an eye blink to these things. The planet was nothing special back then, nothing to recommend it, nothing to attract the other entities, which was why it proved a good hiding place. For a while, anyway. But then, unfortunately for this entity, while it wasn't paying attention, a species of the local fauna developed sentience and became sapient. Now, as far as these cosmic entities are concerned, nothing is more attractive than a sapient lifeform."

"What's so attractive about that? I'd think the universe—or the multiverse, as you said—would be full of them."

"Not so common as you'd think. Lots of life, sure, but we're talking simple, biologically primitive lifeforms. What's known as the Great Filter Theory says an organism has to pass through many, many environmental barriers and evolutionary hurdles to even get near our stage of development, and then it's got to avoid doing something stupid that'll wipe itself out. Only very rare species make it through."

"But why does that attract these entities?"

"They get to play with us." He paused, maybe to let that sink in, then added, "Once we started showing sapience, this place began getting a lot of cosmic attention, which made it impossible for our entity to leave and find another hiding place. So it wound up stuck here."

"How do you know all this?" Danni asked from the rear. Obviously she'd been paying attention.

"Samuel told me."

"Oh, well, that clears it up."

"Samuel knows all this stuff. It's all part of our teachings."

"'Our'?"

"I'm part of a Family. I won't go into the details, but Samuel leads it. Our relationship with the entity is complicated. He understands it, I don't pretend to. Just like I don't understand how these little plaques hide our entity from the other entities. Don't ask me how that's possible. I take the approach that things are what they are and just go with that. It's been hidden away for eons but you guys undid all that. And now a lot of people are paying for it."

... a lot of people are paying for it...

A blade of guilt stabbed Chan. It had been Aldo's doing, but he and Mac and Danni had all been party to it. In fairness to everyone, though, none of them had had any idea of the consequences.

"Let me get this straight," Danni said. "You want us to believe that you work for some sort of gigantic cosmic thingamajig—"

"I just call it 'the Mind.' I find that easier than 'entity.'"

"Whatever. You want us to believe that this cosmic thing came all the way across the multiverse so it could hide out in the Jersey Pine Barrens for millions of years? Seriously?"

"Only part of it is out there. The main part of it is in a mountain hundreds of miles from here. I shouldn't say 'in' the mountain. It *became* the mountain. That's what my Family calls it: *the Mountain.*"

"So, you mean it can divide itself up. Like some sort of amoeba?"

"Get this through your head: It's not a physical thing. It has no substance, but it can affect the physical world, as your friend found out. And as Atlantic City will find out if we don't set this right in time."

Poor Aldo...

"It's an *entity*," he added, "a *mind* with more than one center of consciousness. It can spread its awareness to multiple places."

"Okay, fine," Danni said. "And you want us to believe that by our removing those little plaques—"

"Yeah, if you'd taken just one, or even two, the situation might not have gotten to this point. But you had to take four, which is more than half, which is as bad as taking them all."

"You're saying we exposed your cosmic thing to another cosmic thing that's been hiding out in the ocean and is on its way to kill it."

"Absorb it. You can't kill these things. Its consciousness will go on but it will be part of the bigger one now. And the Owner hasn't—"

"'Owner'?" Danni said.

"I really don't want to get into that. We call it 'the Owner' and it hasn't been hiding out in the Atlantic or anywhere on Earth. It's been *elsewhere*."

"'Elsewhere,'" Danni said. "Fine. But why should we give a damn if your entity is absorbed into this Owner?"

"Because you're fucking responsible!" he shouted.

"Dial it back a little, bitch," Danni said, and Chan recognized Kurt's own words from earlier. Obviously he got the message because he continued in a calmer tone.

"All right, how about looking at it this way: Maybe by saving it you can prevent even more people from dying. Because if what's coming reaches the remote consciousness in the Barrens, it can backtrack from that one to the main consciousness and in the process it'll leave a path of death and destruction like you can't imagine." He banged on the dashboard. "And if we don't get out of this traffic and into the Barrens soon, it'll be too late for Atlantic City."

"Why should it destroy Atlantic City when it's your entity it wants?" Chan said.

"Because it can't resist playing with us. AC is in its way so even though it's headed for another of its kind, it's going to leave a horrifying mess in its wake. Then it sits back and watches us scramble around trying to figure it out."

Their van ground along with the moping traffic in silence for a little while, then something occurred to Chan.

"How come nobody knows about these entities?"

Kurt said, "Because they want it that way. They lurk elsewhere, on other planes. They like to interfere here and watch how we react. We're their play things. Some people glom onto the big picture but are never believed. A guy named Charles Fort had it figured when he said, 'We are property.' And not even valuable property at that. Most people can't handle that and go into denial."

"You hardly seem in denial," Danni said. "In fact you seem pretty comfortable with it all."

"That's because I owe my life to the Mind."

Danni leaned forward. "It saved your life?"

"No, it *gave* me life. It created me—working though Samuel, of course."

"Of course," she said, he voice dripping with sarcasm.

"It's true," Kurt said. "The Mind has to stay hidden so it uses us as its hands in the world."

Chan was skeptical himself, but figured he could get more out of Kurt by playing along. "'Us' being this Family you mentioned?"

"Right."

"And did this Mind and Samuel create everyone in the community?"

"Not the children, but a lot of us adults."

"By 'created' do you mean cloned?"

"Maybe 'created' isn't the right word. More like 'enhanced' in certain ways."

Chan had never been strong in the biosciences—his milieu was code.

"Let me get down to brass tacks here," Danni said. "Are you telling us you're not human?"

"Not saying that at all. I am...mostly. I'm told we've been improved somewhat. I live like any other person. If no one had told me otherwise, I'd assume I was just like you. We were designed for a special purpose which did not work out—we failed in our goal—so we've been repurposed, so to speak."

"What was this goal?" Danni said.

"You wouldn't understand."

"Try me."

"No, I can't."

"After all the fantastic tales you've spun about warring cosmic entities and the like, you can't spin another about this mysterious goal?"

Chan shook his head. So hard to believe, and yet... he sensed that Kurt wasn't spinning fabricated tales. Everything he said about the entities fit so neatly with what he'd been sensing... and with what happened to Aldo... and what was happening right now to the city they'd just left.

Traffic picked up a little after they passed Route 9 and cars got off. Less than a mile later the pace picked up even more as a stream of cars exited onto the Parkway.

They reached Route 50 but when they came to the bottom of the ramp they hit water again.

"This area is lower than the Expressway," Kurt said. "We need to get into the pines and do this."

"I can't believe it's flooded this far already," Danni said.

Chan knew how she felt. "Well, it was already running over the dunes when we were last on the boardwalk. If the damn traffic hadn't held us back all this time, we'd have been here and gone by now."

"We make a turn in about a hundred yards," Kurt said as they sloshed along. "Get ready for a right."

A good thing Kurt had come along. Chan had been a passenger this afternoon and not paying close attention to where Mac was going. Even if he had been driving then, he doubted he would have been able to find the turn in the dark. He followed Kurt's point and the van plunged into darkness as they left 50. The highway had sported a streetlight every few hundred feet or so, not offering a lot of illumination through the downpour, but downright brilliant compared to the Stygian blackness of the side road.

"Thank God for headlights," Danni said.

"And the lightning," Chan added.

The water beneath his wheels turned muddy when the pavement disappeared, and downright slushy as the packed dirt gave way to sand.

"Any chance of our getting stuck?" he said to Kurt.

"Not as long as the engine stays dry."

Kurt seemed sure of his directions. Obviously he'd been out to the spot a number of times before.

"The flood level seems to be dropping," Chan said.

"We're just getting ahead of it," Kurt said. "It hasn't yet risen as high here as it has east of us. But it's coming."

Finally, after seemingly myriad turns in the dark, he held up a hand.

"Okay, we're here."

"How can you tell?"

"We just passed a familiar tree on the corner back there."

Mac's Land Rover pulled to a stop behind them. A car door slammed and seconds later a wet James McIntyre jumped into the back next to Danni.

"This storm is unbelievable! How the hell will we ever get out of here?"

Kurt said, "This place is the target. This is where the storm's headed. If we get these plaques back in place—I should say, *when* we do—the storm will lose direction and retreat." He held out his good hand. "Give them here. Each one has to go back to its own corner, otherwise all this is for nothing."

Chan and Mac fished theirs out and handed them over. Danni had Aldo's as well, and gave both to Kurt. He shuffled through them, then handed one to Mac.

"This goes on the southeast corner. With the way you folks left the wires in pieces, I'm guessing you have wire cutters."

Mac nodded. "Yeah, in my truck."

"Okay. I've got a coil of the special wire we use in the back. Cut yourself a good length with my cutters, then turn your Rover around and point its headlights at the tree on that corner back there. Thread the wire through the little tunnel in the trunk and then through the hole in the plaque and then twist the hell out of it so the plaque stays there. Got it?"

"Got it. What'll you be doing?"

"I'll be guiding these two around the bend where they're gonna do the north and northeast corners. We'll all meet back at the east corner"—he pointed through the windshield—"that's that one right ahead there. We'll give that tree back its plaque and then we're done."

Mac jumped out into the rain again, opened the rear of the van and snipped a length of wire, then ran toward the Land Rover. A flash of lightning showed the flood lapping at the far side of the fire trail.

"Get this moving," Kurt said. "We've got to hurry."

Chan guided the van toward the next corner.

"I've got a Maglite," Danni said. "We can do two at once."

"Okay," Kurt said after a few seconds thought. "He'll drop us off at the northeast corner where I can hold the light for you." He turned to Chan as he rounded the corner. "You point these headlights at the north corner and attach this to the tree there."

He handed Chan a plaque, laid another on the front seat, and kept one for himself. When Chan stopped at the northeast corner, Kurt turned to Danni.

"Reach behind you and grab the machete from the back."

"Machete?"

"Yeah. I got sent out here when they realized something was amiss with the plaques. I didn't know if I'd have to chop underbrush or what. But then I found out they'd been stolen."

Danni found it and held it up. "What do I do with it?"

"Nothing, I hope. We'll bring it along just in case."

"'Just in case' what?"

"You'll know when it happens. Let's go."

Kurt and Danni jumped out into the rain. He hated the idea of leaving her alone with the guy who had held a knife to her throat, but she'd pretty much disabled him and he seemed to want to replace these plaques more than anything else.

After Danni had cut her length of wire from the rear compartment, Chan drove ahead to the north corner and angled the van so its headlights lit up the slim tree there. He checked his plaque and recognized the glyph.

Okay. Had to move fast. Out into the downpour—the hail had mostly stopped but God, the rain was cold—around to the back doors to snip off a couple of feet of coppery wire, then a head-down rush to the tree. Oh, hell, where was the goddamn hole? Then he remembered the plaques had hung somewhere near eye level. The rain increased, coming in sheets now, lashing his face as if trying to blind him. The lightning flashes were brighter and more frequent, the thunder claps so loud they rattled his teeth. His numbing fingers finally found a dimple— the tunnel opening. With shaking hands he threaded the wire through the trunk and then through the hole in the plaque. Quick twists of the wire ends and then he was running back to the van.

He allowed himself a few dripping shivers as he looked for the heater control and cranked it to max, then turned the van around and headed back. Almost immediately the headlights picked up the forms of Danni and Kurt, both looking like the proverbial drowned rats, hurrying toward him. He stopped so they could get in, then got rolling again.

"Get that heat on!" Danni said with a shaking voice. "I'm freezing."

"It's as high as it'll go."

He rounded the north corner and saw Mac waiting at the next turn, his Rover's lights fixed on the tree. Chan pulled to a stop with the van's lights trained on it from another angle. Water swirled around the Rover's tires at hubcap level.

"The flood's here," Kurt said, handing him the last plaque and a length of wire. "I cut an extra piece before. You've got to hurry."

Chan checked the plaque.

This was the one Aldo had given him just a few hours ago, promising him good luck. Yeah, at the tables, maybe. But everything else had gone to hell, especially for Aldo.

The last thing he wanted to do was go back into that rain, but he wasn't about to send Danni. So that left him. He was reaching for the door handle when, up ahead, he saw Mac jump out of the Rover into the water and start toward them. He'd taken maybe two steps when his arms flew up as his feet were whipped out from under him. He landed face first in the water and then was dragged backward.

"Something's got him!" Chan cried.

Danni was already out of the van, running with the machete. "He needs help!"

"No!" Kurt shouted when Chan jumped out and followed.

Mac lifted his head and looked their way as he clawed the ground to slow his course. His eyes were wide with panic and his mouth open in a cry of terror that was swallowed by the storm.

When they reached him they found a thick, black tentacle wrapped around his ankles and trailing off into the darkness. Danni attacked it with the machete, severing it with two swings. But though cut off from the main portion, the severed end hung on. Chan dropped to his knees to help Mac uncoil it from around his ankles, but it simply wouldn't let go.

And then Danni screamed and went down. A new, slimmer tentacle had coiled around her left ankle and was dragging her away. She was trying to chop at it with the machete but couldn't reach it.

"Danni!"

Chan grabbed the machete from her and hacked away at the ropy thing. It parted and slithered away, leaving its distal end still attached to Danni.

"Mac!" she cried, pointing.

Another tentacle had fastened around Mac's throat while he'd been trying to uncoil the remainder of the first. His hands were tearing at it as it dragged him head first across the fire trail toward the darkness. Chan ran after him but lost sight of him as he was pulled beyond the reach of the lights. He followed as far as he dared into the darkness before turning back and running to Danni.

"We've got to get to the van!" he shouted through the downpour as he hauled her to her feet.

"But Mac!"

"We'll never find him in the dark!" It damn near killed him

to say that. "The only thing we'll do is end up just like him. Our one hope is to get that final plaque back in place!" He dragged her toward the van. "Come on! Get moving!"

After he'd pushed Danni into the rear seat he grabbed the plaque and the wire and headed back. His fearful heart pounded wildly as he sloshed to the tree on the corner. He looked for some sign of Mac along the way but found none. At the tree, fortune was with him this time and he found the opening of the trunk tunnel immediately. Fearing that any second he'd feel something wrap around his ankles and tug his legs from under him, he duplicated his movements from the north corner in a rush: Thread the wire through the wood, then through the plaque, twist-twist-twist, then a mad run back to the van.

He climbed back behind the wheel and sat there shivering, panting, and dripping for a moment, then threw the engine into drive.

As the van lurched forward, Kurt said, "Where're you going?"

"To find Mac."

Kurt started to say something but apparently thought better of it. Chan eased past the Rover on the corner where he had last seen Mac and angled the headlights toward the brush and woods on the far side of the flooded fire trail. He could see dark forms darting beneath the rain-pocked surface of the water, but the beams revealed nothing that looked like Mac.

"I'm sorry," Kurt said, "but your friend's gone.

"That's it?" Danni said through a sob. "Mac's gone? There's nothing we can do?"

"If it'll make you feel better you can do a search after the storm when the flood recedes."

*If it'll make you feel better...*Chan got the message: Maybe it will do something for you, but it won't do a damn thing for Mac.

"When will that be?" Danni said.

"Shouldn't be long."

And it wasn't. As the lightning withdrew toward the east, the rain abated and the water level dropped, revealing the sand of the fire trail.

"How is this possible?" Chan heard himself say as some

of the confused thoughts swirling through his brain found his voice. "How can we turn a storm around with little plaques?"

"That's just it," Kurt said, "You didn't do anything to the storm itself. The plaques shield the entity, hiding it from the power behind the storm. With no target, the Owner retreats, taking the storm with it."

"'Shield' it? That's crazy."

"Is it? You're a tairongo, you're somehow attuned to it. You could sense it before. Do you sense it now?"

Chan closed his eyes, searching for the anger of the pinelands entity, and found... not a trace. But he could feel the malignant miasma of the "Owner" receding.

"No. It's not there."

"Because it's hidden again. From the Owner as well as from you."

The rain stopped. The sudden silence after the constant drumming was unsettling.

"What next?" Danni said.

Kurt pointed to Mac's idling Land Rover. "You go your way and I go mine. But first there's someone you need to meet."

Chan looked around. "Who?"

"Here he comes now."

A middle-aged man with longish dark hair pushed through the brush within the septagon and stepped onto the fire trail. He had broad shoulders and a wide face. His pants were damp from the brush but the rest of his clothing was dry.

"Where'd he come from?" Danni said.

"From the Mountain."

"What mountain?"

"I told you about the Mountain."

That didn't make any sense to Chan, but then, nothing about tonight made any sense. As Kurt stepped out of the van, Chan looked at Danni.

"What do you want to do?"

"I want to find Mac," she said, her voice riding the edge of a sob.

He felt the same, but had to face the reality of it.

"I don't see that happening tonight...in the dark."

She gave a disconsolate shrug. "We've got to take Mac's Rover, so we might as well get out and meet the guy." She hefted her Glock, then put it in her shoulder bag. "But I'm keeping this handy... just in case."

They both exited and met where Kurt was talking to the stranger.

"This is Samuel," Kurt said.

"Your fearless leader," Danni said.

"Kurt has been telling me about you two. He extended his hand to Chan. "You're a tairongo, he tells me."

"If he says so." It still sounded like a nonsense word.

"And you," he said, turning to Danni. "You're the one who injured his shoulder."

Danni shook hands with her left, leaving her right in her shoulder bag.

"I won't apologize for that."

"Nor should you. Kurt can be, shall we say, impetuous." He looked at Kurt. "Did you deserve it?"

Kurt winced as he adjusted his arm's position. "I got a little desperate."

Samuel turned back to Chan and Danni. "And speaking of impetuous, the actions of you two and your less fortunate friends have caused untold destruction and loss of life. For our sake and for your own sakes, I advise you to forget about this place and everything connected with it." His gaze grew intense as he leaned closer. "Do you understand? Forget about this place and everything connected with it. Forget the first time you saw it and forget the last time you'll see it tonight, and forget everything between. Is that clear?"

Chan was about to ask how they were supposed to do that but...

8

...he was driving Mac's Land Rover through the night on a puddled, four-lane blacktop highway without a clue as to where he was or how he got there. His clothes were soaked and he had no idea why. Danni, equally wet, sat in the passenger seat. The heater was blowing on max. When he passed a sign saying this was Route 322 and that Glassboro was twenty-five miles ahead, he pulled over onto the shoulder.

"How did we get here, Danni?"

She gave him a dazed look. "I don't even know where we are, let alone how we got here."

"We're headed west on the Black Horse Pike. But why? And how did we get so wet?"

"No idea. This is scary, Chan. The last thing I remember is you and I in the backseat and the sun shining." Her voice rose in pitch as she pointed to the dashboard clock that read *11:52*. "That was ten hours ago! What the fuck, Chan?"

Yeah. What the fuckety-fuck? That was exactly the last thing Chan remembered as well.

"Why are you driving?" she said. "And where are Mac and Aldo?"

"I have no idea. We must have left them back in AC."

"How can we both have ten-hour blackouts? How is that possible?"

"I can't even guess. We need to get back to AC and find out."

He made a U-turn and headed east but ran into a traffic backup in the Mays Landing area.

"What the hell?"

He got out and asked one of the other drivers what the matter was.

"Word is Atlantic City is totally flooded," the man said. "All the way out to here."

"But that's like fifteen miles!"

"Tell me about it."

"What the hell happened?"

"Where've you been all night? There's been a hellacious storm with a freak tide."

He hurried back to the car and told Danni.

"How could we not know about a storm and a flood tide?"

"But look at us. We're both soaked. We must have been out in the storm."

"This is scary, Chan."

More than scary—terrifying.

"If we can't get back to the hotel, we can at least get to my place, but if AC is flooded, Margate is probably underwater as well."

He searched for his phone and was relieved he still had it. He called one of his neighbors in the high-rise and learned that Margate was fine but Ventnor, which was closer to AC, hadn't fared so well. He was told he'd have to approach Margate from the south.

So he took backroads through Egg Harbor Township and Northfield and reached Margate in due time. The only water he found there was in puddles. They'd listened to the radio along the way but didn't learn much because nobody knew much. He still had his car keys, so he was able to park in his spot in the apartment building's garage.

As they got out, he glanced in the Rover's rear compartment and saw a carry-on roller bag.

"Isn't that yours?"

Danni looked and said, "Yes. How'd it get here?"

"Did you check out?"

"Not that I know of."

He popped the rear hatch and lifted it out.

"Another mystery, but a convenient one, since you're spending the night."

"I am?"

"Well, where else are you going to go? We can't get to your hotel.

"Right. I'm not thinking straight."

"At least you've got a change of clothes."

When they reached the apartment, the first thing they did was go to the balcony. The view was eerie: Ventnor's high rises were down and Atlantic City's usual bright lights were dark. Its Boardwalk and enormous hotels and casinos were hidden in a pea-soup mist.

Back inside, he directed Danni to his bedroom where she could change into dry clothes. That bed would be hers for the night.

She returned a few minutes later with two banded stacks of bills in her hand and a dazed look on her face.

"Chan...I found ten thousand in hundred-dollar bills in my bag. Where did I get this?"

Chan pointed to the band. "It says Hard Rock. You must have won big tonight."

"Why don't I remember? How could I forget something like that?"

He had no answer. Not remembering frightened him. Nothing like this had ever happened to him.

He wanted a shower but that could wait. After they changed into dry clothes they sat together on the couch and surfed the TV news channels, but they were no more informative than the radio. Atlantic City was incommunicado. They both dozed off and spent the night spooned there.

In the morning, they returned to the balcony and gaped at the vista of devastation before them. The sun was up and the fog had melted, and Atlantic City... the whole city had simply... vanished.

SATURDAY

1

Pam put down her coffee and stalked to the front door. Who the fuck was ringing her bell on a Saturday morning? Okay, so it was almost noon, but didn't they realize some people didn't like to be disturbed on weekends? That didn't apply to her because she didn't really have weekdays any more, which meant she didn't have weekends, so to speak. If this was one of those Jehovah's Witnesses...

She put her eye to the peep hole and recognized her visitor.

Worse than Witnesses! The fucking FBI again. And not that cute Chinese guy, either. The bitch was back.

Yanking open the door, she said, "Are you fucking kidding me?"

"Good morning, Mrs. Sirman."

She wore pretty much the same outfit she had on Wednesday—white blouse, blazer, and straight-leg slacks.

"What do you want?"

"Just a DNA sample."

She said it so matter-of-factly, with such an innocent smile, Pam could only stare at her a moment.

"A DNA sample?" she said finally. "But you already have one from back when—"

She blinked. "It was compromised in our lab. Don't forget, you gave it seven years ago and our technology has advanced quite a ways since then."

"But my DNA hasn't advanced anywhere. It's still the same now as it was when someone swabbed me back then."

"But we don't have that sample anymore, Mrs. Sirman, and we can do a far more detailed analysis of your genome these days than we could back then."

"What's your name again?"

"Boudreau—Special Agent Danielle Boudreau."

Pam backed out of the doorway. "All right, Agent Boudreau, come in and let's get this over with."

She realized the anger and hostility that flared at the sight of that FBI badge on Wednesday had faded, or maybe mellowed somewhat. Part of that was the result of spending those hours with Chan. He wasn't an agent, just support personnel, but he was connected to the Bureau and seemed an all-around decent guy.

She watched as Boudreau pulled on gloves and produced a long test tube with a long swab. Pam opened her mouth to allow a sample from the inside of her right cheek.

Maybe this Boudreau wasn't so bad either. She seemed too young to have become one of those soulless automatons Pam had had to deal with when Julie disappeared.

Wait…Julie…

"Why do you need my DNA to look for Phil's body?"

Boudreau looked a bit flustered. "A call came to get a fresh sample, so that's what I'm doing."

"A call from whom?"

She blinked. "From on high."

"They sent you out on a Saturday?"

"Well…"

"You know what, Agent Boudreau? You're a fucking terrible liar."

She looked away, then looked back. "Okay, I read the file on your missing daughter. I can't imagine the pain you must have gone through."

"I don't want your sympathy, I want to know what the fuck you're up to."

"I was struck by the parallels: Your infant daughter was stolen away—disappeared without a trace. And then, seven years later, your husband's remains are stolen, also without a trace. It's a little too symmetrical, don't you think? Coincidences do happen, but not all that often. Things that seem like a coincidence can turn out to be connected."

Pam felt like she'd been punched. "You think what happened

to Julie and what happened to Phil are connected?"

"I don't think it's entirely beyond the realm of possibility. I have to keep an open mind about it."

Pam was stunned. Of course it was a possibility. Why hadn't she seen that?

"When did this occur to those brilliant minds at the FBI?"

"This is me talking. I had the advantage of reading the Missing Baby Sirman file with the extra knowledge of what happened to Phil. He disappeared only last week so there was no way I or anyone else could link those two occurrences before then. But it hit me in the face right away."

"And so you brought it to your superiors and they ordered the new DNA test."

She blinked. "Right."

She was lying again. That blink was a tell. She'd been honest about going through the file and seeing that parallel, but...

Pam remembered how Boudreau's buddy, her "consultant" Chan, had reacted when she told him that Phil claimed to have grown up in Alberta in the Catskills. Chan had said he'd been through there just the day before and... what had he said? *I may wind up back there.* And now, two days later, here's Boudreau at her door—on a fucking Saturday morning, no less—looking for a fresh DNA sample.

"There's an expression that goes: 'I may have been born at night, but it wasn't last night.'"

"Sorry?"

"You and Chan the man are doing this on your own, aren't you."

"No-no-no. I'm laying all this out for my superiors first thing Monday morning and just trying to get a head start on everything."

Pam didn't see her blink so what she'd said right then was probably true, or at least partially true. But the pieces were falling together and a picture was forming.

"Chan's up in Alberta, isn't he?" She didn't answer so Pam pressed on. "And he's found something, hasn't he? He—" Suddenly she saw it. "Oh, my God, he's found Julie!" She grabbed Boudreau by her blazer lapels. "Has he? Has he found Julie?"

"Don't go there, Pam. Do *not* go there!"

"Why not, goddammit? Why the hell not?"

"Because the disappointment will break your heart."

"It beyond being broken. It's already been ripped out and shredded."

Boudreau pried Pam's fingers from her blazer. She was damn strong. And she looked pissed.

"All right, Pam, Chan did go to Alberta, but not to find out what happened to Phil, and he certainly didn't go intending to look for your daughter. He went there for us."

"'For us'? What does that mean? Are you two a couple?"

"Hardly. Just old friends." She looked like she regretted saying that. "Look, forget I said that. It's irrelevant."

"No way I'm forgetting anything, sister. An old friend, huh? I'm betting he's not even connected to the FBI—not as a consultant or anything else. Am I right? Because if I *am* right, and I go to your bosses and tell them how you used your badge to bring him to me under false pretenses, I'll bet you can kiss your FBI career good-bye."

Boudreau seemed to deflate a little. She looked away and muttered, "Shit," under her breath.

"Yeah...'shit.' You're not very good at this, Agent Boudreau. If indeed you really are with the FBI."

"I am. That Special Agent shield is genuine and it's mine."

"Well, then, do you want to tell me what fucking game you're playing?"

She took a deep breath. "It's not a game, and it's really, really complicated, but it all comes back to what happened to Atlantic City."

Atlantic City? What the fuck?

"Do your bosses know what happened?"

"Nobody knows."

"Then what the—?"

"Chan and I were in AC through the whole thing but both our memories are blank from early that afternoon to just shy of midnight. Chan thinks your husband is—or was—involved."

"Phil? That's insane! That's Loony Tunes!"

"I know it sounds crazy, but Chan worked out some very

roundabout reasons connecting Phil to what happened. Not that he thinks Phil is responsible—"

"Well, that's good, because no fucking way he could be."

"But too many things connect to Alberta—and your husband's one of them. Chan thinks the key to filling the holes in our memories lies up there, so he made the trip to find a way to get them back."

"'Too many things connect to Alberta,' huh? You can start explaining those things to me right now. And one of those things will be why you want my DNA if it's not to find Julie."

"I'll have to leave that part for him to explain. As for the rest, that'll take all morning."

"That's okay. I'll put on a pot of coffee. I've got the whole fucking day."

"Well, I don't. I'm going to meet Chan and—"

"You're heading for Alberta?"

She nodded and started packing away her DNA-collecting kit. "Straight from here."

"Great. You can explain it on the way."

Boudreau's eyes widened. "What?"

"Surprise-surprise, Agent Boudreau. I'm coming with you."

2

Chan awoke groggy and dry-mouthed.

Last night...either the worst nightmare of his life, or those missing ten hours were back. Nightmare and memory... one and the same in this case.

He groaned. "Oh, God!"

Danni said the FBI therapists had told her those missing hours could return at any time or not at all. Well, his had returned last night.

Poor Aldo...poor Mac. And the city...all of Atlantic City, gone because of what we did. All those thousands and thousands of people dead because of what *we* did!

He staggered out of bed, still in yesterday's clothes. He must have conked out right after the cherry pie last night. Had Ian put something in the pie? No, that didn't make sense. Ian and Erica had been scarfing it down right along with him. The coffee? They'd had tea while he'd had coffee. But why would they want to drug him? What would be the point? He had no valuables. He'd brought a couple of changes of clothes, a paperback thriller, his toiletries, and that was it.

He looked around. Everything seemed the same as when he'd conked out. Lexie's abstract was just where he'd left it propped up on the dresser.

No, it must have been his brain wanting him unconscious while it rearranged the mental furniture to bring back his memories. He'd spent the last two months trying desperately to remember those ten hours, but now that he could...

He almost wished they'd stayed lost.

What about Danni? Had hers returned too? That would be great if they had. He really needed someone to talk to about this, and Danni was the only one who could possibly understand. But right now that understanding was only potential. Because if those hours remained lost to her, she'd be just as clueless as anyone else.

She was scheduled to stop at Pam's to collect a DNA sample this morning, then head up here.

Wait...this morning.

The room darkener shades were down. Had he done that? The light seeping around their edges seemed awfully bright. What time was it? The little digital alarm clock on the night table read *11:30*. That couldn't be right.

He stepped to the dresser for his phone and found it turned off. Had he done that? He hardly ever turned off his phone. He hit the on button and after a vibration or two the screen lit with *11:31*.

Shit! He never slept this late. He checked for missed calls but found none. Where was Danni? He was sure she'd contact him after she got the sample. What would he say? If her memories hadn't returned, should he tell her his were back? He had no doubt she'd want to hear all about it.

How could he saddle her with this crushing guilt?

Should they feel guilty? They could shunt it off on Aldo, all his doing, his single-minded determination to steal those sigils despite Danni's protests and Chan's warnings. Yeah, well, that might fly if Aldo had kept the sigils to himself in his room. But he'd handed them out and they'd each used the luck they brought to clean up at the gaming tables. In Chan's book that made them accomplices and culpable for what followed.

True, none of them had known the consequences or been aware of the forces they'd set in motion, but a simple, damning fact remained: If those sigils had been left in place, Atlantic City would still be lit up and standing, and those 25,000 missing people would still be alive and well and going about their daily lives.

The bedroom walls seemed to close in on him. Air...he needed air. He jammed his feet into his shoes and headed downstairs and out the front door to the parking area. Immediately he felt he could breathe better, but he didn't *feel* better. The guilt had followed him outside.

He walked up to the highway. Which way? West, toward
the mountain? No, he didn't want to see Samuel right now. That
man had looked him square in the face and as innocently as
could be had told him he'd help get his memory back when the
fucker had been the one who'd buried those memories in the
first place. How could he trust him? Then again, did Samuel
owe him the truth? After all, the irresponsible acts of Chan and
his buddies had threatened the existence of the Family he'd
built.

He turned east and started walking. The asphalt was in
poor shape—this stretch of Route 23 definitely needed a fresh
cap—and the shoulders were crumbling in areas. A semitrailer
blew past and the slipstream in its wake damn near sucked him
onto the road. A guy could get killed walking along here.

Well, would that be so bad?

3

Ian sipped his second cup of tea in the breakfast room. Three slices of buttered whole wheat toast rested on a plate before him but he was too tired to eat. Both he and Erica were bleary from lack of sleep. Not total sleep deprivation; they'd each managed to catch a couple hours of kip, but sometimes too little left you feeling worse than none at all. This was one of those times. They'd closed the door to the breakfast room so their voices wouldn't carry, still he leaned close to her and spoke just above a whisper.

"Funny how things work out sometimes, isn't it, pet?"

She yawned. "What do you mean?"

"Here we've sat for years, pretending to be innkeepers as we watched the mountain and its denizens while learning nothing. And then, out of the blue, Samuel himself, the man we were sent to keep track of, sends us a guest who knows all the secrets. We learned more in ten hours last night than in all these years."

Chan's mutterings and ramblings had confirmed what the Order had expected for some time: Samuel was associated with a rogue Player, a squatter that had integrated itself into the landscape—specifically, the mountain itself. If that had been all they'd learned, Ian would have been satisfied. But they also learned how it had been cloaking itself and how to undo that cloak.

"You know," he said, "I have roamed all along that perimeter fence, ducking the drones and looking for weak points, and never noticed those sigils among the foliage. But now that I know they're posted on the corners, I'm going back today and confirm what he said."

"And if they are?"

"I'm not sure yet. But if nothing else, I plan to take advantage of the extra, special, added bonus—if you'll pardon the redundancy—that's been presented to us. You realize, don't you, that our guest is that rara avis, a sensitive."

"But he's Samuel's sensitive."

"Not for long. I'm sure it won't be too long before Samuel's not going to have need for one, or anything else, for that matter."

"Do you think Liao will join your club?"

Ian caught the sneer in her voice. "My 'boys' club.' You mean? Oh, he'll join—whether he wants to or not. A sensitive is too valuable to waste."

He lifted his phone from the table to check the time.

"Speaking of which, I'd have thought he'd be up by now. That witch's brew must have really knocked him for a loop. Go check on him, will you, pet? I don't want him suffering any unanticipated aftereffects from it. Meanwhile I'll start prepping for his breakfast."

"But the kitchen closes at ten."

Erica...how she loved rules.

"We can bend the rules this time, I think. He's the only one here and we are, after all, the reason he missed breakfast."

As Erica left, he finished his tea, but just sat there. The last thing he felt like doing was cooking, but he couldn't abandon the jolly innkeeper role just yet.

He heard Erica's footsteps hurrying down the hall.

"He's gone!" she said as she rushed in. "The bedroom's empty and he's not in the bathroom."

Ian stepped quickly to the window. "But his car's still here."

"He must have wandered off," she said.

"You've got his phone number on the register. Call him!"

Ian followed her down the hall to the desk where she pulled his card and started punching in the number. He continued upstairs to Liao's bedroom where he listened to see if he'd left his phone behind.

After a moment, Erica said, "He's not answering."

"His phone's not ringing up here, so he must have it with him." He hurried back to the first floor.

"He could be anywhere," she said. "Disoriented and lost in

the woods, or staggering down the highway."

"Where he could end up flattened like a bug on some truck's windscreen. Bloody hell! You check the woods out back and I'll take a jaunt down the road."

They both got moving. The Order would be more than a little upset if he let a sensitive slip through his fingers.

4

Chan answered Danni's call and tried to sound upbeat.

"Hey there. I thought I'd hear from you before this."

"And I thought I'd be calling you before this, but the Special Agent in Charge roped us into a mandatory conference call first thing this morning and it dragged on and on."

"No problem. How's it going?"

"Not so great."

Had her memory returned as well? Had to be cautious here. Didn't want to flat-out ask her about it. If her memory was back, fine, but if not, she'd ask about his and he didn't want to get into it over the phone. Didn't want to lie to her either.

"Not so great in what way?"

"Your friend Pam has been giving me a hard time."

No mention of her memories. Damn. That meant they were still locked up.

"Did you get the sample?"

"I did. But we have a problem."

"Oh?" Just then his phone buzzed. "Hang on a sec. Another call coming through." He didn't recognize the number so he ignored it. If it was important they'd call back later. Danni with a problem was a more pressing issue right now. "Sorry. What's the problem?"

"Pam Sirman is insisting on coming along to Alberta."

"Shit. That's not going to work. She could really mess things up."

"Tell me about it."

"Where are you now?"

"On her front lawn while she throws a few things in a bag."

"Why don't you just leave without her? She probably won't make the trip on her own."

"I would, except she's somehow figured out that we're acting on our own and that you're not connected to the FBI in any way, shape, or form. She's threatened to report me to the Bureau."

"Oh, hell."

The last thing he wanted was to jeopardize Danni's career. He didn't know whether Pam would go through with that or not, but... a lot of anger in that woman.

"She wants the whole story and says the trip will give me plenty of time to tell her. What do I do?"

"I don't think you've got a choice. You've got to take her along. Just don't tell her about Lexie. Pam is a loose cannon."

Danni lowered her voice. "She's no dummy, Chan. She knows her DNA is useless in tracking her husband's body. She's already jumped on the idea that you found her daughter. I can only stonewall her for so long. I'm no good at this stuff. What do I say?"

Chan's mind raced. Lying wasn't in Danni's make up. What could she tell Pam? And then he had it.

"If you have to, tell her I found the grave of a little girl who died during the pandemic and she would have been Julie's age now if she'd survived. I wanted to see if I could get a sample from the grave to check against Pam's."

"That's awful!"

"Hey, I'm just winging it here. It's the best I can do on such short notice. Given a little more time—"

"No, I mean telling a mother someone may have found her child's grave."

"All will be forgiven if Lexie turns out to be Julie Sirman."

"That's a big if. Wait. Here she comes. Gotta go."

And then she was gone. Chan pocketed his phone and wondered if he should keep walking or turn around and go back. He knew he couldn't run from the guilt, and with Pam on the way, the situation here had just become way more complicated than it had been yesterday.

He now remembered everything that had happened in those ten hours, but that didn't mean it made any sense. He needed to sit down with someone who knew the big picture. He could think of only one person who fit that bill: Samuel Lamm.

Okay. He knew where he had to go next.

Just then a battered Mercedes pulled to a stop beside him.

"Get in before you get killed," Ian said.

Yeah, not a bad idea, so Chan did just that.

"You gave us a bit of a fright back at the inn," Ian said as they got rolling. "Your car was still outside but we couldn't find you. We feared something might have happened to you."

"What could have possibly happened?"

"After the way you were ranting and raving in your sleep last night, we feared the worst."

Uh-oh. He hadn't realized...

"Ranting and raving about what?"

"About what happened in Atlantic City. You told me you lost your memories of that night, but they seem to be available to your dreams. Do you remember what you dreamed?"

"The memories..." Chan said. "They're back."

Ian slapped him on the shoulder. "Well, cheers, mate. How does it feel?"

"Not good, Ian. In fact, it feels awful."

"As it should, as it very well should. Because you and your laddies dumped a fucking load of shit on all those thousands of people."

Jarred by the sudden change in tone and demeanor, Chan stared in shock at the grim-faced man riding next to him. Gone was the hale-fellow-well-met innkeeper, replaced by... someone else.

"Wh-what?"

"Your ranting last night made it pretty clear that your lot got yourselves between a couple of the Players and paid the price."

Ian pulled off the highway onto a side road and parked.

"'Players'?" Chan said. "What are you talking about?"

"You were calling them entities in your delirium. I call them *Players*, because this is all a game to them."

Chan was stunned. "You *know* about all this stuff?"

"That's why I'm here, after all. I belong to a group that serves one of the major Players."

Chan suddenly remembered a question Ian had posed to him on his first day at Cliff House: *Who do you serve?*

"Let me get this straight: You 'serve' one of these Players? Why?"

"Like I told you before: We all gotta serve somebody."

"Yeah, yeah, fine." Chan hadn't bought into that then and he didn't now. "But if these Players are so big and powerful, what do they need you for?"

"The Game...like Chess, like any game, it has rules. You can't simply sweep the board clean with your arm and grab the king. You've got to make your moves according to the rules, and the rules of the Game say you've got to work behind the scenes. Interfere in the bugs' lives only now and then, and use a deft touch, as in: Don't reveal yourself when you do. They use humans to do their dirty work."

"So you 'serve' them by helping them interfere in human affairs? That's bullshit. Just tell them to fuck off."

"Well, if it makes you feel better, a heartfelt 'sod-off' is all fine and good. It's not like they'll even notice. Plenty of bugs willing to serve."

Chan found Ian's mindset baffling. He called the entities "Players"... while Kurt had called his entity "the Mind." Since they didn't have names, the entities seemed to leave it to their 'servants' to come up with their own designations.

"So you serve these fuckers, do their bidding for what? To curry favor? What do you get out of it?"

Ian sighed and drummed his fingers on the steering wheel. "All right. Let me give you some perspective. Earth is a sapient world. Despite trillions and trillions of planets orbiting trillions and trillions of stars across the multiverse, sapience is not as common as you might think."

This sounded a lot like what Kurt had told him and Danni on that nightmare night, only he hadn't mentioned a Game. Chan wanted to hear Ian's version so he let him rattle on.

"Sapience makes Earth valuable. But before you go getting a swelled head about it, Earth isn't any more special than any other sapient world. Not a jewel in anybody's crown. It's just another marble to add to the collection. Right now our corner of reality resides in the marble sack of a major Player we'll call 'the Owner.'"

The Owner...that clicked. Kurt had mentioned it. He too had obviously served one of the Players.

"Do I assume you serve the Owner?"

"No, I serve another major player, a rival we'll call 'the Contender.' The Contender covets this particular marble and the job of my group is to do whatever necessary to make it change hands from the Owner's collection to the Contender's."

"Then I guess I can assume that Samuel serves the Owner?"

A quick, tight, almost pitying smile from Ian. "Here's where it gets complicated."

"It's not already?"

"Just wait. Samuel serves a minor rogue entity which has been interfering in the Game. It's become known as 'the Squatter.'"

Hadn't Danni asked him if he'd ever heard of something called "the Squatter"?

"I don't know what the Squatter did," Ian was saying, "or what problem the Owner has with it, but the Owner wants it gone, and the way these beings deal with each other is—"

"The bigger one absorbs the smaller one."

Ian looked at him. "How do you know that?"

"A fellow named Kurt who used to work for Samuel—"

"Used to?"

"He's died not too long ago."

"Oh, right. You ranted about him. He's the one who guided you back into the pinelands."

"Sounds like you were listening pretty closely last night."

"What? Oh, hey, I would much rather have been sleeping, but you were loud, mate. I mean, *really* loud. And let's face it, your raves caught my interest. What else did this Kurt bloke tell you?"

"He said the Squatter, as you call it, was both pissed and afraid because we'd exposed it to the other entities, the ones that destroyed Atlantic City."

"Not 'ones,' mate," Ian said. "*One*. All the credit for that belongs to the Owner, the current keeper of this ant farm."

Ant farm...what a view of human civilization.

"Kurt said 'we're property.'"

Ian's lips twisted. "Did he? Well, this Kurt, whoever he is, may have chosen the wrong entity to serve, but at least he got that right."

"But if this Owner *owns* us..." Chan had a hard time wrapping his mind around that one. "If we're its property, why destroy Atlantic City?"

"Well, first of all, I'll state the obvious: They're not like us. They're *so* not like us that we can't begin to comprehend their thought processes. So I'm just assuming my arse off when I say that the Owner's primary objective was to trap the Squatter and absorb it. But these entities like to play games with us, which is why I call them 'Players.' It knew that pulverizing the city that sat in its path would confound, confuse, and frighten most of us, so it had some fun along the way."

"Fun? A city flattened and twenty-five thousand dead?"

Ian shrugged. "You were aghast at the carnage and terrified it might happen somewhere else, right? You were baffled as to how it happened and what could possibly have caused it, right?"

"Of course!"

"Well, then: mission accomplished."

Could this be true? Was this the state of the universe—or multiverse, as Ian called it? Had it always been like this?

"Kurt told me the entity you're calling the Squatter has been hiding out here on Earth for millions of years... arrived here before humans developed sentience and sapience—back when the Earth was of no interest to the other Players."

"Yeah—*squatting.* We just couldn't be sure where. The Players, even the minor ones, possess a multicentric consciousness, so their exact whereabouts can be difficult to pin down. When I heard Samuel and his community talk about 'serving the Mountain,' I began to suspect that the Squatter had merged with the mountain."

"'Merged'? How did it—I mean, what are these things made of, what do they look like?"

He laughed. "You still don't get it, do you. They don't *look* like anything. They don't *have* shapes. What they're 'made of' is pure intelligence, pure *mind.*"

This was so damn bizarre, so hard to grasp. How could it be? A brain didn't need a mind to exist, but a mind couldn't exist without the support of a brain. Or could it?

"This is all making my head hurt. I'm going to need some time to make sense of it."

"Of course you are. It turns everything wonky. You thought we humans were in charge here when in actuality we are, as your mate Kurt said, property."

Well, Kurt had hardly been a friend—or mate, as Ian put it.

Ian added, "If you want help adjusting to your new mindset, my people can help."

"Your people?"

"The group to which I belong. We've been dealing with the Players for countless generations and we have loremasters who know as much as is humanly possible to know about them."

"Well, if they know so much, why aren't they out telling everybody? This is something people need to know."

"The same reason I didn't tell you anything when you arrived and said you were connecting with Samuel and his crew. Tell me true, mate: If I had told you all this when we sat down with that bottle of cab on Thursday, what would you have thought, eh?"

"Well..."

"You'd've thought, 'He's a daft twat! I'm not staying here!' And who could blame you?"

"But—"

"But the real truth of the matter is that *people don't want to hear it*. It's been that way all through history. They're glad to believe in miracles and can blindly accept things like the transubstantiation, but back in the day, if you went around telling people that we're the playthings of vast, nameless, faceless entities that don't give a shit about us, they'd burn you at the stake or stretch you out on the rack. Those dear old days are gone, fortunately, so nowadays they only brand you as a wazzock or dismiss you as a conspiracy nut."

Chan had to admit he had a point.

"But why would your people want to help me?"

"Well, first off, because you've had a direct encounter. You'd know from firsthand experience that they're talking truth. And secondly, your rantings last night made it abundantly clear that you're a sensitive. We're always interested in sensitives."

"I'm assuming by 'sensitive' you mean pretty much the same as Samuel when he calls me a 'tairongo.'"

"'Tairongo'? That's a new one on me, mate. What language is that?"

"No idea. But I'm gathering it's someone who can sense the mood of what you call the Players."

"Well, then, we're talking about the same thing. And believe me, our Lodge would love to have a sensitive as a member."

"Lodge? You mean like the Masons or the Elks?"

Ian made a face. "Hardly. But like them we have lodges all over the world. The closest one is in Lower Manhattan. I'll be glad to take you there and introduce you."

Chan sensed he was getting the hard sell from Ian. Why? Was he that valuable? He didn't want to commit to anything anywhere right now. Too many balls in the air, especially with Danni and Pam on their way here, and that DNA test in the offing.

But something else was bothering him. Now that Ian, via Chan, had confirmed the presence of the so-called Squatter, what did he plan to do about it?

"What's the next step for you and your fellow servants of the Contender, Ian?"

A casual shrug—perhaps too casual? "Dunno. I'll inform my people of the Squatter's whereabouts and leave the rest to them."

"What'll they do with that info?"

"It's a mere point of information more than anything else. We knew the Squatter was trapped and hiding on Earth but we didn't know where. Now we do. And while the Squatter plays *at* the Game, it's not a real contender in the Game, so not of any great importance to us. The Owner seems to be the one with the grudge against the Squatter, and we're not interested in advancing its agenda. If anything, we want to thwart it."

That was good to know. He didn't want to be responsible for yet another disaster. But then again, how far could he trust Ian?

Chan said, "If the Squatter has merged with the mountain, where are the Owner and the Contender?"

Ian swept a hand at the ceiling of the car. "The major Players—the Owner and the Contender and the rest—are out there, frolicking in the dark matter and dark energy, I guess."

Frolicking?

"But isn't the Owner in the ocean? That's where it came from, as part of the Atlantic upwelling."

"It only appeared that way. It directed a miniscule part of its consciousness toward the Atlantic and plowed a path of destruction toward wherever it was you and your lads exposed the Squatter. The Owner arranged for a little fun along the way but the delay backfired. It never reached the Squatter. You can count on it taking a much more direct approach if the Squatter is ever exposed again."

Not while I'm around, thank you, Chan thought. Nor anyone else if I can help it.

"Let's hope that's not today," he said. "I need to lie down for a while and mull all this."

Ian put the Mercedes in gear. "You should be right knackered. I don't think you got much kip last night."

"I don't feel like I did."

He did feel like taking a nap, but had no intention of indulging. His real plan was to drive up to the mountain and beard Samuel in his den, but he wasn't about to tell Ian. Ian would have a dozen or so questions and none of this was his business. Chan had a feeling that Ian knew too much about him already.

5

Ian was removing a block of Semtex from his footlocker when someone knocked on his bedroom door.

"Who is it?"

"Erica."

He unlocked it and let her in, then relocked it behind her.

"Camo?" she said, looking at his outfit. "Really?"

"Yes, pet. Really. I don't want to stick out when one of their drones does its flyby."

She was staring at the Semtex. "You told me you were just going to confirm the presence of the sigils and their locations. What's that for?"

Might as well tell her.

"I've decided on a more decisive course of action."

"Such as?"

"From Liao's experience in the Jersey Pinelands, I gather that I need take out only four sigils to expose the Squatter."

"Don't bring them here. You heard what happened to Liao's friend. I don't want that happening here, thank you very much."

"Worry not, pet. Nothing and no one will be coming after them because I intend to blast them out of existence—into the proverbial smithereens, as it were. And then you and I can just sit back and watch the fireworks."

She stood silent, her expression troubled. "I wish you'd reconsider."

"I see no reason to."

"Then you'll give me advance warning before you start your fireworks?"

"Of course. I wouldn't want you to miss the show."

"Oh, I very much intend to miss the show. I plan to be far away."

"Going on holiday, are we?"

"A brief sojourn to a warmer clime."

"Afraid?"

"Frankly, yes. These Players have a rather cavalier attitude toward collateral damage, don't you think? Twenty-five thousand dead in Atlantic City? I mean, really!"

"We're just bugs to them, pet. You know that. They don't care if they squash some. Plenty more available."

"You'd be wise to plan a trip of your own."

"You might well be right, but before I can go anywhere I must collect the sensitive and deliver him to the Lodge."

"Speaking of the Lodge, have you informed the boys down at your club what you're planning to do?"

"I plan to tell them all about it—once it's a fait accompli."

"So...you're not cleared for this?"

Ian couldn't help bristle at her tone.

"As you damn well know, I've been a member of the Order for most of my adult life. I don't need 'clearance.' I've earned the right to make command decisions in the field."

"Now-now, Ian-baby, don't get your knickers in a wad. I'm just asking if you're sure that's wise. You told me your boys have special members for matters like this."

He'd had enough of this daft cow.

"Shouldn't you start packing?"

Her eyebrows rose. "When are you planning to start your fireworks?"

"Tomorrow morning."

"Why wait?"

"Because I don't want to miss anything in the dark of night. I want to watch it all go down and enjoy every minute."

"Then maybe I should indeed start throwing some things together."

She unlocked the door and let herself out.

So...you're not cleared for this? Damn her. Her comment still rankled, but he shouldn't have let that set him off. She'd asked a good question. And the answer was no, he wasn't cleared for something like this. If he inquired at the Lodge about whether or not he should take action, he knew their answer: *We're sending an Actuator to sort it. Do nothing until he arrives, at which time you will stand ready to supply whatever assistance he requires.*

Bollocks to that. He was the one who had sat up all night listening to Liao's ranting. He was the one who had gleaned all the pertinent facts, like the location of the sigils and how many had to be removed to expose the Squatter. After all that effort was he about to hand over all his intel to some prima donna Actuator and let him take the glory? Not bloody likely.

The Order would want the Squatter eliminated. Though it posed no threat to the Order's mission, it muddied the waters. The fact that they could effect its removal via their rival entity was a definite bonus.

But doing this on his own had its risks. No question about that. If it all went pear-shaped, he would suffer repercussions. The potential for enormous rewards, though, far outweighed the risks involved. If he showed up at the Lodge tomorrow with a sensitive in tow after single-handedly causing the elimination of a pesky rogue player, he'd have proven beyond a doubt that he could take decisive action. Here was a brother who could get things done. His elevation to Actuator status would be assured.

Erica stuck her head back into the room. "I thought you'd like to know, dear brother, that I just saw our guest take off in his car."

"Why didn't you stop him?"

"And how was I going to do that? Besides, he was already on his way out the drive when I spotted him."

"Which way did he turn?"

"Left. Not to worry. He's left all his gear here."

Probably going to the mountain to see Samuel. What Ian wouldn't give to be a fly on the wall of that confrontation. Liao wasn't at all happy about having his memories suppressed.

But Ian had more important concerns. He had to locate four of the sigils and wire them with Semtex, all without being seen. The job might well take him the rest of the day.

He grabbed his remote detonators from their insulated box

and stuffed them in a leg pocket of his camo pants. He needed daylight to get this all properly sorted, so he'd better get started right away.

6

Chan waved to Henry as he stopped at the gate. They exchanged a few pleasantries and commented on the weather, then Chan said, "I need to see Samuel. Is he here?"

"He's pretty much always here, but not today. He passed through on his way out just about an hour ago."

"Where'd he go?"

Henry laughed. "Like he tells me, right?"

"Yeah, okay. I get you. Did he happen to say when he'd be back? I need to discuss a few things with him."

"That he did say: late tonight."

Damn. He'd have to put off the confrontation until tomorrow.

Chan thanked Henry, then turned his car around and headed back.

7

Ian had just reached the top of the fence when he heard the hum of an approaching drone. With no time to climb down, he launched himself backward into the brush, threw his camoed arms across his face to hide it, and lay still.

He heard it cruise past along the inside of the fence at a leisurely pace, and then its hum faded away.

The wankers! When had they changed their drone schedule? Over the years he'd been up here on numerous occasions to time its rounds. It used to run at 10 a.m., 4 p.m., and midnight. Here it was only 2:30. Why had they—?

And then he knew: All the trouble Chan and company had caused by stealing the sigils in the pinelands. That had been a couple of months ago. Ian would bet his last penny that was when the increased vigilance had started. Which meant he'd have to be extra vigilant as well.

He got up, climbed the fence again—the chain link made it easy. And with no concertina wire along the top, getting over was a piece of cake. When he landed on the other side, he found himself face to face with one of the sigils. Like the two he'd already wired, this one was decorated with another odd-looking squiggle.

Before leaving the inn, he'd pre-cut the Semtex into roughly one-inch-square bricks. Now, as with the preceding sigils, he stuck a wad of the malleable, reddish plastique against the rear of the plaque. Then he inserted the business end of the remote detonator cap into the wad and clear-taped it down.

Very risky using a remote-controlled detonator cap in a city where the air was chock-a-block full of RF signals. But out here in the wilds of the Catskills, the chance of a random RF signal matching a detonator's was vanishingly slim to none. He'd left the controller back at the inn sans batteries. No way its signal could ever reach this far, but that was the sort of person he was.

All righty, he had three wired now. The gate was at the south corner, so obviously the sigil there was not a candidate. He'd started on the southeast corner, then moved to the east corner, and now he'd just finished the northeast corner.

For all he knew, that might be enough. According to Chan's rambles, though, his mate Aldo had revealed the Squatter by nicking four of them. Yeah, destroying three might do the job, but Ian wasn't going to risk it. He'd do four for sure.

He climbed the fence again and headed for the north corner. Samuel's security people had cut a path along the inside of the perimeter for when they did foot patrols or needed a closer look at something they'd spotted with their drones, but Ian wasn't about to risk that. The deer trail outside the fence made hiking through here almost as easy. These hills were lousy with deer and every time a herd came up against the Squatter's perimeter, they moved parallel to it, looking for a way past. But they never found an opening. The only break was at the gate and they weren't about to brave that. So around and around they went, following the same path over and over, flattening the undergrowth with their hooves, breaking off branches with their flanks. All of which allowed someone like Ian to move at very near a trot.

The north corner sigil would bring the total of those ready for demolition to four. He had six detonator caps so, just for good measure, he'd wire a fifth at the northwest corner if he found the time before dark.

8

Chan had just pulled to a stop in the Cliff House parking area when Danni called.

"Hey," he said. "I'm almost afraid to ask."

"You mean how it's going? It's actually going pretty well."

He heard Pam shout, "We've bonded! We're fucking BFFs now!"

"Did you hear that?" Danni said.

"How could I not? Color me surprised. Or as Pam would say, 'fucking shocked.' How'd this come about?"

"Well, once she realized I was on her side, we relaxed with each other and found out we had a lot in common."

"Except the lesbo thing!" Pam shouted. "I'm not into chicks!"

Chan tried to imagine the conversation in that car to this point and immediately got a headache.

"What's your ETA?"

"Eighty-six minutes, according to WAZE. That's why I'm calling: Where do we stay?"

"I'm at a nice little B and B called Cliff House. It's off season so I'm their only guest. Plenty of room at the inn, so to speak."

"How do you feel about a B and B?" he heard her say to Pam.

Faintly, Pam said, "Fine with me—as long as you don't think we're sharing a room."

To Chan, Danni said, "Sounds good. Where is it?"

"On Route 23. Call me when you reach Wyndham Mountain and I'll guide you in."

"Got it. Over and out."

Chan went inside. He'd noticed Ian's car was gone so he looked for Erica. When he knocked on her door she opened it a crack and peeked out.

"Can I help you?"

Chan spotted an open suitcase on the bed behind her.

"Yes. I'd like to reserve two rooms for later today. Some friends are coming."

"How nice," she said with a smile. "Reservations are hardly necessary at this time of year, but meet me at the desk and I'll be glad to take their names."

Chan moved down the hall and waited for her as instructed. A few seconds later she joined him and he gave her Danni and Pam's names.

"Going somewhere?" he said as she wrote them down.

Her pen stopped writing, then restarted.

"Yes. A bit of a holiday. I like to get a change of scenery while things are slow."

"Sounds nice. Where?"

"I don't like to plan these getaways. There's a travel agent in Catskill I use. I just pop 'round and see what bargains she can find for me in the southern climes."

"When are you leaving?"

"Tomorrow morning. But not to worry: Ian will be here to take care of everything."

Chan wished her bon voyage and headed for his room. Something different about her today. He'd met Erica only forty-eight hours ago, and she'd struck him as someone who had herself under rigid control. Today she seemed tense and anxious. And the way she'd opened her room door... as if she didn't want him to see that she was packing for a trip. Why try to hide it?

He gave a mental shrug as he entered his room and flopped on the bed. He had more important concerns. Because here in the quiet, without distractions, a deep sadness tightened his throat. With no memory of those hours, he'd been able to deal with his missing friends. Yes, Mac and Aldo were presumed dead, but *presumed* lacked certainty. Hey, they could be alive. Presumed dead wasn't definitely dead.

But any trace of uncertainty he'd been clinging to had fled now. Poor Aldo... Chan hadn't seen him die but he'd seen the aftermath, seen how his entire body—everything except his face—looked like it had been put through a blender. The Squatter—the all-hallowed Mountain—had done that.

But Mac's fate had been worse. Dragged off into the darkness to a gruesome, violent, watery death by creatures released by another entity—the so-called Owner. He squeezed his eyes shut but that did nothing to blot out the memory of a panicked Mac clawing at the muddy ground as a tentacle belonging to some unseen monstrosity dragged him feet first through the storm toward God knows what. And Danni there heroically hacking at it with Kurt's machete and then falling victim herself. Chan remembered hacking at the ropy, rubbery thing around her ankle only to see Mac dragged into the darkness by a third tentacle around his throat.

Chan wanted to scream. Instead, he sobbed.

Is knowing the facts what they call closure? he wondered. Is this what friends and families look for after the loss of a loved one? Guess what? It doesn't help.

And the worst part: He and Danni had never got the chance to help each other over the trauma, had never been able to talk out what had happened to their friends, because minutes later they found themselves on a road miles away with no memory of Mac and Aldo's deaths.

He may have dozed off, but his phone woke him: Danni.

"We just passed the Wyndham Mountain entrance," she said. "How much farther?"

"About three miles, but this place is easy to miss. I'll walk out to the highway and flag you down."

As he ended the call, he went to get a fresh undershirt—his last—from the dresser and spotted the half-chewed wad of Big Red in the baggie... the gum he planned to give Danni, a wad that might contain the DNA of Pam's missing daughter. How had he forgotten that? The trauma of reclaiming the lost memories had blasted it out of his mind.

Forgetting the fresh shirt, he jammed the baggie into a pocket and headed out to the highway. By the time he reached it Danni's Volvo was already approaching from the east. Forcing a smile, he waved her in like a curbside parking lot shill.

He got a hug from Danni when she got out of the car, but

Pam stayed on the far side, giving him a hard look.

"Don't expect a hug from me, Sonny Boy. I've got a bone to pick with you."

Uh-oh. Now what?

"What did I do?"

"You spent that whole fucking afternoon with me letting me think you worked for the FBI when you were really working for yourself."

He held up his hands, palms out. "Guilty. No excuse. I apologize."

Her expression said she'd expected a list of excuses.

"Yeah, well, okay, apology accepted. No harm done, I suppose. And at least I learned a lot about the guy I'd been married to, even though I wasn't exactly happy knowing it."

Chan reached across the Volvo's roof. "Friends?"

"Friends," she said as they shook.

"Great. You and Danni go register while I bring in the luggage."

They didn't have much and he needed only one trip.

After Erica had shown them to their rooms, she handed Chan a bottle of red wine and a corkscrew.

"Ian phoned that he'll be a little late, so would you be so kind as to open this as the five o'clock wine?"

Chan wondered if she was afraid to get that close to an open bottle.

"No problem."

He opened it and set it out to breathe in the breakfast room, then headed for Danni's. She answered his soft knock.

"How much does she know?" he whispered once the door had closed behind him.

"I told her about Kurt Maez being fireproof and his body stolen."

"But not about his child, I hope."

"No. That was a can of worms I wasn't ready to open."

"Good. And on the subject of children..." He fished the snack bag out of his pocket. "Here's a wad of gum straight from the mouth of the little girl I suspect of being Julie Sirman."

She took the bag, stared at it, then at him. "This is perfect.

I won't even ask how you managed it. But I should warn you, I dodged a lot of Pam's questions by putting them off on you. She's got a bundle of them."

"That's okay." He hesitated. He fought an urge to open up to her about his memory, but knew he could do it only by increments. "Look, some of my memory has come back."

Her eyes widened. "Lamm was able to help?"

"No. It seemed spontaneous, but I think seeing Lamm might have triggered it because we both met him that night."

"Where? In the city?"

"No. He and Kurt Maez were out in the pinelands during the storm. It's all very vague. I don't have much more to tell you."

He couldn't bring himself to tell her they were responsible for everything that happened to the city.

"Well, at least it's something. That means there's hope."

No, Danni, he thought. No hope.

After what he'd learned about their place in the cosmos, hope was a fiction.

"Gather up Pam and we'll have some wine here and then find a place for dinner."

"We passed an Italian place in Wyndham we thought looked good."

"Great. Just get it across to Pam that Cliff House is not a good place to discuss private matters and I'll answer any questions I can at the restaurant."

9

Pam had suffered through a couple of glasses of wine at the inn, holding back her questions because Danni had said the walls had ears and didn't need to know their concerns.

Chan had made a big deal of showing them this painting he'd bought, done by "one of the local kids." Her first thought had been who'd spend money on a painting by a kid, especially a painting of nothing? But she'd found the swirls of color interesting, mesmerizing in a way.

After that they'd all made the quick drive in Chan's car to this Italian place.

"Okay," Pam said once they'd ordered their before-dinner drinks, "I've held my tongue this long, so now I want some fucking answers."

Chan leaned forward and spoke in a low voice. "I'll share whatever I know, but the trouble is, I don't know much. That's why I'm up here: to fill in the blanks."

He sounded sincere, so maybe he'd give her an honest answer when she asked about the elephant in the room, though she wasn't sure she wanted that answer. Okay...here goes...

"Why did you ask Danni to get a DNA sample from me?"

He nodded like he'd been expecting that one. "Fair question. I want to be very careful how I answer you because I don't want you taking my words the wrong way and getting your hopes up about a very, very, very long, almost impossibly long shot."

"That's not a fucking answer, Chan."

"I know that. I just hope you heard me."

"Heard and understood. Get on with it."

"Okay. I've become involved with a community that lives up on a mountain in the town where your husband said he grew up with his aunt. Kurt Maez, whose body also wouldn't burn and was also stolen, was working on a property linked to the same mountain.

She couldn't believe this. "That's it? What's my DNA got to do with that?"

"I'm telling you what brought me up here," Chan said. "But this community I mentioned includes about two dozen children of all ages. A couple of them are seven-year-old girls, one of whom did that painting I showed you. I—"

She thought her heart might stop. "You think one of them might be Julie?"

He gave an elaborate shrug. "How can I answer that? That's why I wanted your DNA."

"Have you got DNA from those girls?"

"That's a whole other level of difficulty. I can't just ask their mothers for it, can I? A little subterfuge will be necessary. That's why I wanted to get your sample without telling you why. You can see I've got almost nothing to go on."

Was he telling her he didn't have a sample? She assumed so, but a simple yes or no would have sufficed.

The drinks came then. About time. Chan had a Manhattan, Danni a white wine, Pam took a gulp of her straight-up, three-olive vodka martini without waiting for a toast.

"Bring me another one right now," she told the waitress. "As in *immediately*." To Chan and Danni she said, "Hey, I'm not driving and I fucking need this tonight."

"No problem," Chan said. "I understand perfectly."

After another gulp, she said, "Obviously you've seen these kids. How are they being treated?"

"They're treasured," he said.

Well, that was a relief.

"Pam," Danni said slowly, "let's just suppose that, against all odds, you learn you have a mother-daughter match with one of these girls. What would you do?"

"You mean after I stopped crying my eyes out?" She thought about that a moment. Julie alive and well… an impossible dream come true. "To tell you the truth, I don't know. Chan and I discussed this a little. I guess it all hinges on whether her… I'll call them the 'foster parents' for want of a better term… it would all hinge on how much they knew."

"You mean about where Julie came from?"

"Right."

Chan said, "Not many men around up there. Seems like most of the parenting is done by the women."

"Okay. 'Foster mother,' then. If she thought this baby she received was an orphan or abandoned or given up for adoption by some sixteen-year-old somewhere, that's one thing. But if she knew the baby was stolen away from its natural mother and she kept her anyway…well, that's a whole other thing."

"And that's when you call me in."

"You?"

"The FBI. Going after kidnappers is in our bailiwick."

"Oh, right, right. I've kind of stopped thinking of you as a fed." She leaned back and thought about that for a sec. "Call in the feds… your people didn't do squat when she went missing, but now, if someone finds her for you, I'm sure you'll do a bang-up job of ripping her from the arms of the woman she's called 'Mom' all her life. And I'd be the culprit. She'll hate me, won't she? I know if places were reversed, I'd hate this woman who took my mommy away and now expects me to call *her* mommy. Julie wouldn't understand how she could really be *my* child when all her life she's been that other woman's little girl."

Pam paused to finish her martini and chew on an olive. Danni and Chan watched her in silence. So Pam went on, thinking out loud.

"So whether the foster mother was guilty or innocent, Julie's going to be traumatized. It's a no-win situation for her. As for the mother, if she knows Julie was kidnapped, she can rot in hell. But if she's innocent, if she thinks she got Julie through a legit adoption, then my heart breaks for her. She took in what she thought was an unwanted child and raised her as her own, and she's going to be devastated when she loses her."

Pam remembered how devastated she was when she'd learned Julie had disappeared, and she'd had her for only a day. Okay, she'd been kicking inside her for months before that. But this woman will have had Julie for *seven years*.

She shook her head. "No winners here. Not Julie, not her foster mother, not even me, because I'll be traumatizing my only child, maybe damaging her for life."

She felt a tear start running down her cheek and she quickly wiped it away. Danni reached over and squeezed her hand.

Pam forced a smile that must have looked hideous. "Aren't you glad you asked?"

Her second martini arrived then and she grabbed it and took a gulp.

"I never thought I'd say this," she said, "but maybe no match on the DNA will be a good thing."

Danni gave her hand another squeeze. "Hey, I noticed something while you were talking about Julie. You didn't say 'fuck' once."

"That's because I've always said, if I ever get my little girl back, I'll retire Potty-mouth Pam and be the world's best mother. Gotta set a good example for your children, right?"

Nobody argued with her.

SUNDAY

1

Chan thought about last night as he drove through the morning sunshine toward the mountain's gate. Pam had downed a third martini along with wine at dinner. He and Danni had poured her into bed, then said goodnight.

Neither of the women had made an appearance this morning by the time Chan left for the mountain. A good thing. He couldn't very well explain that he was confronting Samuel on aspects of his recovered memory.

Henry was at the gate again.

"Don't you ever get a day off?" he said as he stopped.

Henry laughed. "I'm only on every third weekend, so it's not so bad. You're looking for Samuel, I'm guessing."

"Yes. I hope he's back."

"Yep. Log book shows he arrived at ten twenty last night."

"Great. Where do I find him?"

Henry scratched his chin. "Well, he lives upstairs at the fort, but he often visits the classrooms during school hours. Seeing as it's Sunday, though, your best bet would be the fort."

Chan thanked him and cruised through the gate into the welcoming warmth of the mountain's aura.

Wait…shouldn't he stop calling it that? After all, the placid atmosphere here wasn't due to the mountain itself but to the amorphous cosmic entity hiding within it. He knew Samuel was aware of it—their encounter at the septagon in the pinelands had made that abundantly clear. And surely the First, whoever that was, was aware as well. But what about the rest of the community? Were the hoi polloi up here—people like Henry and Nicolette and Daphne, for instance—aware of the rogue entity known as the Squatter? Or was that knowledge reserved for the upper echelons? Nicolette seemed too smart to buy into the Magic Mountain mystique, but then, lots of intelligent people held strange beliefs.

Well, this was another question for that bastard, Samuel.

Speaking of Nicolette, he thought as he passed the open areas, there she is.

She was watching some of the boys—Wayne among them—as they kicked a soccer ball around an open area. A car driving through was the exception rather than the rule, so he drew a fair amount of attention as he passed. She recognized him and waved and smiled. He returned both but kept on rolling.

He really liked Nicolette—in bed, of course, but out of bed as well. He liked simply being with her. But what if Wayne was not hers?

Damn, he wished to hell he could get these questions out of his head. But ever since he'd seen that port wine stain on Lexie's fingers, they wouldn't let up. And he couldn't simply dismiss them. They mattered.

Nicolette had said she'd had a husband. Chan had to assume they'd had a child together before he died. That was all fine and he'd be happy to raise Wayne as his own if it ever came to that. But what if he wasn't hers? What if he'd been stolen away like Pam's child, and Kurt's child? If so, did Nicolette know?

"Stop it!" he said to the windshield.

He was making himself crazy. And the only way to quiet the ceaseless questions was to learn the truth. Samuel knew the truth. This was his Family and he damn well knew everything about it.

Farther on, the playground was occupied strictly by girls of varying ages. Chan guessed that if you were segregating the sexes, you'd especially want to keep them apart at playtime.

He parked before the fort. The big wooden door was closed. Did he knock or walk right in. Hell, he was their valued tairongo. Who was going to stop him? He pushed and it swung easily.

The great room inside was deserted. No, not quite. Samuel had just entered the stairwell that led to the second floor. Chan was about to call out to him but decided instead to follow. Maybe he could meet this secretive First.

As Chan entered the stairwell, he saw Samuel pushing through a modern steel security door at the top. He rushed up the stone steps and caught the door just before it latched. As he stepped through, he froze at the sight of the being that stood before him.

He had the heavy brow ridges, sloping forehead, wide nose, and jutting jaw of a caveman, but he was clean shaven with a neat haircut. His barrel chest was garbed in a Ralph Lauren polo shirt; khaki slacks covered his short legs. His feet were shod in leather slippers.

"You're not allowed up here!" he said in a deep voice. "Go back downstairs."

The door latched behind Chan as he took a step back. Shock robbed him of his voice for a few heartbeats, but finally he said, "I-I-I need to speak to Samuel."

"I'll see to it that he meets you downstairs." He pointed to the door. "Now go."

"This won't wait."

"Go!" the caveman shouted.

Samuel appeared from around a corner. "He's already seen you," he said. "He might as well stay."

Chane took in the room. One wall was festooned with monitors. Was this a surveillance center of some sort? And near where Samuel had stopped, an odd artifact hung on the wall, maybe two-foot long, an inch thick, looped on top like an ankh but with a pointed base and its side arms jutting at odd angles, and fashioned of the blackest material he had ever seen. It reminded him of Prince's Artist Formally Known As symbol but lacked the Nike swoosh under the loop.

Samuel casually caressed it with his hand and said, with barely concealed annoyance, "What is so important that you had to invade our private quarters?"

"My memory of those lost hours returned last night," he said, feeling a fury rising. "Along with the memory of how I lost them."

Samuel and the caveman looked at each other.

"They unblocked spontaneously?" the caveman said.

The question threw Chan for an instant. "As far as I know. What sort of question is that?"

"You took no drugs or hallucinogens?"

Chan shook his head. "I don't do that stuff."

"They wouldn't come back on their own unless triggered. You were dosed with something last night."

That would explain the groggy feeling this morning. Ian... had to be Ian. And it had to have been the coffee. But that wasn't important now.

"What I want to know is *why*? Why did you block those hours?"

Samuel said, "I'll answer by asking you how you feel now that you have them back?"

How did he feel?

"I...I feel terrible. I feel...responsible. All those people... gone."

"That was why," Samuel said. "You seemed like a decent man, and none of what happened was your fault, and... you're a tairongo. I didn't want you tortured by guilt."

Chan couldn't tell if that was true or not. He sensed it was, and he could guess why.

"Because you were looking to recruit me for your Family up here?"

Samuel nodded. "That too, of course."

"Here's the thing," Chan said. "I suddenly know a lot of... stuff...facts... but so much of it makes no sense."

Samuel said, "Tell us what you think you know and we'll try to make sense of it for you."

"Do you think that's wise?" said the caveman.

Chan turned to him. "You seem to know who I am, but who are you?"

"This is the First," Samuel said.

"And to spare us both some awkwardness," said the

caveman, "I look like a *Homo neanderthalensis* because that's exactly what I am. But we'll get to that later."

The First was a Neanderthal? Chan realized he was gaping at him and shut his mouth.

"Wait. You can't drop a bomb like that and then just blithely move on to another topic."

"Trust me, it's all connected," Samuel said. "It's better if we settle the big questions first. So... what do you think you know?"

"All right. I know that what you call 'the Mountain' and Kurt called 'the Mind' is really..." He realized he couldn't refer to it as "the Squatter" because he doubted Samuel thought of it that way. "It's really some sort of cosmic entity that has been hiding here for millions of years."

"Hiding from what?" the First said.

"From another cosmic entity that wants to absorb it, the one called the Owner. My friends and I inadvertently removed some of its protections from a part of it and Atlantic City wound up being destroyed by the Owner."

And Chan would carry that guilt for the rest of his life.

"Very succinctly put," Samuel said.

"But what I don't understand is what's going on *here*. Why do I feel so good once I come through that gate, when all the rest of my life I've felt like I had some sort of threat hanging over me?"

"The Mountain—we're used to referring to the entity that way, so let's continue with that, shall we? It deliberately exudes that feeling. We non-tairongos sense it subliminally as a vague, homey feeling, and that makes us want to stay here, but for you it must seem like coming in from a winter storm. The sigils create a two-way barrier that masks the presence of the Mountain, preventing the other entities from sensing it, while shielding all within its borders from outside influences. It's a safe haven for one such as you."

"But that's all very cosmic," Chan said. "Let's get down to the human level. Where do you two come in? I mean, how does a Neanderthal man fit into the scheme of things here?"

Samuel glanced at the First. "Do you want to start this off?"

"I'll give it a try," he said without enthusiasm. "When our

entity—the Mountain—came here millions of years ago, the primates were a long way from developing any intelligence. But eventually they did. We suspect that another of the entities helped them along, but that's neither here nor there. Bottom line: Our entity knew that would attract cosmic attention. To act in this world while hidden, the Mountain needed surrogates, and when my species came along, it chose us."

"Neanderthals."

"It had used primates long before, but we were the first hominids to be chosen, thus my designation. We didn't call ourselves Neanderthals, of course. We called ourselves—" He made a coarse, grunting sound. "Which meant 'the people.' We were saddled with 'Neanderthal' when our remains were first discovered in Germany's Neandertal Valley."

"But wait. If the entity was here in the Mountain, and you were thousands of miles away on another continent, how—?"

"—did it know about us? The Mountain is not a single consciousness. It has centers of awareness here and there around the planet, much like the one you encountered in the pinelands. It didn't need so much protection back then. But as human sapience increased, this corner of reality attracted more and more attention, and the Mountain needed deep cover. Especially when an enemy entity, the very one the Mountain was hiding from, claimed Earth for its own."

"So it used Neanderthals to help hide it."

"Exactly. But unfortunately for the Mountain, we Neanderthals proved an evolutionary dead end. Traces of our DNA still exist in modern humans, but we became extinct as a species. So it next chose Cro-Magnons." He gestured to Samuel. "Which is where you come in."

"Wait," Chan said. "You're Cro-Magnon?"

Samuel nodded. "Yes, though they have fancier names for us now."

The broad forehead, the broad face, the big teeth... the differences from modern humans were subtle, but now that he'd been labeled "Cro-Magnon"... sure.

"But-but-but..." I sound like a motorboat, Chan thought. "But the Neanderthals died out a long time ago."

"Somewhere around forty thousand years ago," the First said. "Not long after the Laschamps excursion when north became south and south became north and the skies came alive with lights every night."

"But surely you're not..."

A slow nod. "Yes, I'm that old. The last Neanderthal. All of my kind chosen along with me by the Mountain have perished from one cause or another over the course of those many millennia."

"But that would make you forty thousand years old."

"Closer to seventy."

"Jesus!" Chan couldn't believe this. "But how is that possible?"

The First spread his hands in an almost priestly gesture. "The Mountain bestows many gifts. Service brings a better brain, a better body, and a long, long life."

"But seventy thousand years! And you never became tired of all this and decided you wanted out?"

The First's smile took on a grim twist. "You don't. That's another gift: boundless devotion to the Mountain."

Chan turned to Samuel. "And you?"

"The last Cro-Magnon," he said with a little bow. "We outlasted the Neanderthals and eventually merged with present-day *Homo sapiens*. But I'm still one hundred percent Cro-Magnon."

"But what about us *Homo saps*? Didn't the Mountain tap any of us?"

"No need to as long as we Cro-Magnons could move freely about your world after you took over. But over the millennia our ranks have suffered from attrition as well. So now, with the First and I as all that's left of the archaic humans who have served it, the Mountain has turned its attentions to *Homo sapiens*."

"You're talking about the men, women, and children who live here on the mountain?" He couldn't help thinking about Nicolette. "Have they been changed by the Mountain?"

"Yes and no. The Mountain is taking a different approach with them."

"Samuel," the First said, "I think you have said enough for

now. You might be straying into a touchy area."

Samuel pursed his lips. "Perhaps you're right."

"No-no!" Chan said, waving his hands. "This is what I need to know before I make my home here. I have to know who I'll be living with."

He hoped that would sway them, because they very clearly wanted him here.

Samuel turned to the First. "He has a point."

"I think it unwise to go any further."

"But he already knows more than his predecessor. He has already confronted a rival entity and survived. I certainly think we can trust him with this."

Trust him? Trust him with what? He had a bad feeling about what might be coming, but he had to *know*, damn it.

The First raised his hands in surrender. "Very well, but I want to go on record as being opposed. Do what you wish. You always do anyway."

It sounded as if these two had butted heads before.

Samuel turned to Chan. "When I was in business, running a corporation—"

"TonaTech," Chan said, then shrugged. "I looked you up."

Samuel smiled. "I should have guessed. Well, anyway, during my tenure as CEO I kept my eye out for the best and the brightest men and women of varying ethnic backgrounds among the youngest job applicants. Whenever I found one, I brought him or her to the Mountain where they were… enhanced."

Kurt had used that term.

"'Enhanced'? Enhanced how?"

"First off, their genomes were cleaned up by removing any harmful recessive genes."

"But if I remember my freshman biology course, recessive genes aren't causing any harm."

"I should have said 'potentially' harmful recessives. They can cause problems for future generations. Also, they received physical enhancements such as stronger bones and tougher skin, and so on."

Something clicked in Chan's mind. "Would that 'tougher skin' happen to be fireproof?"

Samuel stared at him a moment before replying. "Since you've already met Kurt Maez, should I assume that you're aware of what happened to him?"

"You should. I witnessed the crash."

The First stepped forward. "Did you, now? We were not aware of that. What were the circumstances?"

"I encountered him at the sepatgon in the pinelands. I had no idea I'd already met him weeks before. He raced off and I followed him because I had questions to ask. He lost control, slammed into an abutment, and the van exploded."

"Then it was an accident?" the First said.

Strange question. "As opposed to intentional? Sure looked that way. Why do you ask?"

"We were just wondering."

"Why? Was he suicidal?"

"Obviously not," Samuel said quickly. "I am guessing the accident was when you saw that his body didn't burn."

"Yeah. And then when I read that Philip Sirman's wouldn't burn either, I made a connection. So... both Maez and Sirman agreed to be 'enhanced' by the Mountain?"

Samuel shook his head. "No. I brought them here on the pretense of showing them the community I was planning, and asked if they'd be interested. The Mountain enhanced them while they were here."

Chan couldn't hide his shock. "Without asking their permission?"

Both Samuel and the First stared at him with baffled expressions.

"The Mountain does not ask for permission," the First said. "It is the Mountain."

Chan remembered Ian saying the entities thought of humans as "bugs" and that Earth was the Owner's "ant farm." He decided not to mention Ian or his connection to a rival entity.

"Did the enhancements to these people include the 'boundless devotion to the Mountain' you mentioned before?"

The First smiled as if he were discussing a precious gift. "Of course."

To Samuel, Chan said, "You mentioned that you brought

men and women up here. Have Nicolette and Daphne been enhanced as well?"

Samuel nodded proudly. "Oh, yes."

Shit!

He didn't know why he was upset. She'd probably have a longer, healthier life for all that. He should be glad for her. So why wasn't he?

"Was this what you were worried about trusting me with?" he said to the First.

The First gave a puzzled frown. "That they've been enhanced? No, of course not."

"You mean you told them the Mountain changed them?"

"Of course. Once they knew the Mountain wanted them, they were happy they'd been the object of its beneficence."

Oh, right...their "boundless devotion to the Mountain" was in play. Another term for it might be "brainwashing."

"Was Nicolette's late husband 'enhanced' as well?"

"Of course."

"Were their enhancements passed on to their son?"

Samuel frowned. "Their son? No, Nicolette can't conceive. None of the women can."

An Arctic wind blew through Chan and he felt as if he were turning to ice. Because there it was, what he'd dreaded to hear, the awful truth, straight from the horse's mouth, so to speak.

2

Pam was just pouring herself a second cup of coffee when Danni appeared at the door of the breakfast room.

"Morning," Danni said. She wore jeans and a crew-neck sweater. "You seen Chan? I just checked his room and he's not there. Car's gone too."

"I haven't seen a soul since I got up. But this coffee is awesomely strong. What the fuck is this coffee-maker contraption?"

"It's a French press, but I don't recall ever seeing one that big. I'll bet Ian got a hernia pushing on that plunger."

"I think I'm gonna have to get me one," she said as she watched Danni pour herself a cup and sip. "You drink it black?"

Danni nodded and made a face. "Usually, but I might make an exception for this stuff. Wow, this *is* strong." She reached for the cream pitcher.

"Fucking Brits know how to make coffee. Same with scones. Try one. They taste homemade."

A clatter came from out in the hall.

"Well, at least we're not the only ones in the building," Danni said.

Pam waited for someone to show up, but when no one did, she went out into the hall and found Erica struggling with a large suitcase.

"Need help?"

"That's okay, thanks. I've got it."

But she obviously didn't, so Pam grabbed the handle at the underside and helped her out the door to where an SUV sat with its rear hatch up. Together they struggled it into the rear.

"That's fucking heavy," Pam said. "You moving out or something?"

"Oh, no." A nervous laugh. "Going to put some things in storage before I go on holiday."

Pam wondered why she had trouble believing that.

"Why isn't that brother of yours helping? Afraid he'll break a nail?"

After another laugh that sounded even more nervous, Erica said, "No, Ian isn't like that. He's out in the woods somewhere."

"He's a hunter?" He hadn't seemed like the type.

"No, just hiking."

Danni strolled out with her coffee cup and Erica again went through her going-on-holiday explanation.

"Deserting us?" Danni said with a hurt expression. "Was it something we said?"

"Oh, no!" Erica blurted. "I had this trip planned before you arrived. No-no, you two are absolutely lovely people and..." She paused and stared at Danni. "You're winding me up, aren't you."

The picture of innocence, Danni said, "Who me? Whatever could you mean?"

Pam decided she really liked her.

"Oh, posh. Ian will be back right soon if you need anything. Can I do something for you now?"

"No, we're good," Pam said.

Erica slammed the hatch. "Well, I'll be off then. Cheers. Have a good day and enjoy your stay."

They stood and watched her roar off down the highway.

"You know," Danni said, "if I didn't know better I'd say she was running away."

"*Do* you know better?"

She shook her head. "Not at all."

"We'll have to ask Ian about that when he returns."

"Well, I'm not about to wait for him out here," Danni said. "There's a scone in there with my name on it."

"Good idea. I believe I'm due for another."

As they headed back inside it occurred to Pam that Erica looked almost afraid. No, she definitely looked afraid. Fucking scared. What was there to be scared of around here?

3

"Did I hear you right?" Chan said when he'd found his voice. "The enhanced women here in your community can't get pregnant?"

Samuel nodded. "Correct. The plan had been to have the enhanced *Homo sapiens* interbreed and pass their enhancements on to subsequent generations and start a race of *Homo superior.*"

This was sounding worse and worse.

"A master race?"

"No, of course not!" Samuel said with a soft laugh. "Smarter, healthier, more long-lived than the average human, but the goal is not to rule. The goal is to better the lot of those average humans and to counter the machinations of the Owner and its rival entities. But unfortunately the enhancements by the Mountain left the women unable to produce viable ova."

"But the males are fertile?" Chan said, feeling his mouth go dry.

"Yes. Quite."

"So the solution was…?"

As Chan waited for an answer, the First said, "I think this might be a good place to stop. We can return to this subject another time."

"Too late," Chan said. "I already know your solution: You created false identities for your enhanced males and sent them out to impregnate average females, and then you stole their offspring, right?"

"Exactly," Samuel said in a maddeningly casual, matter-of-fact tone. "But we were careful. We spread the males out all over the North and South America and Europe. We limited the harvesting to only a few per year so as not to raise suspicions or attract undue attention."

"'Harvesting'? Do you really call it *harvesting*?"

"It's a rather apt term for the process, don't you think? We plant the seed, wait for it to germinate, then harvest the brand-new sprout."

It took pretty much every ounce of restraint Chan possessed to hold back from launching himself at Samuel's throat.

"But all that aside," Samuel went on in that same matter-of-fact tone, "over the years we've moved nearly a dozen children of each sex here and we're raising them in the presence of the mountain's influence. When they're old enough, they'll intermarry and their children will be *Homo superior*. And when those children mature, they'll go out and change this world into a better place for all people."

He might have been talking about plucking tomatoes from his garden for all the concern he showed for the victimized families. Chan wanted to punch his face.

He was supposed to be a *xiānzhī*, a tairongo, a sensitive. Why hadn't he sensed the ugliness perking under the surface here? Had the Mountain's influence blocked it? A sudden sadness nearly overwhelmed him. This was no place for him. Why did he ever think he could make a life here?

He took a breath. Self-pity sucked. These people had done so much worse to others.

"Do you have any idea of the pain and heartache you've caused those mothers?"

"I'm sure there's been some anguish, but you're talking about a few individuals while I'm talking about benefiting all of humanity. The long-term gains that will accrue to the entire human race far outweigh the temporary distress of a few mothers."

Chan stared at Samuel in wonder. His lack of empathy was almost sociopathic.

"Does serving the Mountain and being 'enhanced' rob you of all feeling?"

Samuel shook his head. "No, it's age. With age comes perspective—the long view. I am somewhere in the neighborhood of forty thousand years old—one loses track after a while. But think about that. The Mountain doesn't rob you of feeling, and the emotions don't simply go away. It's just that across that span of time I've learned that certain feelings must be put on hold if one is to serve the Mountain properly."

"You mean your feelings can't get past your 'boundless devotion' to the Mountain."

Samuel looked at the First. "It's too bad enhancement does *not* rob one of emotions, wouldn't you agree?"

The First nodded. "Quite. If it did, we'd still have our full complement of males."

"What's that supposed to mean?"

The First shook his head sadly. "We've had a number of the males commit suicide."

"From what?" Chan said. "Guilt?"

"We think so."

Chan was taken aback by that. He'd simply thrown that word out as a sarcastic jab, never believing it might be true.

The First said, "Each of them had a child who had been harvested."

That word again...

"A moment ago you mentioned Philip Sirman," Samuel said.

"Yes," Chan said. "I met his wife. It's been seven years and she's still not over the loss of her daughter."

Oh, hell. And she was just down the road at Cliff House.

"Apparently Philip wasn't over it either," Samuel said. "We think the guilt drove him to suicide. He'd been despondent and told one of the other males that he regretted every day the grief he'd caused his wife whom he truly cared for."

"But he didn't commit suicide," Chan said. "He was rammed by a drunk driver."

Samuel nodded. "The truck driver was indeed very drunk. Perhaps that was why, instead of slowing down for a caution light, he speeded up to beat it. But a traffic camera shows Philip jumping the light. It's not indisputable, but his light wasn't green when he pulled out in front of that truck. It appeared deliberate."

Chan realized he could forget the DNA test. These two had

just admitted flat-out that Pam's daughter had been "harvested." And Chan knew exactly who she was.

And Philip...he'd done the unthinkable to Pam. He'd arranged for the abduction of their own daughter. To his credit—only slightly, very slightly—he'd been plagued by guilt over it. In Chan's eyes, that didn't mitigate his heinous act, but it did show that the Mountain's enhancements hadn't completely robbed these humans of their souls.

"Wait," Chan said to the First. "Something you said before: You asked me about Kurt Maez, about whether I thought his death was an accident. Was he depressed too?"

"We didn't think so," the First said. "His wife had passed on from a disease and we assumed he would have less guilt than if she'd been alive. But losing two of our males to vehicular deaths in as many months left us wondering."

"And so you stole their bodies so they wouldn't be post-mortemed."

Two sets of eyes fixed on him.

Samuel said, "You know about the body snatching?"

"Read about it."

"Do you know who might have done it?"

"You mean it wasn't you?"

Both shook their heads. "We have no idea who or why."

If not them, then who?

But at the moment Chan was more concerned about something else. One of them had said—he wasn't sure which one—that the goal of all these machinations and toying with people's lives was not only to improve life for the mass of humanity, but also "counter the machinations of the Owner and its rival entities." That had slipped past him at first, but it had come back to him just now.

Their Mountain, or the Squatter, or whatever you called the damn thing, it was doing more than simply hiding here, it was playing the Game—*while hiding*. Chan didn't know what it was with these entities, but maybe they had their compulsions just like humans, and their big compulsion was playing the Game—finding a sapient world and toying with its inhabitants.

That was what the Mountain was doing. It couldn't reveal

itself so it used surrogates—first Neanderthals, then Cro-Magnons, and now *Homo saps*—to act as its avatars in the Game. The question was, how aware of this were the First and Samuel? Did they merely suspect, or were they fully cognizant and willing participants in the schemes?

He wanted to shove it in their faces, but somehow felt that wouldn't be wise. How would they react? Would they feel he'd become a threat, maybe sound an alarm and have Henry and other security personnel block his exit? They seemed peaceful sorts, but you never could tell.

Samuel said, "I hope this hasn't put you off."

Was he kidding? He couldn't actually be serious, could he? Temporize...temporize...

"Well, I've got to admit, this has given me a lot to think about. Some aspects give me pause, but then there's the profound comfort I find in the presence of the Mountain. I would be loath to say good-bye to that." He needed to steer the talk off the subject of *Homo superior*... his gaze came to rest on the twisted ankh. "Say, what is that thing?"

"It resets the Lever," Samuel said. "Let's hope we never have to use it."

"The Lever? What—?"

"When can we expect your decision?" he said with ill-concealed impatience.

"Tomorrow. You'll know for sure one way or another tomorrow."

While thinking: When I have Danni call in a horde of FBI agents to rescue these kidnapped children, you'll have no doubt about my decision.

"Why don't you come back and join us for our Sunday night community dinner? It's always something of a feast."

How to get out of that? Better to play along.

"I'd love that. Thank you."

Not gonna happen. He and Pam and Danni were getting the hell out of Dodge.

"Wonderful. See you then."

He entered the stairwell, but as the door was swinging closed behind him he heard the rumbling voice of the First.

"We've lost him. Didn't I say you were telling him too much?"

The door latched then and cut off Samuel's reply.

Chan hurried down the steps and out to his car, then headed for the gate.

He hadn't been lying about missing the Mountain's peaceful aura, but nothing could make up for "harvesting"—*harvesting*? He couldn't fucking believe it. "Harvesting" those children.

He approached the gate, mentally chanting, *Almost out... almost out...*

And then Henry stepped out of the guardhouse and raised a hand. Chan couldn't help but notice how his other hand rested on the butt of his holstered pistol.

Shit!

4

Ian pulled the drone out of the boot and set it on the roof of his car. He'd spent well over an hour working on it last night while the inn's guests were out to dinner. He'd finally got the remote detonator controller's switch hooked up to the drone's still photo feature. Now when he pressed the photo button, the drone would send a signal to the detonators instead.

He inserted fresh batteries into the detonator controller where he'd glued it to the drone's underbelly. Even though he stored the detonators in a lead-insulated box, he very deliberately kept the batteries separate from the controller at all times. No accidental detonations, please.

The RF signal the controller emitted had an effective range of a hundred meters or thereabouts, which limited him to destroying but one sigil at a time. How he wished he could have fitted each with a cellphone detonator, allowing him to sit in his room back to the inn and simply place a call to each. *Ring-ring-BOOM!* But the risk that the mountain's security folk would spot the phones before he got to use them was too high.

The drone had been the answer. He'd used it before for looks inside the fence to keep abreast of what they were up to. The results had been uniformly prosaic and a dreadful bore.

If this drone setup didn't work, he'd be faced with the task of detonating one sigil, then dashing along the deer trail to the next corner and detonating another, and then dashing again, and so on. Literally miles and miles of running. He kept in shape, but that would tax him, and someone might well intercept him before he completed the task.

Ah, well. Time to begin.

He started the drone's propellers and watched it lift off.

Using the video feed, he guided it to within about a hundred feet of the southeast corner of the perimeter fence. He pressed the *STILL* button.

The boom was surprisingly loud, even at this distance.

Yes! It worked.

He didn't bother to fly closer and inspect the damage. That sigil was gone beyond all repair. Now on to the next.

He hoped to hell the Order appreciated this.

5

"Hey, Chan," Henry said. "Samuel just called and he said he needs you back at the fort pronto."

The First's words echoed in his brain: *We've lost him.*

And because they'd lost him, because he was now a wild card, they couldn't let him off their reservation. Ever. Was that their thinking now?

Chan lowered his window. "I'm afraid I can't go back right now. I'm supposed to be meeting a couple of friends down at Cliff House."

"I can't help that. Samuel says I'm to send you back, so that's what I'm doing."

Chan eyed the gate. Solid steel, Henry had said, and resting in a concrete cradle. He would have loved to ram it but he didn't think his Sentra was up to breaking through without suffering serious, even disabling damage. And then he'd really be up shit creek. But he couldn't go back.

"Look, henry, I'm coming back later, so why don't—?"

"Sorry, Chan, I—"

An explosion boomed off to the east. Henry froze, then ducked back into the guardhouse. Chan saw him talking excitedly on the phone, then he stepped out again.

"What's going on?" Chan said.

"Explosion of some sort." His dark face looked troubled as he stared off through the trees to the east.

Duh! Chan thought. I could have told you that.

"That was no firecracker," Chan said. "Who has—?"

A second explosion then, as loud as the first.

"Shit!" Henry cried. "The sigils!"

He took off toward the sound at a dead run.

Chan wasted no time. He hopped out, dashed to the guardhouse, found the gate button, and pushed it. Then he drove through and headed for the highway.

Henry's parting words struck him as he left the Mountain's comfort zone. *The sigils!* Could someone be blowing up the sigils?

"Aw, no!" he said and banged on the steering wheel. "Ian!"

Ian had listened in on his delirium last night. He knew what had resulted when Aldo removed four of the seven sigils, and Ian served another of the Players. He'd said his entity had no beef with the Squatter, but why should Chan believe that. What had Ian said?

The Contender covets this particular marble and the job of my group is to do whatever necessary to make it change hands from the Owner's collection to the Contender's.

Maybe his group had decided to stir things up by setting the Owner against the Squatter. Maybe they wanted to be rid of the Squatter as well and were inciting their rival to do the dirty work.

Whatever the reason, if Ian destroyed enough of those sigils, another Atlantic City caliber disaster would be on the way.

As he stopped at the highway, he heard a third explosion.

Was it possible? Was Ian actually blowing up the sigils? Seemed so farfetched. Where had he got the dynamite or whatever he was using? Destroying them put them beyond recovery. Did Samuel have replacements handy?

No matter. He had to warn Danni and Pam to pack up and get out. Because it was too late to stop Ian.

When he pulled into the Cliff House lot he saw only Danni's Volvo. He'd expected Ian's Mercedes to be gone, but the SUV that had been sitting there was missing as well. Had Erica known what was coming and fled? Of course she had.

A fourth explosion sounded as he stepped out of his car.

Okay, he thought. If that signaled the destruction of a fourth sigil, then we are now officially fucked.

He hurried inside, calling for Danni. She and Pam stepped out of the breakfast room.

"Chan!" Danni said. "Where have you been?"

"Up on the mountain. Where's Erica?"

"Gone," Pam said, then added, "'On 'oliday,'" in a bad accent. "But if you ask—"

A loud rumble shook the floor beneath their feet. What had Ian done now?

He rushed back outside and stood frozen in awe watching the black, roiling clouds massing over the mountain. A supercell was forming—in the Catskills. The clouds piled higher and higher in the otherwise flawless morning sky.

That hadn't been an explosion...

"What the fuck is *that*?" Pam said as she and Danni came up behind him.

A massive bolt of lightning speared the mountain from the supercell's base, followed by another thunderous, ground-shaking rumble.

"Those clouds..." Danni said in a shaky voice. "I've seen clouds like that before."

So had Chan. He and Danni had watched them gather offshore during the lost hours. Was Danni remembering?

"Where did you see them, Danni?"

Her expression was tortured. "I...I don't know. But they frighten the hell out of me."

"They should. They're the same clouds we saw over the ocean shortly before the assault on Atlantic City."

"I thought they looked familiar. You remember?"

He nodded. "Yeah. And I'm pretty sure the same thing's about to happen here so we'd—"

"To the mountain?" Pam said. "Like Atlantic City?

"Afraid so."

"Weren't you talking last night about a bunch of kids up there? Maybe Julie?"

Oh, shit! He'd been so intent on getting free of the Mountain, he hadn't been thinking about anything else. The Owner was coming to absorb the Squatter and in the process it would destroy everything around it, including the children.

"There are!" Chan cried. "We've got to get them clear!"

Danni started for the inn. "I'll get my keys."

"No time!" Chan said. "And it might be better if we all go in my car. They should be used to seeing it by now."

"Fine," she said, "but what about my nine? Should I bring it?"

Her Glock...yeah. He prayed she wouldn't be called on to use it, but better to have it than not.

"Yeah, maybe you'd better."

"Be back in a sec."

"Her 'nine'?" Pam said as Danni ran back into the inn. "What—?"

"Her FBI pistol. Come on, get in the car and I'll start her up and be ready to go as soon as she comes back."

"You really think she'll need a *gun* up there?" Pam said as she jumped into the shotgun seat. "What good's a gun against *that*?"

"We don't know what we'll be getting into. Might have some panicky people to deal with. Just showing it could help."

He couldn't get into what the storm might be bringing besides rain and lightning. The Owner couldn't flood the Mountain like AC, so swimming predators were out, but he had no idea what else it might have up its sleeve.

Danni was gone no more than thirty seconds but the storm doubled in intensity during the interval. The clouds thickened further and rose higher, forming that too-familiar anvil top, lancing more and more lightning bolts into the mountain as it began to descend upon it.

As soon as Danni leaped onto the rear seat, he gunned out of the lot and raced up the highway.

Pam was twisted around to face Danni. "Is that thing loaded?"

"Of course. Otherwise it's little more than a big paperweight." To Chan, she said, "What were those explosions before?"

"Our host blowing up things."

"What things?"

"It's complicated. Hang on,"

Chan screeched into the turn onto the road up the mountain. The bright morning quickly faded to a grim twilight as the supercell's flat base blotted out the sunlight. Then came the rain in what could only be described as a tropical downpour as the trees rocked back and forth in the roaring gale.

The gate and guardhouse were exactly as he'd left them: open and deserted. He blew through and continued on up the hill, half expecting that peaceful, easy, welcoming aura. But he wasn't all that surprised when he felt just the opposite: the same anger he'd sensed in AC, and also the underlying fear. Only the fear seemed stronger now. Did the Squatter know the jig was up?

To the right they passed the Family's homes but few were lit. Power failure?

Just then a massive lightning bolt lit up the plateau as it struck one of the houses, dissolving it in an explosion of flaming embers.

"Oh, God!" Danni said. "I hope no one was home!"

Chan didn't slow. If the community had any sense they would be gathered at the fort, even though that couldn't stand against the forces that flattened Atlantic City.

As they approached the playground, a blinding bolt exploded atop a swing set with a July Fourth burst of sparks, followed instantly by a deafening blast of thunder.

Pam screamed and lurched away from her window, banging against Chan.

"Sorry," she cried, "but I was not fucking expecting *that*!"

"Just hang in there," he told her. "It's gonna get worse."

Through the driving rain he spotted lights ahead. Could only be the second floor windows of the fort. He aimed for them.

When he reached the fort he pulled up next to the vans and left the engine running.

"Come on," he said. "Inside."

"All of us?" Danni said.

"I may need you."

"Gotcha."

As she got out she tucked the Glock under her shirt at the small of her back and the three of them raced through the downpour to the big door. Once inside, with the door closed behind them, the sound of the storm receded, but only a little. Thunder shook the stone walls and the floor.

Chan looked around for a familiar face and saw Nicolette on

the far side of the great room with a group of boys. She spotted him just then and they headed toward each other.

"Chan, what are you doing here?"

"You've got to get off the mountain," he told her.

Her expression was baffled. "Leave the Mountain? No way. And who are those people?" she said, pointing to Pam and Danni, still by the door. "They shouldn't—"

"Friends. They'll help you load the kids into the vans."

"We're not leaving, Chan. The Mountain is our home. It'll protect us."

"Like it protected Atlantic City? It's all over for your Mountain, I'm afraid."

But he could see by her expression that she wasn't buying that. He looked around for help but saw only women and children.

"Where are all the men?"

"Samuel sent them out to fix the fence, but that was right before the storm hit. I hope they're all right."

Most likely they were anything but.

"Okay, then where's Samuel?"

"He just went upstairs." As Chan started toward the steps, she said, "You can't go up there!"

"Watch me."

He entered the stairwell and took the steps two at a time. The door at the top was locked so he started pounding on it.

"Samuel! Open up! It's Chan! It's an emergency!"

He kept it up until the door swung inward and Samuel stood there, his expression furious.

"Are you responsible for this?"

An accurate answer would be yes and no: Ian had learned from Chan what would result from loss of the sigils, but Chan had had nothing to do with their destruction.

"Ian from Cliff House—I learned that he serves another entity. He—"

The First appeared behind Samuel, his coarse features twisted in shock.

"Ian Carroll? The innkeeper serves the Owner?"

"A contender, I think. Don't ask me what he hopes to

accomplish with this, but the hard truth is, everyone here is going to wind up like Atlantic City: dead."

Samuel said, "We sent out the men with new sigils—"

"Too late. You've all got to get off the mountain."

Both men shook their heads. "No," the First said in a tone laden with certainty. "We will not abandon the Mountain."

Well, no big surprise there.

"Okay. That's fine if you want to make some grand gesture, but at least save the kids. After all, that's what this horrendous scheme is all about—what your Family is about. The kids, right? Save them!"

Both stared at him.

Samuel said, "Why would you want to further our 'horrendous scheme,' as you call it?"

"Because they're just kids! Give them a chance to live. Don't make that choice for them!"

Samuel and the First looked at each other and Chan could pretty well read their thoughts: If the kids could survive and intermarry, they could still produce *Homo superior*. The Mountain could live on through them.

"Take them, then," Samuel said.

"I can't. The mothers won't let them go. They think they're all safe here because the Mountain will protect them. But you and I know your Mountain is outgunned here. There can be only one outcome: absorption for your entity, annihilation for whatever humans are in the vicinity. So it's got to come from you."

Samuel pushed past him and hurried down the steps. Looked like he'd bought into survival of the kids as the only way to go.

He clapped his hands as he entered the great room and shouted, "Listen, everyone! We must evacuate the Mountain."

Gasps and cries of dismay rose from the mothers.

"Everything will be all right," he continued, "and you can come back when it's safe. We've had drills to prepare for this eventuality, so everyone should know what to do. Now let's get to it before the storm damages the vehicles."

Both Chan and Samuel knew there would be no mountain

to return to when this was over. The mothers got moving right away, herding the children toward the door.

Samuel said, "I'll check the back rooms to make sure we don't leave anybody."

He reached Nicolette as Danni and Pam hurried up to him.

"What can we do?" Pam said.

Nicolette said, "We can always use help with the toddlers."

As Pam hurried off toward a group of children, Danni held back. "Who was that man who made the announcement?"

"Samuel?"

"I've seen him before."

Was all of this triggering Danni's memories?

"We met him in the Pines that night."

Her face hardened. "He was part of that?"

"No. He was a victim like most everybody else."

She shook her head. "I'm getting all these flashes…"

"Look, you and I will sit down and go over all this, but right now we have to get these kids to safety."

"Right."

As she hurried off to help Pam, Chan turned to Nicolette and said, "And me? Do you need a driver?"

"Thanks, but we're covered in that department. I'll be driving the lead van, Shonda will have the second, and Cheryl the third. We'll swing by the houses to pick up whoever's still down there."

"You mean you're not all here?"

"We were supposed to be, but I'm sure some mothers don't want to take their child through this storm. Could you help herd the kids to the vans?"

"You got it."

The community had obviously paid attention during their drills and things went smoothly—well, as smoothly as guiding a bunch of frightened kids through a raging, lightning-slashed tempest could go. Soon three vans were loaded with wet women and children. Chan had kept an eye out for Daphne and Lexie, and saw them get in the middle van.

He hung back by the fort door and said to Samuel, "You and the First can ride with me."

"No, we can't leave. If this is the way it ends, then so be it. Neither of us will feel cheated of any years."

You've had far too many already, Chan thought. He couldn't forgive what they'd done to mothers like Pam.

Samuel added, "I want to give you the resetter for safekeeping."

"The what?" What did it reset?

"That object on the wall upstairs. It's indestructible but I don't want it falling into the wrong hands. I'll be right back."

As Samuel hurried for the stairs, Chan ran back into the storm. He found Pam and Danni standing by his car.

"I'd like you two to go with them and I'll follow."

"Why don't we come with you?" Danni said.

"Those kids are scared. A couple of extra adults will help keep them calm."

Nicolette ran up. "I'll lead the way down to the houses for the stragglers."

"I'll follow and we can fit any overflow into my—holy crap!"

A bright bolt of lightning had revealed a twister churning among the houses, scattering them into flying debris. Screams from within the vans as they saw it too.

"Aw, shit!" Danni said. "I've seen that before too! Things are coming back to me, Chan!"

He watched in horror as the funnel cloud mowed along the row of houses, leveling them. Whoever had stayed down there didn't have a chance. Those poor kids!

Shaking it off, he shoved Danni and Nicolette toward the first van. "You two get in there! We've got to get these kids off the mountain!"

Hurrying away, Nicolette said, "Where's Samuel?"

What to say? If he told them Samuel was staying, some might want to stay with him.

"He's coming with me. We'll be right behind."

He pushed Pam toward the second van. "You squeeze in there. Go! Go!"

"Don't have to tell me twice!"

As the vans started rolling, Chan dashed back to the doorway to the fort. Where was Samuel? He spotted him just exiting the stairwell, holding that thing he'd called the "resetter," when an intolerably bright flash lit the night and bleached the colors out of the great room—and brought down the ceiling on Samuel with a horrendous blast that blew Chan backward into the storm again.

He struggled back to his feet and saw that the entire interior of the fort was little more than a pile of rubble. Samuel and the First—and the resetter, whatever it was, were goners. He staggered to his car and followed the vans, keeping his eye out for that twister. To his relief, another bolt of lightning revealed that it had changed direction away from the road and was weaving toward the remains of the fort. The clouds were lower than ever, swallowing the top of the mountain. They'd left just in time.

The gate was still unmanned and open and the vans wheeled right through, Chan close behind. The rain was merely a drizzle down at the highway. The storm seemed to be strictly limited to the mountain where it still raged.

Nicolette's van led the others into a right turn, heading west. Chan would catch up to them later, wherever they were going. He'd call Danni and find out where they landed. Meanwhile, he had some unfinished business back at Cliff House.

6

After what he'd heard from Samuel and the First this morning, Chan harbored no doubts that Ian had drugged him Friday night. He'd mentioned the blank spot in his memory that first night at the inn and Ian—in the service of the Contender—decided to find out if those memories held anything that could be used against the Squatter. The result: something in the coffee he'd served with the cherry pie.

Samuel and the First had said the memories wouldn't return spontaneously, but Danni had encountered a number of triggers up on the mountain. Who knew how many would come back on their own? He wanted to give her the option of recovering all of them, and to that end he was going to find out if Ian still had any of whatever he'd used on Chan.

He covered the three-quarters of a mile to Cliff House in no time and found the parking area empty except for Danni's Volvo.

Great. He'd expected no cooperation from Ian, nothing beyond denials, in fact. This gave Chan a chance to search his room.

As he got out of the car he glanced back and gasped. The supercell had engulfed almost the entire mountain. Flashes lit its interior. He could only imagine the hell that must be raging inside that storm.

He hurried inside and found Ian's door unlocked. The room was a mess. Looked like he'd left in a rush. A footlocker sat on the bed, obviously not its usual spot. Since that too was unlocked, Chan went right to work searching it. He found a brick labeled *Semtex*. Wasn't that an explosive? He didn't know much about demolition, but he also came across some things that looked like detonating caps.

Here was indisputable proof that Ian had blown up the sigils. But Chan had already been sure of that. Where was the drug he'd used to free Chan's memory? He kept pawing through the trunk and came upon a padded envelope addressed to Ian and stamped with Friday's date. No UPS or FedEx logo. A private delivery service? Inside he found a bubble-wrapped vial of clear liquid and a thumb drive.

This had to be it.

"Well, well, well," said Ian's voice behind him. "So you found the witch's brew."

He turned to find himself eye to eye with the large muzzle of a revolver.

"Shit, Ian!" he said, jumping back. "Put that down!"

"Got a better idea, mate." Ian wore a blue work shirt. He pulled a pair of handcuffs from a breast pocket. "Put these on. Start with your left wrist."

"No fucking way."

He jammed the revolver's muzzle into Chan's cheek—hard—and it hurt like hell.

"Now!"

Chan dropped the vial on the desk and snapped the cuff around his left wrist.

Ian waggled the gun. "Okay, now, sit in the chair and snap the other cuff around the radiator pipe running along the wall there."

Chan complied.

"Good."

"Where are you going with all this, Ian? You're wasting time when you should be on the run."

"On the run from what?"

"The law. You killed people up there."

"Not me. That's the Owner's work, just like Atlantic City—which I believe can be laid on the doorstep of you and your mates, right?"

Chan spotted movement behind Ian as a very wet pair of jeans and sneakers appeared in the open doorway. He recognized them as Danni's. Did she have her pistol out?

Chan kept his eyes off the doorway and focused on Ian's face as he said, "Maybe you can make a case for that, but we had no idea what would happen. You knew exactly what you were setting in motion when you blew up those plaques. When you deliberately unlock a lion's cage, you're responsible for anyone it kills."

He shrugged. "Then so be it. They chose the wrong side. Down with the ship and all that."

"We're talking men, women, and children here, Ian—*children*."

"Well, I'm sure you know the old saying about omelets and breaking eggs, so I won't bore you with it. Where's your perspective, mate? Haven't you gotten it through your thick skull that we don't matter? That we're playthings... property. We're *owned*. Only the Game matters and we're just pieces on the board." He picked up the vial of what he'd called *witch's brew*. "What were you going to do with this?"

"I'm assuming that's what you slipped into my coffee Friday night."

"Good guess. The memory restorer. You don't need it anymore, so I've got other plans for it."

"Like?"

"Well, it's also a sedative. I've got plans for you, as well, you being a sensitive and all. The Order will find you very useful."

"'The Order'?"

"My people—the ones who sent me here."

"I'd rather save it for a friend who can use it."

"One of those women who joined you yesterday?"

"Exactly. She has the same problem I did."

"Really?" He grinned. "My, my. Nicolette Thursday night, then these two last night. Quite the ladies' man, aren't we? I never got the chance to meet them."

"Easily enough remedied. One of them's right behind you."

Ian's smile broadened. "Even if I did turn around, what can you do? You can't reach me cuffed to that pipe."

Chan saw the sneakers step forward and Danni say, loud and clear, "Feel this against your back? That's a Glock Nineteen. Do not move."

Ian's startle reaction was almost comical, but then his expression took on a more calculating look.

"Shoot me and I'll shoot your friend here."

Danni was still blocked from Chan's view; he couldn't see her face but her voice was coldly matter-of-fact.

"The Glock is loaded with nine-millimeter hollow points—Winchester one-twenty-four-grain PDX-ones, to be specific. I've got the muzzle pressed within inches of the backside of your heart. Do you know what one of these hollow points does once it gets inside you? You won't be shooting anyone. Understood?"

Ian's expression was still tense and calculating as he said, "Understood."

"Okay. Toss your that big old Webley on the bed and raise your hands."

Unable to see Danni's face, Chan had to watch Ian's and saw his features slacken. He might have entertained making a move but Danni's casual mention of "that big old Webley" signaled loud and clear that he wasn't dealing with an amateur. He tossed the gun onto the bed and raised his hands. Danni backed up a step as he made a slow turn but still remained between her and Chan.

"Hello, pet. You're a pretty one, even when all wet. What do you plan to do with that?"

"Shoot you," came the cold reply. "Shoot you dead."

Was that really Danni?

"Now, now. You don't mean that."

"Don't I? You should see what's happening to that mountain. It's… it's dissolving. There's no hope for anyone up there. And you did it."

"No, not me, pet. You must have been listening when I was trying to straighten out your fellow here. That's our Owner come in to evict a squatter. Hear that? *Our Owner.* There are forces at work here that are far beyond our ken. I'm irrelevant… you're irrelevant…"

Her tone became uncertain. "I-I've remembered some things, memories I thought were gone forever. My life… I've spent it battling chaos, but chaos is the rule, isn't it?"

"Ah, so you've seen the light…or the dark, rather."

"Don't listen to him, Danni!"

"No, no, he's right, Chan. I've realized how irrelevant I am. How worthless we all are." She leaned against the door jamb. He could see her now. He features slack, her expression lost. "My life... I thought it meant something, but it's pointless... so pointless... and it will only get more pointless." She lowered her gun arm.

Ian made his move then, angling left and grabbing for her. And Danni... she simply raised her forearm and fired three times, point blank. One of the slugs came out Ian's back and spattered Chan with blood. Ian spun and collapsed onto the desk, then slid to the floor to come to rest lying on his side, sightless eyes staring at Chan.

He fought a surge of nausea. Danni...she'd killed him. Just like that. A moment ago he was alive, now he was dead. Chan had never seen anyone die before. Okay, he'd seen Kurt's car explode and burn, but Kurt hadn't been visible. He hadn't actually *seen* him die. Not like Ian...

And the *sound*. He'd never been this close to gunshots before, never imagined them this loud. His ears were ringing.

He looked up at Danni. The lost expression of a moment ago was gone like it had never been, but the one that had replaced it was unreadable. .

"You shot him!"

Her mouth twisted. "You noticed, huh?" He could barely hear her through the ringing.

"But..."

She nudged the body with her sneaker, rolling it onto its back. "Who's irrelevant now?"

Danni...he'd never seen her like this, never imagined she could *be* like this.

Without a word she turned and walked out—with Chan still cuffed to the pipe.

"Danni?"

No answer.

Chan rattled the cuffs. They weren't heavy duty but still plenty heavy enough to hold him. He straightened from his cringe in the chair and looked around for a key. During his reconnoiter he spotted a fresh hole in the room's rear wall.

Holy shit. That could have wound up in him.

His gaze came to rest on the right breast pocket of Ian's shirt. He'd pulled the cuffs from there. Maybe the key...?

Blood from the three bullet wounds in his chest and upper abdomen was soaking much of Ian's shirt and pooling on the floor beneath him. It hadn't reached the breast pockets yet. Chan reached over and wriggled his fingers inside the right one and found the key. Seconds later he left the cuff dangling from the pipe and scrambled out of the room.

He found Danni, her face in her hands as she sat at the table in the breakfast room, her Glock, the remnants of the scones, and the cold, half-full French press on the table before her.

Reflexively he said, "You okay?" and immediately regretted it.

She looked up. "Do I look okay?"

"Sorry. Stupid question. You're obviously not okay."

"I just killed a man, which puts me about as far from 'okay' as I can get. I've never shot at anyone before, let alone killed them."

"You almost had a two-fer," Chan said, and immediately regretted that too. He was running at the mouth here. Was it shock?

"What do you mean?"

"One of the bullets hit the wall. Good thing I wasn't behind him, I guess."

"Oh, I made sure of that."

It took Chan a few seconds to process that.

"You mean that sagging against the door and all the 'pointless' talk was a ruse?"

"Well, yeah. I had to get him out from between us. Even though they issue us hollow points, at that range I was afraid one might go all the way through, so I had to get him to move."

"You...you intended to shoot him all along?"

"Well, not if he didn't make a move. Give me a *little* credit. And I did warn him."

Yeah, she did. When Ian had asked what she planned to do with her Glock, she hadn't minced words: *Shoot you... shoot you dead*. And that was just what she'd done.

He said, "But all that little-girl-lost talk. You knew he couldn't resist."

"Look, Chan, I didn't *know* anything, except maybe that no one would ever be bringing him to trial. He killed people, Chan. I heard him admit it. And he didn't care one bit. 'They chose the wrong side'? What is that?"

"He says the entity did it."

"Yeah, and I can say I didn't kill him, the Glock did. But what was anyone in the real world gonna charge him with? Exploding a few plaques on a mountainside? He needed to be dead, Chan—*deserved* to be dead. And now that he is... I didn't think it would be like this."

He needed to help her past this. And then what she'd said just seconds ago registered.

"You know about the plaques? You remember?"

"A good deal," she said with a nod. "More and more kept coming back as we rode down the hillside. When I saw you turn in the opposite direction, back toward the inn, I knew—just knew—you were going to get yourself in a bind. So I had Nicolette let me out and I walked here."

"In the rain?"

"Just a drizzle down here. And along the way, as I looked up at the storm engulfing the mountain, more and more kept coming back to me: what happened to Aldo, Kurt talking about how the plaques protected the entity in the pines, what happened to Mac..." Her voice thickened here for a second. "Those poor guys."

The stone-cold executioner of a moment ago was now puddling up talking about her dead friends. This was the Danni he knew.

She looked up at him, her expression tortured. "We'll never get them back, will we?"

He shook his head. "No. Never."

"I still don't understand, Chan. What happened back then? What happened this morning?"

He remembered how Ian had put it. "The Owner came to evict a squatter."

"'Owner'? Are we really owned?"

"According to people like Ian, we are. And from what I've seen lately, I think he may be right." He thought of something. "Feel like stepping outside? I want to check on the mountain."

She rose and followed him. Both of them froze one step outside the door.

"The storm..." Danni said. "What is happening?"

The clouds still shrouded most of the mountain, but they'd thinned and lost their shape. They appeared to be drifting off in various directions.

"Looks like it's breaking up."

As the storm continued dissipating, Chan waited to see what it had done to the mountain, expecting to see trees flattened like matchsticks, similar to how it had left a section of the pinelands trees. But instead, the dispersal of the clouds revealed...nothing.

The storm was gone, but so was most of the mountain.

"My God," Danni said. "Where's the mountain? Where'd it go?"

The community's homes, the fort, countless tons of earth and rock and vegetation, all gone, along with every human and animal with the bad fortune to have been there.

"All I can say is it looks like the Owner not only removed the Squatter, but its squat as well."

Danni sagged against him. "What's happened to the world, Chan? This isn't the world I grew up in."

He put his arm around her shoulders. "Yeah, it is. We just didn't realize. The reality's been hidden from us—the hidden history of the world. A lot of people have suspected, only a few know. We're now among the few."

"I was happier not knowing. And damn them all anyway! They killed Mac and Aldo!"

Chan could only agree, so they stood for a moment in silence, staring at the clear sky that had been blocked by a mountain earlier this morning.

Finally Danni straightened and said, "I have to call in this shooting. How the hell am I going to explain about the plaques and the entities and all that? They'll think I'm crazy."

"*Don't* explain. Leave all that garbage out and let the scene speak for itself. You came back and found me handcuffed to a pipe with Ian standing over me with a gun. When you told him to drop the gun, he made a move against you and you fired. End of story."

"But his revolver is on the bed."

"If you'll give me half a minute's head start, it will be on the floor next to his body when you get there."

Without waiting for permission, Chan headed back inside.

"I can't let you do that, Chan."

"What did you say? I can't hear you."

He wasn't about to let Danni get into hot water for saving his butt. When he entered the room he went straight to the bed, reached under the covers, and bumped the pistol onto the floor. Then he kicked it over toward Ian's body.

"There. Done. I never touched it."

"But..." Her jaw worked as she stared at the pistol, then she said, "But what about you? Why did he have you...?"

"Captive? Let me ask you first: Do you want any of that memory-restoring potion?"

She shook her head. "I don't see that I need it. I'm remembering plenty, and more keeps coming."

"Okay, then. We'll tell them Ian was going to force that witch's brew, as he called it, into me. That's true. He told me that. For what purpose, I have no idea. We'll let the crime lab figure out what's in it. I sure as hell don't know."

"That'll fly," she said, nodding. "I'll get on the phone and report it."

"Good. Meanwhile I'll call Pam to see where they are and let them know the bad news."

"What's that?"

"That they've got no place to come back to."

"Oh, damn, that's right. Those poor kids."

"Who're you gonna report this to? The town doesn't seem big enough for a police department. Are they covered by the county sheriff?"

"I don't know. I'm calling my boss to make sure I do this right."

As she jabbed at her phone's keypad, Chan stepped out into

the hall. Pam had given him her cell number so he called that. It went straight to voicemail. He tried again with the same result. Okay, he tried Nicolette's number and that too went straight to voicemail.

Odd that they'd both turned off their phones. Maybe they were someplace without a signal. He'd try again later.

But later his calls were still going to voicemail. Something was up. He left a message for Nicolette saying that Samuel had stayed behind and how the mountain had been completely destroyed. Call him ASAP.

7

Nicolette said, "I'm going to have to ask you to make a choice, Pam."

The chaos of taking all these kids into a thruway rest stop for a bathroom and food break had quieted to a dull roar as they all settled into their seats and stuffed their faces.

Most of the adults were still too much in shock to eat. Everyone in this extended family had known each other, and they'd lost all the mothers and children who'd stayed huddled in their houses. Everyone had turned their phones off as a safety measure, but when Nicolette checked her messages, she found one from Chan telling her that their leader had stayed behind on the mountain which was no longer there.

Well, no one could believe that, so Nicolette turned the vans around and they all drove back to the mountain—which, indeed, was no longer there. But the National Guard was, plus the entire sheriff's department, and a ton of other law-enforcement types were swarming in. The vans kept moving. The children didn't grasp what had happened, but the adults certainly did. Lots of tears in Pam's van.

And now at the rest stop, Nicolette had pulled Pam aside for "an important decision."

"We have a destination," Nicolette said in her French accent. "Samuel knew this day might come and he prepared for it. He prepared *us* for it. He put a *lot* of money aside for us—enough for all of us to stay together as a Family. He bought and furnished a whole condo complex in New Hampshire. We will have it all to ourselves. Would you want to be part of that?"

"I would," Pam said without an instant's hesitation.

Nicolette blinked. "Don't take it lightly. You might want to think about it a little."

As they'd driven away from the mountain and the storm that engulfed it, a little red-haired girl on Pam's bus had been upset that she'd had to leave all her paintings behind. Pam learned that her name was Lexie and hers was the painting Chan had shown them back at the inn. Pam's heart had damn near stopped when she'd seen the port wine stain on the child's fingers. Could it be? Could it really be? Was this why Chan had pushed her to ride on this bus?

Having seen Lexie's painting gave Pam an entrée to talk to her mother, who obviously adored the child. Was this woman, Daphne, her natural mother or was Lexie adopted? Pam hadn't wanted to press because many parents keep that fact from their kids.

But no way was she going to let that child go off into a new life without her along for the ride.

"It's an easy decision," Pam told Nicolette. "My husband died last week in an auto crash and—"

"Oh, I'm so sorry!" Nicolette said, grabbing her hand.

"It's okay. I've accepted it. But it's left me with no one. My parents are gone, I have no children, so a new life is perfect for me."

Well, the "no children" bit was up in the air at the moment—maybe—but the rest was sadly too true. What reason did she have to go back to Lincroft?

"You're welcome to join us, but if you do, you'll have to adjust to a little paranoia."

"I'm perfectly comfortable with paranoia."

I should be, she thought. I was married to a man whose whole life was a lie and whose body was inflammable.

"Here's the fact: We were attacked. All our men are probably dead. We might still be targeted so we have to disappear. That means we don't communicate with anyone outside the Family, which means we keep all our phones turned off and destroy the chips and buy burners. I know you know Chan and that other woman—"

"Danni. I've known her and Chan for less than a week, so it's no great sacrifice."

"Good." Nicolette held out her hand. "Phone, please."

She shrugged. "I don't have it. I left it back at the B and B when we rushed up to the mountain to save the kids." And hadn't missed it. No one she wanted to call anyway. "Left my wallet too, with all my ID and credit cards. I'm officially nobody now."

Nicolette smiled. "Well then, welcome to life on the run."

Pam found herself loving the idea. And she couldn't wait to get back on the bus with Lexie.

8

It turned out Alberta didn't have a police department, so Danni called the Greene County Sheriff's Office. She told them as little as possible until agents from the FBI's NYC Regional Office arrived and took over. The sheriff didn't complain. He had his hands full. This whole area of the Catskills was in complete chaos over the disappearance of the nameless mountain and everybody on it. The National Guard had been called in from the Joint Force Headquarters in Latham, along with DHS and the FBI. Danni didn't know any of the NYC agents who questioned her but they gave her every courtesy. If she hadn't been an agent, the shooting investigation would have been more involved.

Even so, the Bureau naturally had lots of questions. First off about the details of the shooting, and lots more when they found the Semtex in Ian's foot locker. She and Chan had agreed to play dumb. They were old college friends on a weekend getaway. They knew nothing about Ian and his sister. Chan told them he suspected Ian might have cuffed him up because he'd spotted the Semtex but he didn't know for sure. No, they didn't know how many people had been living on the mountain or if any of them survived, blah-blah-blah and on and on. She was sure they were backgrounding Chan for any terrorist connections or links to Antifa or Proud Boys and all that, but she wasn't worried because there'd be nothing to find.

And then suddenly the agents backed off and stopped with their debriefing. She and Chan bided their time in his room at the rear of Cliff House until one of the NYC agents showed up wearing a mordant grin.

"Looks like you hit the jackpot, Boudreau."

"Oh?"

"Some NSA nut jobs have arrived and want to interview you."

She knew immediately who he meant. "R3A?"

He nodded. "You got it. You know them?"

"We've met."

"Well, you're about to meet again. They're outside in the biggest goddamn RV I've ever seen. Let's go."

Chan looked totally confused as the agent escorted them down the hall.

"'NSA nut jobs'? R3A?"

She lowered her voice. "Remember earlier when I was worried how I was going to explain about the plaques and the entities and all that? How they'd think I'm crazy? Well, I remembered some folks who'll buy right into all that, and so I put in a call."

She was glad she'd held onto Zina's card.

They stepped into the parking lot which was now occupied by what appeared to be a huge, windowless mobile home festooned with antennas and rooftop dishes. A door slid open as they approached and closed after they entered. The Troika waited within among more screens and blinking electronics than Danni had ever imagined could be squeezed into one vehicle.

"Told you we'd meet again," Zina said. "And this is your Mister Liao."

They all introduced themselves, then Zina said, "I must congratulate you, Boudreau, on your talent for being in the wrong place at the wrong time. Or does weird shit happen simply *because* you're there?"

"The former," Danni said. "Definitely the former."

"But consider what's just happened to your status. You started out categorized as a lucky survivor who just happened to be an FBI agent. Now you're not only a material witness but a person of interest in both of the most calamitous mysteries that US law enforcement and intelligence agencies—make that the *world's* law enforcement and intelligence agencies—have ever faced."

"Lucky me."

Zina smiled. "You've got some explaining to do, young lady. And since you called us, why don't you begin."

Danni looked at Chan. "You'll help, right?"

"Absolutely," he said, nodding vigorously. He looked at the Troika. "I'll give you what I remember from the Upwelling, what Ian told me, and what Samuel and the First told me."

"By 'Samuel' I gather you mean Samuel Lamm. We're very familiar with him. But who is the First?"

"You won't believe it."

All three nodded and spoke in unison.

"Try us."

"Well, then," he said, "get your recorders going."

Zina's smile had a sardonic twist. "What makes you think they ever stop?"

9

Chan did most of the talking. It took a while but they finally got the whole story out, with Danni learning a lot herself along the way. Some of it shocked her. To her relief—no, make that to her delight—she saw no dubious frowns, heard no disparaging chuckles from the Troika. Mostly their story was met with knowing nods.

"We've suspected a lot of this," said Zina when they finished, "but the Squatter was something we knew nothing about. At least now we know what 'touched' you, Boudreau. What you call the Owner is also known as 'the Ally.' That's not our term. We sort of inherited it. It's better than 'Owner' because the Owner can change. The current Owner is an ally only in the sense that it blocks the Otherness, which your friend Ian referred to as the Contender, and which is totally inimical. We never knew which side Samuel Lamm was associated with but I must say, we never suspected a third entity."

"Well, there are only two now," Chan said. "Did you know about Ian Carroll working for—what do you call it? The Otherness?"

"No. His cover was good. He never pinged our radar, and I wish he had. He sure made one hell of a mess up here. At least the death toll is nothing like Atlantic City," she added with a pointed look at Danni and Chan.

"Thanks for the reminder," Danni said.

Chan let the AC dig slide. "There's another mystery I'd like solved. Samuel and the First told me they didn't steal the Sirman and Maez corpses and I believe them."

"As well you should," Luka said, all in black as before. "*We* took them."

Chan looked surprised. "But why?"

"Well, we wanted to know why they didn't burn."

"And did you find out?"

He nodded. "Their genes are a unique tangle. But we're more concerned about the genes they passed on."

"To the Family's children?" Danni said. "What do you know about the kids? All abducted?"

Ilya nodded. "Every last one."

She shook her head, disgusted. "That's monstrous. Do the foster mothers know?"

Ilya shrugged. "Maybe, maybe not. We've never been able to get close enough to them."

Did Pam realize her Julie was there with her, maybe sitting a few feet away?

"Are you going to return them to their natural parents?"

His expression was hard to read through that thick beard. "We have to find them first."

"You've lost them?" Danni couldn't believe it.

He said, "The storm that assaulted the mountain and the Squatter monopolized surveillance assets in the area while it lasted. When we had eyes again, we looked for the Family but they'd disappeared. They seem to know what they're about when it comes to hiding. They've ditched their phones and parked out of satellite view. But they can't have traveled very far, so it's only a matter of time before we locate them."

"And we want very much to locate them," Zina said. "Philip Sirman and Kurt Maez have genomes with unique features that we're still teasing out. And their kids... who knows what those kids will turn out to be? They're a total question mark."

10

The surviving mothers were gathered in the condo clubhouse. The remnants of the Family had crossed Vermont to an empty condo complex just outside Keene, New Hampshire, where they parked the vans in the building's basement garage. The property manager had broken down and wept when they arrived. Pam was told, "His name is Rick and he's one of us."

So now he and the mothers were having a strategy meeting about various matters—new vehicles and so on. They'd invited Pam to join in but she begged off. Instead, she took some of the older kids, those six and up in age—making sure Lexie was among them—out to the fire pit in the courtyard. The night was barely cool enough, but kids always liked a fire.

The manager kept a supply of wood off to the side which Pam arranged in a pyramidal pile to allow for the best draw. Her place in Lincroft had a fireplace and she knew how to make a good one.

"Does anyone see any kindling?" she said.

The kids made a quick search of the fire pit area but came up empty.

"Does this mean we can't have a fire?" Lexie said, looking disappointed.

"Not at all, honey. I'll find something and we'll get it going."

She had her butane cigarette lighter, so all she needed was something easy to burn. She remembered seeing a stack of newspapers by the recycle bin.

As she wriggled an old issue of the *Union Leader* free, she thought about the DNA test Danni had mentioned. How were they ever going to arrange that now? She was going to have to give her situation some thought. Because if she did manage to get it done and it turned out a non-match, she saw no reason to stay with these people. They were talking about life in hiding, which was something that didn't interest her unless she had a pony in the race.

When she returned to the fire pit with the paper, the wood was already ablaze.

"Who started the fire?" she said.

The kids just looked at her.

"Did the manager come by and start it for you?"

Again, just stares.

Shaking her head in bafflement, Pam pulled up a chair and tossed the newspaper into the flames. As it caught and curled and turned black, one of her carefully stacked logs fell over onto its side. Pam looked around for tongs to get it back in place but saw none. When she turned back she bit off a scream as she saw Lexie bending over the fire with her hand in the flames, righting the log. Lexie looked at Pam and gave an easy smile, as if to say, *It's okay. I took care of it.*

Then, brushing off her hands, she came over and plopped onto Pam's lap.

"I like you," she whispered.

Pam had the arms of her chair in a death grip. She released them and slipped her own arms around Lexie and fought to keep from bursting into tears. All her vacillation about remaining with the Family had vanished. The DNA test had just become superfluous.

Pam was staying.

<end>

ABOUT THE AUTHOR

F. PAUL WILSON is an award-winning, bestselling author of seventy books and nearly one hundred short stories spanning science fiction, horror, adventure, medical thrillers, and virtually everything between.

His novels The Keep, The Tomb, Harbingers, By the Sword, The Dark at the End, and Nightworld were New York Times Bestsellers. The Tomb received the 1984 Porgie Award from The West Coast Review of Books. Wheels Within Wheels won the first Prometheus Award, and Sims another; Healer and An Enemy of the State were elected to the Prometheus Hall of Fame. Dydeetown World was on the young adult recommended reading lists of the American Library Association and the New York Public Library, among others. His novella Aftershock won the Stoker Award. He was voted Grand Master by the World Horror Convention; he received the Lifetime Achievement Award from the Horror Writers of America, and the Thriller Lifetime Achievement Award from the editors of Romantic Times. He also received the prestigious San Diego Comic-Con Inkpot Award and is listed in the 50th anniversary edition of Who's Who in America.

His short fiction has been collected in Soft & Others, The Barrens & Others, and Aftershock & Others. He has edited two anthologies: Freak Show and Diagnosis: Terminal plus (with Pierce Watters) the only complete collection of Henry Kuttner's Hogben stories, The Hogben Chronicles.

In 1983 Paramount rendered his novel The Keep into a visually striking but otherwise incomprehensible movie with screenplay and direction by Michael Mann.

The Tomb has spent twenty-five years in development hell at Beacon Films.

Dario Argento adapted his story "Pelts" for Masters of Horror. Over nine million copies of his books are in print in the US and his work has been translated into twenty-four languages. He also has written for the stage, screen, comics, and interactive media. Paul resides at the Jersey Shore and can be found on the Web at www.repairmanjack.com.

REPAIRMAN JACK*

The Tomb
Legacies
Conspiracies
All the Rage
Hosts
The Haunted Air
Gateways
Crisscross
Infernal
Harbingers
Bloodline
By the Sword
Ground Zero
The Last Christmas
Fatal Error
The Dark at the End
Nightworld
Quick Fixes—Tales of Repairman Jack

THE TEEN TRILOGY*

Jack: Secret Histories
Jack: Secret Circles
Jack: Secret Vengeance

THE EARLY YEARS TRILOGY*

Cold City
Dark City
Fear City

THE ADVERSARY CYCLE*THE KEEP

The Tomb
The Touch
Reborn
Reprisal
Nightworld

OMNIBUS EDITIONS

The Complete LaNague
Calling Dr. Death (3 medical thrillers)
Ephemerata

NOVELLAS

The Peabody-Ozymandias Traveling Circus & Oddity Emporium*
"Wardenclyffe"*
"Signalz"
*

THE LANAGUE FEDERATION

Healer
Wheels Within Wheels
An Enemy of the State
Dydeetown World
The Tery

OTHER NOVELS

Black Wind*
Sibs*
The Select
Virgin
Implant
Deep as the Marrow
Sims
The Fifth Harmonic*
Midnight Mass

COLLABORATIONS

Mirage (with Matthew J. Costello)
Nightkill (with Steven Spruill)
Masque (with Matthew J. Costello)
Draculas (with Crouch, Killborn, Strand)
The Proteus Cure (with Tracy L. Carbone)
A Necessary End (with Sarah Pinborough)
"Fix"* (with J. Konrath & Ann Voss Peterson)
Three Films and a Play (with Matthew J. Costello)
Faster Than Light – Vols. 1 & 2 (with Matthew J. Costello)

THE ICE TRILOGY*

Panacea
The God Gene
The Void Protocol

THE NOCTURNIA CHRONICLES
(with Thomas F. Monteleone)

Definitely Not Kansas
Family Secrets
The Silent Ones

SHORT FICTION

Soft & Others
The Barrens and Others
Aftershock and Others
The Christmas Thingy
Quick Fixes—Tales of Repairman Jack*
Sex Slaves of the Dragon Tong
Secret Stories
The Compendium of F (Three Volumes)

THE RX MYSTERY SERIES

Rx Murder
Rx Mayhem

THE DUAD NOVELS

Double Threat
Double Dose

THE HIDDEN
*
The Upwelling
Lexie

Curious about other Crossroad Press books?
Stop by our site:
http://store.crossroadpress.com
We offer quality writing
in digital, audio, and print formats.

Made in United States
Orlando, FL
17 August 2024

50459676R00236